DEATH'S PALE FLAG

A NOVEL

GARY SIMONDS

BQB
North Carolina

Published in the United States by BQB Publishing
(an imprint of Boutique of Quality Books Publishing, Inc.)
www.bqbpublishing.com

979-8-88633-004-5 (p)
979-8-88633-005-2 (e)

Library of Congress Control Number: 2023932223

Book design by Robin Krauss, www.bookformatters.com
Cover design by Rebecca Lown, www.rebeccalowndesign.com

First editor: Caleb Guard
Second editor: Andrea Vande Vorde

PRAISE FOR GARY SIMONDS AND DEATH'S PALE FLAG

"... The author did a marvelous job of portraying some of the norms of society and breaking them. He wants the readers to have a peek at what the life of a so-called 'Hero of People' looks like without downright degrading it... There's a norm fixed deep inside our minds—heroes don't need saving. But here's what's wrong with the theory, Everything. Everybody may need saving at some point, if not by others then by themselves....

– Book Nerdection

"... This is a compelling book with a realistic plot woven into a fantasy story. *Death's Pale Flag* by Gary Simonds is an excellent book, combining elements of a thriller, medical drama, comedy, and paranormal themes. It's a worthwhile read, and I recommend it to fans of supernatural thrillers."

– Literary Titan

"This book is magnificent. While weaving a fascinating para-normal mystery tale, Gary Simonds has artfully depicted the pain and poignancy (and nobility) of life in neurosurgery, both for the surgeon and his/her spouse/family. Like all good art, he engages the reader, then takes them on not just a narratively-described, but an emotionally-cathected journey; the relentlessness of brain surgeon, Ryan's work/life and existential/humanistic conflicts are grueling to experience, as is the endless compassion and questioning that his wife, Kelly, must live with. In fact, despite the increasingly unsettling paranormal events and the heart-racing peeks into the neurosurgery universe, the heart of this novel lies in the Brenan's struggle to save their marriage.

The writing is sensational. The characters are compelling—the reader thirsts for evermore info about Kelly and Ryan; the wordsmithing of contexts and settings is eloquently intelligent; and the drama of the story is well-paced.

Descriptions of in-the-trenches experiences of a neurosurgeon and the interplay with other members of the team and the variety of patients dealt with (their brief stories describing the circumstances that lead tot he tragedies that resulted in their injuries) are nothing short of fascinating and galvanizing.

The theme of 'that which you focus on and immerse oneself in magnifies; what you ignore in life shrinks' is powerful. We readily come to understand that much can be lost in that cauldron of duty to endlessly needy constituents, ego gratification, going where the affirmation is, the reflexive avoiding of the tensions of a failing home life, etc.

The vignettes that offer a glimpse into life in the E.R., ICU's, and operating rooms are 'grab the reader by the shirt and shake them into paying attention' effective. They are fast-paced, fascinating, educational, and awe-inspiring. The leave the reader's head spinning.

Lovers of medical thrillers will enjoy the accurate portrayal of the minute to minute critical decision making involved in caring for the tidal waves of sick and injured patients crashin gupon our hospitals every day. Lovers of ghost stories will savor this story of a man who is relentlessly and inexplicably haunted, rather than a dilapidated house or mist-laden hollow. And, this is a novel that should be assigned reading for anyone who wants to explore the fallout of workaholic overcommitment to even the most noble of causes, and those who wish to TRULY understand life in medicine and life in a 'medical family.'"

– Wayne M. Sotile, Ph.D. Sotile Center for Resilience

For Cindy who has put up with far more than just ghosts.

And to the patients and their families who must suffer through the ravages of neurological disease and injury.

ACKNOWLEDGMENTS

Many thanks for all the input from Cody Sisco, Wayne Sotile, Cindy Simonds, Caleb Guard, and Andrea Vande Vorde.

O, my love! My wife!
Death, that hath suck'd the honey of thy breath,
Hath had no power yet upon thy beauty:
Thou art not conquer'd; beauty's ensign yet
Is crimson in thy lips and in thy cheeks,
And death's pale flag is not advanced there.

—William Shakespeare, *Romeo and Juliet*

CHAPTER 1

HEMORRHAGE

Perhaps it had passed the point of futility, but neurosurgeon Ryan Brenan persisted in packing pristine white cotton balls into the gaping hole. And again, the white turned to red and blood began to stream out of the little girl's head. With a sigh, Ryan peeled the now spent cotton balls away and tossed them with a dripping wet splat into a nearby stainless-steel basin. He took a shot at several of the bleeding points, the acrid smoke of cauterization mixing with the smell of blood and brain, but quickly abandoned the effort and packed in more cotton.

The evening had started peacefully enough. Ryan had just sat down for dinner at the kitchen table with his wife, Kelly, and their three daughters, Ava, Riley, and Erin, when his phone erupted. He took a last look at his plate of grilled vegetables, then pushed himself away from the table as he answered.

"Hey there, Eric . . ."

"Hey, sir. Sorry to bug you again so soon." It was ginger-haired Eric Edmundson, third-year neurosurgical resident, known throughout the hospital as "Eric the Red."

"No sweat, buddy. What's up?" asked Ryan, as he slipped into the dining room.

"We just got called on a two-year-old girl, Olivia Spencer. Head injury from a bad car accident. Reported awake at the scene, now in coma. She just dilated her right pupil. They're bundling her up for a scan as we speak."

Ryan's coal black eyes narrowed.

"Okay, I'm on my way. Meet you in CT."

Kelly looked up from her dinner, a subtle frown crossing her lips. "Really, Ryan? You *just* got home."

"Sorry, honey," replied Ryan as he kissed each daughter on the top of her head. "They've got a kid who's in big trouble. I doubt I'll be back any time soon."

This was code that he was likely headed to the operating room. It was greeted by a chorus of theatrical sighs from the girls.

"But, Dad, we were supposed to carve pumpkins tonight," protested seven-year-old Riley. "You promised. We've been waiting all weeken—"

Ryan was out the house and jogging to his jeep before she could finish. He arrived at the CT scanner just as Eric, two Pediatric Intensive Care Unit nurses, and pediatric critical care specialist Hugh O'Connor pushed Olivia's hospital crib into the suite. He helped the team load the little girl into the giant, gleaming-white miracle of modern electrical engineering. Within a couple of minutes, pictures of her brain appeared on the monitors. Ryan took one look and pulled out his cell phone, speed-dialing the operating room.

"OR front desk," came a cheerful response on the second ring.

"Hey, there. Brenan here—"

"You again, Dr. Brenan? I thought we just got rid of you."

"Yeah, well, we've got a little girl in CT who needs to come up right away. Crani—right side—big bleed." As Ryan spoke, phone held between his ear and shoulder, he helped remove Olivia from the scanner and return her to her crib. Soon, he and Eric were wrestling the bulky apparatus toward the elevators.

Operating room twelve was pulsating with activity when he pushed the crib through its swinging doors. The scrub nurse was laying out an assortment of stainless-steel instruments on tables draped in sterile blue disposable sheets. Other scrub-attired personnel were hooking up drills, suction systems, and electrocautery devices. The anesthesiologist and his assistants were filling various syringes and hanging IV bags, and two circulating nurses were tearing open bundles of sterilized tools and drills. All activity paused for a moment, however, as Ryan lifted Olivia to the operating table, and everyone in the room let out an anguished groan as her bruised and battered body was laid bare.

Ryan shaved a large patch of Olivia's hair and slathered the exposed scalp with a fluorescent-orange solution. He left the room for only a few seconds to rub antibacterial lotion into his hands and arms, then burst back in, arms held away from his body, impatiently waiting to be gowned. With the scrub nurse's assistance, he donned his sterile gown and two pairs of gloves, draped out the operative area of Olivia's head, and picked up a scalpel.

"Okay, guys. Time-out!" he barked. This was an institution-alized nod to patient safety, where the surgeon would normally run through an accounting of his or her surgical plans, needs, and concerns with the rest of the personnel in the room before starting the procedure—like an airline pilot running a pre-flight checklist before a take-off. But with a dying child under his scalpel, he cut short the exchange. "This is miss Olivia Spencer, and we're about to open the right side of her head for a big-assed bleed. If anyone has any objections, speak now or forever hold your peace."

He cut into the child's scalp directly behind the widow's peak, fashioning a giant question-mark-shaped incision, encompassing the entire right side of her head, while Eric applied blue plastic clips to the cut edges to stop them from bleeding. After a few minutes of operating, Ryan addressed a couple of nursing students who were watching the procedure.

"So, this little girl's got a large accumulation of blood deep in her brain that's crushing the surrounding tissue. The longer the brain gets crushed, the more it shuts down and dies. The blood solidifies into a clot or, as we call it, a 'hematoma.' Dr. Edmundson and I are trying to get the hematoma out before it's too late. We'll see how lucky we are tonight . . ."

The two surgeons continued to operate, peeling the scalp off the skull. Ryan then stepped on a metallic pedal on the floor. An eighty-thousand rpm drill in his right hand leaped into action with a high-pitched scream. With it, he made dime-sized holes in the skull, then switched out the drill bit.

"So, we just made what we call 'burr holes.' This new drill bit cuts on its side, so if we insert it into a hole and push it against the bone, we can make nice thin cuts from one hole to another."

He maneuvered the drill about the child's head, creating a six-by-five-inch window in the skull. He lifted the freed-up flap of bone and passed it to the scrub tech. Underneath lay a purple-red glob of what looked like currant jelly. Ryan pointed it out to the students.

"So, what do you think this is, guys?"

"Um, is it a subdural hematoma?" replied one of the students who was so tall her scrubs ended halfway down her shins.

"Close!" replied Ryan. "It's an *epidural* hematoma. The brain and spinal cord are contained in a bag of fluid called the 'dura.' This clot of blood is on the outside of the dura and thus is '*epi*-dural.' If it were under the dura, it would be '*sub-dural*.' The problem is, it's not this little girl's problem. The clot that we're really after is in the brain itself. It's known as an '*intra-parenchymal*' hematoma."

Ryan swept the clot off the underlying tissue with his gloved finger. "So, here's the dura—the leathery bag of fluid that the brain sits in. It feels tight as a drum. That's not good. It means the pressure in this girl's head is off the scales."

Eric incised the dura with a scalpel. A geyser of bloody fluid shot out and hit him in the chest. With further opening, large lumps of clotted blood presented themselves. Eric suctioned them away only to be greeted by bubbling mounds of the child's brain.

"Normally, guys," remarked Ryan, "the brain is kind of gray-white in color, with the consistency of overcooked pasta. As you can see, this child's brain is all yellow, orange, and purple; and is way too mushy—almost to the point of being runny."

A section of such brain percolated up through the opening in the dura like a volcano rising from the sea, crimson lava coursing down its sides. Ryan incised the apex of the peaking mound, and volumes of clotted and liquefied blood spewed forth. The two surgeons suctioned this away and then worked to remove lumps of clotted blood from well below the surface.

"This is the hematoma we're after," said Ryan. "Once we have it all out, we'll likely have some bleeding to contend with."

He was proven correct. He and Eric were now facing fierce whirlpools of hemorrhage deep within the cavernous opening in Olivia's brain.

"When the brain is badly injured, the body's clotting mechanisms can get all screwed up, and bleeding can be a challenge to control," continued Ryan, his voice remaining calm despite the constrictive bands tightening around his chest. He had been in the same position just a few nights before with a badly beaten baby. He had been unable to save her. "Dr. Edmundson and I are cramming these sterile cotton balls up against the brain tissue to hold pressure against the bleeding sources," he continued. "This is known as 'tamponading.' We're hoping our anesthesia colleagues can give our patient enough clotting factors to help us eventually get things under control."

On the other side of the surgical drapes, the anesthesia team worked at forcing volumes of assorted blood products into Olivia's veins. Unfortunately, every time the lead anesthesiologist leaped from his supply cart back to the operating table, he bumped into it, jouncing the operative field.

"Of course," commented Ryan, "we'd be most obliging were they to refrain from kicking the table . . ."

Ryan went silent for a period, but the voice in his head kept chattering away. *Come on, you little witch, this is ridiculous. Give us a freakin' break here, will ya? One dead kid's enough for the week.*

Through the ambient noise of anesthesia machinery, positive-pressure air exchange, and muted chatter, he noticed an increase in the rate of electronic beats coming from the heart monitors. Without taking his eyes off the operative field, he asked, "How's it going over there, guys? We keeping up on her blood?"

"Christ, I hope so," came the reply from the other side of the drapes. "You guys're losing a lot up there."

"Yeah. I know, I know," replied Ryan, as he sensed a warm, sticky liquid soaking into his socks.

"Ah, crap," he mumbled as he shuffled his feet into another position. He looked up at the students for a moment, blinding them with his fiber-optic headlight. "So, guys, we use special drapes for this sort of operation. They have an attached plastic bag and suction system that's supposed to whisk away all the icky stuff like irrigation, blood, pus, spinal fluid, bits of brain and the like. As always seems to be the case, though, much of said stuff must have skirted the bag and run down the drapes into our shoes. Or at least my shoes. How about yours, Eric?"

"You bet, sir!" replied Eric, as he too shifted his feet.

Ryan went silent again as he and Eric continued their minuet of removing supersaturated cotton balls from the crater in Olivia's brain and replacing them with fluffy dry ones. *God, my eyes are on fire,* he thought. *I bet I haven't blinked since we started the case.* He deliberately opened and closed them several times, refocused, and went back to work. After what felt like several days, the rapidity of cotton-ball replacement began to slow. The scarlet pool diminished in depth. And soon, upon the removal of spent cotton, instead of a raging torrent, they were greeted by an anemic trickle.

"Much better," remarked Ryan, as he began to breathe again. "Not good enough yet, but better. The factors seem to be taking hold. We may get out of this little girl's head after all."

Within another half hour, Ryan and Eric had the bleeding stopped.

"Hey, Joan," said Ryan, as he lined the cavity with antibleeding materials, "Do me a favor and call out to the family. Tell them, if you would, that we're closing, and that I'll be out to talk with them as soon as we're done." He glanced up at the clock. *Shoot,* he thought. *The kids are in bed. So much for carving pumpkins. I wonder if they went ahead without me.*

"How do you think she'll do, Dr. Brenan?" asked one of the students, interrupting Ryan's musing.

"Hard to know. Kids' brains are unpredictable. Anything and everything's possible. She might be brain dea—" Ryan choked up for a moment, thinking about the baby from earlier in the week. "Or, she might be left in coma. Or, if we got the pressure off her brain in time, she could come right around. But even if that's the case, she might be paralyzed on her left side. We really won't know until we see what she does."

Soon, Ryan was entering the pediatric intensive care waiting room, scrubs soaked with sweat, mask hanging from his neck. Stuffed into the small airless space were twenty-five to thirty terror-stricken people. Mom, who he had yet to meet, was immediately identifiable. There didn't appear to be a dad.

"Ms. Spencer?" he asked.

"Yes," replied the woman looking so fragile she might shatter.

"I'm Ryan Brenan, the neurosurgeon caring for Olivia. I'm sorry we haven't met yet, but we had to take Olivia straight to surgery."

"How's my baby, Doctor?" asked Ms. Spencer, eyes nearly swollen shut from continuous crying.

"We don't know yet, Ms. Spencer. She was in big trouble when she got here. But the surgery went as well as we could hope for. We're waiting to see how she responds."

Tears were streaming down Ms. Spencer's face. "When will we know?"

"It could be very soon, or it could drag out. I promise you, though, we will keep you informed every step of the way."

Ms. Spencer collapsed around Ryan. An older couple, probably grandparents, joined in, half hugging Ms. Spencer, half clinging to Ryan as if he were a life preserver thrown into a raging sea. If there was an elixir that fueled Ryan in his efforts, it was this. The humanity of it. The crystalline purity of it. The ripping away of all pretenses and social contrivances. Right down to the bare bones. Right down to the heart. Where a primal connection was forged, a communion of souls. They continued to hug him, raining their unbridled gratitude upon him. Not for any miracle—the outcome was too much in doubt—but for the effort. For doing his best. For being a pillar of strength, of calm, of competent order, in a tempest of mayhem. He never felt more like a doctor than in moments like these.

Ms. Spencer and the grandparents eventually released their grips and began to ask questions—mostly technical in nature. What did he find? What did he have to do? In how bad a shape was her brain? What were the next steps? And so forth. Time stood still, yet time evaporated. In the middle of it all, Eric stepped into the room. He put his hand on Ryan's shoulder and spoke in a hushed tone.

"Uh, Dr. Brenan, she's waking up. Moving all extremities . . ."

The room broke open with light, and sighs, and tears of relief. Again, Ryan was engulfed in suffocating hugs. This time, in addition to gratitude, there was love. Immediate, unrestrained, everlasting love. After several minutes, he broke free and took his leave, heading for Olivia's bedside. He found her to be in good shape. He sat down nearby, released a heavy sigh, and dictated an operative note.

When he hung up the phone, he considered going straight home in the hopes of getting some sleep, but instead, went about checking on some of his sickest patients. They were scattered among five of the medical center's twelve ICUs. On finishing, he met up with Eric and tagged along for a couple of ER consultations: a young man with a broken neck, and an older woman with a small, deep brain hemorrhage—neither requiring surgery. He then felt compelled to pay one more visit to Olivia. Despite a black eye on the operative side, she looked great. It was a nice punctuation to the night's work, and he walked out of the hospital, smiling.

By the time he pulled into his driveway, it was very late. All lights in the house were out. It was a dark corner of the universe, and the streetlights on Avenue G were well obscured by large oak trees still jealously clinging to their orange-yellow leaves. Fall had definitely made its appearance, though, and he sat in the jeep for a few moments to savor its crisp, spicy air. Suddenly, his heart jumped. His head reflexively jerked toward the side porch. Something there had moved.

"What the hell was that?" he said to the empty seat beside him.

He had only caught a glimpse out of the corner of his eye. He would have sworn it was a person, a woman, but it—she—had disappeared before he could be sure. He grabbed a flashlight out of the glove compartment, eased out of the jeep, and probed the trilling darkness. Nothing. No one hiding behind a tree or slinking away down Avenue G. He turned his head and listened with all his might. Nothing again. No snapping of twigs or retreating footfalls tucked in among the calls of treefrogs and katydids. He made one further sweep with the flashlight, shrugged his shoulders, and headed for the door. But then stopped. *Shoot.* What if it was some local delinquent looking to score some cash or opioids. Jesus, with Kelly and the girls asleep upstairs? Perhaps he should take a better look around.

He wandered about the property, shining the flashlight in every potential hiding spot: around the various collections of trees, through the many bushes, in the old icehouse and outhouse, and finally, in the barn. There, he tried the light switches without success. The fuse must have blown again. He stumbled through the bottom floor, then climbed the stairs into the loft and flashed his light on the discarded family goods lying about. Goods that in daylight would offer no threat whatsoever, but in the darkness seemed full of menace. The hairs on the back of his neck stood on end and he shivered. His hands began to shake. *Jesus, Ryan. What's your problem? Chill out, will ya?*

He left the barn and strode into the house in as manly a manner as he could affect, but his pounding heart betrayed his growing anxiety. *Sheesh*, he thought. How easy a shot of Jameson's would go down right now. But he was still on call. And yet, why not? He was sure some did it. Sneak in a little nip here and there over a weekend like this. And if he did, who would ever know? He wouldn't skip a beat. But no. He couldn't do it. What a freaking scandal it would cause if someone found out.

He sighed, opened the refrigerator, and reached for a carton of orange juice. After slugging down several glasses, he entered the front hallway, intent on heading upstairs. But on his way through, he glanced at the front double doors and froze. A dark silhouette was visible through the stained-glass panels. A dark female silhouette. Grabbing an umbrella from a nearby stand, he undid the deadlock and threw himself out onto the porch. Nothing. No one. Lungs heaving, he turned and noted a somewhat anthropomorphic shadow on the doors cast by a moribund birch.

"Ridiculous," he mumbled. "You're really spooking the hell out of yourself tonight, aren't you, Ryan?" Sleep deprivation. That had to be it. He was dog-tired. He hadn't seen the backs of his eyelids for what now, forty-two hours? Perhaps sleep had momentarily overcome his weary brain and made him see things that weren't there: things resurrected from the hellscapes of his childhood nightmares; old "friends" who used to visit in the blackest of nights and render him unable to move. He shook his head to clear the memories, closed the doors, and bolted the locks.

Moments later he was upstairs watching his girls sleep. When did he last spend any real time with them? Tuesday? No, he had that meeting in Bellemonte. Monday? Nope, he was still working on that acoustic neuroma. *Holy hell, has it been a week?* It couldn't be. But it could. It had been a week, an entire freaking week. *God, I hate this.*

He made his way down the hallway to his bedroom. After undressing, he crawled up to Kelly, hoping she'd turn and envelop him within a sheltering embrace. But she failed to stir. She always failed to stir. At least they had spent some quality time together on Thursday. Or was it Wednesday?

He rolled onto his back and tried to will himself to sleep. But he was filled with dread. A darkness was gathering around him. And with the darkness, bad things. He shivered as he imagined hearing whispers—the whispers of beings crouching in the closet and under the bed, beings awaiting his surrender of consciousness.

"Ridiculous," he grumbled, shaking his head.

He sat up, took one last look around the room, then retreated to the safety of his spouse.

CHAPTER 2

A DAY IN THE LIFE

Ryan's eyes popped open at 5:25, half a second before the soporific voices of NPR climbed to an audible level on the clock radio. He reluctantly took his leave of his slumbering wife, cursing the morning, cursing the hospital, and cursing neurosurgery. He turned off the radio and was downstairs in minutes, dressed in his usual uniform of a white oxford shirt, a nondescript tie, khakis, loafers, and a sport jacket. He threw down his usual toast and coffee while skimming the news headlines online. A quick run upstairs to kiss the heads of his sleeping girls, and he was out the door. The dark drive over to the medical center was so short that he had little chance to clear his residual unease from the previous night. He was in the Neurotrauma ICU by six, where he was greeted by one of the neurosurgery residents, two physician assistants, and an unfamiliar face.

"Hey, Dr. Brenan," said fourth-year resident, Lisa LeClair, former starting guard for the UConn Huskies. "This is Darla Sutton, a neuroscience major at Penn State. She's doing a paper on 'A Day in the Life of a Brain Surgeon.' You said she could tag along with you today."

Crap. He'd forgotten. Now he had to perform. *Well, buddy, this is what you signed up for.* Ryan forced a smile and reached out his hand. "Oh, yeah. Welcome aboard, Darla. I hope we don't bore you to death." He turned as all systems within his consciousness lit up into full functional configuration. "Come on then, let's see what the morning's brought us."

The group went about visiting a good dozen ICU patients. Ryan briefly reviewed each patient's progress, checked key components of their exams, and then discussed an action plan for them with the team. Between each visit he gave Darla a quick encapsulation of the patient's diagnosis and neurosurgical issues. At six thirty, the group shot down a series of long corridors and six flights of stairs, to land upon the pediatric pre-anesthesia unit; Darla, in heels, racing to keep up. They stopped in on a smiling butterball of a baby boy whose head was too large for his body. Ryan spoke reassuringly with the parents, signed a couple of papers, then slipped out into an adjacent hallway.

"Little Jason there has hydrocephalus, or 'water on the brain.' The brain and spinal cord are contained in a bag of crystal-clear fluid—the same fluid you take out in a spinal tap. That fluid, known as CSF, is made in little sacs deep in the brain, called ventricles. The fluid percolates out of those sacs down thin little channels to holes at the bottom of the brain, from where it's released into the surrounding bag. If the channels or those holes block up, the sacs, or ventricles, fill with the fluid, get bigger and bigger, and squish the brain against the skull. If this goes on long enough, it enlarges the baby's head and, eventually, kills him. We tried to open up some channels for Jason with a TV scope, but it didn't do the trick. So, we're going to put in what's known as a VP shunt. That *should* take care of things." He smiled and then said, "Come on then. Let's go listen in on checkout."

They ducked in on a collection of neurosurgical residents and PAs in a small room down the hall. The group was going over a list of about sixty patients, periodically reviewing associated MRIs and CT scans on a computer. At seven, they dispersed, leaving Ryan and Darla alone in the space.

"Theoretically," remarked Ryan, "we're supposed to be in the operating room at seven, all ready and raring to go. But with kids and big cases, putting the patient to sleep and getting them ready for surgery can take forever. We call this period 'May-Fat.'"

"May-Fat?" asked Darla.

"Mandatory Anesthesia *F* Around Time," replied Ryan with a smile. "They'll call us once they've gotten through it with our baby."

To kill the time, Ryan signed in to the electronic medical record system on a nearby computer and worked his way through dozens of tasks. As the minutes passed he jiggled his right foot faster and faster. When it reached the point where it was shaking his whole body, he popped out of the chair.

"Okay, let's go see what's taking so freakin' long."

They headed into operating room twenty-two. The room's air was thick with heat and perspiration. Three anesthesia personnel were hunched over the baby while a fourth held a mask over the baby's face. Stuck into the table's cushion were a couple dozen spent IV needles. Alcohol pads and two-by-two cotton sponges were scattered all over the table and the nearby floor.

"How's it going, team?" asked Ryan with an air of teasing enthusiasm.

"Fucking fat babies and their fat fucking limbs. Can't find a decent damned vein anywhere," came the reply from a drenched, disheveled anesthesiologist, his mask having slid under his nose.

"Mind if I take a shot?" asked Ryan, needle in hand as he reached for a leg.

"Good luck. I tried that drumstick for the last forty-five minutes," grumbled the anesthesiologist.

In the blink of an eye, Ryan had the IV in a vein and was taping it in place.

"Oh, fuck you, Brenan," came his only thanks. With this, the anesthesiologist pushed a bunch of medications into the IV, and then passed a breathing tube down the baby's throat.

Ryan retired to the back of the room and watched with Darla.

"How'd you do that?" asked the wide-eyed undergraduate.

"Pure luck," chuckled Ryan in a whisper. "I couldn't see or feel a thing. But it sure helps with the ol' neurosurgery mystique," he added with a wink.

Ryan and Lisa were soon operating on the baby.

"A VP shunt is basically a tube that diverts excess fluid out of the brain and dumps it into the belly. The child will need it for life," said Ryan. "They aren't perfect—they can block up. When they do, we have to replace whatever parts are blocked. But the damned things have saved thousands and thousands of kids."

The two surgeons passed a long shish-kebab-like rod just under the skin from an incision in the baby's head to one in his belly.

"Pretty gruesome, eh, Darla?" asked Ryan. "But it's how we get tubing from point A to point B."

Within half an hour, the operation was done, and Ryan was dictating an operative summary into a phone on the wall. As he finished, his cell phone sounded.

"It's uncanny, Darla," remarked Ryan. "It's as if the world can sense the second you throw the last stitch. The phone goes nuts. The office attacks with a bunch of messages from outside docs. Pre-op has a million questions. Post-op, a million more. Then watch, the minute we step out of the room, the residents and PAs will be all over us, each with an inconceivably critical issue. You'll see. There's no time to think, ponder, or cogitate." *Or remember you have a family, or life, outside of this twisted existence,* he thought.

Things unfolded just as he had predicted. His phone erupted into a series of nonstop calls and texts. Through the barrage, the two bounced all about the hospital. They checked on an ICU to see why a drainage tube in someone's brain had blocked up, then dashed to the clinic to see a patient with back pain who was demanding buckets of narcotics. Next, they spoke with the anxious family of a comatose victim of a car accident. Then they stopped in to greet and reassure their next operative patient. They scaled several flights of stairs to a stroke unit to see a patient with a new brain hemorrhage, and ran back down the stairs to radiology to review an MRI scan with a neuroradiologist. Next came a long slog over to the children's hospital to check the VP shunt of another hydrocephalus patient who was intermittently vomiting. Then up the stairs to the neonatal intensive care unit to see a comically tiny baby with a hemorrhage in its ventricles. Afterward, they sat down at the computer to do some further documentation but were jumped by a couple of physician assistants who wanted to complain to Ryan about one of his partners. Apparently, said partner hadn't checked on her patients for several days. After this, the two made their way to another ICU to help pronounce a nineteen-year-old patient with a head injury, dead. All the while the phone wouldn't stop ringing.

"This is why the OR can be a refuge, Darla," remarked Ryan, as they climbed another staircase. "During an operation, we can't really multitask like this. We have to focus on one thing, and one thing only: the surgery. Not that they leave us alone in there— problems that are deemed too dire to wait an hour or two will be piped in. But in the middle of an operation, all you can do is answer questions."

Eventually, they were back in the OR with the high-pitched scream of the surgical drills echoing off the tile walls.

"So, Darla," yelled Ryan, eyes fixed through surgical loupes on the operative site, "this super nice woman has a brain tumor that's almost certainly going to be a glioblastoma multiforme, or GBM. They're nasty buggers. Surgery, radiation, chemotherapy, immune therapy, gene therapy, you name it, and she'll most likely be dead within a couple of years—probably much sooner. Right now, it appears that surgery buys several months, but I always tell the patients the tumor's like a weed. We can take out the 'plant' that you can see, but it has microscopic roots that spread out all over the brain, and we can't go after those roots with a knife. You have to use weed killers, so to speak. That is, radiation and chemotherapy."

"That's so sad," said Darla.

"Isn't it? They come in, in an endless line. One after another. Decades of research and experimental treatments, billions of dollars, and the disease is just as deadly as it was in the twentieth century."

The surgery lasted about two and a half hours and, again, the minute Ryan and Lisa placed the last staples in the patient's scalp, Ryan's phone detonated. Watching nearby, Darla asked, "So, Dr. Brenan, you operate on kids *and* adults? Does everyone do that?"

"No, I guess I'm kind of an anomaly. In general, pediatric neurosurgeons stick to kids, and the adult neurosurgeons stick to adults. Technically, my specialty is pediatric neurosurgery, but after training, I went into the Army. In the military you really have to be a jack-of-all-trades. I guess I never broke out of the habit of taking on whatever comes my way."

"Does that mean you do twice as much surgery?"

"God, I hope not," chuckled Ryan.

"Don't let him fool you, young lady," interjected the anesthesiologist. "He probably does do twice as much surgery as anyone else around here. He's a glutton for punishment."

"Ha!" replied Ryan as he wrapped the patient's head in gauze. "Always good to have your PR team around."

Despite Ryan's scoffing, the characterization was pretty accurate. His procedural output was pegged at the far end of the bell-shaped curve of surgeon productivity. He had become a victim of his own competence. As a resident, and then a faculty neurosurgeon, he was quickly identified as a "natural." His outcomes were excellent, his complication rates low. In addition, he was fast, very fast. And, as word of his prowess spread, referrals compounded referrals. The reward: more patients, more operations, more time spent in the hospital.

"Wow, you must really love what you do," remarked Darla.

"Every minute of it," replied Ryan. *But do I really?* He pondered the question for a while, realizing he was oddly ambivalent. Sure, he enjoyed helping people, or at least trying to help them. And he recognized that his restless mind was kept satisfactorily engaged throughout each day. But he had to admit, he didn't adore being a neurosurgeon. He didn't live for it, breath it, savor it, or revel in all its trappings—like so many of his colleagues—he was simply good at it. And in his soul, there forever waged a desperate tug-of-war between work and the four women in his life. He so ached to be with Kelly and the girls, that just thinking about them proved insufferable. Yet, somehow, neurosurgery always won out. How? Why? He had no idea. But it did. Thus, he would force himself to ignore the torture of separation, clear his mind of all related thoughts, lower his head, and drive, day after day, year after year.

Despite the magnitude of the surgery, the patient came round nicely, and the two surgeons and the anesthesiologist wheeled her into the post-anesthesia care unit. After taking their leave, Ryan and Darla were off again in a crisscrossing blitz throughout the hospital. An hour and a half later, Ryan and Lisa were operating through a tiny incision on the lower back of a middle-aged man.

"This patient has a herniated disk, or ruptured disk, or slipped disk—they all mean the same thing," commented Ryan to Darla. "A chunk of crabmeat-like material rips out of the cushion between two vertebrae and smushes a nerve that's trying to leave the lower back. The nerve gets all upset, and the patient gets severe shooting pain everywhere the nerve goes. That is, all the way down the leg. What do you think the best treatment for this is, Darla?"

"I would have to guess surgery."

"Ha! Trick question! The best treatment is time. Ninety percent of the patients will get completely better on their own. The crabmeat doesn't move, but the nerve learns to put up with it. We only operate when the nerve refuses to feel better after several weeks. If that happens, we sneak in, find the nerve—that's it on the screen right now—protect it, then get the crabmeat out. The results are often instantaneous for the patient."

Indeed, when they visited the patient shortly after surgery, he thanked Ryan for a "miracle cure." Then Ryan and Darla were at it again, frenetically racing about the hospital. Somewhere between ICUs, Darla asked, "Hey, Dr. Brenan, when do you eat . . . drink . . . go to the bathroom?"

"Oh jeez. Thanks for reminding me. Some days you kind of forget. It's stupid, really. I even got a kidney stone when I was in the Army from not staying hydrated enough on OR days. You'd think I'd have learned my lesson. Come on . . ."

They shot down a set of stairs and ended up in the cafeteria. Ryan paid for Darla's meal, and the two sat down at an empty table, Ryan's phone still buzzing. Within two minutes Ryan's plate was clean and he was fidgeting. Darla choked down the remainder of her salad and they were off again. Soon, they were back in the OR.

"So, Darla, we'll knock out this last case, check on our post-op and ICU patients, and get out of Dodge at a reasonable hour," commented Ryan, as he and Lisa went about driving screws into the neck of an eighteen-year-old girl. She had sustained a fracture in a diving accident. The team had attempted to treat the fracture with a brace—allowing the bones to heal themselves—but it became obvious that the spine would need some surgical help.

"Is this your typical day, Dr. Brenan?" asked Darla, with a note of incredulity.

"Pretty typical. It can be calmer . . . or crazier. Call days tend to be quite a bit crazier."

"Crazier than this?"

"Oh sure. Imagine today with anywhere from five to fifteen additional patients to see, one or two maybe needing immediate surgery. It's the joy of working at a level-one trauma center. And then you have the night to look forward to. That's when things really heat up. It seems that the worst disasters—strokes, fractures, bleeds, etc.—always occur after midnight. We can get twenty or more emergency consults in the middle of the night."

"Sounds awful."

"It kind of is . . . at least for the residents. Isn't it, Lisa?"

"Oh, no," replied Lisa with exaggerated enthusiasm. "Love every friggin' minute of it."

"And it's not just the surge in consults," continued Ryan. "They're getting bombarded with calls. Worse, believe it or not, than what you're seeing today, because the whole service gets focused down onto one person—the on-call resident. Needless to say, they get zero sleep. But at least they get the next day off. We faculty neurosurgeons stupidly roll right on through into another full day of work."

"So, what's *your* night call like, then?" asked Darla.

"Certainly better than the residents. I go in for any surgery, of course; and if a resident is having difficulties. I'd say, on average, I get two to three hours of sleep on call nights. But you tend to sleep 'with one eye open,' if you know what I mean. And then there's what I call "call psychosis.""

"Call psychosis?"

"Yeah, when you're on call you feel utterly vulnerable, unable to relax, constantly on edge. And there's good reason. Any attempt to play, or hang out with friends, or do something fun, is invariably interrupted by an emergency. Thus, when on call, you kind of go into a cocoon—afraid to do anything—your phone just sitting there, pulsating evil, waiting for you to enjoy yourself in any way. Am I exaggerating, Lisa?"

"Nope," replied Lisa. "I'd say you've got it pegged, Dr. B."

"How often are you on call?" asked Darla.

"Every fourth or fifth night."

"But aren't there, like, a dozen neurosurgeons here?"

"Yeah, but two will only cover kids, three only cover strokes, and two have aged out of night call. So, those willing and able to cover general call aren't all that plentiful. But no call for Lisa *or* me tonight, so it won't be long before we're both chillin' with a nice glass of cabernet, eh, Lisa?"

"Got that right, sir."

As if on cue, sixth-year resident Cara Klein, valedictorian graduate of Rutgers University, popped into the room.

"Hey, Dr. Brenan, remember that shunt kid?"

"The one we just operated on?"

"No, the seven-year-old over on peds who was vomiting."

"Got you. Looked okay when we stopped by . . ."

"Yeah, well, he's worse. We got another MRI. Vents are bigger. I know you're not on call anymore, but I thought you'd probably want to do it."

"Well, Darla, so much for an early evening," said Ryan. He looked up at Cara. "Yeah, get her down as soon as you can, will ya? We'll go speak with her parents as soon as we're done here."

When they got out of the spine repair, Ryan told Darla she was certainly free to leave at any time. He noted that she had gone well above and beyond the call of duty. Darla, however, insisted on staying, despite having developed an obvious limp from blisters on her feet. Noticing this, Ryan had her sit down alongside him at a computer bank as he attacked the fifty or so emails that had stacked up over the past few hours. Soon they were back in the OR.

"See, Darla," remarked Ryan, "this is a VP shunt that was working fine for several years in this sweet little girl. But protein, and cells, and whatever, has blocked it up. We've disconnected a couple pieces of it, and it's clear that the blockage is in the piece going into her brain. We'll have it replaced, and this case done, in minutes."

And so they had. But they had surprised the anesthesia team with how fast the procedure went, and thus it took an unnerving hour for the girl to wake up.

"Yeah," remarked Ryan to Darla, "one of the joys of operating on the nervous system is never being 100 percent sure that all is well until the patient can show you that it is. All sorts of complications can be hidden from you until you can examine your patient awake. So, we kind of sit on pins and needles until they wake up, even though we're pretty sure things are okay. This is why I never tell my wife when I'll be home." Ryan looked up at the clock, his eyes darkening. "Any time I've ever said that I'd be home by a specific time, I've ended up being off by a mile. And God help me if there's a kid's event that I'm planning to get to. Invariably, a post-op patient will go sour, or a sick kid will come in, and the next several hours are filled with CT scans, ICU interventions, and family discussions."

The girl eventually woke up and looked good. Ryan and Darla headed out to speak with the parents, then made some more rounds.

"Come on, Darla, time for you to get out of here," commanded Ryan between ICUs.

"Are *you* leaving now?" asked Darla.

"Me? No. I've got to hit the computer for a while."

"But didn't you work all weekend?"

"Yeah. But that's the thing. There's always so much left to do after a weekend of call."

"What do your wife and children think about your schedule?"

Ryan shuddered for a moment. *Direct hit,* he thought. "Yeah, well, I'm not sure they're too happy with it. But you get swept up into these days. And all these sick and broken people. I guess you make compromises for their sake."

"It seems like a pretty one-sided compromise."

"Yeah, I guess you kind of shortchange your loved ones a fair amount. But maybe that's narcissistic. You're presuming you're something worth having around ..." replied Ryan with a sad smile.

"There isn't a way to get out of here at a more reasonable hour?" persisted Darla.

"Not that I've figured out," said Ryan with a sigh. "Anyway, get out of here before you turn into someone like me. Or your feet fall off!"

Darla took him up on the offer and, after expressing her gratitude for an "amazing day," limped away down a darkened hallway. Ryan shuffled to a nearby ICU and slumped into a chair. He sat for a good ten minutes looking at nothing, thinking nothing, then resumed his battle with the ever-ravenous electronic medical record. Finally calling it quits, he made his way to the changing room and threw on his original outfit for the day. He checked on the last surgery patient and then shuffled his way toward the doctor's parking lot through 4 West.

He was shocked to find the usually hopping ward silent and lifeless. No personnel at the nursing station. None of the constant din of beeps, alarms, and chatter. No nurses, no ambling patients, no ubiquitous blue-green TV light emanating from any of the rooms. He looked into several—all empty. He continued down the ward's long, jaundiced hallway, drawn to the very last room. He pushed the door open.

"At last, Dr. Brenan, we've been expecting you."

The room was filled with begowned personnel, several restraining a female patient on an exam table. Ryan could see her legs kicking furiously but, despite his considerable height, couldn't see past the mass of heads and shoulders obscuring her body and face. Someone in the crowd, presumably a nurse, handed him a scalpel, and the crowd parted to allow him access to the patient's head. He looked down, as he prepared to incise the scalp, and saw that it was Kelly.

"Hey, Dr. Brenan. Are you okay?"

Ryan came around to someone shaking him by the shoulders.

"Huh? What?" asked Ryan. His eyes coming to focus on the nursing station of the Four North ICU.

"You were asleep . . . and crying. And saying, 'no, no, no,'" said a young ICU nurse in maroon scrubs. "Sorry to startle you, but you looked like you were having a nightmare. I was worried you might fall off the chair."

"Sheesh, sorry about that. Thanks for waking me. I guess I better get home."

He stood up on shaky legs and made his way to the doctor's parking lot, but dropped down to the ground floor, giving wide berth to 4 West.

CHAPTER 3

HALLOWEEN PARADE

The dream clung to Ryan's consciousness for several days. In the hospital he avoided less populated wards once darkness fell, and looked over his shoulder as he went out into the parking lot each night. At home he was skittish, jumping with every creak of a floorboard or groan of a closing door. And he came down with a major case of the heebie-jeebies every time he ventured into the basement or out to the barn. It all threatened to put a damper on his fifth Halloween in the family's adopted hometown, New Bethany, Pennsylvania.

Straddling the flood-prone Susquehanna River, New Bethany strained to reach a population of ten thousand but was home to the Carriere Clinic, a sprawling hospital complex designed to bring state-of-the-art medical care to a vast, rural section of Pennsylvania. Very rural indeed, Pittsburg lay four hours to the west; Philadelphia, three hours to the east; and that was about it. Unless you counted Scranton, but most did not. New Bethany was a picturesque little town full of anachronistic mom-and-pop shops, unimposing but well-kept homes, and finely manicured parks. To the kids growing up there, it was just as lame and uninteresting as any other corner of the United States. Lost on them was the unrushed and kindly nature of the town's shopkeepers, the lack of violent crime, the associated freedom of movement without hovering parental supervision, the superlative public schools, the always-accessible athletic facilities, and the surrounding hillsides of verdant forests and well-tended farms. But it wasn't lost on Ryan and Kelly, who instantly fell in love with the place.

Both Ryan and Kelly were the products of military families and had thus grown up in an array of locales. After college and professional schools, both ended up working in Washington D.C. There, they fell in love, married, and brought three daughters into the world. When Kelly was pregnant with their third, the couple sought to get away from the crime and bustle of D.C. and settle somewhere "out in the country." Kelly, an environmental lawyer, could work remotely from anywhere. Ryan was more of a challenge. Hospitals featuring top-of-the-line neurosurgery departments were generally found in the hearts of big cities, not out among a bunch of fields and streams.

After an intensive search, the two found precisely what they were looking for: an archetypical American small town, well distant from the madding crowds of the Eastern Seaboard megalopolis but featuring a major medical center. They therefore pulled up stakes and headed for New Bethany. They settled into a rambling old farmhouse just across the river from the town's business section. A busy work schedule soon swallowed Ryan whole, but he did find his way to the occasional Sunday afternoon pickup game of soccer. Said games served as a nexus for a growing social life, and the Brenans were quickly absorbed into a fun-loving group of thirty- and forty-something-year-olds.

Over time, Ryan and Kelly came to recognize some short-comings in their new home. Ignorance, inequity, and bigotry ran deep within its veins. And rather than sharing a small-town joie de vivre, many of the locals seemed to marinate in a pervasive sense of town-grown resentment and aggrieved entitlement. But one thing that could always be said for the place was that "it kept Halloween well."

To celebrate the holiday, shops and residences would be

decked out with elaborate displays ranging from the tacky, to the whimsical, to the macabre. Entranceways would be adorned with cobwebs and jack-o-lanterns. Front lawns would be littered with tombstones and skeletons. And displays of hangings, headless beings, witches, ghosts, ghouls, and goblins could be viewed down every lane and side street.

The highlight of the season, though, was the Halloween parade; and yearly, on the Saturday before Halloween proper, people from across the region would line up three and four deep along its route to partake in the festivities. The parade consisted of every regional civic group, high-school band, preschool class, scouts' den, sports club, volunteer fire department, cheerleading squad, teenage guitar band, sheriff's department, church choir, knitting circle, and stamp club, all marching in full Halloween regalia. Elaborate floats were perched, in a most teetering fashion, upon the beds of old pickup trucks. The town's mayor (and popular hairdresser) waved to the crowd from atop a John Deere tractor. Fellow dignitaries rode behind in a hay wagon. The celebration lasted a good three hours as the procession inchwormed down Main Street, eventually disbanding in the parking lot of the town hardware store, a block away on View Street. Before reaching the parade's end, though, every float, pickup truck, Chevy convertible, tractor, police car, ambulance, and fire truck disgorged itself of a cornucopia of candy. Said bounty was shed upon every inch of the parade route, only to be eagerly scooped up by throngs of children and not a few adults.

Ryan adored the event and, each year, sold his soul to his partners in order to be off work for it. This year was no different. And so, with someone else facing the slings and arrows of neurosurgery call, he and Kelly headed out to the parade. The girls were already there, in the company of family friends Hugh and Dianne O'Connor, and their five children. Freed of shepherding the kids for the evening, Ryan and Kelly leisurely crossed the New Bethany Bridge on foot. With the Susquehanna churning thirty feet below, the two paused halfway, and took healthy pulls of Irish whiskey from a stainless-steel flask. After disembarking from the bridge, they took a circuitous route into town. They first walked away from the fanfare along a series of fog-draped levies overlooking the river, then doubled back along High Street, voyeuristically peering into the front parlors of the old Victorian mansions there in a state of unbridled antique-envy. They eventually lighted on a spot at about the midpoint of the parade route.

As the bands and floats passed by, and sugar-fortified mana rained down upon the delighted throngs of children, Ryan settled into a state of well-being: loving wife under his arm, and his own happy, healthy children marching by in an all-but-extinct example of small-town Americana.

Honk!

A blaring horn snapped Ryan out of his trance, and he alerted to an immense diesel-powered fire engine as it rolled up the parade route. His throat closed as he spotted a little girl darting out into the street to snatch a fallen Tootsie Roll immediately in front of the truck's oversized right front tire. To his horror, the driver, busy mugging at a covey of teenage girls, failed to notice the child. Ryan tore himself away from Kelly, scythed through the crowd, and threw himself out into the street. There, he came face to face with a canine hood ornament as the truck came screeching to a halt. He bolted around the side of the vehicle and frantically searched for its victim. With a sigh of confused relief, he noted no human detritus under the wheel or in the adjacent gutter.

The fire engine's driver jumped out and grabbed Ryan by the shoulders. "Hey, buddy, you all right? I almost ran you over."

"Yeah, I'm okay," replied Ryan, heart slamming against his ribcage. "A little kid almost went under your wheel, though."

The driver froze and his face turned ashen. He looked all around the truck, then back at Ryan. "You saw a kid too close to the truck?"

"She must have just made it to the other side. Scared the hell out of me, though," replied Ryan, noticing he was trembling.

By now Kelly was out with them. "Ryan, what is it? What's the matter?"

"Oh, just some little kid trying to meet her maker. Where the hell were her parents?" growled Ryan as he squatted to take one more look under the truck.

The driver stooped down by Ryan again, then stood up with a smug smile on his face and put a hand on Ryan's shoulder. "Well, buddy, I'm glad *you* didn't end up under my wheel. Maybe next time it'd be best to leave the drinkin' 'til after the parade, eh?"

Ryan looked up at the guy, eyes narrowed.

"It's on your breath, friend . . ." said the driver with a wink.

Ryan started to protest, his chest tightening, but thought better of it and signaled to Kelly that it was time to head home. Meanwhile, the driver climbed back into the truck and moved along to close the fifty-yard gap that had been created in the parade.

CHAPTER 4

ANY MORE ?

For the rest of the weekend, Ryan struggled with images of the little girl darting out in front of the fire truck. In actuality, though, he struggled more with the driver's admonishment. *What a freaking jerk*, thought Ryan. It had been only by the grace of God, or more likely by blind luck, that the inattentive idiot didn't roll right over the kid. Screw him.

It took reentry into the work week to divest Ryan of his anger and injured pride. And reenter he did, right back into a busy day of call. Day became night, and he didn't come up for air until well after midnight. Any respite was short lived, though.

"Hey, sir, it's me again." It was fifth-year resident Cam Carlson, Ryan's unofficial favorite. Cam had been a safety at Clemson University, and a Rhodes Scholar before heading off to medical school.

"Hey, Cam. What's up?" asked Ryan as he exited his jeep back at the house.

"A ten-year-old girl, Heidi Mueller. Had a bad headache, then collapsed tonight at home. Been in coma since. Big bleed in the cerebellum. AVM on CTA. Intubated. Minimal response to pain. Pics should be in your phone."

Ryan looked at the girl's scans and whistled. "Sheesh. What do you want to do, Cam?"

"Get the bleed out, as soon as possible. But I suspect we're gonna have to tackle the AVM while we're there."

"Agreed, buddy. Meet you there."

Ryan made it to operating room twelve, just as Cam was pushing Heidi's stretcher through the swinging doors. The two surgeons hovered impatiently as the anesthesia team fiddled around taping up her breathing tube and placing additional IVs. Cam then grabbed a vice-like device and clamped it onto Heidi's head, sharp stainless-steel pins puncturing her skin and embedding into her skull. Multiple members of the team lifted and flipped her onto her belly as Ryan guided the positioning of her head. Cam contorted his way under the operating table and secured a set of chrome-plated arms to the device, assuring the stricken girl's head would stay firmly in place throughout the procedure.

Ryan turned to the anesthesia team, hair clippers in hand. "Okay, guys, I hope you've got blood on the way up. This could get messy."

"We're working on it," replied the always-anxious anesthesiologist, Dermott Morgan. "And how the hell do I always manage to be on call with you, Brenan?"

"Born under the right star, I guess," replied Ryan as he shaved a large patch of the back of Heidi's head and upper neck, and then prepped the skin. Soon, he had completed his abbreviated Time-Out and was making a straight up-and-down incision in the area. He and Cam then started dissecting the muscle off the underside of the skull. Without looking up, he addressed a medical student who had scrubbed in with them.

"Okay, Madeline, this young woman has an AVM that's hemorrhaged in the cerebellum. What do you know about AVMs?"

Third-year medical student, Madeline Ador, had been transplanted to America from Haiti at age ten after her parents and brother died in a hurricane. She was diminutive and soft-spoken, but there was steel behind her dark brown eyes. "I believe that 'AVM' stands for 'arteriovenous malformation,'" she answered. "Arteriovenous malformations are tangles of abnormal blood vessels where arteries flow directly into veins without any capillaries in between. The veins aren't equipped to tolerate the pressure of the blood coming through the arteries, so they can tear open and bleed. I think they can go unnoticed for years, then 'rupture,' causing severe bleeding and brain destruction."

Cam and Ryan looked up at each other.

"Sheesh," said Ryan, "not bad, Madeline."

"Yes, well, I had to do a report on them last year. I guess it stuck."

"I guess it did. Well, this one is in the back of this girl's brain, and it indeed bled. The blood is pressing on the brain stem. Doesn't matter how good a shape the rest of your brain is in, if the brain stem's shot, you can't turn on the computer, and you'll be in coma or brain-dead. We'll get the blood out of there as quickly as we can, but Dr. Carlson and I suspect the AVM will let loose when we do. So, be prepared for some bleeding."

And bleed it did. As soon as Ryan and Cam opened the dura, blood spurted out of Heidi's head. The two surgeons suctioned away flowing and clotted blood, and then held pressure on the source with cotton balls. After some tense minutes and some swearing under their breaths, they had the bleeding stopped and were demonstrating the AVM to Madeline.

"Okay, Madeline, you can see that the darned thing did let loose. But we got it under control pretty quickly. To remove it, you've got to be gentle and patient. Approach an AVM at all roughly, and you can bleed someone out. Our goal is to *gently* clip and cut all arteries leading into it. But we leave alone the big veins coming out of it, until all the arteries have been cut. Do you know why?"

Madeline was watching the operation on a huge wall-mounted TV screen. Displayed in high definition was the AVM, looking like a bag of pulsating red worms—a bag of pulsating red worms that might explode at any moment and flood the room with blood. "I guess because you need the veins to drain blood out of the AVM. If you clamp them off while there's still blood pumping in, it will explode."

"Precisely," replied Ryan, "I hope you got an A on that report."

"Oh, Dr. Brenan," replied Madeline. "You know we don't do grades, just pass-fail."

"Yeah, well, good job anyway," said Ryan, admiring the spirit of this survivor of life's all-too-often ruthless capriciousness. "Watch closely, now. In a few moments, Cam is going to clamp off and cut the last artery going in. When he does, the AVM will turn blue and go all limp."

And so it did. And it was subsequently removed from Heidi's brain with little fanfare. The two surgeons closed up the wound and waited to see if there was any chance she would come around for them. Morgan was an abrasive and twitchy anesthesiologist, but he had a gift for waking up patients on demand. Within minutes, Heidi was awake, the breathing tube was out, and she spoke her first words: "I'm hungry."

Ryan and Cam fist-bumped and, after depositing Heidi in the recovery room, headed over together to speak with her parents. The two collected their hugs from the vast and shell-shocked family of farmers but were soon called away to the ER for a seventeen-year-old who had shot himself in the head with a .38.

The young man proved to be unsalvageable. Ryan spoke to the boy's family, shook the tragic nature of the scene out of his head, and left for home. He made it there shortly after 4:00 a.m. Too wound up to go to bed, he flopped onto the family-room couch and flicked on the TV.

Halfway through a sitcom, the scene changed from some absurdly spacious apartment in New York City to a dark, fog-enshrouded graveyard. The camera zoomed in on a deep pit in the ground. It was apparently a mass grave, judging from the lifeless children who lie there. The view shifted out of the grave and onto a veiled, dark-clad woman who looked directly into the camera and asked, "Any more for us, Ryan?"

"Wake up, Ryan. Wake up . . ."

It was Kelly. She was shaking his shoulders. He was still on the couch, tears flowing down his face.

"Jeez, Ry, I could hear you crying from upstairs. Another nightmare?"

"Yeah, I guess so," replied Ryan, trying to reorient himself to the safe confines of his home.

"Well, why don't you go take a quick shower—you're covered in sweat. I'll make you some breakfast. It's late. You need to head back in to the hospital soon."

CHAPTER 5

WHO IS THIS GUY?

"What are you talking about, Ryan?" asked Kelly, her blue eyes flashing. "You love mischief night."

They both did. It had become a Brenan tradition. For the past four years, they and their closest friends would strike out on the night before Halloween and play sophomoric pranks on some of their stodgier acquaintances. This year, however, Ryan begged off. This had become a disturbing pattern. Something at work—he would never explain what—would precipitate several days of malaise and withdrawal. He would then slowly emerge from his funk and be more himself, although each time a little less so.

"Just not feeling up to it, honey," replied Ryan.

"Does it have to do with that little girl?" asked Kelly.

She was referring to a phone call she had partially overheard a couple of nights before. It sounded like some girl in the Pediatric Intensive Care Unit had taken a turn for the worse—something about needing re-intubation. Kelly had queried Ryan about it at the time but, as always, was offered only a sanitized summary of the situation and an empty reassurance that things should turn out all right.

"No . . . she's okay."

"Is it all the nightmares? I mean, they seem to be coming so frequently anymore," pressed Kelly.

"No, Kelly," replied Ryan, a little sharply. "I just don't feel so hot. Maybe I'm coming down with something. I just feel like crashing tonight."

This, in Kelly's mind, was code for him wanting to collapse onto the family-room couch and stay there all evening. "Come on, Ryan. It'll do you good. We haven't hung out with the gang for ever."

"Please, Kell, let's just enjoy each other tonight."

This was more code, for her having to sit silently, nestled under his right arm, watching some insipid movie, or worse, watching him flick aimlessly from one station to another. But she told herself, the guy did work insanely hard and, with the girls all away at a sleep-over, he probably deserved some "fire-gazing" down time. If only he didn't need it all the time. With a sigh of resignation, she made some popcorn, poured some wine, started up one of his beloved cabin-in-the-woods-teenage-slasher movies, and applied herself to his rigid torso on the couch. Before the first gory death, however, the Brenan's two dogs, John and Paul, exploded into a barking frenzy at some gentle knocking at the side door. It was Ryan's closest friend, Matt Wolfe—Plant Manager at a nearby pharmaceutical factory, soccer teammate, and denizen of New Bethany since birth. He had stopped by with his wife, Juleen for "just one" quiet drink together. Fifteen minutes later, Dianne and Hugh O'Connor did the same. When word got out that a group was congealing, three more couples materialized.

With this, Ryan kicked back into gear. Soon he was making killer margaritas and telling tales of raids of yore. A consensus soon built among the group: they simply must hit the residence of good friend, fellow soccer player, and Presbyterian minister/ clinical psychologist, "Reverend Ron." Ryan disappeared for a few minutes and then burst back into the room with face paint, temporary tattoos, and boxes of his old Army Combat Uniforms.

The group suited up and prepared for battle. Juleen Wolfe, by far the most sober of the group, was conscripted into chauffeuring the raiding party in Kelly's van. Soon, a slapstick loading of the vehicle ensued with arms, legs, and buttocks sticking out every window; and a sliding door that couldn't be fully closed. The heavily laden troop carrier crawled across the New Bethany bridge toward the other side of town.

A mile away from Reverend Ron's, Juleen let out a squeal of distress—a police car was on her tail. Ryan, sitting on Matt's lap, suggested that she make a series of turns to see if the police car was definitively in pursuit. It was. Or so it seemed. The tension and giddiness among the intoxicated sardines rose to an intolerable level. The police car fell back a distance at a stoplight. Ryan and Matt seized the opportunity to obviate at least half a dozen of the rapidly accumulating moving vehicle violations. On the next turn, they bailed out of the van as if they were members of a parachute stick over Normandy. They hit the ground and rolled into a nearby ditch. Kelly, Yasan, Ivan, Helmut, and Sasha soon followed. The van took off in Reverend Ron's direction at a slow, careful clip.

On the ground, the deposited troops realized they had grossly missed their intended drop zone. Reverend Ron's split-level firebase was still a several-minute forced march away. Short on alcohol provisions, the team made the agonizing battlefield decision to switch their assault to a secondary target—the home of Matt's brother, Mitch. Although of less strategic value, this enemy lair was within easy striking distance. So, they hit it, and hit it hard.

The initial incursion involved repeatedly ringing the front doorbell, then circling to the poorly patrolled rear. There, the strike force bedecked a small orchard of apple trees with toilet paper and opacified all the house's ground floor windows with soap. They then set off a rainbow of colored smoke bombs, hit the dirt, and laid in wait with their pump-action squirt guns.

Mitch and his wife, Kirsten, confronted by the opacifying fog of purple, orange, and green, were drawn out into the unmerciful outdoors. Suddenly, the strike force pierced the kaleidoscopic veil and fell upon them. Mitch, under an intense barrage, commando-crawled to a hose with an attached power washer, and drove the aggressors into an adjacent forest. Flush with his apparent victory, he continued to fire into the thickets and taunt the vanquished invaders. Only, the invaders were no longer there. They had circled back, two houses down, and returned on hands and knees to the front door. Soon, they were inside. They secured the entrances, activated all indoor and outdoor lighting, blasted out death metal on the sound system, and plundered the stores of ale.

Assessing that all was lost, Mitch and Kirsten surrendered and were taken prisoner. With the fall of the stronghold, the jubilant victors hailed Juleen, and she, the remainder of the raiding party, and Reverend Ron, soon joined in on the armistice celebrations.

As the revelry reached a fever pitch, Kelly sat quietly in a kitchen chair, transfixed by the main catalyst of the affair, her husband, her Ryan. He was so full of life, and joy, and creative adolescent mischievousness. He filled the room with his incandescent personality. Everyone around him seemed to sparkle in his light. She frowned. A tear formed in her right eye. Who was this guy? Where had he been hiding? Why did he show up so rarely? How long before he would disappear again?

CHAPTER 6

BRAIN-DEAD

He didn't stick around for long, but it probably wasn't entirely Ernest Nobleman's fault. Ryan loved all the Carriere neurosurgical residents, and delighted in teaching them, but one or two of them could definitely test his patience, Ernest being the most adept. Ernest, a holder of an MD and a PhD from Harvard, was a brilliant but distractible first-year resident. The guy knew his neuroscience back to front, but sometimes had trouble applying it to the real world. He had called Ryan down to the emergency room shortly after 1:00 a.m., several days after Halloween. A Penn State student had run his car into a tree at seventy miles an hour, reportedly trying to avoid a deer.

"Hey there, Dr. Ryan . . . I mean, Dr. Brenan," started Ernest. "I think we need to go on this one . . . he has a bad fracture dislocation of the neck. He was avoiding a deer, and he has a ruptured spleen . . . and—and he isn't moving, and—"

"Hold on, hold on, Ernest," interrupted Ryan, holding up his palms. "You're firing a bunch of non sequiturs at me. Can we start at the beginning, please?"

"Um . . . yeah. Well, there was a deer . . . and the guy broke his neck, and—"

"Is that what we lead with, Ernest?" asked Ryan, trying to help his resident organize his thoughts.

"Um, no sir. Um . . . uh . . ."

"How old? Male or female? Type of accident. You know the drill."

"Oh, okay, Dr. Brenan. I'm just concerned that we need to take this guy to the operating room right away—"

"That's why we're having this conversation," answered Ryan, examining the patient.

"Um, okay, uh . . . we have a nineteen-year-old male, who was a restrained driver in a high-speed motor vehicle accident, with a protracted extraction and multiple trauma . . ."

"See, that wasn't so hard, was it?"

Ernest clearly couldn't hold back the whirlwind of additional information swirling around in his head a millisecond longer and blurted, "No, but the guy has a bad neck fracture, and it's compressing his spinal cord, and—"

"And, what's his exam?" interrupted Ryan.

"Well, nothing's working, sir . . ."

"Oh, Ernest, you're killing me. Describe his neurological exam—like a neurosurgeon."

"Well, he's in coma and's showing no response to voice or pain—"

"Aha! There's a start. Go on."

"And he has a broken neck, and—"

"Goddamn it, Ernest, if you mention his broken neck one more time, I'm going to slit my wrists," responded Ryan, turning scarlet. "I want to know the status of his brain! Stay on the neurological exam!"

"Okay, um . . ."

Ernest was so agitated he was hopping from one foot to the other. If he were a puppy, thought Ryan, he'd be peeing on himself. Perhaps he was, anyway.

"Come on, Ernest, what comes next?" pressed Ryan.

"Um . . . well, there's no eye opening, or attempts at verbalization . . ."

"Cranial nerves?" prompted Ryan.

"Um, not so good . . ."

Ryan almost leaped over the gurney to thrash Ernest, but recognized he was making the guy nervous—short-circuiting his brain—and eased up. "Remember, buddy, you've got to be specific. On my exam, the patient has dilated, oblong, and unresponsive pupils; no corneal reflexes, no gag, and no breathing over the ventilator. What does that tell you, and what further information would you like to know?"

"I want to know if he can move, because he has a bad cervical fracture dislocation . . ."

"Oh Ernest, you're ripping the soul right out of me. Stay in the head. His spinal cord's no freakin' good without a brain. We don't even know if he's alive, do we? We need to figure out if he's brain-dead. What else could we do to help determine this?"

"Oh shit, yeah, Dr. Brenan. Um, how about cold calorics?"

"Bingo! Have you performed those?"

"No, I forgot." Ernest burst toward the equipment cabinets to start setting up for the test, which involved flooding the eardrums with ice-cold water and looking for certain reflexive eye movements.

"No, not now, Ernest, that can wait. But we do have to suspect that in addition to his cervical fracture he has a devastating brain injury, don't we?"

"Yes, sir."

"So, what did the CT show?" asked Ryan.

"Um, yeah, no major bleeds . . ."

"Let's take a look then."

The two accessed the scans on a nearby computer.

Ryan cleared his throat. "Um, Ernest, how would you describe the patient's hemispheres?"

"I think they look a little swollen."

"Swollen, eh? How's the gray-white distinction? How does the overall anatomy look? Here, stand back a couple of feet." Ryan took Ernest by the shoulders and moved him away from the screen.

"Shit. Oh shit. You're saying his brain looks like 'ground glass,'" replied Ernest.

"So, what does that mean to you?"

"Maybe that the kid's stroked out his whole brain . . ."

"So, he's screwed. Isn't he?," asked Ryan.

"I guess so, sir."

"Okay, let's look at his spine now . . ."

The spine was a mess, with a bad fracture of the neck, as advertised. But this indeed proved to be the least of the young man's problems. A vessel study of his head showed no discernible blood flow above the neck. His brain was dead.

"So, do you still think we should drag this poor kid off to the OR to fix his neck?"

"No. I guess not, Dr. Brenan."

"All right, let's go break the awful news to the family."

The large collection of stricken faces were packed into a small consultation room like rush-hour commuters on a Japanese subway. The room reeked of sweat-saturated polyester. Ryan sandwiched himself inside and addressed the young man's parents.

"Mrs. Franklin, Mr. Franklin, I'm Dr. Brenan. I'm the neurosurgeon covering emergencies here tonight, and I'm going to tell you all I can about DeShawn's injuries. First of all, though, can you tell me what *you* know?"

Everyone was crying or outright weeping, but as Ryan had witnessed a thousand times before, the parents stepped up, exhibiting supernatural courage and grace. Mrs. Franklin took the lead. "Not much, Dr. Brenan. Some doctors came in a little while ago and said DeShawn was in bad shape—"

"Shawnie was tryin' to save a deer," chimed in a little girl in pigtails, face stained by tears.

Ryan pulled up a chair and positioned himself immediately in front of Mrs. Franklin, who sat literally on the edge of her seat—a dingy, coffee-stained, burnt orange, relic of the early 2000's. "Mrs. And Mr. Franklin." Ryan looked about the room at all faces. "Guys, I have nothing but rough things to tell you. But please bear with me. I'll tell you everything I know. And you can ask me anything. *Anything.* Got it?"

Mrs. Franklin nodded. The rest swayed with anguish at the new and horrific reality that was surely coming their way.

"I am so sorry to have to tell you this, but DeShawn is not going to survive," began Ryan.

There was a cry of agony from the back of the room. Several people sat down on the floor.

Ryan shifted in his chair and continued, "He sustained what we call 'multiple trauma.' That is, many parts of his body were badly injur—"

"How can that be?" blurted out a big, powerful, middle-aged man, possibly an uncle. "His car has all the safety features. This is bullshit, man, what's the point of all that safety shit if it can't save you from hitting a tree."

Mrs. Franklin shot the apparent uncle a "settle-down-and-let-the-doctor-speak" look. The uncle shrunk back into the crowd.

Ryan addressed him nonetheless: "You know, I've been working in trauma for many years. The simplest things can cause freak accidents, horrible accidents, and terrible injuries. It *never* makes sense. And you're right." Ryan had shifted his gaze to the little girl. "He was trying to avoid hurting a deer . . ." He went on to explain that although DeShawn's heart was still beating, his brain had permanently ceased working, and that he was thus considered brain-dead.

Tears flowed down Mr. and Mrs. Franklin's faces, but both maintained rapt attention.

"So, are you saying that nothing can be done to help DeShawn get better, Dr. Brenan?" asked Mrs. Franklin.

"Yes, Mrs. Franklin. I'm afraid so," replied Ryan, feeling tears forming in his own eyes. "There are no medicines or surgeries that will bring him back."

Another burly uncle stepped forward out of the crowd. "But you always hear about someone coming out of a coma months, even years, after a head injury . . ."

"That's true," replied Ryan, "but it's actually very rare. That's why it makes the news. And it never happens in people with the type of injuries that DeShawn has sustained; that is, when their brain has died."

"What should we do then, Dr. Brenan?" asked Mrs. Franklin. "I mean, what comes next for my boy? Does he just get unplugged?"

Ryan held up his hands. "No, Mrs. Franklin. We don't need to rush into anything. His neurological exam right now is consistent with brain death, but we purposefully wait several hours before performing another formal exam in case there is the slightest possibility that we could be wrong. So, right now, we should move him to an ICU, support his lungs and heart, and see if anything changes. I don't believe it will, but I would love to be proven wrong."

"But you won't be, will you, Dr. Brenan?" asked Mrs. Franklin.

"No, ma'am. It's not going to happen in poor DeShawn's case. I'm so very sorry."

Mrs. Franklin nodded slowly but knowingly. Others in the crowd still bore expressions of doubt and hostility. Ryan fielded scores of questions. Anger and distrust gave way to unbridled grief.

"The nurses told us you're the best, Dr. Brenan, and I believe them," remarked Mrs. Franklin once everyone had run out of queries. "You've been very honest and kind, and I can see that it grieves you not to be helping my boy."

Ryan looked at the ground for a moment and then returned his gaze to Mrs. Franklin. "It absolutely does. And you and your family are being so amazingly brave. I should tell you, though, that there's another component to this whole dreadful situation that you need to be aware of, so it doesn't come as a shock..."

"What is that?" Mrs. Franklin asked with obvious trepidation in her eyes—as if she were questioning, how could this get any worse?

"Well, in situations like DeShawn's, an organ donation team will automatically be contacted, and they'll want to talk to you."

Mrs. Franklin shot a warning glance at the murmuring crowd and then asked, "About taking De Shawn's organs?"

"Yes, ma'am."

An agonized rumble arose from the crowd. Disgruntled conversation mixed with crying and prayers echoed about the small room in a cacophony of horror and despondency. Mrs. Franklin shushed the crowd, paused for thought, then asked: "Is it possible, then, that my baby's organs could help someone else?"

"It is, Mrs. Franklin. It's very possible. He's so young and healthy..."

More rumbles, more crying.

"Dr. Brenan, do you have children of your own?" asked Mrs. Franklin.

"Yes, ma'am, three little girls, who I love dearly, like you love DeShawn," replied Ryan, who was struck dumb by how much he meant it, and by how unimaginable, yet wholly imaginable, this type of tragedy befalling one of his angels was to him.

"Then you know what we're going through here," stated Mrs. Franklin.

Ryan choked up on this one and had to restart his response. "Oh no, Mrs. Franklin, I don't. I can't. I can't imagine what you're going through right now. I can't fathom your loss. It's clear to me, though, looking around this room, that DeShawn is a very special and a very loved young man."

"He is, Dr. Brenan. But if you, as the loving father that you seem to be, are telling me that there is no hope of getting my boy back, I think we have to pray that some good can come out of this, somehow," said Mrs. Franklin as she sought through eye contact, and received, a nod of acquiescence from her husband. "So, if my baby's organs could help someone else, please, make sure that the organ people do come speak with us."

"I will, Mrs. Franklin," assured Ryan. "And please, understand, DeShawn has experienced no pain throughout any of this."

Mrs. Franklin touched her eyes with a handkerchief.

"I appreciate that, Dr. Brenan. Thank you for making that clear to all of us." She stood up. "Can I see my boy now?"

"Absolutely," said Ryan.

Ryan, Ernest, and a nurse led Mr. and Mrs. Franklin to the room where DeShawn awaited transfer to the Neurotrauma ICU. Ryan took his leave. He felt completely drained and didn't think he could bear witnessing this saintly woman tending to her dying son.

CHAPTER 7

AUTUMN LEAVES

Mrs. Franklin's parental grief was still haunting Ryan on a Friday evening, two weeks before Thanksgiving. He felt drained and, on arriving home, plopped down on the family-room couch and sipped some Irish whiskey. A sporting event on the TV held his attention for all of a minute, and then the world blurred and went dark.

"Oh no, mister, wake up. The gang'll be here any minute now."

It was Kelly. Ryan looked up at the clock and realized he had been asleep for at least half an hour.

"Go collect the girls. They're in the study with Ben," ordered Kelly, pulling Ryan up by the arms.

The study was a small room filled with floor-to-ceiling, glassed-in mahogany bookcases just to the right of the front entranceway. Ryan dutifully made his way there and peered in. Ava, Riley, and Erin were seated on the floor around a bearded old man dressed in tweed. He was sitting in a wingback leather chair and was showing pictures to the girls from a large, leather-bound book. Only the pictures depicted dark, gruesome, gratuitous scenes of torture, mutilation, and dismemberment. The girls were all quaking with terror, pleading for the old man to stop, and grasping and clutching for one another. Ryan leaped toward the doorway but as he did, the old man slammed the door shut with a cane. Ryan reached for the knob, but it broke off in his hand as the girls' screams scorched his ears.

Ryan's eyes sprung open. He was still on the family-room couch. Kelly was standing over him, shaking him.

"Oh no, mister, wake up. The gang'll be here any minute now."

It had been a brutal couple of weeks since Halloween. Long hours, lots of calls, physically taxing surgeries. And, since pronouncing the Franklin boy brain-dead, it seemed that every time he fell asleep, this same nightmare struck. Ben, whoever the hell *he* was, and his grisly book. But it was Friday night, and everyone was headed to the high school's last football game of the season. As Ryan started to stir, the front doorbell rang.

Excited calls of "Come on, guys," bounced about the downstairs hallways in three-part harmony. "Everyone's here!"

New Bethany was short on formal entertainment for adults, so even the most mundane of events could take on the luster of a Broadway play on opening night. The high-school football clashes certainly fit the bill. Each game drew a sizable collection of the local populace despite a guaranteed mediocre performance by the home team. The New Bethany Crusaders just couldn't compete with some of the powerhouses from nearby "coal country." Many of the teams, such as Coalville, Fracktown, and Shamaqua, were notorious for their liberal deployment of "red-shirts"—boys who had been started in kindergarten a year or two later than normal in anticipation of their eventual physical maturational edge on the high-school gridiron. Nonetheless, the affair was a major social event—for all ages. Other than a few hard-core dads who stood as close to the action as allowable, bleating out their violent inanities, most adults could be found around the end-zone concession trailers, dressed in heavy parkas, gabbing over steaming cups of coffee, or better yet, hot apple cider, enlivened with Wild Turkey Bourbon. Teens distanced themselves from the adults, but mimicked their parents' behavior of congregating, chatting, and spiking their drinks. Preteens traipsed around the field in expanding and contracting amoeboid clumps. And the game would start and finish without the crowd taking much notice.

The stadium itself was crouched in a flood-prone bowl and consisted of crumbling and soon-to-be-condemned concrete stands for the home fans and, on the opposite side of the field, sagging, splintered, wooden bleachers for the visitors. On game nights, there was an otherworldly aura to the place thanks to its sunken nature, its hyper-echoic surroundings, and a fog that would creep up from the river and swallow it whole.

The Brenan clan was joined by the Wolfes and their four children, and the O'Connors and their five. Soon they were crossing the bridge on foot, the adults passing around a couple of flasks of Jameson. After exiting the bridge, the group moved along the levees toward a telltale yellow glow in the mist-laden atmosphere and the sounds of high-school marching bands violating outdated hip-hop standards. Kelly, Dianne, and Juleen were engaged in their usual rapid-fire discourse, into which Hugh kept trying, unsuccessfully, to insert himself. Matt played with the children, joining them in dramatic tumbles down the slopes of the levees. A taciturn Ryan drifted along at the rear, deep in thought, or in no thought at all. At a T-intersection below, however, something caught his eye. He wasn't a natural-born worrier, but, after years of witnessing every permutation of what should be innocuous human fun result in unthinkable tragedy, he had developed a keen radar for prospective calamities, and a series of shrill alarms were now sounding deep within his chest. A pickup truck had raged up to the intersection, whipped hard to the left onto Susquehanna Avenue, and roared away from the fanfare of the game. In the truck's bed, five or six teenage bodies bounced along, all leaning out over the side as if they were deckhands on a heeling America's Cup sailboat.

"Morons," growled Ryan under his breath. *Jesus.* How many times had he needed to tell some mother that her dear progeny had split their head open doing crap like that? How many times had he—

He halted, as the group continued on.

"What the . . ."

Something wasn't right. The truck was from another era, yes, but that wasn't uncommon in these parts. It was something else. Maybe it was that the vehicle, and its occupants, looked a little fuzzy, a little indistinct, maybe even a little transparent. No, that wasn't it. It was foggy, and the fogs around the region were notorious for playing tricks on the eye. Then it hit him. As the truck had screamed down Susquehanna Avenue, it had slammed into a great stack of leaves. Yet, as it blew its way through, not a single leaf stirred. The stack was left unmolested.

Strange.

"Yo, Ryan!" It was Matt, now fifty yards ahead with the rest of the crew. "You comin'?"

"Huh? Sure," replied Ryan as he began to walk, eyes still scanning the undisturbed pile.

CHAPTER 8

STORIES

Untroubled leaf piles disappeared from Ryan's top ten list of concerns the second he entered the Monday morning fray of the hospital. By the afternoon, they would have been lucky to make the top hundred. Now in first place had to be Benjamin Rush University junior Ann Hodges, and her boyfriend Jonathan Brandis. By report, Ann had just turned twenty-one. She and Jonathan had planned to go out that evening to a bona fide restaurant—one with tablecloths, fawning waiters, and wine lists—once she was cleaned up from three hours of field hockey practice. But Jonathan had painstakingly arranged something else altogether. A huge surprise party awaited Ann at the apartment she shared with four other women. Jonathan had apparently timed the event to the second. He had stationed a friend at the entrance of the building who would notify him of Ann's arrival. As Ann scaled the five flights of stairs to the apartment, he would position the merrymakers and douse the lights. Upon her opening the door, he would lead the group in a unified cheer of "surprise," and hit the celebratory playlist.

As fate would have it, though, Ann's practice ended twenty minutes early due to the head coach being assaulted by a gastro-intestinal virus. Ann therefore made it to the apartment building twenty minutes early, at the exact moment Jonathan's friend temporarily abandoned his sentry post to decompress his beer-distended bladder. Undetected, Ann reached her apartment, turned the key in the door, and stepped into the crowded living room, surprising her friends more than they were able to surprise her. Although not as shocked and awed by the gathering as she might have been, she was deeply moved. She cried, and hugged and kissed multiple attendees, then called out to her beloved. A fissure formed in the mass of young bodies, creating an unobstructed pathway to Jonathan, who was standing at the back of the room leaning up against a large picture window. The two locked eyes. Ann broke into an athletic sprint and leaped into Jonathan's arms, wrapping her legs high around his waist.

Unfortunately, the leap was a little too athletic. She impacted the rather slight Jonathan with enough force to throw him backward. They crashed through the window and plummeted to the ground, still locked in their embrace. An hour later, they were in adjoining trauma bays at the medical center.

Ann was awake but bruised from head to toe. She had sustained multiple long bone fractures and injuries to her spleen and liver. Of greatest concern, however, was the fact that her thoracic spine was shattered. Jonathan harbored no cuts or bruises or fractures but was in coma. The going theory was that the two must have turned in mid-air, with Jonathan's body being protected from impact by Ann's, but his head clipping the back end of a sports utility vehicle on the way down. One way or another, the left side of his skull was caved in, and his brain showed severe pulping from one end to the other on a CT scan. Ryan rushed him off to surgery and cleaned things up as much as possible but sighed as he surveyed the macerated mush that once was the boy's thoughtful and loving brain. He couldn't conceive of Jonathan doing anything but dying, and then only after a protracted ICU course of coma, multiple complications, and transformation into a bloated and discolored "living" corpse.

Ann could and should fare better—physically, at least.

Miraculously, she wasn't paralyzed. She needed a night of trauma team attention, but then in the morning, Ryan and his team would be free to piece her spine back together.

———

"So, here's a great example of the world of trauma," commented Ryan to a small collection of nursing students the next morning, as he operated on Ann. "Two happy, healthy college students joyfully celebrating one of life's epochs, and then all hell breaks loose. In an instant, one becomes slated for death and the other becomes damned to a lifetime of horrible memories and guilt over killing the love of her life. Yep, working in a trauma center can be pretty grim..."

"What types of injuries get to you the most, Doctor?" asked one of the students.

"Well, I'm afraid I've become pretty hardened to the actual injuries—no matter how gruesome. I suppose you have to, to be able to do your job. But I'll tell you what does get to me..."

"What's that?"

"The darn stories."

"The stories?"

"Yeah, like this young woman," replied Ryan as he turned a large titanium screw in Ann's back. "They all come in with an attached story about how they ended up the way they ended up. Then every member of the care team embellishes the story—fills in little pieces—the more gut-wrenching, the better. Others sprinkle in what a wonderful person the victim was. Most of the time we're so focused on the neurosurgical problems at hand that we forget there's a human being attached to them." *And that's probably a good thing—for us . . . and them,* thought Ryan as he bent a long metal rod with some medieval-looking tool.

"But the stories drive home the point that we're dealing with very real people," continued Ryan, placing the rod into screw heads in Ann's back. "People who have hit the wrong number on the great roulette wheel of life; people who have been, for some reason, abused by the cosmos. And I have to say, it gets to me. So, frankly, I don't ever wanna hear their stories. I don't want to know who they are. I don't want to know about their accomplishments. And I certainly don't want to know the Rube-Goldberg way in which they met their fates."

Ryan and second-year resident Michelle Sawvell kept working on Ann's back, locking with bolts the metal rod into the heads of several screws.

"I imagine stories like this girl's can stay with you for a long time, can't they, Doctor?" asked the student.

"You'd think so," replied Ryan. "I mean, can it get any nastier than this? But it can. A kid comes in with a malignant brain tumor, a young mother blows an aneurysm, a toddler accidentally shoots his little sister. And soon, Ann here blends in with all the other horror shows. Every time you hear a helicopter landing on the roof, it's pretty much a guarantee that someone's life has just been turned completely upside down."

As if on cue, the operating room "squawk box" came to life. This was a communication device apparently installed during the First World War, judging from its acoustic fidelity.

"Hey, Ryan, it's Loren Sykes down in the ER. Got a minute?"

"Sure."

"We've got a twenty-year-old woman down here—about sixteen weeks pregnant—ruptured aneurysm, sure looks brain-dead to me. She's hypotensive and not responding well to resuscitation. The baby's too young to be delivered. What do you want us to do with her?"

"Jesus," blurted Ryan. "Um, see what you can do to get her stabilized. We'll get down there as soon as we can. Thanks, Loren."

Ryan worked for a minute or two, then looked up at the nursing student. "See what I mean?"

But Ann's story did stick with him. For an unusually long time. It was god-awful for sure, but so were so many others. Perhaps it was because he had looked into Ann's eyes several times a day, over several days, and saw the terrible toll the event was taking on her psyche. How future birthdays would forever be marred by what had happened. How they would serve as mileposts pointing back to the worst experience of her life, resurrecting all the associated anguish, guilt, and loss. How future relationships would be tainted, even inhibited, by a sickening sense of vulnerability—vulnerability to a cruel and capricious world. How this "life event," this "period of adversity," wouldn't simply leave some scattered scars—scars that might gradually fade, scars that might strengthen her, build her resilience, mature her—but instead would likely leave gaping wounds, wounds that would never heal, wounds that would open and pour out their vile contents whenever they so chose.

His only solace was that Ann *would* eventually blend in with the others, into the great amalgam of tragedies that was his professional memory. Her name would likely leave first. It always did. Then her anguished face would fuse with the many others into almost no face at all. The distinguishing features planed away. Then her operative site of torn and bloody muscles and smashed and splintered bone that at one point seemed burned into his retinas, would merge with hundreds of others into one great tapestry of anatomic disarray. Finally, details of the story, particularly the nastier ones, would begin to blur and cross over with others so that he would come to question whether specific elements were part of her story, or someone else's; or were creations of his own novelty-seeking mind.

CHAPTER 9

BAND PRACTICE

He was gone again. There was no doubt about it in Kelly's mind. He had made that lovely appearance on mischief night, then seemed to struggle to hold on over the next few weeks. Then, shortly before Thanksgiving, he disappeared. And *this* funk had settled in for weeks on end—well into December. Not that he was home much, but when he was, he was barely communicative and had set up camp on the couch, eschewing any suggestion of social engagements. She had tried to draw him out on several occasions but was rebuffed with his usual platitudes that he would be just fine once he had a chance to recharge his batteries. She teetered on the edge of suggesting he see a psychiatrist. He had done so a couple of years back but bailed after he became convinced that the "shrink" was more depressed than he was. She decided to try something else first. She would call a band practice. If anything could resuscitate him back to the old Ryan, back to her Ryan, it would be a band practice.

The origin of said occasions dated back to the couple's second year in New Bethany, at a bonfire in Matt Wolfe's capacious backyard. Matt had turned the several-acre expanse into a rustic playground with a go-cart course, quoits pits, volleyball courts, trampolines, mini-soccer fields, a BB gun target range, and an above-ground swimming pool. At its very back, close enough to the woods to hear owls and coyotes call, he would erect towering pyres and, on frosty fall evenings, set them ablaze. The gang would congregate, toast the gods of autumn, and cook potatoes wrapped in aluminum foil in the glowing coals. A group of kids, the Brenan girls included, would alternate between the many outdoor amusements and toasting sandwiches in iron presses thrust into the fire.

Ryan was a passable rhythm guitarist and, one night, Kelly prodded him into bringing his father's old Taylor to a bonfire. Once the gang had warmed up internally as well as externally, Ryan began to play. The effect was beguiling. Everyone started to sing along. Matt ran inside and came back out with a fiddle. Mark Dike drove home on screeching wheels and came back with a portable keyboard. Jim Kassal pulled out a harmonica. Gary Shepler kept time with two sticks and a plastic pale. And several of the women sang into an ancient karaoke machine.

A garage band had been born. More like a barn band, though, because the group employed the Brenan barn for their "practices." The somewhat canted, blood-red building was once a horse stable with room for a couple of stalls and a buggy downstairs, and a hayloft upstairs. It was old and decrepit, but it warmed up nicely in the winter with a couple of milk-house heaters and seemed to keep the noise well contained within its rough-hewn walls.

In the best of times, the band would congregate in the lower level once a month and run through scores of oldies—ancient oldies. About one out of every five or six selections would come off passably and would be toasted as a "keeper" by the band with a shot of Irish whiskey. Thus, the practices were set out upon immutable arcs of improving performance with diminished inhibitions, short periods of peak performance, and then precipitous declines into dystonic caterwauling. But the members had the time of their lives and, with the barn doors closed, the police were rarely summoned.

Kelly adored the practices. She loved how, in their initial hours, they served to bring her girls and Ryan together in a fun and joyful activity, well away from TVs, phones, and computers. She loved how they served to gather all of their friends in one happy place. And she particularly loved how they served to resurrect that guy she had married; that happy, neurosurgery-free guy of whom she once couldn't get enough. On this night, resurrect him it did. By the second set he was in full Ryan form, and Kelly savored singing alongside him, often into the same mic.

During a beer break, Kelly ran into Reverend Ron. Reverend Ron wasn't a band member, but he derived great pleasure from the practices through hanging out with any and all of the non-musically-inclined wives and girlfriends in attendance.

"Hey there, gorgeous," said Reverend Ron. "So wonderful to see the gang back together again. Is everything all right in the Brenan compound? Ryan doing okay?"

"I guess so," replied Kelly, a little taken aback. "Why do you ask?"

"I dunno. I pass him every so often in the hospital, and he always looks so harried and hassled. He rarely even notices me—just blows right past. And he's not making it to any of our soccer games. And these silly band practices are getting further and further apart. To be honest, I'm worried about him. His personality type puts him at high risk, you know."

"His personality type?" responded Kelly, eyebrows raised.

"You know. Hero type. Indestructible. Lone Cowboy. Keeps everything bottled up. Hyper-intense. Perfectionistic. Relentless self-improver. Intolerant of his own weaknesses and foibles . . . I could go on."

Kelly let out a big sigh. Ron had reached right into her bucket of worries without any preamble whatsoever. "Yeah, well, I'm worried about him too. Is there any way you might speak with him? He's so stubborn about sharing any problems with me.

Thinks he's protecting me or something. But maybe he'd open up to you. I would have to think he's right up your alley. Or he will be, if he ends up blowing a gasket . . ."

Kelly was referring to Reverend Ron's ascension to the status of a nationally acclaimed "Doc Whisperer." It had all started with a couple of Carriere "disruptive physicians." They had been sent his way after having been given a choice between psychological counseling or dismissal. They chose the former, but insisted on a non-Carriere shrink. Reverend Ron was a full-time minister and part-time psychologist, and he took the two docs on because they were "C&E" members of his flock. He found the docs to be good people who had acted out after reaching work-related states of emotional exhaustion. He had them both back on the job and feeling much happier after just a few sessions. Soon there was a regular lineup of other troubled Carriere physicians at his door. From there, it didn't take long for other assorted healthcare systems to catch wind of the miracle work he was doing and gleefully dump their problem children on him. Over the span of a dozen years, he had treated hundreds of tortured souls, written multiple related papers, and published a couple of books. He even periodically made the morning TV talk-show circuit, after one physician suicide or another—his black handlebar mustache seeming to add psychological gravitas to his assertions.

"I can try, Kelly. But like you said, he's a stubborn guy. And so damned prideful—at least with respect to his grit. He could be a tough nut to crack."

"Yeah, well, if he keeps going like he is, I'm afraid he might *become* a cracked nut," quipped Kelly with a forced smile.

"Well, Kelly, often these physician problems start on the home front—or at least are exacerbated there. How's it going in that realm? If you don't mind my prying."

"Hmm. I'd have to sa—"

"Come on, Kelly," interrupted Ryan. "Stop talking with that washed-up old striker. Get back to your mic. We're about to do the Beatles!"

"Shoot," said Kelly as she stood. "I've gotta go. You know how Ryan is about the Beatles."

Kelly knew that Ryan had a near mystical attachment to the band. They were apparently his father's favorite, and their music used to fill the Brenan household when Ryan was a child. She also knew that "Across the Universe" was playing on a stereo when Ryan learned of his father's death, and that ever since, the poor guy couldn't hear the opening chords of the song without breaking into tears.

The band had recongealed and started playing. Kelly shrugged at Reverend Ron and joined them.

"I'll work on him," mouthed Reverend Ron, as "I Saw Her Standing There" exploded out of the amps.

The band sawed their way through a good fifteen Fab Four pieces, including three keepers. Halfway through "Get Back," Ryan stopped playing. He looked as if he was straining to hear past the music. Kelly sidestepped over to him and asked what was up.

"Did you hear that?" Ryan asked. "Upstairs in the loft. People walking around. Moving things . . ."

"Could be a couple of the gang goofing around," replied Kelly.

"I hope not. It's a disaster up there. I barricaded it off for the night." Ryan's expression turned to concern. "It's not the kids, is it?"

"No, honey. They went back down to the house a couple of hours ago. I'm sure they're in bed. Allisa runs a tight ship." She was referring to Allisa Wolfe, Matt and Juleen's fifteen-year-old daughter.

"I better have a look anyway."

Kelly watched as Ryan made his way to the stairs in the back of the barn. A few minutes later, in the middle of "Hey Jude," the music cut off and lights went out. From above, there were a couple of loud thumps followed by a moan.

"Ryan, you okay up there?" Kelly called out into the darkness, only to be responded to with another moan.

Kelly pushed open one of the barn doors, encouraging some illumination from a streetlight out on Avenue G. She grabbed a couple of large flashlights from a shelf by the entrance and addressed to the gang. "Hold on a sec, guys. We must have blown a fuse again. Matt, can you get down to the house and see?" She handed Matt one of the flashlights. "I'm going upstairs to check on Ryan."

Soon she was up in the loft, a beam of light running over Ryan as he sat on the floor rubbing his head.

"Ryan, what happened? You okay? What was that thump?"

"Probably my head."

"Your head?" asked Kelly.

"Yeah, when the lights went out, I heard a creak in the floorboards behind me and felt someone tap me on the shoulder. I turned around and thought I saw someone, a woman, right behind me. Scared the crap out of me. I jumped back and slammed my head against one of the beams. Almost knocked me out."

"Ouch," remarked Kelly.

The lights came back on.

"See, there's my lady," said Ryan, nodding toward an old sewing mannequin in a black slip.

"What did you think it was, a ghost?" teased Kelly.

"Or an axe murderer, I guess . . ."

"Well, come on then," replied Kelly, helping Ryan up. "Let's get some ice on that noggin."

They started walking toward the stairs, Kelly supporting a woozy Ryan. She looked over at the mannequin again. "Ha! Doesn't take much to spook you, does it, honey?"

CHAPTER 10

CHRISTMAS SPIRIT

The truth was, there wasn't much that did spook Ryan. But on occasion, the house sure could.

It wasn't spooky per se, but it was a rambling 160-year-old former farmhouse, and its age, its echoic spaces, its creaky knotted-pine floorboards, its slanted upstairs hallways, and its oil-craving nineteenth century door hinges gave it the potential for a spectral feel at night, or when occupied alone. To further the effect, the house was surrounded by imposing trees that, on moonlit nights, cast cavorting shadows upon the walls through warped, oversized windows. Certainly, the girls never ventured out of the family room or kitchen without sisterly or canine escort. No matter how creepy it could be, though, the house demonstrated supreme competence in hosting Ryan and Kelly's annual Christmas party. And said party always proved to be a riotous affair full of laughter, debauchery, and singing. In fact, the singing was mandatory. After the revelers had toasted the season with several shots of Irish whiskey, Ryan would sit down at an antique player piano, load up a music roll, and pump his legs furiously. The holiday standards would fill the house, and the merrymakers had no choice but to gather and bellow.

So, a week before Christmas, Ryan found himself pumping out one holiday treat after another to a room packed with revelers. After ten or so, the muscles in his legs had filled with lactic acid, and he gave up the pumping station to the always game Matt

Wolfe. He then slipped to the back of the room and sipped some hot chocolate spiked with peppermint schnapps. During a rousing version of "O Holy Night," he glanced across the front hallway into the study. There, seated in the wingback chair, was an elderly gentleman. For some reason, Ryan couldn't help but study the guy. There was something familiar about him. As if sensing the attention, the gentleman turned his head, made direct eye contact with Ryan, smiled, and nodded. Ryan smiled and nodded back, but still couldn't place the guy.

In truth, this was par for the course. Kelly had a habit of inviting multiple nearby neighbors to the party, her theory being that it would be harder for them to be offended by the hijinks of the affair if they were complicit in them. It seemed to work. The year prior, for example, several partygoers thought it amusing to place all the neighborhood's Christmas lawn figures in indelicate positions. This proved particularly risqué with a series of animated reindeer and reached its greatest level of indecency with a group of orally fixated elves. No complaints were lodged, however, and the figurines were restored to their more reverent attitudes by church time the following morning. Thus unfamiliar faces at the party were common to Ryan. But there was something about this guy that unnerved him. Kelly was across the room, so he decided to grab her and inquire about the identity of the old geezer.

He swam through the torrent of well-lubricated well-wishers. He made it halfway when he froze and began to tremble. The guy, the old guy. It was him. Different outfit. Beard more trimmed. Hair a little more gray. But it was him. At least it sure looked like him. The old man from his recurring nightmares. The old man with the gore-fest children's book. The old man who liked to trap and torment his girls behind the library door. What the hell was going on? *Christ,* thought Ryan, *am I asleep and in another nightmare? Has this whole evening been a twisted dream?*

He pinched the webspace between his thumb and index finger. Dug in his fingernails. Hard. Drawing blood. The mass of bodies, the pine-scented air, the music from the piano, the laughter, the singing, the happy faces all remained. He bit down hard on his lower lip. Same. *Ridiculous*, he told himself. *Booze. Fatigue. That has to be it. You're just letting your imagination too far off the leash. Go back. Have another look. You'll see. It's just a freaking neighbor. One of Kelly's strays.*

He had to will himself to take the first step. But soon he was swimming back. It took some work, but he made it to the library. The chair was empty. The room itself was empty—save their neighbor, June Haley, obliviously making out with someone other than her husband in a far corner. Ryan smiled, but then was seized with a wave of panic.

Christ, the girls!

He sliced through a thicket of guests in the hallway and then bounded up the front staircase, three steps at a time. He sprinted down the hallway and slid to a stop at the playroom, grabbing hold of the doorknob. The door was stuck. He threw his shoulder into it. It popped open and twelve smiling faces looked up at him. Ava, Riley, and Erin; the Wolfe's children, and the O'Connors, all happily watching Christmas movies. He smiled through constricted lips, then pulled the door closed and stumbled back down to the party. *Jesus, man*, he thought, *get a grip*. What was wrong with him? Maybe he needed to get checked out. Thank God Christmas break was almost here.

CHAPTER 11

HOME FOR THE HOLIDAYS?

"You've gotta be kidding me . . ." remarked Ryan into his phone. He was in the Neuro-ICU, visiting a post-op patient.

"Not kidding, sir. Want us to give it to Dr. Hindley? I know you're off for the holidays starting tomorrow." It was fourth-year resident, Lisa LeClair. She was calling about a child with a newly diagnosed brain tumor.

"Starting in five minutes, to be exact. I can already taste the Shiraz," replied Ryan. "But no, I'll take a look. Holy Christmas, though, it's like clockwork . . ."

"I know, sir. I couldn't believe it when the call came in. I contemplated not telling you, but thought you'd be pissed."

Ryan was aware of the standing joke among the residents that whenever he was preparing to leave town, a child with some horrible tumor would hit the doors. They would laugh at how he would go ahead and operate on the kid, stick around for a few days to make sure that all was going smoothly, and then, having finally taken his leave, call and check in on things at least a couple of times a day. He couldn't argue the point. The phenomenon proved remarkably consistent. And sure enough, it was happening again. It was 4:54 on December twenty-first, and Ryan's Christmas Vacation was slated to start at five.

"Yep, I'd be pissed, all right," replied Ryan. "So, go ahead. Hit me with it."

"Kid's name is Tsutomo Yamaguchi—a.k.a. 'T.T.'" Twenty-two months old. Normal perinatal history, normal development, no major health issues. Started becoming irritable in the mornings and would vomit several times after a fair amount of fussing. Afterward, he'd be his regular happy self for the rest of the day. The pediatrician thought it was a GI virus—one's apparently going around—but when it persisted for over two weeks, he ordered an MRI. Kid's got a big-assed fourth ventricular tumor compressing his brainstem."

"Got it," replied Ryan. "Let's go see him."

Ryan spent the next two hours discussing the situation with the child's shell-shocked parents. T.T. would need to undergo surgery first thing in the morning. It was a big, dangerous procedure—lots of potential complications, including coma and death—but there really weren't any viable alternatives. The parents acquiesced to their new reality and peppered Ryan with dozens of what-if questions. Ryan eventually broke free, collected his gear, and left for home.

―――

"Oh, Ryan, not again. We're supposed to leave for New Jersey first thing in the morning," said Kelly, responding to the news of the surgery. The girls had been secured out of earshot in the family room.

"I'm so sorry, honey, but the kid came in today. What was I supposed to do?" replied Ryan, holding up his palms and frowning.

"Yeah, probably came in at the last minute, like always," noted Kelly, rolling her eyes. "But you're on vacation. Why not turn him over to one of your partners?"

"Well, Jim's already left town, and Leslie isn't keen on doing any more fourth ventricular tumors after getting sued twice over them last year. And I can guarantee, none of the adult guys would touch the kid with a ten-foot pole . . ."

"But good ol' Dr. Brenan will pick up the slack—like he does for everything over there," replied Kelly, now pacing. "This is nuts, Ryan. You need a break. *We* need a break. We need to get away now and then. Away from Carriere, away from New Bethany, away from neurosurgery."

"But we do get away, Kelly. You know that."

"Not nearly enough, buddy," said Kelly, coming to stand in front of Ryan, hands on hips. "Your partners are always cutting out—one, two, three weeks at a clip—with you sucking up the extra call. And whenever we do get a break, *this* happens. We live parallel lives anymore, Ryan. Both busy as hell, but never intersecting, never intertwining. We need some time together. *Real* time together."

"I know. I get it, honey," replied Ryan. "I promise I'll do a better job."

But it was an empty promise. The truth was, no matter how much he loved time off with his family, it ultimately proved more stressful than just plowing head with his work. An extended break acted like a wedge hammered into the middle of a month's already-overloaded calendar, compressing the same volume of work into a fraction of the time. What was worse, though, was the profound dysphoria he would experience at the end of the break. He would ache for Kelly and the girls with such ferocity that throughout the last day of vacation, and the first several days of his return to work, he would constantly be on the verge of bursting out into full-fledged weeping.

"Well, I'm not holding my breath," said Kelly, fiery eyes fixed on Ryan. "If you meant it, you'd start right here and now, and let one of your dozen partners take care of the child."

"You know I can't do that, Kelly. But it won't be bad. The case'll only take a few hours—first thing tomorrow morning," replied Ryan, escaping Kelly's stare and pouring her a tumbler of whiskey as a peace offering.

"But Ryan, we were supposed to be heading out to your mother's first thing tomorrow morning," noted Kelly, accepting the whiskey.

"Well . . . how about you and the kids go ahead and go, and I'll meet you there later in the day as soon as everything's stable."

"Oh no, mister, I know you too well to bite on that." Kelly waved her index finger. "There's no way you'll leave town the day of a big operation. Nope, you won't even consider it until a couple of days after surgery. And you know what day that is, right, Ryan?"

"Um, I guess it's Christmas Eve," replied Ryan, pouring his own glass of whiskey.

"That's right, it's Christmas Eve. So, no. We'll go with you when you're ready."

"But Kelly, the girls will be so disappointed if we cut short their time with Mom."

"Did you ever stop to think about how disappointed they already are at how often their time with *you* is cut short?" said Kelly, forcing eye contact. "You do realize they're growing older every minute you're away from them, don't you? That you're going to turn around one day, and those sweet little girls will no longer exist. Three adult women will have taken their places. The here and now is a most precious time to be around them, and you're missing it all."

"I know, *Kelly*," replied Ryan, emphasizing her name. "I'm doing my best. I *know* how precious this time is, but people *do* get sick, no matter how inconvenient it is for the Brenan family."

"You can get mad at me, Ry, but I'm just trying to save you from a world of regret ten or twenty years from now."

"I get it, Kelly. I truly do. I'll work on it. I will . . ." Ryan said, downing his whiskey in one gulp.

———

Ryan was soon back within the antiseptic embrace of the operating room, prepping the back of T.T.'s neck and head. Soon his entire world would zero in on the few inches of anatomy that played host to yet another desperate battle for life. The troubled thoughts that had plagued his sleep, or lack thereof, the preceding night—thoughts of rushed holidays, of disappointed spouses, of disappearing little girls—retreated under the brilliant light of the operating microscope. For a few hours, what went on under that light was all that mattered in the universe.

"So, guys," he commented to a couple of nursing students, "we have a little toddler here with a large tumor in the back part of the brain called the cerebellum—the part that's responsible for coordination. The tumor's crushing another part of the brain called the brainstem. The brainstem is the on-off switch for the whole shootin' match. If you knock off your brainstem, you can't turn on the computer—that is, the rest of your brain—and you're either left in coma or you're dead.

"Is the tumor cancerous?" asked one of the students.

"It certainly can be. Some are highly malignant. Some less so. *All* will kill you if we don't stop them."

After an official time-out, Ryan and Lisa began operating.

"To get to the tumor, you've got to get up and under the back of the skull through some thick neck muscles," explained Ryan. "But that's much easier in kids—much less muscle, much thinner bone . . ."

The two surgeons worked silently for a period, then Ryan spoke up again.

"Okay, guys, we've opened the head and worked our way under

the cerebellum. The big purple mushy thing you see there on the screen is the tumor. We'll take some biopsies first and send them down to pathology for a quick read. Then we'll go about getting out as much of the tumor as is safely possible."

Half an hour later, the pathologist called in on the squawk box.

"Hey there, Dr. Brenan. It's Eva Williams in path. I've got a frozen section for you on Too-soo-mee Yum-oo-gotti—or whatever his name is." A frozen section is a rapid, but not always accurate, laboratory study of a biopsy specimen performed by flash-freezing the tissue and then staining it for microscopic inspection. Final pathological diagnosis requires a more labored process, and takes a day or two, or more, to come back.

"Fire away, Dr. Williams," bellowed Ryan over the ambient electronic beeps, mechanical humming, and sound of rushing air.

"I'm afraid we've got fields and fields of small blue cells. Sure looks like a 'medullo.'"

"Got it. Thanks, Dr. Williams," replied Ryan. "Well, guys," he remarked, addressing the students, "sounds like this is going to be a 'medulloblastoma.' These are highly malignant tumors. But if you accomplish an aggressive resection in surgery, and it's the right genotype, it can be cured—80 percent or more of the time."

Over the ensuing hour, the two surgeons removed, in a piecemeal fashion, the gooey tumor off a gleaming-white structure that Ryan explained was the brainstem. After demonstrating the lack of any visible residual tumor, he pushed away from the microscope, rolling backward in his chair. "So, that's it," he remarked. "The tumor's out and we're going to close. Dr. LeClair has done a fantastic job, and soon we'll all be home drinking eggnog and eating mincemeat pie, or whatever we're supposed to do."

Ryan left the hospital at one in the afternoon. He had to remind himself that he was, and had been all day, on vacation, as he weathered waves of guilt for pointing the jeep toward home in broad daylight. Over the next two days, he spent a couple of hours each morning with T.T. and his family. Then, on Christmas Eve, with T.T. looking stable, he packed up the minivan and struck out with Kelly and the girls for his mother's home in New Jersey. Kelly had been most accurate about his subsequent behavior, though. He was on edge throughout the remainder of Christmas Eve, calling in to check on T.T. every few hours. On Christmas Day, when he was told T.T. was a little less alert than anticipated, and that an urgent CT scan had been ordered to rule out any problems, he almost jumped into the van to drive back to New Bethany. He was assured by resident Cara Klein, though, that T.T. was fine and that she would castrate him if he did something as stupid as returning to the hospital during his vacation. So, he sweated out the next hour awaiting the CT results.

"It was all bullshit," reported Cara. "Apparently, a moron peds resident gave him a whopping dose of narcotics because 'he was a little fussy.' He's much more alert now. I texted the CT to you—looks perfect."

By Boxing Day, Ryan had finally begun to relax. With the release of his work-related tension, though, all drive to remain conscious vanished, and he collapsed on a couch, plunging into a deep, impenetrable sleep. The next day, a happier, more animated Ryan made an appearance. The morning report on T.T. had been great. The child was out of the PICU, up and walking. Ryan was ebullient as the family packed up the car and left for Kelly's parents' house in Arlington, Virginia. He sang Christmas songs and exchanged silly jokes with the girls all the way down to the DC Beltway. On reaching their destination, he carried his youngest, five year-old Erin, under one arm and a case of his father-in-law's favorite scotch under the other, and burst into the O'Connor house, brimming with holiday cheer.

For a good thirty minutes, he was Ebenezer Scrooge—the day after his spectral visits—repeatedly hugging his always reticent in-laws, chasing the girls in loops about the house, and sweeping Kelly into passionate kisses under the mistletoe. Then his cell phone sounded, and he reflexively scooted upstairs to his and Kelly's assigned bedroom to field it.

"Okay, gotcha, Cara," said Ryan after a minute or two of exchange. "And they're absolutely sure?"

"Yeah, Dr. Brenan. I'm sorry, sir," replied Cara. "I'll go ahead and talk to the family before peds oncology gets to them, if you don't mind. You know what bleak pricks they can be."

"Sounds good, Cara. Thank you."

"Hey, Dr. Brenan . . ." said Cara, after a pause.

"Yeah?"

"Don't sit there and stew. You didn't give the kid his tumor. Go enjoy your family. The shit show will still be here when you get back."

"Got ya, Cara. Thanks for calling."

Ryan put his phone back in his pocket and turned toward Kelly, who had tiptoed into the room. He could feel the color drain from his face and bile crawl up his throat.

"Ryan, what is it? Did something happen to the baby?" asked Kelly.

"No, but the final path just came back. It's a death sentence. Something called an 'ATRT'—an awful tumor. No one survives it."

Ryan sat down on the bed, eyes filling with tears.

Kelly sat beside him and put a hand on his now-rigid shoulder. "I'm so sorry, honey. I know it must be crushing. But you have to remember, you just gave him the best shot he could get—the best surgery he could get—I'm sure of it."

Ryan didn't respond. He wanted to tell Kelly how gutting it was to do his utter best for the child only for it to not be good enough. How sickening it was to so often bear witness to the ravages of a disinterested, if not gratuitous, god; how furious he so often was at said god, for all the senseless carnage inflicted upon the innocent; and how a little divine intervention—or at least assistance—would be so very appreciated every now and then. But he wouldn't. He couldn't. Instead he buried his head in her chest and accepted her fingers stroking his hair.

CHAPTER 12

PIETÀ

After the Christmas break, Ryan plunged back into the neurosurgical world with a three-day weekend of call. And it didn't disappoint. Friday was filled with broken spines; Saturday, with brain hemorrhages; Sunday, with newly diagnosed brain tumors. By Monday, he was spent. Nonetheless, he had two brain tumor operations and a spinal fracture repair to get through before he could head home. They all went smoothly, and after the last operation, he and two medical students walked down to the coffee shop for celebratory chocolate chip cookies. They were just finishing up when Cara Klein came bustling through and spotted him.

"Hey, sir, you done already?" asked Cara.

"Yep, piece of cake," replied Ryan, eyes sagging. "Where you going in such a hurry?"

"Trauma bay. They've got a twofer for us. Wanna come along?"

"Happy to. But if they need surgery, I'm not on call."

"Don't think that's going to be the case," replied Cara. "Kendah says they're brain-dead."

"Lovely." Ryan rolled his eyes as he pushed away from the table.

The group trooped off to a staircase leading to the ER. The trauma bays were abuzz with dozens of professionals tending to a man and a woman laid out on adjacent stretchers. Ryan spotted Nichole Kendah, lead trauma surgeon.

"Hey, Nicki, what's up?"

"Hey, Ryan. I think they're both brain-dead, but it'd be great if you guys would give your benediction," said Dr. Kendah, making a sign of the cross in the air.

"Jeez, they look young," replied Ryan, standing on his tiptoes to get a peek.

"Yeah, newlyweds on their honeymoon. A drunk in a mega-pickup truck hit their compact head on. They've been doing nothing since the accident. No meds. Pupils fixed and dilated. The drunk, of course, came through without a scratch."

"Wonderful," replied Ryan as he waded into the mass of medical bodies attending to the two. He quickly confirmed that both were indeed brain-dead, and grimly took his leave, medical students still in tow. As he scaled the nearest staircase, he fielded a call from Pediatric Oncologist, Jeff Price. After hanging up, he turned to the students.

"Well, that was about a long-term patient of mine, Dylan Thompson. He's seven. I operated on him for a brain tumor when he was two. The tumor was highly malignant. We thought we had the damned thing beat, though, with no evidence of recurrence for over four years. But then it came back with a vengeance. He went through further surgeries, and aggressive chemo, and molecular therapies, but it kept coming back. It's now spread throughout his brain and spine. He's in the children's hospital, dying."

As the group trudged up the stairs, Ryan continued, "Mrs. Thompson has no living relatives, and her husband took off with another woman when Dylan was three. That's pretty par for the course among the parents of severely ill children. The fathers are only able to handle about a year of the associated intensity and lack of attention, and split. The moms become lost in their sacred duty, the unrelenting terror, loss, and self-sacrifice hacking years off their lives."

Ryan's heart rose in his throat as he and the students approached Dylan's room. There, they found Mrs. Thompson, seated in a vinyl easy chair, cradling her skeleton of a child, stroking his wispy hair, and cooing to him that everything was all right. She looked up and parted the curtain of misery to offer a subtle but genuine smile to Ryan. The anguish in her eyes pierced Ryan's armor and caused his knees to buckle. He had to steady himself by reaching for a nearby sink. He tried to speak but had to clear his throat several times to get the words out.

"Hey there, Mrs. Thompson. I hear Dylan isn't doing so well."

Dylan was in deep coma, but his bones writhed beneath his paper-thin skin. He breathed in disjointed gasps, and periodically released a vocalization somewhere between a sigh and a cry.

"I couldn't do it, Dr. Brenan," replied Mrs. Thompson, looking up at Ryan. "I'm so sorry. I know everyone worked so hard to make it easy and peaceful for us at home. But I just couldn't face it alone. And Dylan so loves everyone here. This is his family. He would want to say goodbye to his fam—"

She couldn't finish, breaking down into silent sobbing.

Ryan kneeled in front of her and touched her arm. "It's all right, Mrs. Thompson. Everyone here adores Dylan. Everyone here adores you. This is the place to be."

"They tell me tomorrow or the next day. And did you know, Bill's not coming? He says it's too much for him to bear."

"I'm so sorry," replied Ryan with a faltering voice. "There'll be better days ahead. I promise."

"You've been so good to us, Dr. Brenan," said Mrs. Thompson, looking up at Ryan. "And Dylan so worships you. He tells me all the time that he's going to be a brain surgeon when he grows up, just like Dr. Bren—"

She dissolved into spasms of tears. Ryan held her forearm until she could settle and take some breaths.

"You've been an angel to us, Dr. Brenan, a guardian angel," offered Mrs. Thompson. "I'll never forget it."

"If anyone's an angel around here, Mrs. Thompson, it's you. No one could have taken better care of Dylan. No one would have treated him so . . . so darned normally. He's happier than any kid I know. You've done a miraculous job, the job of an angel."

The two went quiet. Ryan gave the medical students a glance that conveyed the message to leave—that he was going to stay for a while with this grieving mother. The students backed out, clearly grateful to be removed from the suffocating pathos of the room. Ryan pulled up a stool in front of mother and child and held Dylan's left hand. The three sat there together without exchanging a word for the next few hours. The silence was punctuated only by Dylan's sonorous breathing and the occasional nurse who would materialize, move about the room on tiptoes, and then dissolve back into the walls.

It was late. Darkness had long since fallen, and the room was lit solely by the green glow of meaningless readouts on useless monitors. Ryan was thus treated to the diorama of a star-strewn sky in a large picture window directly behind Mrs. Thompson. He alternated between watching Dylan—helplessly, hopelessly— and staring out upon the incomprehensible expanse of the Milky Way. Suddenly, his eyes were drawn by a flash of light. A meteor. A brilliant fireball that streaked across the sparkling heavens. In the same instant, Dylan drew in a deep, stridorous breath and flexed at the waist. He then settled back into his mother's arms as he released all the air from his lungs. His body became limp, and he sunk even deeper into his mother's embrace. Mrs. Thompson looked up at Ryan and, instead of bearing the tortured visage of the mother of a dying child, her face had relaxed and had become ageless. Maternal love filled the room. There were no further sobs, no further whimpers, no further tears. She smiled serenely and nodded. Ryan could feel her grace wash over him, embrace him, elevate him.

Two nurses appeared. Unintelligible questions and answers were exchanged, and it was clear that Mrs. Thompson intended to remain in place, holding her son, for quite some time. Wires were removed, monitors shut off, and Ryan somehow found himself out of the room, well down the hallway, reliving the parting image of Mrs. Thompson's beatific face, lips pressed to the forehead of her only child.

CHAPTER 13

HALLUCINATIONS

After leaving the hospital, Ryan sat in his jeep and cried until the January cold seeped into his bones and insisted upon his retreating home. It was too late for the girls to awake but as he approached the house, a single lamp threw its light out onto Salisbury road. Kelly must still be up and working in the study. Ryan stumbled out of the jeep and slipped in the side entrance. He quietly poured himself a shot of bourbon. After downing a second, he tiptoed up the back staircase. He was startled, as usual, by two dolls sitting in an antique chair on the landing. Antique, porcelain Victorian dolls, in age-appropriate attire, that Kelly adored but always gave him the creeps. After settling his galloping heart, he made his way down the long hallway, slipped into the girls' room, and watched them sleep for the better part of an hour. Then he crept to the master bathroom, stepped into the shower, and stood under its stream, sizzling water pounding the back of his neck.

Suddenly, the curtain burst open.

"Holy crap, Ryan." It was Kelly. "I didn't hear you come in. The house was as quiet as a morgue. Then I heard the shower running. Scared me half to death. Why didn't you say hello?"

Ryan looked at her but was at a loss for words.

"Jesus, Ry, what's the matter?" asked Kelly.

"Nothing. Just a bad day," replied Ryan, unable to make eye contact.

"Want to tell me about it?"

"I'm okay. Like I said, it was just a bad day." Ryan turned off the shower and wrapped a towel around himself.

"Honey, it's obvious it wasn't 'just a bad day.' By the look on your face, it was an awful day, a horrible day."

"It's really not that bad, Kell. Just tired from the weekend."

"Come on, Ryan. This is happening all too often. You need to share these things with me. You can't hold it all inside."

"I'm fine. I just need to get to bed," replied Ryan, toweling off.

"Ryan, if you won't speak with me, why not see a psychiatrist again? Or Ron?"

"Maybe I will. If things get bad."

"I think we might already be there, honey," said Kelly, hands gently brushing hair from his forehead.

———

Ryan couldn't clear the dark clouds that had closed in around him during the following week. To make matters worse, Ben returned to the study each night, holding his grisly book club for Ava, Riley, and Erin. Ryan would awaken with a start each time the study door slammed shut in his face and then would be unable to go back to sleep. By Saturday, he was feeling so disjointed that on returning home from hospital rounds, he headed out to the barn to affect a major cleanup rather than interact with the family. When working in a back corner, he tripped over the girls' bicycles for what seemed like the ten thousandth time. The bastard bikes were in the habit of lying about in the shadows in grotesquely contorted positions like the dead of Antietam. There, he was sure, they conspired to ensnare his feet and send him plunging into a collection of rakes and pitchforks. He decided that a public hanging was a just fate for the malicious pricks, so he got into the jeep and drove out to the New Bethany hardware store to pick up some rafter hooks.

The weather for the short trip was foul. A warm front had slipped up from the Gulf along the Appalachians and collided with the frosty Pennsylvania upper atmosphere. This initially resulted in two-inch-wide clumps of snow dropping all over the region with the thuds of rotten apples. The snow soon gave way to sleet, then freezing rain, and then to the all-too-familiar "mixed precipitation." But Ryan's antique jeep—originally his father's—had no problem making its way through the mess. After securing his purchase, Ryan headed back toward home, windshield wipers shrieking at him in bitter confusion about what they were supposed to clear. As he crossed the bridge, he noticed a man dressed in a trench coat shuffling his way along the sidewalk. The man leaned into an onrush of wind, holding one hand over his head to keep in place a levitating fedora. He weaved and stuttered as if drunk. Ryan chuckled at the guy's early start to the evening's libations. The guy, however, proceeded to slip, stumble, dance an off-balance jig, and then pitch headlong into traffic.

Ryan slammed on his breaks, precipitating the sound of screeching tires and blaring horns behind him. The two vehicles ahead made no such effort. The man bounced upon the hood of the blue Toyota sedan in the vanguard, tumbled over the roof, skipped off the trunk, and landed face-first on the road where the second in line, a large Dodge pickup truck, ran over him with both the front and back right-sided tires. The crumpled body lay motionless on the round, blood pouring from a head that had taken on the shape of an acutely angled parallelogram.

Ryan exploded out of the jeep, feet slipping on the icy steel grating as his hand reached for his phone. Only he fumbled it, and it slid under the jeep. "Jesus." He dropped to his knees, and through straining his shoulder girdle, got hold of a corner. He hit 911, then popped up and made a dash for the front of the jeep. On rounding the hood, however, the pancaked drunk was gone.

Ryan looked all about: under the jeep, over the sidewalk, and even in the ice-laden river below. Nope, no mangled body, no pieces of flesh, no entrails, and not a drop of blood.

"What the hell's going on?" Ryan queried an indifferent stanchion nearby. *Jesus.* He was hallucinating. The woman on the porch. The kid and the fire truck. The old guy in the study. Now this. Christ, he must have a brain tumor. How ironic would that be? He needed to see someone. He needed a scan.

CHAPTER 14

SHRINKS AND NEURONS

A fter the incident on the bridge, Ryan immediately contacted his favorite neurologist, Malcolm Whitehead. He didn't admit to experiencing full-blown hallucinations, but did confess to the "very occasional episode of distorted visual perception" and asked Whitehead to have at him. And have at him he did. MRIs, PET scans, EEGs, blood tests, spinal taps, and the like. Afterward, Whitehead went over the results.

"So, Ryan, I've run every test I can think of, and everything's absolutely clean. If I had to put money on it, I would bet your visual disturbances are related to your constant state of sleep deprivation."

"You think?"

"Sure. I see the hours you keep. And the amount of call you're taking. It was bound to catch up with you. Your poor brain is probably always on the edge of sleep—trying to drop off whenever it can. I have to think that whatever you're experiencing is related. Something that would respond to some sleep, real sleep. I'm not talking a good night every week or two. I'm talking months of attention to your sleep hygiene: real recovery after your crazy nights of call, reasonable bedtimes and wake-ups, dark and cool surroundings, no screen time before bed, no spicy foods, no caffeine after noon, and cutting way back on, or eliminating all together, your alcohol consumption."

"Oh God no, not the alcohol!" replied Ryan with exaggerated horror.

"I'm serious, Ryan. I think you need to do everything you can to improve your sleeping conditions, and alcohol will only screw that up. And for God's sake, all of you need to abandon those absurd three-day weekends of call you take. How can anyone establish normal sleep patterns with them? And if none of that works, we should admit you to the sleep center and really go to town on you."

"Hmm. I think I'll hold on that for now . . . You don't think it's seizures, then?"

"You can never be 100 percent sure with seizures. But your EEGs are clean, and the symptoms don't match up well. We could have Randy Woodfield check you over, though . . ." added Whitehead with a smirk, aware of Ryan's low opinion of the Harvard-trained epilepsy specialist. The two were known to medically butt heads on occasion.

"Uh, thanks but no thanks," replied Ryan, with a roll of the eyes. "Should I try some sleeping pills?"

"I wouldn't. The more naturally you can establish normal sleep cycles, the more sustainable they'll become. Let's go with the improved sleep hygiene for now."

———

With brain tumors and other major neurological disorders ruled out, Ryan also sought evaluation by a psychiatrist. This time, he admitted to the hallucinations. Once again, he was subjected to an exhaustive battery of tests.

"So, I'm not cracking up, then?" asked Ryan after Dr. Leopold Larkin, Chief of Psychiatry at Carriere, summarized his findings.

"Now Ryan," replied Larkin, "let's be precise in our term-inology. There's no question that you're suffering from situational depression and PTSD. And you're a hair's breadth away from a full-blown clinical depression, although I've never met a neuro-surgeon who wasn't. But you've passed with flying colors every assay I've thrown at you. So, you're not showing any evidence of severe mental illness or compromised reality testing. I must concur with Dr. Whitehead's assessment that your episodes are most likely sleep-related, perhaps hypnagogic—occurring in transitional states of consciousness."

"Could they happen in surgery, then?" asked Ryan. The thought terrified him. Were any to occur in the operating room, or frankly anywhere near the hospital, he told himself, he would have to stop working immediately. He couldn't risk harming his patients.

"Probably," replied Larkin, "if you don't start effectively addressing your sleep deprivation. And frankly, it's beyond dep-rivation. I would call it 'sleep starvation.'"

"But, with some better sleep I should be good to go?"

"Not necessarily. As I said, you have some pretty substantial emotional issues to deal with. Normally, I would recommend some antidepressants—just to take the edge off, restore the serotonin levels in your brain—but they could interfere with your sleep. I think it's best to try one intervention at a time. So, let's go with Dr. Whitehead's regimen for now. You should definitely keep up with your sessions with me, though."

———

Next stop was Reverend Ron. Ryan thought it might be worthwhile to "nibble at the edges" of his difficulties with his friend. For one more opinion. He didn't want to disclose too much, though—having someone that close rummaging around in one's psyche could get uncomfortable—but perhaps he could pick up some helpful tips from the guy. He therefore "curbsided" Ron at an indoor soccer game they were playing in, rather than subject himself to a formal visit.

"So, Ron, what are your top three tricks to prevent coming unhinged at work?" asked Ryan as his and Reverend Ron's line took a breather off the pitch.

"Tricks?" repeated Reverend Ron, watching the game from behind a plexiglass window. "There are no tricks, Ryan. Building emotional resilience takes focus and work; and commitment to one's self-compassion and self-care."

"Yeah, I get that," said Ryan. "But you must have some tried and true . . . um . . . strategies. I mean, what do you say in your books?"

"You might read one and see," responded Reverend Ron, turning toward the considerably taller Ryan and punching him in the chest.

"Sure. On my next vacation. But come on, Ron, how about a freebie for your star midfielder?"

"What's up, Ryan?" pressed Reverend Ron, studying Ryan's face. "Feeling burned-out?"

"No, I'm good. It's just that it's been crazy up on the hill of late. And Kelly's been on me about being withdrawn and overcommitted."

"Ah, the curse of being a doctor."

"Eh?"

"Yeah. By the nature of the business, the better a doctor you are, the worse a husband, father, and friend you become. That's why you guys burn out. Medicine can soak up every ounce of your being, leaving nothing for those you love. The 'trick,'" explained Reverend Ron, making air quotation marks, "is to find a way to be fueled by your work rather than drained by it, so you have the emotional energy to engage with those you care about when you get home."

"Easier said than done."

"It certainly is for someone like you, my friend," replied Reverend Ron, placing a hand on Ryan's shoulder. You may feel beaten up by your work, but you need it, you live for it. The question is, can you tone it down enough to prosper from it, rather than be dragged under by it?"

"Jeez, Ron. I was just looking for a few simple suggestions, not psychoanalysis."

"Okay, okay." Reverend Ron held up his hands. "Here's some 'tricks' to hold you over. But we really should get together, formally. You're at high risk, my friend."

"Got you. I'll make an appointment."

"I'm not holding my breath," replied Reverend Ron with a frown. "But for now, try going through your day harvesting some uplifts. I know there's a lot of bad stuff going on around you, but there's also a lot of good stuff. Great saves, smiles from patients, thanks from grateful families, effective teamwork, surgeries that go well. You know. Write a few down. Share them with Kelly and the girls. Reflect on them when you go to bed at night. Try to collect three for every major hassle you encounter."

"You must be joking," replied Ryan, raising one eyebrow. "There's got be a thousand hassles an hour up there."

"I get it. But try to notice some of the uplifts, rather than stewing over the hassles. If you force it for a while, your mind will train itself to start logging them in automatically."

"Okay, will do," said Ryan as he started to step away, signaling he was finished with the conversation. But Reverend Ron grabbed him by the shirtfront and continued.

"And stop indulging in the classic neurosurgeon suffering-contest."

"Meaning?" asked Ryan.

"Meaning you guys are forever trying to top one another in

who can suffer the most for their cause. Get in the earliest, leave the latest, have the most overbooked clinics, take the most call, do the most operations. Toxic medical machoism if I've ever seen it. And you're a poster boy for it, Ryan."

Ryan was about to respond, but his and Reverend Ron's line was waved back into the game, and the conversation came to an abrupt halt.

CHAPTER 15

SNOW BOWL

For much of February, Ryan did everything he could to follow his marching orders. He stopped drinking altogether, practiced reasonable sleep hygiene, and sought to celebrate the many highlights of his life. And it was paying off. The whole house seemed more upbeat. As an apparent reward, the heavens dropped a good foot of powdery snow on the region, transforming it into a sparkling winter wonderland. Ryan got up early and shoveled out the cars, intent on hitting the hospital after a quick breakfast. On reentering the house, however, he was set upon by three effervescent young girls.

"Ooh, Dad, can we go play soccer in the snow like we did last year?" pleaded the usually cool, collected, and analytic Ava, Ryan and Kelly's oldest.

"Yeah, Daddy, can we? It would make my dreams come true!" added their middle child, Riley, the couple's most theatrical.

"Can we, Daddy? You totally promised we could, next big snow!" said their youngest, Erin, the couple's most litigious.

The girls ratcheted up their pleading to ear-piercing pitches and danced around Ryan as he poured himself some coffee.

"Ah, girls, I can't right now. I'm just about to leave for the—"

Ryan caught himself as he witnessed the countenance of each girl shift from joy to disappointment; and worse yet, to resignation. *Well screw it*, he thought. Kelly was right. They were all growing up so fast. How many more mornings would he get like this in his life? Snow falling gently, the girls all fresh and eager. A snowy day is a wonder to them—nature's amusement park, waiting to be experienced in all its delightful simplicity. Things weren't so bad over in the hospital. He could always go in later in the afternoon. The truth was, he never had to go in on his off-call weekends. Whoever was *on call* was supposed to round on the whole service and field all emergencies. It was a lot of work, but, theoretically, it meant you got the next three weekends off completely. But Ryan just couldn't stay away that long. So, on his off-call weekends, he would go in anyway and visited his patients, on both Saturdays and Sundays. Sometimes it only took an hour. Sometimes it took four. But today, for his girls, he would forgo it. At least for the morning.

"Okay, girls, let's do it," said Ryan. "I'll whip us up some chocolate chip pancakes, and then we can hold the Brenan World Cup of Snow Soccer!"

The proclamation was greeted with squeals of delight and anticipation. Soon, the crew was all bundled up and working their way toward the door.

"Isn't Mom coming? I can't play if she's not," sniffed Riley.

"Yeah, can Mom play too?" chimed in the other two.

"I don't think so, girls," replied Ryan. "Mom's been up *all* night on the phone. If she does manage to break free, I think she'll want to hit the sack—don't you?"

"All-nighters" were a rare event for Kelly, but something nasty was going down out in the forests of Oregon. Panicked phone calls were coming in from all over, and video meetings were stacking up like delayed jets at a snowbound LaGuardia. The group was disappointed, but nonetheless trudged across the street to a sizable field adjacent to a Methodist Church. Thankfully, the girls were unaware that the field had once been a graveyard.

The four Brenans were soon joined by two boys and a girl from neighboring homes, and it was game on. After fifteen minutes of play, Ryan's side was well ahead, but the match's fortunes took an abrupt turn as Kelly strode out onto the fluffy pitch. Kelly had never played soccer formally, but there was no question about it: at nearly six feet tall, lithe and toned, she was an athlete.

For some time, the contest became deadlocked, but as Ryan's legs turned to Jell-O, Kelly's team began to net goal after goal. Determined to put his team back into the scoring column, Ryan took on Kelly right in front of her goal and tried a spin move. She stuffed him, stole the ball, then dashed forty yards downfield with Ryan in hot pursuit. Ryan caught up with her and took a mad swipe at the ball. Kelly countered with a quick move that left Ryan swinging at air. This caused him to slip, stagger several yards, then face-plant into a virgin drift behind the goal. Meanwhile, Kelly rolled the ball into Erin's path setting up her youngest for an easy score. She then went into a hip-hop dance celebration, soon to be joined by all the other players on the field.

Watching, Ryan drifted above the scene among the waltzing snowflakes, and contemplated the magical fabric of this most magical being. Kelly had grown up in a strict and disciplined, but not unloving, household. Tall and stunning, with a gloriously American mix of ethnic bloodlines, she was olive-skinned but blue-eyed and auburn-haired. She was the runaway valedictorian at her high school, and an all-state athlete in both volleyball and lacrosse. She went on to attend Dartmouth College and then Yale Law School where she graduated second in her class and was lead editor of the Yale Law Journal.

Although not of the usual Ivy League lineage of money and elite private schooling, Kelly saw herself as immensely privileged: privileged for having loving parents, privileged for possessing a smoothly functioning body that seemed immune to disease and injury, and privileged for being bestowed a ravenous brain that perpetually demanded new knowledge and novel problems to solve. But her life wasn't without challenge. Her father was an Army Ranger, and she moved with her parents every year or two from one Spartan Army base to another, preventing the development of any sense of permanence or lasting friendship. She lost her mother to breast cancer when she was ten. She was then bullied mercilessly in her early teens for her bookishness and her late entry into adolescence. And, through her adult years, had weathered more than her share of sexual harassment—some, quite threatening. But she took it all in stride. She was on a mission. She was committed to leaving the world a better place for future generations. A cleaner and more sustainable place.

So, with every high-powered and incomprehensibly lucrative law firm in the country offering her sensational positions, Kelly accepted a laughably low-paying job with a nonprofit environmental organization in DC. She was so effective in her role there that when she told the firm she was moving to New Bethany, they restructured her work so that she could manage it entirely from home. There, she would put in five to six unbroken hours of high-efficiency effort in the middle of each weekday. There, she would also put in countless hours for an array of local charitable organizations, yet seem to be able to effortlessly attend to every want and need of each of her children. This, in spite of her functioning for all intents and purposes as a single parent.

"What's on your mind there, mister?" asked Kelly, now standing over her snow-enshrouded husband, holding the ball on her left hip, her long hair whipping about her face in the brisk wind. "You look a million miles away."

It took a minute for him to answer.

"Oh, just thinking..." started Ryan, continuing to stare off into the distance.

"Oh, yeah? What about?"

A long, pregnant pause ensued.

Then Ryan sprung to his feet, knocked the ball out of Kelly's grasp, dribbled it madly down the field toward the other goal, and yelled back over his shoulder: "Revenge!"

CHAPTER 16

PERCHANCE TO DREAM

For Kelly, things at the Brenan household seemed to be improving, and she could feel her nervous system shift into a more relaxed and happy mode. Ryan had informed her that he had started seeing a psychiatrist and a neurologist, and that they were working on his sleep. And he definitely appeared to be less fatigued and skittish. He was even trying to modify his after-work routine. While he still never made it home in time for dinner, when he did get home, he didn't immediately fix a drink and plop down on the couch, hand glued to the remote. Instead, he actively engaged her and the girls. And he was trying to be creative and playful—giving each non-call evening an interactive theme. Monday might be family art project night; Tuesday, musical instrument night; Wednesday, home-improvement night; and so forth. And he was going to bed at a reasonable hour instead of staying up until after midnight watching war documentaries. In addition, he started discussing things with her, even work things—tidbits of the life that had always been securely locked away from her. Tiny and insubstantial tidbits, yes; but hey, Rome wasn't built in a day. He even made vacation plans with her. The old Ryan was trying to resurface. Until one frigid night in late February.

As darkness fell that night, gale-force winds lifted newly fallen granular snow off the ground and hurled it against the house's storm windows. The girls were unsettled by the persistent patter on the panes and the angry howling of the naked trees, but eventually were coaxed to their beds and into uneasy slumber. Kelly and Ryan, their breaths billowing out into the air of their miserably insulated bedroom, crawled under a full-throttled electric blanket and read their respective books side by side. Kelly soon felt herself drift off. Suddenly, though, she was recoiling from an apparent fist thrown into her right eye.

"Jesus!" she blurted as she looked over at Ryan. He was a shocking sight. He was sitting bolt upright, eyes open and roving wildly, arms flailing as if he was fending of a rabid bat. And he was screaming. More shrieking than screaming. And sobbing: a gasping, sputtering, retching form of sobbing. She jumped out of bed to avoid another punch in the face and watched in stunned silence. It took a few moments, but she realized that Ryan was still asleep. She circled the bed, timed her move, then dove in between the swinging fists and tackled him onto his pillow. She shook his shoulders and yelled, "Ryan, Ryan. Wake up. It's just a nightmare. Wake up!"

He continued to screech and flail. She grabbed a glass from the bedside table and threw water into his face. "Wake up, Ryan. It's just a dream. Wake up!"

"Okay, okay. I'm awake. I think," replied Ryan, wiping his dripping brow. "God, what the hell happened? Why are you rubbing your eye?"

Before Kelly could answer, a series of high-pitched screams came echoing along the plaster walls of the upstairs hallway. Ryan and Kelly exploded off the bed, sprinted down the hallway, and burst into the girls' room. All three were huddled together in Ava's bed. All were weeping, the littlest throwing in squeals at every inhalation. They had heard Ryan's shrieking and were terrified. It took a solid couple of hours, a lot of milk and cookies, some cartoons, and lots of hugs and back rubs to get them settled down. Kelly finally got them all back into bed while Ryan poured a couple of tumblers of Irish whiskey in the dining room and brought them upstairs. The two reunited back in their bed. Kelly gratefully accepted her glass, as well as an ice pack for her now black-and-blue right eye. They pulled up the electric blanket around their necks and clinked glasses.

"Whew, no wonder the girls were freaked out—hearing their dad scream like that," remarked Kelly. "I mean, if it weren't for the storm, I'm sure you would've woken up the whole neighborhood. What were you dreaming about?"

"I don't know. I can't remember a thing," replied Ryan. "Did I actually hit you?"

"Well, there was no one else in the room, as far as I know."

"Jesus, I'm so sorry."

"I'll live. But boy, will you have a lot of explaining to do with the gang," quipped Kelly, eyeing Ryan carefully, trying to read between the lines of the incident. "What the heck was that, Ry, a flashback to Afghanistan?"

CHAPTER 17

WRONG PLACE

To the best of his knowledge, Ryan had never experienced an Afghanistan-related flashback—or even a related nightmare—although he had plenty of reason to do so. He had grown up in a military family. His father had been a Navy fighter pilot who, at six-four, liked to joke that his most dangerous mission was clearing the many door jambs of his aircraft carrier. He was struck and killed by a drunk driver, however, at the Norfolk Naval Station. Ryan was ten. The military had taken such good care of his mother at the time, that he swore he would someday repay them. When he was offered a military scholarship for his medical schooling, he saw it as a perfect opportunity to do so. The Army would pay his tuition, and, in return, he would serve as a physician for them. Thus, upon finishing up his neurosurgery training at the University of Pennsylvania and the Children's Hospital of Philadelphia, he was commissioned as an active-duty Army Major, and assigned to Walter Reed National Military Medical Center in Washington, DC. After only nine months there, however, being the low man on the totem pole, he was deployed to Afghanistan.

The conflict in Afghanistan, however, proved to be sedate, and Ryan had little medically to do. After several startlingly boring months, he was befriended by a marine colonel, Robert Jessup. One day, Jessup invited Ryan to accompany him on a "mission" that he and his crew made every month out to a remote mountain village. They would bring electronics, weapons, and other trinkets to the town leaders and reap scouting information about insurgent activity in the surrounding mountains. Jessup maintained that the region had been quiescent for years, and that the trips had essentially become good-will junkets. What made the excursions special, however, was the stunning scenery along the way and some "spectacular sunsets" over a tableau of endless mountain ranges. Not long thereafter, Ryan found himself flying over barren terrain toward the mountain stronghold, shoulder to shoulder with a bunch of burly, foul-mouthed marines. Upon arrival, Ryan's helicopter stayed aloft, and Ryan noted that Jessup had been accurate. The sun began to set, and the already breathtaking landscape shifted in hue from brown, to orange, to red, to purple, to indigo, and then to a starlit black.

Soon, all three helicopters were speeded home. Ryan watched the other two in the bright illumination of a newly risen moon. It was a stirring scene, the stuff of happy "war memories." And, from his vantage point, he had a perfect view of the two rockets that slammed into the other choppers' midsections. To his horror, one helicopter disintegrated in midair, and the other burst into flames and pitched downward. He couldn't follow its path, however, because a moment later, a third projectile hit his own craft. Somehow, the rocket didn't explode on impact, but rather had punched through the cabin like a BB shot at an empty milk carton. But it did clip the rotor blade, and the helicopter plummeted toward earth like a winged grouse.

The chopper hit the ground with shocking force. Ryan blacked out. He had no idea for how long. When he came to, every part of his body screamed with pain and blood was streaming into his eyes. He was just coming to grips with his situation when a booming voice invaded his befuddled consciousness.

"Hey, Doc—you're awake. How bad you injured? Can you move?"

It was Anthony Mason, a massive African-American staff sergeant.

"Um, I think so."

Mason undid Ryan's safety belts and eased him down to an acutely angled cabin floor. Ryan seemed able to bear his own weight, though he wobbled like a newborn fawn.

"Great," said Mason. "Think you can help me move these injured marines outside?"

"Um, I'm not sure that's a good idea, Sergeant. They could have spine fractures . . ." slurred Ryan.

"I get it. But if those fuck-heads come after us, this bird'll be their first target. We gotta get everyone out. Got it?"

"Yeah . . . I think so."

"Great. I lucked out and didn't get torn up too bad in the crash—"

"Fuck you, Sarg. That was a goddamned baby-soft, three-point landing," came commentary from the cockpit.

"Yeah right, baby soft. Hey guys, can you help move the rest of the men?" asked Mason.

"No can do, Sarg. I'm wedged into my seat, and Billy's pretty beat-up. Do what you need to do, then come for us."

"Great, will do." Mason turned back to Ryan. "Look, Doc, we're kind of lucky; we have steep-assed canyon walls on three sides of us. Right behind us is some sort of gully. It's a great defensive position. I've already moved a bunch of ordnance out, but we need to get these marines out there ASAP."

"Gotcha," replied Ryan.

Ryan and Mason teamed up to pull seven injured marines out of the wreckage. Afterward, Mason looked Ryan in the eyes.

"Look, Doc, if the shit hits the fan, I'll work from the right flank, and you make your way to the left."

"Okay . . ."

The sergeant handed Ryan an M4 rifle and asked, "You do know how to shoot and reload, don't you?"

Ryan nodded.

"Great," replied Mason. "Now listen. If you do have to engage, do not—I repeat—*do not* shoot from a fixed position. They'll blow you to pieces."

Ryan nodded, not really processing much of what the sergeant was saying.

"Great. Remember: shoot and move. And *no* automatic. Semiautomatic only. Got it?"

Ryan nodded.

"Okay, then. Can you start doing whatever needs to be done to free up the pilots? I'll settle my gear out in the flank and then get back to you."

Ryan nodded.

"Great. Now, Doc," said Mason, grabbing Ryan by the shoulders and shaking him a little, "if they come at us, don't be a fucking rear echelon pussy, right? These injured marines are depending on us. Got it?"

Ryan nodded.

"Great."

Ryan shuffled into the helicopter and crept his way toward the cockpit. He could hear the pilot communicating with a base somewhere. It all seemed dreamlike.

"Shit, here they come!" The pilot's words snapped Ryan into raw wakefulness.

An instant later, hot metal buzzed about the cabin, and the air exploded with rich sprays of crimson. Ryan hit the floor. He tried to crawl to the pilots but stopped when he realized that they were already dead. He managed to turn around and low crawl several feet toward the chopper's doorway. There, he threw himself out and onto the ground, rolled over the side of the gully, and dropped five feet to the embracing dirt. He lay there for some time, hugging the earth and praying that this was all some awful nightmare. When he heard Mason open up, though, he made himself get to his feet and move in a limping crouch down the gully.

After passing the injured marines and giving them a couple hundred feet of separation, he scrambled to the edge and peered out. Down range, there was a furious exchange of fire going on between Mason and what looked like a battalion of insurgents. It was a mesmerizing sight. More like a surround-sound summer blockbuster than an actual desperate fight for life. After several minutes, Ryan shook his head. *Shit, I'm ball-watching. I better do something.*

He popped his rifle muzzle over the gully edge, sited one of three insurgent pickup trucks off in the distance, and squeezed the trigger. A burst of at least a dozen rounds exploded out of the muzzle, and the rifle leaped up out of his hands. He fumbled for it, and watched it tumble to the ground.

"Goddamn it, Ryan. You idiot. You had it on automatic."

He retrieved the rifle and again pushed the barrel over the edge and refocused. With the weapon now set to semiautomatic, he fired. And then fired again. Then again. He kept at it—picking targets and firing. The poor bastards were so focused on Mason that he had clear shots at several. He thought he may have even hit one.

The ground around him erupted.

"Christ, Ryan, are you *trying* to get yourself killed? You were supposed to shoot and move."

From this point on, he followed a pattern of popping up, taking one quick shot, then crawling twenty yards or so to his left or right for his next. He maintained this for an eternity. But it was effective. He and Mason seemed to be holding the insurgents off. Things took a nasty turn, though, when an explosion off to the right of the helicopter stopped all fire coming from Mason.

"Christ. They killed the Sargent . . ."

Ryan froze. He pictured his mother back home, being approached by an officer and a chaplain, for the second time in her life. He slumped down the gully wall and collapsed into a ball of shivering flesh. *Jesus Christ, I'm going to die*, he thought. *God, please, please don't do this to Mom.* Then his mind shifted to blind rage. "What the fuck's wrong with these pricks?" he barked at the darkness. "Haven't they killed enough for the night?"

He pushed himself back up to the edge, took aim at a large machine gun mounted on one of the pickup trucks, and squeezed the trigger. Down went an insurgent. He moved farther down the gully, popped up again, and shot—possibly hitting a creeping insurgent just a hundred yards away.

And so it went. For another eternity.

At some point in the haze of the exchange, he found himself all the way out on the left flank, aiming at a crouching insurgent, or perhaps a bush. But before he could pull the trigger, an explosion went off somewhere out in front of him. He was blown backward and slammed against the back wall of the gully. He dropped to the still quivering ground and felt around for his rifle, but it was gone.

"Well," he remarked to no one, "I did what I could. Nothing to do now but die, I guess."

He crawled up to peer over the gully edge, too impatient to wait for the next event to unfold. He didn't cry, he didn't shiver, but he watched with morbid fascination his own impending demise.

The blinding phosphorescence hit him well before the deafening crack of thunder. In an instant, the insurgent trucks were atomized. Then, all over the valley, streams of tracers picked out human flesh and annihilated it. The calvary had arrived, in the military's latest low-noise choppers. Next came the more conventional attack helicopters that set up an airborne perimeter. Then came the troop carriers, and a good hundred marines were disgorged into the canyon. Ryan slid down the gully wall and sat on its littered floor. The sudden waves of fatigue were overwhelming. The already dark night went black.

———

He awoke to a flinty voice coming from down the gully.

"Don't move an inch, motherfucker. Identify yourself."

"Um . . . Ryan. Ryan Brenan . . . and, uh, I'm a major . . . a major in the Army. The US Army . . . in the Medical Corps."

A marine corporal stepped forward out of the darkness, his rifle aimed at Ryan's chest. He looked Ryan over for a few moments, smiled, and lowered his weapon.

"Well, shit, sir. What the hell are you doing here? I guess that explains the fucked-up uniform. I thought you were one of those dipshits for a minute!"

He dropped to his knees by Ryan.

"Shit, sir, you're pretty banged up, aren't you? Well, hang in there; you'll be okay. We'll get you all patched up." Then he added with a wink, "We've got the best docs in the world . . ."

The corporal flipped a switch on his vest, and summoned the medics and his commanding officer. The medics got to Ryan first. Within minutes they had two wide-open IVs in his arms, and had patched up a jagged laceration that ran across his forehead. Soon, another voice echoed its way down the gully, a voice with a pronounced Texan drawl.

A towering marine captain appeared and saluted Ryan. "Well, hey there, major. My name is Pickett, sir—no relation, 'case you were wonderin'—and I am so goddamned glad to meet you."

Pickett took a knee and put a hand on Ryan's shoulder. "Sir, the boys down the gully tell me that you held off that band of shitheads for the better part of an hour—all by your lonesome."

"Uh . . . no, Captain. There's a Sergeant . . . Sergeant Mason . . . who did most of the work. But I guess . . . I guess he's dead . . ."

"No, sir, the sergeant's alive and kickin,' just pretty concussed. Says you're some kind of action hero, though. Says you aren't even in combat arms—that you're some kind of panty-waist doc. Could that possibly be true?"

"Yeah . . . I guess . . ."

"Well, shiver me timbers and blow me down! You're a doc and you just fought off a good thirty of those little pricks yourself? Jesus, Joseph, Mary, and Moses, I am duly impressed. And not even a marine doc at that . . ."

CHAPTER 18

SCREWING THE POOCH

"**W**ake up, Ryan. Wake up!" The words sunk in to Ryan's rising consciousness.

"Huh . . . what . . . another one?" he mumbled, blink-ing repeatedly, as the room came into focus.

"Yep. And it was a doozie," replied a frazzled Kelly.

They were initially sporadic but now, in late-March, were hitting four to five times a week. Kelly made the diagnosis, with the help of Dr. Google. They were called "night terrors," a diagnosable sleep disorder. The pattern was classic—right down to the thrashing and screaming, and the lack of recall of the preceding dream. It didn't come as a total surprise. Ryan had suffered from another disorder, sleep paralysis, for several years as a boy after his father had died. No matter what they were, though, they were proving destructive to the only recently restored "normalcy" of the house. And tonight, as had become the routine, Ryan and Kelly spent the next hour settling down the freaked-out girls and cowering dogs, getting everyone back to sleep, then calming their own nerves with a shot of whiskey. Once back in bed, Kelly was out in a minute. Ryan took a good hour.

———

"Come on, Ryan. Wake up!"

Ryan surfaced again to Kelly shaking him. "I'm awake, I'm

awake," he replied as he realized it was the same night. "Christ, another one?"

"Nope. It's your phone."

Apparently, his phone had been howling out its own primal screams for some time, and he, most uncharacteristically, had slept through it.

"Sheesh, what time is it?" asked Ryan, still trying to focus.

"Uh, 3:20 . . ."

"What in the world could they want with me at this hour? They know I'm not on call," remarked Ryan as he squinted to see the readout on the screen. It was Cara Klein. "Crap. This can't be good. It's one of the residents." He swiped the screen and answered. "Cara?"

"Hey, Dr. Brenan, sorry to wake you."

"No problem. What's up?"

"It's Mr. Dunton, sir, he's in big trouble." Ryan had operated on the forty-five-year-old father of three the previous day for a malignant brain tumor.

"What's going on?" asked Ryan, pulling on his clothes.

"I guess sometime late in the night, he got agitated and was complaining of a bad headache," replied Cara. "One of the newbie ICU nurses called the critical care fellow instead of me. The fucking moron ordered an IV pain killer and a sedative without ever seeing the guy. Mr. Dunton settled down and fell asleep. Thinking it was best to 'let sleeping dogs lie,' the nurse didn't do any sort of neurological exam for the next couple of hours. I came by and found him in coma with fixed, dilated pupils."

"Jesus . . ." was all Ryan could muster, now hurrying out to the jeep.

"I'm so sorry, Dr. Brenan. I was on my way to check on him earlier and would have caught this before it turned to crap, but a bunch of emergency pages came pouring in, and I ended up having to go to the OR with Dr. Apple. I even had the circulator call the ICU about the guy while we were in there, and they told us he was 'resting comfortably.' By the time I got to him, he looked like crap."

"And both pupils are blown?" asked Ryan.

"They were, but we intubated and hyperventilated him, and one came down. But the best I could get out of him was some decerebrate posturing." She was referring to an abnormal reflexive stiffening of the body to pain, indicating a cataclysmic event going on in the brain.

"And you say he got narcotics *and* sedatives?"

"'Fraid so, sir. And it was enough to bring down a rhino."

"Christ," winced Ryan. "Meet you in CT."

Ryan shivered his way through the crisp March air, his father's old jeep unable to muster a single BTU from its antique climate control system. He arrived at CT just as the brain images appeared on the monitoring screens.

"Shit, Dr. B., no clots," observed Cara, "just a very pissed-off brain."

"Yep, no good shall come of this," replied Ryan. "What do you want to do, Cara?"

"I'd say go to the OR."

"And do what?"

"All we can do, really, is remove the bone flap and let the brain swell."

"And what if the brain comes out on our laps, as it's wont to do?"

"Well, then I guess we'd be screwed."

"Or, more appropriately, he would be. Anyway, get him up to there. I'll go speak with his wife."

Ryan made it down to the OR just as Cara had begun to remove the staples from the previous day's scalp closure. Within minutes, the two surgeons had the bone flap out and were reopening the coverings of the brain. A third-year medical student rotating on the service was also scrubbed in, and Ryan directed his commentary her way.

"So, Anna, this unfortunate man has a glioblastoma multiforme, or 'GBM.' We took the bulk of it out yesterday in an awake craniotomy. With that diagnosis, what do you think his life expectancy is?"

"Um, isn't it less than two years?" answered the student.

"Right! And that's with aggressive surgery, chemo, radiation, gene therapies, experimental protocols, reoperation—you name it. So, basically, we're fighting a retreating action—trying to buy the patient some extra months with his loved ones. So, tell me this, surgically speaking, what do you think's the worst thing we can do to a patient like Mr. Dunton?"

"Uh . . . not take out enough tumor?"

"Yeah, well, it does no good to just 'peek and shriek' at the tumor—as they say. But I would argue the worst thing you can do is to hurt the patient neurologically; leave them paralyzed, unable to speak, or in coma, for their last months of life. So, it sure looks like we failed this poor gentleman."

"Why do you say that, Dr. Brenan?"

"Well, this kind of thing can happen no matter what you do—even when things go perfectly. But in this case, I think we screwed the pooch. I think he was beginning to show signs of trouble last night and needed aggressive management of his brain swelling. Instead, he got sedated. That caused the brain to swell even worse. When that happens, the brain crushes itself up against the skull and starts to die. That causes it to swell even more. And so on . . ."

Ah, Jesus, thought Ryan as he and Cara went about dealing with the disaster at hand. Mr. Dunton's brain had leaped out of the opening in the skull like an alien bursting from a hapless victim's chest in some science fiction movie. Having to throw caution to the wind, the two surgeons began rapidly coring out boggy brain tissue from the region where they had previously removed the tumor. *Christ*, thought Ryan, biting his lip to fight back a sense of nihilistic nausea. *Feels like we're taking out half his freakin' brain.*

Serving only to rub salt in the wound, the medical student piped up. "Um, Dr. Brenan, won't removing so much brain leave this patient devastated?"

"Well, let's hope not," replied Ryan, who had to swallow back down bile that had crawled up into his mouth. "We're trying to stay away from critical areas, but it's hard to tell their boundaries in situations like this."

The two surgeons kept at their bloody, messy work. After what felt like several hours, they presided over a "relaxed" brain—all contents pulsating away back within the skull. They left the bone flap out and started to close.

"So, Dr. Brenan," persisted the medical student, "about the sedation and the brain swelling, will you go after the critical care fellow and the nurse?"

"I'll certainly have a long talk with both of them. But I don't want to 'go after' anyone. I want them to learn from this and do better next time. And ultimately, it's the fault of my team and me. We're the experts. We're the ones who let Mr. Dunton down. We're the ones who have to do a better job."

"Will you tell the family . . . about the mistakes?" followed up the medical student. Cara shot her a withering glance, but it went missed.

"Absolutely. I've got to, right? But it has to be measured. It may help assuage our own guilt, but I'm not sure spewing a bunch of mea culpas will do *them* any good."

"So, will they sue you?"

"They could. You can get sued for just about anything—

even when things go great. But most people aren't looking to sue anyone. They get it—better than we do—that it's an imperfect world, that everyone's doing their best, that *everyone's* human."

After surgery, Ryan did explain everything to Mr. Dunton's family. And he prepared them for the worst. But Mr. Dunton ended up surprising everyone. He rapidly regained consciousness and, although weak on the left side of his body, was on his feet and walking within three days. Ten days after surgery, however, Ryan received a call from the emergency room. Mr. Dunton was down there, in bed forty-seven, dead. He had apparently been doing well in a rehab facility when he complained of severe pain in his chest while working with Occupational Therapy, and keeled over. He was dead by the time he made it to Carriere. The presumptive diagnosis was a pulmonary embolism—a massive clot of blood thrown into the bloodstream from a vein in the leg that goes on to block a major artery in the lung.

"Well, nothing we could have done about that," remarked fourth-year resident Frances Boateng on hearing the news. The team was rounding over in the pediatric hospital. "We had the guy on SCDs and appropriate anticoagulants, and had rapidly mobilized him. Just bad luck, I guess."

"Oh, Frances, don't take that attitude," responded Ryan. "We have to accept that we're responsible for Mr. Dunton's death."

"But sir," replied Frances, "people with glioblastomas are prone to throwing clots. We even checked his veins with doppler just before discharge."

"You're missing the point, Frances. He had to go through a whole second operation because of us. We set him up for disaster in a situation where only superlative care will get a patient through in good shape. So, I would motion that we're *absolutely* responsible for Mr. Dunton's death."

"But sir," persisted Frances. "We can't be at every patient's bedside every minute of every day. We're at the mercy of others to help provide that 'superlative care.' We can't hold the hand of every nurse and fellow in the hospital."

Frances had hit on a sore point, perhaps the crux of much of Ryan's ever-present angst. He recognized that he had to depend on others—the nurses, the residents, other specialists, his colleagues. But he so often found them to be lacking: in their attention to detail, in their vigilance, in their caring. So, he felt personally responsible for every mishap or complication that occurred. He knew it was irrational, and that it was a critical driver behind why he stayed so late in the hospital each evening, and why taking time off—even on weekends—proved so difficult. But he couldn't overcome the anxiety that seized him every time he stepped out of the medical center, blind to what was happening there, impotent to fix things that were going wrong. *And then some fiasco like this happens,* thought Ryan, *and only proves the point.*

Ryan shook his head to clear such thoughts and responded. "Let's not be so quick to blame others for this, Frances. Perhaps Mr. Dunton's brain wouldn't have swollen up so badly if we'd done a better job in surgery, or treated him with more preoperative steroids, or pushed his sodium higher immediately post-op. Maybe then a little sedation would have been harmless."

"But sir, it was hardly 'a little sedation.' And one way or the other, the guy had a GBM. They love to swell. Sometimes we're at the mercy of the tumor . . ."

"Oh, Frances, it's such a slippery slope to blame the disease for a bad outcome rather than our own actions—or inactions, as the case may be."

"But, sir, I'm just saying that sometimes the odds are stacked against us . . ."

"I get it, Frances. But it's hard to blame the odds when we're responsible for tipping them the wrong way."

Ryan broke off the discussion to track down Mrs. Dunton. He found her in an ER consultation room surrounded by weeping relatives. He approached her, heart in mouth, and offered his condolences. Mrs. Dunton hugged him, cried on his shoulder, and thanked him profusely, and emphatically, and soulfully, for all that he had done for her beloved husband.

For Ryan, nothing could be worse: to be thanked so sincerely for a job so poorly done. His stomach turned. His chest tightened. His head pounded. He broke out in a cold sweat. On departing, voices in his head viciously berated him, calling him a failure, a joke of a doctor, an impostor, a fraud. No hallucinations necessary this time. The voices were his own, welling up from deep within his soul.

CHAPTER 19

DARK LADY

On arriving home later that evening, Ryan trudged past a happy welcome from the girls and headed for the shower. He stayed under the hot spray until it went cold, cursing the ICU nurse, cursing the critical care fellow, cursing the residents, cursing the medical center, cursing himself. Kelly came into the room and queried what he was mumbling about, but all Ryan could offer was that the day was "less than ideal." Upon finally emerging, he made a bee-line for the couch in the family room. There, he was jumped by the girls who eagerly started setting up a game of Clue.

"Hey, guys, what's this?" he asked.

"It's family game night, Dad. Don't you remember?" replied Ava.

"Oh jeez, guys, not tonight. Okay? Your dad's pretty beat."

"But Dad, I had my heart set on playing games with you all day," whined Riley.

"Yeah, Daddy, you promised. You don't want to break a promise, do you?" litigated Erin.

"I know, guys, but maybe we could take a rain check. *Please*? How about over the weekend?" Ryan tried to smile behind his words, but it proved more of a grimace.

With the dark clouds that were gathering around him, the girls cleared out of the room. Hardly noticing, he remained planted on the couch, flicking stations. Minutes, or perhaps hours later, Kelly poked her head in the room.

"You coming to bed? It's pretty late, you know."

"Is it?" replied Ryan, eyes fixed on the TV.

"You haven't eaten, you know. You didn't even say good night to the girls."

"Oh . . . sorry, Kell. I got caught up in a documentary," said Ryan, who was still flicking channels every few seconds.

"Well, I'm headed up. Lots of meetings tomorrow."

"Okay, honey. Good night then," said Ryan, still staring at the TV.

Kelly turned and walked away. Ryan remained immobile, save his one thumb on the remote control. He dozed off several times, but each time was awakened by dreams of Mrs. Dunton thanking him for all he didn't do; or worse, of Mr. Dunton's brain exploding out of his head. After a particularly vivid rendering of the event, he looked up and saw that it was 3:00 a.m. He was overcome with thirst, so he made his way into the kitchen and downed two successive pints of orange juice as if he were in a collegiate chugging race. Upon rinsing his glass, he happened to glance out the window over the sink and spotted, not ten feet away, a dark figure, a dark female figure.

He jerked back, the cranberry-colored glass falling from his hand to the terra-cotta floor and shattering into hundreds of pieces. He shook his head, advanced back to the sink, leaned forward and pressed his face to the window. Again, he was pro-pelled backward, this time tripping over a chair. A shrouded face had stared back at him now, only a couple of feet away.

"Holy Christ," he sputtered.

He scrambled to his feet and looked at the window. The woman was now up against it, peering into the kitchen, hands flanking her face. Ryan backpedaled and frantically massaged the kitchen wall, feeling for the outdoor light switches. He managed only to turn the kitchen lights off. Heart turning upside down in his chest, he kept fumbling for the right switch. Finally, he turned on both the kitchen lights and the outdoor floodlights. He advanced back to the window.

The woman, or hallucination, or whatever it was, had retreated a few feet but was still there. Ryan could make out her appearance better now, although her outline was blurred—perhaps due to a fog that was hanging over a freshly fallen spring snow—perhaps due to an odd flickering quality to her substance, like the sputtering flame of a tallow candle. She was quite tall, and was attired in multiple layers of black filigree lace over a black sheath dress. She sported a black pillbox hat with overhanging veil. Her face was too obscured to make out any details, but he sensed that she was young. Around her neck was a strand of black pearls.

He was at a loss for what to do. Could she be real? *Of course not.* It had to be a dream. He must still be on the couch. At least it wasn't Ben torturing his children, or Mr. Dunton's exploding brain. He tried pinching his skin and biting into his lip, certain that he would awaken, still in front of the TV. But he didn't. He remained at the window, and the woman remained in the snow-draped driveway. His next response was all reflex. He bolted into the family room, grabbed a hiking pole, and burst out through the side door. He leaped out into the snow, brandishing his ersatz weapon. But she was gone. No trace of her. Not even a footprint in the snow.

"Christ..."

He reentered the house and dropped back down on the couch. "Well, shit," he commented to the blank TV screen. The hallucinations were back. Whitehead and Larkin must have been right—it was all sleep related. "Wonderful..."

CHAPTER 20

DROP DEAD

"**W**ell, there's no doubt about it. We need to get you into the sleep center," remarked Dr. Whitehead. Ryan had tracked him down immediately after the hallucination of the dark lady, offering only information about his night terrors.

"Sheesh, can't we try some meds first? My schedule's jam-packed," replied Ryan.

"Ryan, if this keeps up, you won't be able to attend to your 'jam-packed' schedule. You'll be in a coronary care unit . . . or a psych ward."

"Yeah, I get it. But I know what will happen. We'll do nights and nights of recording, and then ultimately try some medication, won't we? So, why not just go with a sleep med first?"

"It'd be nice to know what medicine to go with," replied Whitehead. "We do try to be scientific, you know."

"Sure, but in the end it'll still be a matter of trial and error, won't it? So, let's just get started on a trial of *something*."

"I don't know, Ryan. I really think you need a formal evaluation by the experts. Meds may only screw everything up. Let's at least get you on the books. It takes a few weeks to get in."

Ryan allowed Whitehead to schedule him for three nights in the sleep lab the following month. In the meantime, he raided the local natural food store and started a regimen of low-dose melatonin every night. It helped him fall asleep but had no effect on the terrors. He doubled the dose. But if anything, the terrors worsened. He tried valerian root, then magnesium, then passionflower extract. All were total failures. Next came tryptophan, then ginkgo biloba, then other assorted "witch doctor" concoctions—all to no avail. CBD proved no better. Switching to the pharmaceutical world, he gave antihistamines a try. Then serotonin reuptake Inhibitors (a.k.a. SSRIs). Then other antidepressants. Finally, having postponed his sleep evaluation twice, he talked Whitehead into bona fide sleeping pills. They seemed to help but left him too "hungover" the following days.

Throughout this time, the repetitive nighttime disruptions had the entire Brenan household on edge, even John and Paul, the family's border collies. Ryan started coming home later and later to lessen the obvious irritation he seemed to cause everyone. When he was at home, he overcompensated. He indulged every wish of the girls: playing any game they chose, giving them sweets and junk food, letting them watch one insufferable prepubescent comedy after another, and allowing them to stay up well past their bedtimes, night after night. He tried to assuage Kelly's obvious consternation by diving into her world with great fervor: begging her to share every detail of her days, sharing his own in-depth online research about her current projects, enacting short-term fixes for every long-term structural and cosmetic problem of their ancient house, and jumping in to take over any household chore she initiated.

One such chore was the acquisition of a new outdoor grill. Their previous workhorse, a wedding present, had given the couple years of unselfish service until it rusted out from below, rendering it as dangerous as it was useless. Ryan insisted that he accompany Kelly when she went to purchase a new one. Thus, on a late-April Saturday afternoon, after some protracted hospital rounds, he headed home intent on executing the mission. Only, it was uncharacteristically beautiful outside, so he decided to take a circuitous route home, crossing the river five miles east in Catamount. Along the way, he opened the jeep's sunroof and allowed the rare springtime sunshine to wash over him.

He passed a large and well-kept farm—most likely a rich person's horse farm judging by the immaculate nature of its endless lengths of whitewashed four-rail fencing. Sure enough, an attractive woman in expensive-looking equestrian gear materialized off to his right and paralleled his drive. She was riding atop what was, by all measures, a slapping stallion. Ryan couldn't help but admire the graceful union of human and beast on the gallop. Then the elegant rider dug her heels into the horse's side and the two accelerated, veering off toward a gate between adjoining fields, clearly intent on jumping the obstacle. The horse, however, had no such inclination and abruptly pulled up short. The woman was shot into the air like a skeet released from its house. She cleared the fence by several yards and then plowed headfirst into the freshly tilled Pennsylvanian topsoil on the other side. The speed and trajectory of her descent, and the inelegant landing, left little doubt that her neck would be snapped in two.

Oh bullshit, thought Ryan. It had to be another freaking hallucination. He brought the jeep to a stop, got out, and ambled over to the fencing, expecting the woman to have vanished. And, indeed, the faultlessly attired body was gone. The horse, however, remained, lazily chewing on some weeds by the gate.

Ryan arrived home, cursing his brain's recent penchant for the fantastical. He collected his impatient wife and headed, at flank speed, for a big-box megastore in Bloomsbury. Soon he was loading a large, unwieldy box onto a shopping trolley. Having succeeded, he looked up at Kelly, anticipating some gratitude for his manly assistance in the expedition, only to find her attention focused on a host of gleaming stainless-steel grilling instruments. He turned back to the trolley and noted an ashen, Santa Clausbellied, store clerk staggering his way. The guy clung to the store shelves like they were railings on a heaving ship. Ten feet away he stopped, clutched his chest, grunted, and sunk to his knees. He teetered there a moment, gurgled, and collapsed face-first onto the concrete floor. *Here we go again,* thought Ryan. He grabbed the handle of the trolley and pushed it toward the front of the store.

"Ryan, aren't you going to help that poor man?" It was Kelly, looking at him as if he had gone mad.

"You saw that?" asked Ryan, eyebrows raised in surprise.

"Of course I saw it. Shouldn't you *do* something?" replied Kelly.

"Oh, yeah, sure . . ." responded Ryan. He walked over to the fallen clerk and nudged him with his foot. The guy had substance, and failed to disappear. Ryan dropped to his knees and laid his hands on him. He seemed of flesh and blood. And the blood, as indicated by a lack of a carotid pulse, was no longer pumping through his arteries.

"Christ," growled Ryan. If this was a hallucination, it was a good one. He turned to Kelly. "The guy's arrested. Call 911. I'll get started on him, but the sooner we get a rescue squad in here the better. And see if they have any defibrillators in the store."

Kelly took off on a sprint, phone to her ear. Ryan turned to the downed man, flipped him onto his back, and started CPR.

Jesus, I hate CPR, thought Ryan. And he did. At least out in the field. In the hospital, there were "code teams" assigned to handle any sort of cardiopulmonary arrest, so he never had to get involved. And the teams had all sorts of assistance, medicines, and fancy equipment. Out in the field, it was always an awful experience. And was seldom successful. He'd only had to do it twice in the past, but that was more than enough. The first was on a very old woman, back when he was a medical student. The woman's osteoporotic rib cage crackled and snapped under his chest compressions; and she vomited into his mouth as he administered rescue breaths. The second had occurred just the past summer. A middle-aged man in Bermuda shorts and T-shirt had been mowing his lawn around the front bushes of his house. It was later revealed that the man was deathly allergic to bees. Why on earth he would choose to mow so close to the intensely floral azalea bushes, all pulsating with bees, would forever remain a mystery; but he so chose, and was stung, and had an anaphylactic reaction, and arrested. Ryan was simply driving by when he saw the guy drop. He ran over and initiated CPR. No fracturing of ribs this time, but the guy had apparently just eaten because he vomited volumes of partially digested pizza into Ryan's mouth. Ryan had not eaten pepperoni since.

After an eternity and a half of Ryan working on the clerk alone, people began to show up. An off-duty EMT took over the chest compressions. Shortly thereafter, a rescue squad came roaring down the Exterior Illumination aisle and pounced on the scene. Defibrillators were fired and within a few minutes, the guy had an EKG tracing and a thready pulse. Soon he was whisked away in a wailing ambulance.

Back in the jeep, with the grill secured in the rear, Kelly put Ryan to the third degree. "Ryan, what the heck was that all about? Were you truly going to walk away from that man?"

Ryan was on his heels but didn't want to own up to the whole hallucination thing. Kelly was already pissed at him for forgoing formal sleep evaluations and "winging it" with his endless lineup of medications. He was certain if he told her about seeing things, she would freak out—probably have him committed. And it was so unnecessary. He would get things squared away. It was just a matter of time. It wasn't like he was crazy—just sleep deprived.

"Uh, jeez, Kelly, I don't know. I'm so freaking tired from the terrors and all the call lately. I guess I just wasn't processing well. I think I thought I would go get help."

"With the shopping cart?" pressed Kelly.

"Like I said, I don't think I was processing all that well . . ."

"Because you're so tired."

"Yeah."

"Then how can you possibly do brain surgery in this state?" asked Kelly with arms crossed.

"Oh, I wake up fine for that."

"But not for someone who collapsed right in front of you?"

"It's not the same, Kelly," responded Ryan, eyes purposefully glued to the road so he didn't have to meet Kelly's paralyzing stare. "When I'm not working, my systems kind of shut down, and I get terribly sleepy."

"Well, that would explain a lot," said Kelly with a roll of her eyes.

"No, seriously. I just don't think I'm firing on all pistons today— kind of sleepwalking my way through things."

"Sounds like crap to me, Ryan Brenan. But if you don't want to share with me what's really going on in that head of yours, so be it. When we get home, we'll put you to bed, and I'll put the grill together." Ryan started to protest, but then thought better of it and shrank deep into his seat.

CHAPTER 21

FALSE ADVERTISING

"**A** few good weeks in February—then the night terrors began, and he disappeared completely," remarked Kelly to her best friend, Dianne O'Connor, as the two walked along the New Bethany levies in early May, the swirling waters of the rain-swollen Susquehanna mirroring Kelly's rising sense of turbulence within her marriage. "I mean, for that brief period, it felt like I got the man I married back, or at least some approximation of him. But maybe I've been fooling myself all these years. Maybe that man never existed."

"What do you mean by that, Kell?" asked Dianne.

"Well, I've only ever known Ryan since he was a doctor. I never actually got to know the man he was before the neurosurgical world started layering all its twisted ways on him. I never got to know the person underneath all those layers."

"Like?"

Kelly picked up a stick, threw it into the rushing river, and stared at it until it was swept downstream. She turned back to Dianne and tried to smile. "Oh, you know: the perfectionism, the need to constantly excel, the need to perpetually function at peak performance, the need to always have the answer, the need to never ask for help, the need to act rather than listen. And then there's all the horrific ego-battering."

"Ego-battering?"

"Absolutely. I think all of their egos are in tatters," replied

Kelly, continuing to watch the stick until it disappeared from sight.

"I don't know, Kelly," said Dianne. "I mean, you ask anyone what strikes them most about neurosurgeons and they're liable to say: 'their titanic egos.'"

"Yeah, I get that. Perhaps their baseline self-worth is pretty strong. After all, you've probably got to have a pretty high opinion of yourself, of your abilities, to plow into peoples' brains every day. But believe me, Di, you should see the damage all those bad outcomes, all those complications, do to them. Not that Ryan would ever share that sort of thing with me. But when several of them get together and have had a few drinks, it comes spilling out, in all its gory detail. It's horrifying to listen to. It's incredible what they weather, really."

"Well, you sound more sympathetic than angry, at least."

Kelly paused again and this time picked up a stone, throwing it far out into the rushing water. "Sympathetic? I guess so. I certainly feel bad for him at times. But it does get me wondering: this bizarre being who comes home late every night—is this the actual Ryan Brenan? I certainly don't think it's the person I fell in love with. But like I said, maybe I was fooling myself back then. Maybe I was just overcome by romance, and hero-worship, and lust. Maybe all this time I've been projecting onto him the person I wanted him to be, the person I kept telling myself was underneath all those layers. I keep expecting the real Ryan to surface. But what if this is *the real Ryan*, the actual Ryan, the only Ryan? What if this is all he'll ever be?"

"And that would be bad?"

"Yes, that would be bad," replied Kelly turning toward her friend, eyes flashing. "The guy's so freakin' . . . unidimensional."

"Unidimensional?"

"Yeah. He eats, sleeps, and breaths neurosurgery," replied

Kelly, throwing her hands into the air. "To the exclusion of everything else. He feigns interest in me and the girls, but there's no question whatsoever where his priorities lie."

"Do you think that's a little harsh? I mean, it's an extremely demanding job."

"We all have demanding jobs. Hugh has a demanding job. Matt Wolfe has a demanding job," said Kelly. "You and I have multiple demanding jobs. But Ryan has taken dedication to his 'demanding job' to whole new levels."

"Was he this way in DC?"

"He's definitely been much worse since we got here," replied Kelly, gesturing north toward the town center. "But the telltales were there back at Walter Reed: missed dates, nights where he just couldn't let go of the day's events, always checking in, constantly fatigued, falling asleep in the middle of a dinner out. But at least he was making an effort then. It felt . . . I don't know . . . heroic. I wanted to soothe him and support him. But I worry now that I sold myself a false bill of goods."

"Meaning?"

"I guess I believed he'd make adjustments for me—out of love— come to a compromise between his work world and, well, me. And I also believed I'd be invited into his life, live through the highs and lows with him, experience the medical world vicariously. Instead his entire work life, which is 99 percent of his actual life, is an absolute black box, totally sealed off from me."

"And you've discussed this with him?" pressed Dianne.

"Sure, a million times," said Kelly.

"And how does he respond?"

"Well, he can get defensive when he's all tired and beat-up, and reminds me that I knew what I was getting myself into when I married him," replied Kelly with a frown. "But most of the time, he's all apologetic and promises to do much better. Which only makes me feel like a selfish bitch, and like I'm doing nothing but adding to his stress."

Dianne paused for a moment in thought then asked, "Does Ryan seem stressed out a lot?"

"Absolutely. He comes home emptied every day, near collapse. Then he attaches himself to me—all evening—not for intimacy but for succor, for repair. And he's constantly on edge, jumping at every creek of the house. And don't get me started on his sleep—"

"Jeez, Kelly, this sure sounds like depression to me."

"There's no doubt he's depressed, how can he not be? And you should see how dark he gets if he's had a little too much to drink," noted Kelly, her eyes narrowing. "It's awful."

"Do you mean he gets . . . abusive?" asked Dianne, studying Kelly's face.

"Oh God, no," replied Kelly, holding up her hands. "Just so horribly dark. It's like a light switch—from playful to morose. It's scary, really. I worry that he might . . . might . . . hurt himself someday."

"Is he seeing anyone about all this?"

Kelly glanced up at Carriere, presiding over the town on a high hill. "Yeah, he's seeing a psychiatrist right now, and a neurologist, apparently. They're working on his sleep. But he saw a psychiatrist before and blew her off when she suggested he take some time off from work. Heaven help anyone who tries to interfere with his mighty work schedule. And I'm sure that's what's at the root of it all. The man is never home."

"And he can't modify things at all?"

"I'm sure he can," said Kelly with a sigh. "The point is, he won't. And, you know, I get it. At work, he gets nothing but approbation for his efforts. At home, he gets grumbling and demands. At work, he's a big man on campus, a star brain surgeon, a hero. At home, he's just a parent. A second-string parent, at that. The girls almost see him as a visitor, not a father."

"Sheesh, Kell. So, what are you going to do?"

"Keep at him, I guess," replied Kelly throwing another rock into the river. "But it's exhausting, Di. I'm running out of the energy and the desire to reel him back in."

"I don't like the sound of that."

"I don't like the sound of it myself. But at some point, you have to cut your losses. If he constantly empties me of all I've got, what do I left to give the girls?"

CHAPTER 22

WAS THAT YOUR FOOT?

On parting from Dianne, Kelly immediately felt guilty about what she had said; or, more accurately, about what she was feeling. What had happened to her relationship with Ryan? It had once been so intense, so incandescent, so irrepressible. As she walked across the bridge and watched the Susquehanna seething below, she thought back to those days, and back to the night they first met.

It was at Whispers, a DC dance club, a stone's throw from the White House. She had been chatting with friends on a vast elevated platform overlooking the dance floor. She was standing next to a short staircase when she felt a sudden pain in her left foot. She reflexively jerked it back, then watched helplessly as a man on crutches tumbled down the stairs.

Kelly ran down and helped the man to his feet. "Are you all right?" she yelled over the oppressive music. "I am so, so, sorry."

"I'm okay, ma'am," replied the man, "but why on earth would *you* be sorry?"

"I tripped you. I mean, I didn't mean to. I just turned, and next thing I knew, you were falling.

"Wait, was it you who I crutched?"

"That would be me," replied Kelly, annoyed at the fact she could feel herself blushing.

"Hey, it wasn't your fault. Someone bumped into me as I was getting ready to negotiate the stairs. I tried to catch myself.

Unfortunately, the crutch landed on your foot rather than on terra firma."

"But you hit the ground so hard. And you're already so banged up. What in the world happened to you?"

"An accident."

"Looks like it was a nasty one."

"You can say that again."

Kelly found herself inexplicably attracted to this tall, dark, could-be handsome man. It was an odd feeling. She had been badgered by friends to accompany them to the club. This was not her thing, not her thing at all. She had no intention of hooking up with anyone. She wore a business suit and black librarian glasses to signal her lack of carnal interest in any potential suitors. A couple of drinks with her friends and she would head home to bed—alone. But here before her was this guy—this battered, beleaguered guy—with coal-black eyes that bespoke a rare depth and intelligence; and a sadness and sense of loss; and, perhaps, a deep—

Oh, bullshit, thought Kelly. She was going all Florence Nightingale just because this guy took a spill. *Don't get all soft, sister. Remember, injured or not, all men are pigs.* But those deep, dark, pensive eyes, and that embarrassed grin, and that nasty cut on his forehead. He was just so vulnerable and adorable. "I'm sorry you're so banged up, or I'd ask if you wanted to dance," she heard herself shout. Perhaps it was the Macallans talking.

"I'd be delighted. Just no swing dancing," came the answer.

The man leaned his crutches against the railing and stepped toward Kelly. The two took hold of one another and started swaying, well out of sync with the Euro Middle-eastern hip-hop booming from nearby speakers. They chatted, or rather, bellowed at each other through several songs, trying to create piecemeal biographical sketches of each other. But the music climbed in decibels and made it next to impossible. The man looked uncomfortable and seemed to be wincing with the loudest booms from the speakers, so Kelly asked if he would be interested in a drink in a nice, sedate bar just around the corner. The man was all in.

The two made it out into the blessedly quiet night air. Kelly turned to the man. "Well, that's much better, isn't it? You know, in all that noise, I don't think I fully caught your name."

"It's Ryan. Ryan Brenan."

"Well, delighted to meet you, Ryan Brenan. I'm Kelly, Kelly Connolly."

The two shook hands, then made their way to the small, sparsely attended wine bar. After settling in, they kicked into a rapid-fire exchange of information. They quickly covered their youths and found they had much in common, both having grown up in military families, both having lost a parent at a young age. Kelly then steered the conversation to Ryan's injuries.

"Nothing too bad," explained Ryan. "Some broken vertebrae in my back and neck, and a shattered knee . . . oh, and some kidney and lung injuries. I guess I was kind of lucky."

"You don't look very lucky."

"Oh, it could have been much worse."

"Surgery?"

"Yep, I've got my share of titanium in various places."

"Ouch. What about that?" asked Kelly, touching a fresh scar running across Ryan's forehead.

"Oh, yeah. Forgot about that. I guess a bit of a depressed skull fracture—but no surgery."

"Coma?"

"Missed out on that one."

"Well, that's something at least. Are you able to work?" asked Kelly, feeling drawn deeper and deeper into this battered man's universe.

"Hopefully soon. But I'll have to pass a physical first."

"Oh, what do you do?"

"Well, I'm in the Army. What about you, Ms. Connolly, what's your chosen profession?" asked Ryan, eyes riveted to Kelly's.

"My 'chosen profession,' sir, is the law," replied Kelly, riffing on the formality of his inquiry. "I happen to be an attorney."

Ryan visibly cringed.

"What's the matter? Got something against lawyers?" asked Kelly with a smile.

"Only some, I guess. Or . . . well, yeah. Probably most."

"What, are you a doctor or something?"

"Why do you ask?" replied Ryan, his dark eyes widening with surprise.

"Well, it's been my experience that only doctors have such a reflexive negative reaction to encountering a lawyer."

"Well, as it turns out . . ."

"So, you *are* a doctor," said Kelly with a triumphant smile. "An Army doctor, then?"

"Yep ," replied Ryan, looking down into his glass of Syrah.

"So, what kind of doctor are you?" asked Kelly, taking a large sip of her cabernet.

"A surgeon. What kind of lawyer?"

"Environmental."

"Cool," replied Ryan with an approving nod.

"A surgeon, huh?" asked Kelly, studying Ryan's eyes.

"'Fraid so."

"What kind?"

"Um . . . a neurosurgeon," mumbled Ryan, shifting in his chair as if embarrassed by the admission.

Kelly paused for a moment, then leaned forward, fixing her eyes on Ryan's, and exclaimed, "Holy shit . . . *holy shit!* Let me get this straight: Army neurosurgeon, all beaten to hell . . . You're him, aren't you, Ryan?"

"I'm who?"

"You're that Army neurosurgeon who was all over the news a few weeks ago. 'The fighting brain surgeon,' or whatever they called you."

"Well, that's better than the 'killer doc,'" offered Ryan, looking down at his shoes.

"Indubitably. But you lied to me! You told me you were in an accident," reproached Kelly, hands on her hips.

"Well, it was a kind of accident, wasn't it?"

"Holy shit!" exclaimed Kelly. "Sorry for the profanity, but it is *so* surreal to meet you. I didn't recognize you—all beat-up as you are. I mean, the pictures of you they showed on TV were from prior to the crash. And my God, you must've lost fifty pounds since then. You look like you've been in a POW camp."

"Probably would've been better food . . ."

"How did you end up at Whispers tonight? I mean, you don't look quite ready to really hit the dance floor—so to speak."

"Yeah, well," replied Ryan with an eye roll, "my residents grabbed me in rehab and dragged me down here. They insisted it would do me good. But honestly, even when I'm in one piece, it's not my thing."

"Yeah, mine either," said Kelly. "But Ryan, I have to say, it's truly an honor to meet you. You're a freaking hero; an old-fashioned real-life war hero!"

Kelly realized she was gushing like a starstruck teenager, and this annoyed her. Frankly, despite her love for her Army-ranger father, she was no particular fan of the military. And she was unimpressed by its supposed "heroes." The stories behind their alleged acts of heroism always seemed hyperbolic, too far beyond the norms of basic behavior, too out of keeping with human narcissism. And the stories about this guy sitting across the table from her seemed utterly implausible—outrageous, really—how could they be true? Yet, there he was, looking so broken and so in need of some tenderness.

Ryan broke in: "Please understand, Kelly, I'm no hero. Your dad's a hero. He's a real soldier. I'm certainly not. If I knew what I was getting myself into that day, I would have never gone. And I was scared out of my mind every second of it all. I spent most of the time crying, and praying to any god that would listen to save me."

"You're way too self-effacing, Ryan," said Kelly. "Most people who did what you did would be marching around, chests out, bragging about it, letting people buy them drinks and dinners."

"What I did was kill people, literally kill my fellow man—to save my own life. I hate that I did it. I hate that I hated them when I did it."

"But you had no choice. Everyone would've been killed. All those injured marines. You were doing your duty, as a soldier, as an American," said Kelly, surprised that such words could ever leave her lips.

"Yeah, it sounds much better here than it did there, that's all I can tell you," said Ryan as he wiped from his eyes the thick pools of moisture threatening to run down his cheeks.

Kelly noticed the action and that Ryan was trembling. She reached out and lightly brushed hair away from his scar with her fingertips. "You poor man. You poor, sweet, lovely, man," she whispered. She had no idea where the words were coming from, but she meant them with a depth of sincerity that shocked and frightened her.

Within six months the two had moved in together. Their

lives became a happy, hectic mix of long hours at work; frequent separation due to Kelly's travels and Ryan's nights on call; late evening dinners out in the Irish bars of DC, Georgetown, and Alexandria; and long runs together through Rock Creek Park. Every Saturday morning, Ryan would come home from hospital rounds with a small bouquet of flowers he had bought for her from a street vendor. And every time he did, the adoration behind the gesture would make Kelly cry. She couldn't imagine being more in love. She couldn't imagine being happier. Within a year, they were engaged. Within two, they were married. After four, their first child, Ava, was born. Then, in rapid succession, Riley and Erin. Then came the move to New Bethany. Somewhere in there, though, thought Kelly with a sinking heart, in the rush of professional commitments, changes in location, parenthood, and parallel existences, they'd lost hold of one another.

CHAPTER 23

SLEEP AID

"**S**hit!" exclaimed resident Cara Klein as blood detonated out of the patient's head and splattered across the lens of the operating microscope. She jerked her head away, shuddered, and leaned forward to look through the "scope's" eyepieces again. "Jesus Christ! I can't see a fucking thing!"

"Stay cool now, Cara," remarked Ryan in a low, monotonic voice. "Take a deep breath. Remember, the patient depends on you remaining calm and collected, right?" Ryan was in his element on this mid May morning. The world of night terrors, hallucinations, and unhappy spouses was a million miles away. He had sealed it up in a vault and was focused solely on the work at hand. This level of compartmentalization of one's life was a critical skill that most surgeons acquired during their training. Without it, they could be rendered useless when the proverbial shit hit the fan, as it was now for Cara.

"Right, Dr. Brenan, but I can't see a damned thing!" replied Cara.

Ryan grabbed the release button for the magnetic locking system that held the several-hundred-thousand-dollar microscope in whatever conformity the surgeon wished. He swung the device's arm away from the operative field and returned his attention to the opening in the patient's skull. It was nothing but a percolating pool of crimson.

As Ryan began to suck away some of the blood, he addressed

the circulating nurse. "Hey, Elynne, do me a favor and throw my loupes and headlight on me, will ya?"

The nurse hurried over and placed operating loupes over Ryan's eyes, and then cranked down a fiber-optic headlight around his head.

"Cara, help suck some of this blood out, if you will."

Cara grabbed a suction device, and the two surgeons removed standing blood until they came to a region deep in the patient's head that was the source of the scarlet jets. With a pair of forceps, Ryan grabbed a flat, one-by-one-centimeter square of cotton from the scrub nurse's Mayo Stand and guided it down to the bottom of the dissection, placing his sucker on top of it. This helped control the sprays of blood, but it didn't stop them. He grabbed another and laid it over the first. Again, he placed his sucker on top of it. With this, the raging torrent was downgraded to a trickle.

"Right, Cara, wash out the field while I keep this plugged, and then let's get the scope back in."

Ryan held the cotton squares in place as Cara rinsed the field with flushes of sterile saline. Then he limbo-danced under the microscope's arm as it was swung back into place over the field. Cara replaced his sucker with her own, and he stepped away. He had his loupes and headlight removed, then settled back behind the observer eye pieces to watch Cara work. The rest of the room turned their attention to a giant-screen TV on the wall with the operative image projected upon it in HD.

Cara began to dissect around the offending agent—an aneurysm: a balloon-like bulge off a blood vessel wall that can tear open with devastating consequences. When treated surgically, they're dissected free of other structures and clamped shut with a tiny spring-loaded titanium clip.

As Cara worked, Ryan made small technical suggestions here and there, but mostly offered a series of *uh-huh*s, *yep*s, *good*s, and

I don't think so's. After an hour or so, the aneurysm was ready for "clipping." Cara took a long "applier" with an aneurysm clip loaded at its end and passed the jaws of the clip around the base of the big, broad, pulsating monster.

"Okay, Cara. Do it," encouraged Ryan.

Cara let the jaws slowly close, then released the clip from the applier. After a long sigh, and with tremulous hands, she poked a hole in the aneurysm with a spinal needle. A small trickle of blood ran out and the aneurysm deflated. It was dead.

Ryan looked away from the observer eye pieces and turned to the profusely perspiring resident. "Great job, Cara. How'd it feel?"

Cara pushed back from the microscope, let out a huge exhalation, and looked over at Ryan. "Jesus Christ, Dr. Brenan, I felt like I was gonna vomit in my mask the whole damned time."

After the two surgeons had closed the wound, deposited the patient in the Neurovascular-ICU, and spoke with the patient's anxious family members, Ryan turned to his still-rattled resident and said, "Come on. It'll take them forever to turn over the room after that. Let's call the gang and hit the coffee shop."

Soon a gaggle of residents and physician assistants were sitting around Ryan and Cara at a large table, going over the patients on the service. Once they had exhausted the medical issues of the day, a rambling general conversation got off the ground. It eventually landed on the subject of sleep difficulties. They were apparently ubiquitous amongst the crew. When the discussion made its way to Ryan, he reluctantly confessed about his night terrors. A feeding frenzy of questions and observations ensued.

Throughout the subsequent inquisition, he failed to mention the associated hallucinations. But he thought about how they seemed to be percolating up with great frequency of late. All fleeting. All vague. But so many seeming to involve his dark lady friend. He would spot her late at night—or think he spotted her—out in the field across the street. The field he and the girls used for snow soccer. The field that was once a graveyard.

"Jesus, Dr. B," remarked Cara, breaking into Ryan's thoughts, "if I were your wife, I'd make you sleep in another room."

"Tried that. Started sleeping in the family room. But I guess my screams would echo up to the girls' room and become kind of demonic on their way. I can tell you, *that* was not well received."

"Sheesh, sounds like you need to hit the sleep lab," offered Cara.

"Yeah, I know. But it seems so self-indulgent, when you consider all the horrible crap our patients and their families face. I mean, why use up valuable specialists' time over a few nightmares.

"Oh bullshit, Dr. B. You just don't want to be benched for several days for a bunch of sleep studies!" countered Cara. The table erupted into hearty laughter and ribbing of Ryan for his workaholic tendencies.

———

A week later, Ryan was wrestling with the electronic medical record in the post-anesthesia care unit when he was approached by Ariana Salazar, a physician assistant on the neurology service.

"Dr. Brenan, got a minute?"

"Sure, Ariana. Problem with a patient?"

"No, sir. A problem with you," replied Ariana.

"Oh?" said Ryan, a little taken aback.

"You must forgive me, but I couldn't help overhearing the discussion about your sleep disorder in the coffee shop last week," said Ariana. "We were at the next table."

"Not a big deal, Ariana; it's just some nightmares."

"It will be a big deal if you don't get it under control, Dr. Brenan. Anyway, I talked to a friend of mine about you. He's a shaman. And he sent you this." Ariana reached into a backpack and pulled out a box, handing it to Ryan. Ryan opened it, revealing an elaborate dream catcher.

"This is for me, Ariana?"

"Absolutely. I told my friend what a wonderful doctor you were. He made it specifically for you. He guarantees it will help. And I believe him. He's a very powerful shaman."

Ryan knew that Ariana was into weird stuff. New-wave, earth-mother type stuff. There were even rumors that she was into witchcraft. So, the gift didn't necessarily shock him, but it did leave him tongue-tied.

"Well . . . thanks, Ariana. What do I do with it?"

"You hang it in a north-facing window."

"Then what?"

"You sleep!"

CHAPTER 24

WINNING WHEN YOU THINK YOU'RE LOSING

The dream catcher only made it as far as the back of the jeep. Ryan had tossed it there on exiting the hospital that night, but forgot about it with the arrival of another weekend of call. Soon he was immersed in the care of one severely injured teenager after another. Late Saturday night, however, the nature of the caseload dramatically shifted.

"Hey, Dr. Brenan." It was Cam Carlson. "Got a big ol' spinal epidural abscess. The guy's been totally out from the neck down since Thursday. Pics are on your phone."

Ryan looked at the MRI images and whistled. "Well, Cam, no good shall come of that, but let's see what we can do for the guy."

Within an hour, the patient was laid out on the operating room table, prone, and Ryan and Cam had made several small incisions in his back. In each incision, the two surgeons had exposed the spine and were removing bone.

"So, guys," noted Ryan to two nursing students. "This nice gentleman shoots up and must have gotten bacteria into his blood. The bacteria have caused a huge collection of pus to form in the spine, crushing the spinal cord and paralyzing him. We have to get to the pus and clean it out, up and down the entire length of the spinal cord. But after being crushed for a couple of days, the chances of his cord kicking back into gear are near zero."

An hour later, Ryan was explaining the situation to a room full of overtly angry family members. A couple of large men in biker jackets crowded Ryan and demanded to know why it had taken so long for their brother "to get fixed."

"Well, guys, we operated on him pretty much right away," offered Ryan.

"That's bullshit, man. Bernie was here for two and a half fucking hours before you guys did anything!" replied one of Bernie's brothers.

"Believe it or not, that's pretty quick," replied Ryan, gagging a little on the brothers' body odor. "It takes time to get things figured out. The ER docs did a really good job. And we had him in the operating room within twenty minutes of the diagnosis. That's near record time!"

The brothers closed in another inch, affecting some sort of primal threatening posture. "Still seems like a long fucking time to get workin' on someone who's paralyzed, Doc."

"I know it feels that way, and I have to admit, there are times when things get maddeningly delayed. And it can really piss me off. But that wasn't the case this time. Your brother's in trouble, there's no doubt about it. I'm very worried that he won't regain any movement. But it's just bad freakin' luck. Honestly, I would tell you if I thought we screwed up."

After some further exchange, the brothers backed off and asked reasonable and goal-oriented questions. Eventually, Cam and Ryan escaped.

"Crap, Dr. Brenan, I thought for a while there you might have to pull some of your Army Green Beret shit on those Hell's-Angel dudes," remarked Cam.

"Are you kidding, Cam?" replied Ryan, "I thought I might need my Clemson safety to lay them out."

"Don't give me that, Dr. Brenan," responded Cam. "We've all looked you up. We know all about you and your medals. I'm sure you could've gone all SEAL Team 6 on them."

"Far from it, my friend," replied Ryan, chuckling.

Two hours later, Ryan received another call from Cam. "Bad news, Dr. Brenan. Got another sick addict for you."

"What goes, buddy?"

"Twenty-nine-year-old male in coma. CT on its way to you. It shows a big-assed right parietal abscess that's ruptured into the ventricle. I think he's toast, but I thought you might want to clean him out."

Ryan looked at the CT images that came up on his phone.

"Yeah, let's do it, Cam. I agree, doesn't look good."

Cam and Ryan had the patient in the OR within half an hour. The two nursing students were still hanging around, so Ryan launched into a tutorial.

"So, abscesses are infected balls of pus that form in the brain tissue itself. Without treatment, they get bigger and bigger, squishing and killing the surrounding brain. With surgery and antibiotics, patients can often make good recoveries, but in this gentleman, a dire complication has occurred. Some of the pus broke out of the abscess and spilled into the fluid-filled chambers in the center of the brain called the ventricles, causing an instantaneous and overwhelming meningitis. This is usually fatal."

Cam and Ryan made short work of the opening in the skull and were soon making a two-centimeter cut into boggy, purple-red brain tissue. After dissecting for a couple of minutes, yellow-green pus, with the aroma of rotten eggs, came pouring out of the patient's head. The grossly contaminated drainage alluded the clear plastic bag below and ran down the drapes into Ryan and Cam's shoes. Hardly noticing, they cleaned out the cavity and began to close. Just as they were stapling up the scalp, the circulating nurse put an ER doctor on the squawk box.

"Hey, guys; Potter here." It was Gary Potter, who everyone liked to call *Harry* Potter because of his unmistakable British accent. "We have a thirty-two-year-old woman, prostitute, drug addict, found down. She's got the biggest brain abscess you've ever seen. She looks pretty far gone."

Cam and Ryan looked at each other. "Shit, Dr. Brenan," remarked Cam, "the bacterial world is on the march tonight."

"Sure seems to be," replied Ryan, glancing at the clock and hoping it would move quicker.

An hour later, the two were again washing out vast volumes of foul-smelling, yellow-brown pus from deep within someone's brain. The surgery went well, but neither surgeon expected the patient to recover. With that happy thought, they parted, Ryan hoping to catch a few winks of sleep at home.

He never made it there. He was on his way to the jeep when Cam called yet again.

"Another brain abscess, Cam?" Ryan asked with a note of sarcasm.

"Not quite. This one's a subdural empyema, and the girl's sick as shit." A subdural empyema is a rare, pus-forming infection on the surface of the brain. It is rapidly fatal.

"You sure, Cam?" asked Ryan, hoping more than questioning.

"Yeah, Dr. Brenan, pretty nasty shit. Pics in your phone. I've already notified the OR."

An hour later, the two had the girl's head open and were washing out another vast collection of putrid pus.

Thankfully, the remainder of Sunday call proved more gen-teel. But junior resident Ernest Nobleman was on, and he managed to call Ryan every fifteen minutes throughout the day and the night, precluding any hope of real rest. Monday, Ryan was slated for an all-day "outreach" clinic in Bellemonte. There, he sleepwalked his way through thirty patients, then left for home. On the hour-and-a-half drive back, he called in to Cara Klein to get an update on all of his patients.

"Well, Dr. Brenan, all your infections from the weekend look like shit," noted Cara.

"Lovely."

"Yeah, the spinal abscess is still intubated and sedated due to shitty lungs, the two brain abscesses remain in deep coma, and the subdural empyema gal is seizing like a hooked fish."

"Wonderful . . . "

———

Early the next morning, Ryan was coming out of a pediatric patient's room when Cam came running down the hallway and grabbed him.

"Hey, Dr. Brenan, you're not going to believe this, but—"

"Oh God, Cam, who's crashed this time?"

"No, sir, nothing like that—"

"All right, what disaster have you dragged in off the street?"

"Nothing like that either. But you're still not going to believe it. I promise you."

"Okay, Cam, let me have it."

"Well, remember those four infection disasters from Saturday night?"

"How can I forget? They all dead?" asked Ryan, cringing in anticipation.

"Nope. Quite the opposite," reported Cam, unable to hold back a massive smile. "All three brain infections are awake and following commands. And the spine guy's already walking."

"You're talking about the four we operated on this weekend?" asked Ryan, his eyes narrowing with skepticism.

"Yes, sir. The very same."

Ryan made a double-take. "Well, hell. Let's go see them, then."

They made their way to the main Neurosurgery-ICU and visited the brain infection patients first. All three were still intubated but were awake and moving under their own volition. Ryan and Cam fist-bumped and made their way to the patient with the spine infection.

"You the guys who operated on me?" came their greeting. The patient was seated in a chair, wolfing down some rubbery eggs.

"Yes, sir. Dr. Carlson and I performed your surgery," replied Ryan, anticipating an embarrassing flood of gratitude for his and Cam's miracle work.

"Well, fuck you both, then!" yelled the man, food falling from his mouth and onto the floor.

"Um . . . I'm sorry. What seems to be the problem? Are you hurting?" asked a wide-eyed Ryan.

"Of course I'm fucking hurtin', but that's beside the point. The nurses tell me you pricks are refusing to let me smoke."

"Um . . . well, I mean, you've got to understand th—"

"I don't have to understand shit! I need a smoke!"

"Well, sir," tried Ryan, clasping his hands together, "smoking isn't very good for you right after major surg—"

"I don't give a rat's ass if it kills me. It's my right to have a fucking smoke. Do I have to call a goddamned lawyer?"

Ryan held up his hands in a defensive posture. "Okay, okay, sir, I get it. There's a lot of red tape to doing that when you're an ICU patient. Let us see what we can do."

"Well, get on it, or I'm fucking out of here!"

Ryan and Cam cleared out and hurried to a secluded stairwell.

"Holy shit, sir, can you believe that?" asked Cam.

"Not the first time I've been yelled at, but this one certainly makes the yearbook."

"Well, sir, despite Mr. Brenvold's heartfelt gratitude, not a bad collection of outcomes from the weekend, eh?"

"Not bad at all, Cam. Thanks for finding me this morning. Huh, who would have believed it?"

"Well, you know what Dr. Martin says?" Dr. Martin was the oldest member on the Carriere team, and he was a wellspring of pithy aphorisms.

"What does Dr. Martin say, Cam?"

"In neurosurgery, sometimes you're losing when you think you're winning, and sometimes you're winning when you think you're losing."

"Amen to that."

———

When Ryan finally got home that night, he was beyond exhausted. He made a concerted effort to engage with the girls but went to bed right after they did. Two hours later, he awoke to his own screams and Kelly shaking him.

"Good God. How can it happen when I'm this tired?" he asked after coming fully around.

"You've got me, Ryan."

The two went about settling down the girls. When they returned to bed, Kelly dropped off immediately. Ryan did not. *Okay, that does it*, he thought. He had to get those sleep studies. Then, an image of Ariana's dream catcher flashed into his head. He'd forgotten the stupid thing. It must be still out in the jeep.

Why the hell not give it a try? It was even shaman-guaranteed. *Oh, come on, Ryan, really?* he thought. *A dream catcher?* What was next, burying a toad under a full moon? On the other hand . . .

CHAPTER 25

BARN DANCE

The effect was instantaneous. No nightmares, no wakeups in the middle of the night, and no night terrors—for weeks on end. And, hallelujah, no more hallucinations. Yes, Ryan still had a grueling summer call schedule to contend with, but he was actually getting a chance to catch up on his sleep on the intervening nights. He was ecstatic and grateful.

Thus, on a balmy late June morning, he burst into Ariana's office—his grin taking up half of his face—and presented her with a case of top-of-the-line cabernet sauvignon and a bouquet of orchids. Not that he thought that the dream catcher was actually catching dreams, but the thing must have had one hell of a placebo punch to it, because he hadn't slept this well for . . . well, since his father died.

"Oh, Dr. Brenan, you shouldn't have . . . ," responded Ariana.

"Are you kidding? I owe you a lifetime supply of both. I'm forever indebted to you," gushed Ryan.

"You're too kind," said Ariana.

"No, you're too kind, Ariana. It was such a sweet, and apparently effective, gesture."

"I'm delighted it's worked so well for you. But I did tell you, my friend is a most powerful shaman."

"You did at that. You'll have to thank him for me."

"I'd be happy to."

"It's a miracle, Ariana, a freaking miracle!"

"It sure sounds like it. But I should warn you about something," replied Ariana, with an anxious expression that unsettled Ryan.

"Oh?"

"Yes, well, my friend—the shaman—he told me that your nighttime disturbances . . . well, that they might be more than just bad dreams."

"Oh?"

"Yes, he said they might be symptomatic of a deeper, more complex problem."

"Oh, I get that, Ariana," responded Ryan, raising a hand. "Depression, anxiety, PTSD and stuff. I'm working on it all with a shrink."

"No, that's not what he means," responded Ariana, raising her preternaturally green eyes to fix upon Ryan's. "He's talking about something else entirely. He's talking about the spirit world. He thinks your disturbances may be the result of restless beings trying to get to you, interact with you. And your dreams are the easiest portal."

"I see," remarked Ryan, trying not to sound dismissive.

"I tell you this because, with the dream catcher working so well, I don't want you to be surprised if they try to connect with you in other ways."

"Uh, meaning what, Ariana?" asked Ryan, struggling to sound respectful.

"Well, my friend says that sometimes if you block their access to your sleep, they may become insistent on interfacing with you when you're awake."

"Who does he think might wish to 'interface' with me when I'm awake, Ariana?" asked Ryan, one eyebrow raised.

"The restless beings. That is, specters, ghosts, the undead . . ."

"He can't be serious," slipped out of Ryan's mouth.

"He's very serious. Have you had any such experiences, Dr. Brenan?"

"Um, no. Not that I know of."

"Well, be on the lookout. They can be subtle. But they can be very persistent if they don't get what they want."

———

Ryan continued with his week, but he couldn't quite shake off Ariana's admonition. Specters, ghosts, the undead? Ludicrous. He had a perfect physiological explanation for it all. The experts had all agreed: His scattered "apparitions" were sleep-induced brain hiccups. Well, they hadn't quite put it that way, but it meant the same thing. His brain was misfiring. Occasionally. Because of sleep deprivation. Hell, more than that—because of sleep starvation. And now, with his sleep under much better control, they were gone and all would be well. Yet her words insisted on rattling around in his brain: "specters, ghosts, the undead."

They were so insistent that a couple of days later, he sought to suppress any such thoughts with a good long run and some jacked-up hip-hop in his earbuds. He had made it home early after his last operation of the day was canceled due to an abnormal liver function test. Kelly and the girls were off at a dance class, so with his dogs John and Paul leading the way, he headed out on Salisbury Road. Soon, he was well out of town, passing acre after acre of rapidly filling cornfields. As he cleared a small berm, his eyes fixed on a tall, handsome, quintessential Pennsylvania barn. Atop the roof strode an old man in overalls, shingles on a shoulder, hammer in the opposite hand. But the guy looked way too old to be up there. Ryan couldn't help but picture him toppling off the roof. If lucky, thought Ryan, the fall would kill him outright. If unlucky, the old fool would break his neck, among various other body parts, and die a protracted and decaying death over in the medical center.

"Jesus," Ryan commented to the dogs. "What's wrong with everyone around here? Do they all harbor some sort of death wish? All that guy needs to do is catch his toe and—"

And over the guy went. From the very crest of the roof.

He tumbled out and down in an elegant summersault, and then managed to spread out his arms and legs as if skydiving. He bellyflopped into the compacted barnyard dirt and bounced. Not like a tennis ball, per se, but he bounced nonetheless—like a medicine ball thrown at a gym floor—a single, deadened bounce. He came to rest on his face and knees, in a position of prayer, as scattered shingles twirled down about him like falling maple seeds.

"Ah, screw this," muttered Ryan, as he turned away from the scene. "And I got a decent sleep last night."

But John and Paul had alerted and strained at their collars toward the downed man. Ryan tried to pull them in the opposite direction, but they fought to get to the guy. Ryan reluctantly capitulated and followed their lead. He recognized that if the guy was indeed an actual living being, he was now a dead, "actual living being;" but he figured it was best to check. As the dogs anxiously dragged him toward the downed farmer, he watched for any sign of movement. There was none. The crumpled-up hulk of perhaps previously animate flesh was motionless, save a shock of gray hair that swayed in the cooling evening breeze.

Ryan tied up the unnerved dogs and scrambled over a flat-boarded fence, carefully negotiating an apex that featured an array of rusty nails and stiletto-sharp splinters. He jumped to the ground, landing harder than he had anticipated, causing some pain in his partially metallic right knee. He bent over, rubbed the incensed joint for a few moments, and looked up toward the old man.

But the old man was gone. No blood, no impression on the ground, no hammer, no shingles. Just a few disinterested hens.

"Yep. I knew it," he commented to the chickens, shaking his head in disgust. But he looked over at the dogs. They were yelping and barking and orienting to the spot where the hallucinogenic farmer supposedly impacted. "What the . . ."

The mind chatter kicked back into gear: *Specters, ghosts, the undead.*

CHAPTER 26

EVIE

Ryan quickly excommunicated all paranormal references from his thoughts. One last brain hiccup was all it was. It had nothing to do with the "spirit world." It was all about sleep deprivation. Nothing more. He had only been getting decent sleep for a few weeks. It might take months for his brain to fully chill out, to fully reconfigure. Maybe more. Ariana was a kind and lovely person, but she was obviously a little on the looney side. Looney, yes, but the placebo effect of the dream catcher was still holding and that's all that mattered. Everyone was sleeping. Everyone was happier. The family was healing.

To convince himself of his return to normalcy, Ryan headed out to the Sunday afternoon pickup game of soccer at Nelson Park. The site was a couple of miles north of New Bethany and was surrounded by a dense forest. The field was in rough condition, but it sufficed for this collection of lumbering dad-bodied men, all in their fourth and fifth decades of life. The group gave Ryan a prodigal-son welcome as he assumed a position in the left midfield—he hadn't made an outdoor game since the previous autumn. It took half an hour or so for him to shake off the cobwebs and adjust to the July heat, but he eventually became confident in his play and spent much of his time on the pitch looking to set up teammates with scoring opportunities.

His principal target was Reverend Ron. Reverend Ron was an enthusiastic if not a particularly skilled player, and he certainly had a flair for the dramatic. Halfway through any game, he would usually pull up lame with a hamstring injury. From that point on, he would hobble about the field braving indescribable pain, until a nice through ball would set him off on a high-speed vector toward the opponent's penalty box. He would get off a shot—generally wide and high by a dozen yards—then crumble to the ground and roll about in near-extremis, until assisted off the field by teammates. Shortly thereafter, he would be back out on the pitch, reeking of Ben-Gay, his ailing thigh swaddled in several coils of Ace Bandage. One could set their watch by the pantomime. And so today, as if not to disappoint, the good reverend went down.

With the break in the action, Ryan's eyes were caught by a young woman who approached the field from the parking lot. From a distance, she was quite fetching. As she moved closer along the touchline, she became more so. When she reached midfield, she stopped, sat in the shade of a towering oak, and casually watched the game. Ryan was, and would always be, hopelessly in love with Kelly, but he wasn't dead, and he found the woman to be bewitching. He couldn't help stealing a glimpse of her at every opportunity. Eventually, though, the game came to a close, and Ryan jogged over to a dilapidated set of bleachers on the opposite side of the field. After fist-bumping a number of players and engaging in an end-of-combat hug with Matt Wolfe, he approached Reverend Ron. "Hey Ron, who's the blonde over there?"

"What blonde?"

"The girl over there on the far touchline. You had to have seen her. She's been there all afternoon," said Ryan with some incredulity. Reverend Ron possessed particularly fine-tuned sensors for the fairer sex.

"What girl?" asked Reverend Ron, swiveling his head about like the radar unit on a guided missile destroyer.

"*Over there,*" repeated Ryan, nodding his head in her direction, but Reverend Ron exhibited no signs of a target acquisition. Ryan snuck a peek, but the woman was gone. "Well, she must have just left. I can't believe you didn't notice her. She was just your type."

"My type?" asked Reverend Ron with feigned innocence.

"Yeah, young and alive!" The two shared a chuckle.

"So, what did your disappearing lady look like?"

Ryan described her, vividly.

"Are you sure you didn't see a ghost, my friend?"

This caught Ryan off guard. *Oh crap!* Another goddamned hallucination. But how could it be? All the previous ones were so fleeting. And, in retrospect at least, they always had a dreamlike, reality-stretching quality to them. Their edges were blurry, their coloration off by a shade. But not this one. This woman looked as real as any other person in the park. She was sharp and in-focus—even up close. Her coloration was, well, enchanting. And there were beads of summer sweat on her lips. Her eyes blinked with appropriate timing. And she remained there, in his waking consciousness, for over an hour. He swallowed hard, then turned to Reverend Ron and asked with faltering prosody, "What do you mean a ghost?"

"Well, you do know you're standing on Nelson Field, don't you?"

"Of course . . ."

"Named after a one Evie Nelson."

"And I suppose you're going to tell me that she was some favored daughter of the community who suffered an untimely death, and now haunts this spot every third Sabbath of every third month of every third year . . . ?"

"Close. Your physical description sure fits her, I guess. Matt can tell you more about her. Reverend Ron called Matt over. "Hey, Matt, Ryan here just saw Evie Nelson."

"Evie? Well, you wouldn't be the first," replied Matt. "She likes to hang out here, you know."

"That's what I'm telling our resident brain surgeon, here," replied Reverend Ron.

"Yeah, well, she hung herself right over there." Matt pointed to where the woman had been sitting throughout the game.

"Yeah, yeah," said Reverend Ron, "tell him the whole story, though."

"Well, Evie lived here during the Great Depression," started Matt. "A young, very pretty girl. One day, she presented to the police station, swearing that she'd been raped by the town's Baptist minister—right here in what used to be all woods. Soon it became apparent that she was pregnant, and everyone in town assumed she had made up the rape story. Her father kicked her out of the house, and she was shunned by the community. Ron's good ol' First Presbyterian came to her rescue, though. They took up collections for her and her baby. Even gave her a job and an apartment. That same winter, though, the baby died of diphtheria, or something. She fell into a deep depression and ended up hanging herself."

Ryan shifted uncomfortably.

"Eventually," continued Matt, "the Baptist minister was caught in the act with a fourteen-year-old and confessed to a series of rapes. Well, the town elders were overcome with guilt, so they converted this spot into a nice little park. They named it after Evie. This pitch used to be a baseball field. And there used to be a pool and carousel over there. You can check out the whole story over in the library. They have a little memorial to her there with all sorts of pictures and artifacts."

It was a hot and humid day, but Ryan couldn't overcome the bone-cracking chill permeating his body. He had to know. Was it in any way possible that he could have witnessed a ghost? As preposterous as it sounded, he had to consider it. He had never heard of Evie Nelson before, knew nothing of her story. Yet today's protracted hallucination—or brain short-circuit, or whatever it was—might be rooted in an actual historical event, a historical being. He had to know. He had to see if Evie Nelson was the girl from the game.

That night, he feverishly searched for her online. The story was there in all its lurid detail. But any picture of the girl was too grainy or washed out to make out her features. So, a trip to the New Bethany Library was definitely in order. It took until the following Friday for him to get to the place before it closed, and by then, he was crawling with nervous energy. On arrival, he burst into the ancient stone building and marched straight toward what looked like its original librarian. The tiny, wizened corpse of a woman listened to Ryan's pressured inquiries, then led him to an enormous oak bureau at the back of the main reading room. With some effort she pulled open the top drawer.

"Yes, Dr. Brenan, Evelyn Nelson died at only twenty-one years of age, the poor dear," offered Elisabeth Sladen, New Bethany librarian for almost fifty years. Her voice, if it could be called that, hissed and sputtered as if the air from her lungs had to run a gauntlet of cancer cells before it could amass enough force to rattle a single leathery, cigarette-stained vocal cord. "It was a very sad chapter in New Bethany history. It was a rougher, nastier place back then. There were many sad stories. Evelyn's probably sticks more in the collective consciousness because she's believed to still frequent some of its locations.

"You know," she continued, with an unsettling smile, "she and her baby were buried out in a pauper's graveyard without headstones. No one knows where now. But she's been seen out at her park many times. Some say her spirit is trying to find her little baby. But that's just people talking."

Ryan wondered for a moment whether Ms. Sladen herself

was a ghost. She certainly fit the bill. She was so frail, so thin, so lacking mass, that light coming from the stained-glass windows high in the room's outer wall seemed to pierce right through her. And had he even introduced himself as a doctor?

"Thank you, Ms. Sladen, You've been so very helpful," he said, squeezing her shoulder—in part to confirm its earthly density.

The cadaveric librarian smiled in response. "It is my pleasure, Dr. Brenan. I'm so pleased you've come to see us, and to have taken an interest in poor Evelyn."

"Are there pictures of her in here, Ms. Sladen?" asked Ryan, rummaging through the drawer.

"Oh yes. There are some of her in the papers, but there are several of the originals under them." She lifted a pile of papers out of the drawer—the top one reporting Evie's death in bold headlines—and placed them on a nearby table. Underneath lay a large manila envelope. In it were several black-and-white photos depicting a scene in front of the First Presbyterian Church. There, standing on the front steps, accepting a food basket from the minister, was an attractive young woman smiling, defiantly, at the camera.

And, there was no doubt about it, it was her.

Ryan was suddenly lightheaded. His mind strained at its confines. This thing, this entity, this whatever, was once a person—a real person—an actual living being. She wasn't a figment of his imagination, a contrivance of a sleep-starved mind. She had existed, walked this earth, felt, breathed, and loved—at least at one time. And now she was a spirit, a wraith, a ghost. A ghost that he had witnessed. With his own eyes.

Did this mean that all of his other sightings were ghosts too? Did they all have real pasts, real lives, real histories as well? Were they all manifestations of identifiable former beings? How about the little girl at the parade, or the ill-fated equestrian, or the old geezer at the Christmas party? Were their stories also buried in the newspaper pages of New Bethany's past?

CHAPTER 27

GHOSTS

Ryan took his leave of the near-spectral librarian and hurried home. After a cursory greeting for Kelly and the girls, he headed for a desktop computer in the study and slammed the door shut. There he sat, right through dinner, and right through the girls' bedtime routine. Hour after hour, he sifted his way through New Bethany's history, searching for threads that he hoped would lead to the identities of his many visitors.

At eleven thirty, Kelly crept in. "Ryan, what's up? What's going on?"

Ryan shut down the screen as if he had been cavorting on a most rancorous porn site. "Just work stuff, honey. I just need some quiet time on the computer."

"But you barely acknowledged the girls. You haven't even eaten or kissed anyone goodnight. What's up?"

"Just some administrative stuff. I'll be up soon." He turned back to the computer in a clear nonverbal declaration of his desire to be left alone.

"Okay, Ryan," sighed Kelly through a forced smile as she turned and exited the room.

Ryan dove back into his search engine. Unfortunately, not much was turning up. He had been obsessing about the little girl and the fire truck. He kept linking any sort of related key words with New Bethany and Laurel County. But he got nowhere. At 3:00 a.m. he crawled into bed but couldn't sleep.

The following morning, after several hours of hospital rounds, he was back at it again. Frustrated, he struck out on another tack. He researched all previous owners of what was now the Brenan residence. Perhaps the little old man from the Christmas party or the funeral-attired lady would turn up. After chasing multiple fruitless leads over the better part of the day, he finally hit pay dirt. There he was on the computer screen—the old man from the Christmas party—the old man from his recurrent nightmares. Benjamin McFadden.

Benjamin was the brother of Grover McFadden, a former owner of the house and a local judge at the turn of the twentieth century. Benjamin, a religion professor and apparent pedophile, had lived in nearby Lamington, but was a frequent visitor to his brother's home. Only, the guy had died nowhere near New Bethany. He was on a year-long "sabbatical" in France when he succumbed to influenza. He was interred in Paris.

"So, the guy's not even buried around here," mumbled Ryan. "Yet the son of a bitch chose to come back and haunt the place anyway. All the way from freaking Paris."

A thunderclap hit him: if McFadden didn't have to die in New Bethany, then perhaps none of his other friends had to either. "Who knows," he said, shaking his head. "I didn't make the rules."

He attacked the search engines with new vigor, scanning for the various tragedies with no location attached. "Bingo, I've got you, you little witch!" announced Ryan at about 1:00 a.m. to the image of a smiling little tow-headed girl on the computer. The sad 1957 headlines from Denver, Colorado reported the awful tale of three-year-old Dorothy Rydell who darted out into the procession route of a local parade and went under the wheel of a fire truck.

The teens in the pickup truck were more of a challenge. Stories of deaths from riders catapulting out of the beds of such wayward vehicles were a dime a dozen. Eventually, however, he found one in 1979 that sure seemed to fit the bill. A truck filled with teenagers ran a railroad crossing in Morristown, New Jersey, and was creamed by a speeding train. To seal the deal, there was a New Bethany connection: decapitated victim, seventeen-year-old Mary Sellig, had moved with her mother from New Bethany to New Jersey when her parents divorced.

Ryan continued the search, plowing through the night, forgoing his visit to the hospital Sunday morning, and any sleep or sustenance. He wanted the swan diver from the barn and went after him with an almost religious fervor. Eventually, he settled on one David Van Nie, a farmer in Hendersonville, North Carolina. He had performed his tumbling exercise back in 1984 but had done so on the same day of the same month as he made his appearance to Ryan.

Next was the equestrian. And there she was, Emma Patterson, 2001 graduate of New Bethany high school. She died after breaking her neck in a jumping accident in Charlottesville, Virginia. She wasn't discovered until several hours later. And she apparently didn't die instantly. It was suspected that she lay out in the field and slowly asphyxiated due to paralysis of her breathing muscles.

Ryan was stoked. He found himself enthralled by the macabre treasure hunt. Only he stumbled on the next quest: the woman, the "dark lady." There were no real leads. Way too many hours wasted on her. Nonetheless, he was elated. He had tracked down several of his "friends." He felt vindicated. Yes, vindicated. This proved he wasn't going crazy—a real concern considering all that had been happening. And it wasn't sleep deprivation and "hypnagogic hallucinations," for Christ's sake. Ariana's friend was right. It was ghosts. The undead. Beings from another dimension. And he was amassing incontrovertible evidence of it. Why the hell said ghosts were interested in him, he couldn't venture a guess.

But the fact that all of them had once been actual living breathing beings confirmed that he wasn't hallucinating, that they weren't constructs of his addled brain, but real entities, real people—dead people, but real people nonetheless.

And what about the existential implications of all this? If ghosts, spirits, specters, or whatever, were real—Jesus Christ, the inferences about existence, about the afterlife, about God, and heaven and hell, and all that stuff, were profound. Weren't they? They were proof that *something* occurred after death, other than bleak nothingness. He needed to discuss this with Kelly. He needed to share with her the good news. He needed her razor-sharp mind to help him plumb its depths, divine its meaning.

Or . . . maybe not.

Not yet at least. Maybe he should wait until he had had a chance to sort it out in his own head. He was just getting a handle on it himself right now. Right now, he might only come across as a raving lunatic. She had been none too happy with him this past year. Things were finally settling down, finally getting back on track with the resolution of the night terrors. Something like this might tip her over the edge. Better to explore it with other less emotionally-invested individuals—maybe Matt or Ron—and get it figured out before he presented his thesis to her.

CHAPTER 28

DEATH'S PALE FLAG

A ny further in-depth metaphysical investigation would have to wait, however. The work week had arrived with its endless outpatient clinics, late-running operating rooms, and busy night calls. Each day rolled into the next and suddenly, it was the weekend again. But there would be no rest for the weary. Ryan was conscripted into child transport, all three girls going in separate directions to soccer games, dance practices, music recitals, play dates, and sleepovers. It was exhausting, and he found himself longing to get back into the medical fray.

He got his wish. Before he knew it, he was fully submerged in another action-packed Monday. And it got off with a bang. One disaster after another. He blinked and it was 4:00 a.m., Tuesday morning. He, Cam Carlson, and a medical student were deep in the brain of a young woman. Her frontal lobes had exploded into hemorrhage during the delivery of her first child. Ryan was working on an area of persistent bleeding as he replied to the squawk box.

"Right, we'll get down there as soon as we can."

The ER had called about a forty-eight-year-old man, James Gordon. Mr. Gordon had bad atherosclerotic vascular disease and had presented with a large stroke in the back part of his brain. He was in coma but was purported to be "otherwise stable." One catch, he weighed over four hundred pounds. After ten minutes or so of further operating, an increasingly fidgety Ryan looked up at

Cam. "Jeez, Cam, I can't take it anymore. Every minute we don't get to someone like that, I get worse chest pain. Looks like we've got things under control here. I'm going to run down and lay eyes on the guy. God knows what they're doing with him."

"Probably not much," replied Cam with a roll of the eyes.

"Yeah, well, that's what worries me. Back in a flash."

"Got you covered, Dr. B.," replied Cam, continuing his work deep in the women's brain.

Ryan broke scrub, tossed his bloodied gown and gloves into the trash, and disappeared out of the room. A few minutes later he burst back in through the swinging doors.

"Well, you called that one right, Cam. They hadn't done a thing: no intubation, no blood pressure control, hadn't even raised the head of his bed. Just basically ignored him, waiting for us to get there."

"Jesus," responded Cam.

"Anyway, he's in bad shape. Huge stroke. I've got them opening the room next door. Care to join me?"

"Sure, sir. Things are looking good here."

Ryan scrubbed in for a few minutes to help get the closure started and then hopped over to the next room on Mr. Gordon's arrival, bringing the medical student along with him. He took a look at the now-anesthetized man and whistled. "So many Americans anymore, Sophia, are morbidly obese, and positioning them for surgery is a major challenge. There's no easy way to move an extremely heavy patient who is out cold—they're nothing but awkwardly distributed dead weight. And the problems don't stop there. Once you have a patient in the position you want, their weight continues to threaten their welfare through excess bleeding, difficulties in ventilation, blood-clot formation in the venous system, compression of the arterial system, pressure sores of the skin, pressure-related nerve injuries, bad wound healing, post-operative medical complications, and more. So, Mr. Gordon here's gonna be a challenge. Anyway, what do you think we're going to do in this operation?"

"I'm not sure," replied Sophia. "Restore blood flow to the cerebellum?"

"Ha! Nothing so complex. Unfortunately, the horse is already out of the barn for that sort of thing. The tissue in question is already dead. But the back part of the head is a very crowded place under normal circumstances. So, the swollen, stroked-out cerebellum has nowhere to go except up against the brainstem, shutting it down. We'll go in and remove enough dead tissue to take the pressure off the brainstem and hope it can switch back on."

Despite the predicted monumental struggle getting Mr. Gordon into a manageable position, the surgery moved right along. The two surgeons quickly accessed the back part of Mr. Gordon's skull through his very deep upper neck and then opened a large window in the underside of it. When they cut open the underlying dura, brain tissue squeezed out like playdough through a press.

"Pretty straightforward stuff now we're down to the brain, Sophia. As you can see, infarcted cerebellum is just squishing out of the head. We're going to suck away dead stuff until things back here completely relax. You can see that, because it stroked, it doesn't even bleed much."

The remainder of the procedure moved quickly. Soon they were bandaging up Mr. Gordon's head.

"How will he do, Brenan?" asked Sophia.

"Hard to say," replied Ryan. "Cerebellar strokes are unpredictable. Sometimes they do amazingly well. Like a miracle. Sometimes they never come out of coma. And with someone as unhealthy as Mr. Gordon, here, God knows what curveballs he'll throw at us post-operatively.

Ryan proved most prescient on the last point. Mr. Gordon came out of coma immediately and had been looking great in the Neurovascular ICU, but two days after surgery sustained a massive heart attack. Ryan had been passing through when it happened. He noticed several nurses and doctors running into Mr. Gordon's room and followed them.

"Oh God, I'm not going to die, am I?" pleaded a crying and writhing Mr. Gordon under an oxygen mask.

"You're going to be okay, Mr. Gordon. Just take some slow, deep breaths," reassured one of the nurses.

"Oh God, I'm dying. I know it. Please don't let me die," cried Mr. Gordon, who began to panic and bolted upright, pulled out his IVs, and fought off the many hands trying to settle him back into semi-recumbency.

Now a dozen people were in the room trying to reassure Mr. Gordon as they sought to hold him down and get the IVs back in. Ryan pitched in and grabbed one of the man's massive legs. It was all he could do; the critical care specialists were running this show.

"Please don't let me die. Oh my God, what about my family? Please, please don't let me die. I'm going to die. I know it." His voice was raspy now, and he started choking on a pink froth that bubbled up from his lungs.

"He's going into failure. Get a tube down," commanded the critical care doctor in charge.

Mr. Gordon was anesthetized and a breathing tube was placed. The "code team" continued to labor frenetically at his care. But more and more pink froth was coming up out of his breathing tube, despite frequent suctioning by the nurses. His heart was dying. It could no longer pump blood out of the lungs, and they were filling with bloody fluid. Then his EKG tracing went flatline, and they were doing chest compressions. After an hour or more of compressions, in a room that looked like it had been hit by a tornado, the team "called the code." That is, they ceased all efforts to resuscitate Mr. Gordon and declared him dead.

———

"Ryan, I don't think you heard a word I was saying."

It was Kelly. Ryan was home. He had little recollection of getting there, or what he did after he arrived. He had showered, for sure. And ate, maybe. And probably helped get the girls to bed. But it was all a blur. Kelly was incorrect, though. He had heard a word of what she was saying, maybe a few. Something about Joshua Tree National Park and too many tourists. But that was it. All he was really hearing, though, was Mr. Gordon's plaintive cries as he lay there dying.

"Ryan, where are you? You've been an utter zombie tonight. What's up? Talk to me." Kelly was now sitting before him, fixing her ever-penetrating eyes on his own.

God, he'd love to explain. To share with her. But how? How could anyone appropriately describe stuff like what happened tonight? Seeing, hearing, feeling a lovely, grateful, gracious human being transform so rapidly, so disgustingly, so appallingly, into inanimate flesh? Do you describe how you still felt Mr. Gordon's thrashing, dying leg in your hands, for God's sake? Or the crackling sensation of his skin under your fingers as you took your turn doing chest compressions? How do you describe that mix of sickly scents—the bodies, the sweat, the urine, the feces, the antiseptics, the blood—that's still there, lingering in your nasal passages? How do you describe the sense of Death, as a being, lurking about the room, looking down from the ceiling at you all, watching greedily, waiting for the patient's skin to drain of all blush, of all color; to hoist the pale flag of mortality? How do you do justice to it all? And why would you share such things, anyway? Why would you transfer your feelings of grief, and repulsion, and desperation, and terror, and helplessness onto anyone, let alone someone you loved? To soothe your own angst? To assuage your own sense of vulnerability—for yourself, but especially for your loved ones? How selfish. How narcissistic. Weren't these things better left unsaid? Better buried and forgotten?

He did manage to choke out some answer. Kelly had backed him into a corner. But he couldn't remember what it was. He was sure it was sanitized and cursory at best. And not long thereafter, he slipped into bed and turned out the light, the images of the day still playing out in his retinas, and Mr. Gordon's pleas for salvation still ringing in his ears.

CHAPTER 29

ENOUGH SENSE

Mr. Gordon's pitiful cries continued to haunt Ryan into the weekend. On Saturday, he sought to subdue them by indulging in one of his greatest pleasures: checking out the sizable selection of new and used acoustic guitars at Elementary Strings, a shop housed in an old one-room schoolhouse. The girls were all away at sleepovers, and Kelly had gone out for a run and some coffee with Dianne and Juleen, so he felt at ease to lose himself in the smell and feel of the many finely crafted instruments. He fell in love with a used Martin Auditorium and was itching to buy it, but he had splurged on a brand-new Baby Taylor back in March and had yet to play it. Such a level of conspicuous consumption was just too much for him to bear, so after reluctantly relinquishing the instrument, he purchased some strings and shuffled out of the store in a state of non-buyer's remorse.

During his time in the shop, the afternoon had morphed. It had been nearly perfect when he had gone inside. The humidity was low, and a honeysuckle breeze pushed cotton-ball clouds across an azure sky. Now, however, the heavens were dark and cancerous, and a series of agitated late July storms were marching up the valley. As he got into the jeep and made his way down Bloomsbury Road, the marauding invaders opened fire and pelted the countryside with grenade-sized raindrops. The malignant sky strobed with repetitive flashes of blinding light, and the landscape quaked with a near-constant celestial roar. As he strained to see through his waterfall-obscured windshield, he noticed two figures in the distance making their way toward New Bethany on foot. As he drew nearer, he could see that they were an old man and a gray-muzzled black Labrador, stumbling along the weeds at the side of the road. There were no houses for at least half a mile, so Ryan pulled up alongside the saturated pair.

"Hey sir, could I give you two a lift? The jeep's pretty used to wet dogs. It'd be no trouble at all . . ." offered Ryan, leaning toward the passenger-side window.

The old man ignored him and kept moving.

Ryan was used to this type of behavior from the farmers of the region. They were a hardy bunch—fiercely independent, and righteously indignant about any perceived need of assistance. The dog, on the other hand, looked up and rolled its eyes at the obstinacy of its master.

Ryan pulled up to the pair and tried again. "Seriously, sir, it's not safe out there. Let me drive you home. It's no problem, really."

There was a flash and a deafening cannonade that seemed to destabilize the very ground beneath the jeep. The old man stopped walking, turned to Ryan, and nodded. He stepped to the back right door of the vehicle and tried the handle, but the door was stuck. Ryan sprang out into the deluge to assist. As he struggled with the door, another incendiary explosion rocked the earth and blinded him. When he blinked his vision back to some level of functionality, the man and his mournful dog were gone. He stood by the jeep, absorbing a full-scale dousing, hands clenching and unclenching, head slowly shaking back and forth.

"Holy Christ, not again. And the dog too?"

As the rain slashed at his head and face, he began to tremble. He wasn't sure if it was out of fear or rage. He felt his chest collapse and a terrifying air hunger seize his lungs. He gasped and sputtered and sank to his haunches. *Breathe, Ryan. You're all right*. But God, he was seeing ghosts . . . ghosts! But that was crazy. He must be freakin' crazy. What the hell was going on? The world began to spin. Then, there was darkness.

———————

He awoke, face half-submerged in a puddle. He looked at his watch. He'd only been out for a few minutes. He must have hyperventilated himself into a dead faint, so to speak. *Jesus*, he thought, *this is insane*. He needed to talk to Kelly. She would know what to do. She was so calm, so collected—in the face of anything. But not this. No, not this. This would be too much. Ghosts and goblins, angels and devils, gods and prophets simply didn't exist for her. *She'll have me committed. She'll literally have me locked up in a psych unit.*

CHAPTER 30

ANY YOUNG GIRLS?

"Ryan, what the heck happened to you?" asked Kelly. He had come home from his trip to the guitar store looking like he had gone through a car wash. But more than that, he looked unsettled and ghostly pale.

"Yeah, well, the goddamned back door on the jeep got stuck again. I have no idea why I hang on to the freaking thing."

"You know why you hang on to it," said Kelly, offering Ryan a towel. "But that's beside the point. Why are you soaked to the skin?"

"Just trying to be a good Samaritan. But you see where that gets you," replied Ryan, teeth gritted.

"You're not making any sense. What do you—"

"Jesus, Kelly, I don't need the third degree. I got caught in a downpour, that's all." He turned and marched toward the front of the house, stopping in the dining room for a shot of bourbon. Soon he was upstairs in the shower.

Kelly made no further attempts at inquiry but observed her husband through the remainder of the day with growing frustration. He was agitated and jittery. Every groan of the house was greeted with wide eyes and a rapidly pivoting head, as if he expected a particularly violent home invasion. He downed two more shots before dinner, then went about canceling plans to get together with the Wolfes. The evening was to be their first together without the girls in months—all three were at sleep-overs. Rather than take advantage of the rare freedom, however, all Ryan could do was collapse around her on the couch, hand fixed to the remote. No conversation. No interaction of any kind.

The next morning, he disappeared without a word into the hospital and didn't reappear until late afternoon—no calls, no updates. So, as they drove through downtown New Bethany on their way to pick up the girls, a disaffected Kelly ignored any of his feeble entreaties for some generic conversation and buried herself in emails.

The van climbed and crested Laurel Ridge, the principal elevation flanking New Bethany to the north. They passed through a development of oversized McMansions, each one indiscriminately dropped onto three-acre lots of clear-cut forest. Kelly hated the spot, and normally would comment on its senseless violation of the natural world, but she was lost in a haze of work concerns.

"Christ, the poor little thing," mumbled Ryan, his words piercing Kelly's numbed consciousness.

"Huh? What poor little thing?" she said.

"Oh, we just passed a little girl. She had the look. She's clearly got one horrible cancer or another, and is probably getting tortured with chemotherapy. She was out by a storm grate, dropping sticks into it. And when I caught her in the rearview mirror, she doubled over and vomited. I mean power vomited. All over herself. Anyway, it just broke my heart. Ah, crap!"

"What is it?"

"Oh, it just hit me. I didn't see any parents or other kids around. No one. And she was obviously very sick. I mean, puking up bile. So slight, a strong wind would pick her up and carry her off. She shouldn't be out there on her own. She must have slipped away from her family, and now she's getting sick in the gutter all alone."

"Well, let's go back and check on her then. Get her back to her parents," suggested Kelly, noticing tears forming in Ryan's eyes. No matter how conflicted her emotions might be about him, she couldn't help but feel a surge of respect for this man who was so clearly moved by the suffering of others.

Ryan turned the van around, but when they reached the spot where he had seen the girl, she had disappeared. He stopped the van, and he and Kelly got out. They canvased the area, but the girl was nowhere to be found.

"Well, I guess she went back to her house, the poor thing," suggested Kelly.

"I guess so," replied Ryan. "But we should make sure. She looked so miserable." He looked up at the imposing property facing them. "Let's just go check."

They walked up a long, curving, immaculately groomed driveway to the main house on the property. It was an overwrought brick federal. They rang the front doorbell and were greeted by a torrent of dogs that collided teeth-first with the glass storm door. A late-middle-aged woman in a fine woolen dress swam through the roiling canine waters and stepped out onto the porch.

"Hello, can I help you?" asked the refined woman in a refined accent.

"Hi. My name's Ryan Brenan. And this is my wife, Kelly. We were wondering if any young girls live here?"

"I beg your pardon?"

"Sorry, that didn't come out right. We were driving by, and we saw a little girl out by the street. She looked too young and too sick to be out there unattended."

The woman offered no reply, just knit her brow and stared

down at Ryan, even though she was at least ten inches shorter than him.

"You see . . . um . . . I'm a doctor over at the medical center," offered Ryan.

"Oh?"

"Yes, and we were worried about her, the little girl. We just wanted to make sure she was all right."

"I see, and what did you want from me again?" asked the women.

"We just wanted to know if there's a young girl living here or in any of the houses nearby. A young girl who's sick . . . with cancer . . . undergoing chemotherapy. We just want to make sure she's safe at home with her parents. I'm a doctor. A surgeon. Over at Carriere."

"Well, I'm sorry, Doctor . . ."

"Brenan."

"Yes, Dr. Brenan. I'm sorry, but there are no little girls living here or anywhere else in the neighborhood that I know of. I think the youngest children anywhere in this development are in junior high. And none would fit that description."

"Are you sure, ma'am?" asked Kelly.

"Quite sure. Little Caryn Wofford, who lived three doors down, did have a nasty bone cancer, but she died three or four years ago. I'm sure no one else around here has anything like that. I would have heard. Poor Caryn, it was an awful thing. We did raise ten thousand dollars for her parents, though."

Ryan mumbled, "Christ," abruptly thanked the woman, and started back down the driveway without waiting for a response.

"Do you want to try the next couple of houses?" asked Kelly, who had to jog to keep up with him. "We could split up."

"No. You heard her. No one fits the description. There aren't even any young girls in the neighborhood." Ryan was already back in the car, starting the engine. His eyes had darkened, and his face had gone gray. "Come on, let's go get the girls."

Kelly studied him as she slowly climbed into the van. "Ryan, don't you want to check at least another house or two? Maybe this lady doesn't know her neighbors."

"Oh, she was pretty goddamned definitive, don't you think, Kell? Let's go get the girls. We did our good deed for the day." He shifted into gear and left in a spray of gravel.

Kelly continued to study his colorless face. His strange and sudden loss of conviction managed to quell the waves of love that had been washing over her earlier, leaving her feeling that he was yet again locking his inner world away from her. Now only waves of annoyance crashed down on her.

CHAPTER 31

FLASH THUNDER

"**B**ut why me? What could they possibly want from me?" asked Ryan. He had tracked down Ariana and related the stories of the vomiting little girl, the farmer and the dog, and Evie Nelson. He then pressed her on all she knew about visitations from the dead and what to do about them. She didn't know much.

"I'm so sorry, Dr. Brenan. It's not my thing. I wish I had the answers for you."

"Is there any way to block them during the day like we did from my sleep? Some sort of daytime dream catcher?"

"I don't think so, but I'll ask my friend. I can certainly put you in touch with some psychics. Perhaps they might have more answers for you."

"I might resort to that if they don't back off. But what do *you* think is going on, Ariana?"

"If I had to guess, I would say the spirits are still trying to connect with you. I mean, they're being pretty persistent about it, aren't they? I think they'll keep at it until they make it clear what they want from you."

"Wonderful . . ." replied Ryan, with a shiver.

Under any other circumstances, this would be crazy talk. But he had such undeniable evidence that it was all real, and that terrified him. And Ariana's suppositions didn't help matters. Could these things truly want something from him? Would they really keep at it until they got what they wanted? And why couldn't they just explain to him what exactly it was? Wouldn't that be far easier than all the freaking drama? And again, why him? What made him so freaking special? Thankfully, he had plenty to divert his attention away from all the possible permutations. He was neck-deep in trauma season.

There was no true off season for horrible things befalling the populace of central Pennsylvania, but there was an on-season: summer. The day winter's dense gray shroud had finally lifted from the rural landscape in late May, citizens of the region would crawl out from under their collective seasonal affective disorder and celebrate the approaching solstice by engaging in a harrowing array of self-sacrificial rites. The favored instrument of expiation this year was the all-terrain vehicle. And with no more protective gear than a T-shirt and a six-pack of beer, every man, woman, and child took to their awaiting chariots and attacked at full throttle the region's most hazardous forests, fields, and glens.

The resultant carnage was stunning, even to the jaded. Popular among the crowd was auto-garroting on barbed wire fencing, made most spectacular when said fencing was electrified. Dramatic ejection into various stationary objects also proved a very sought-after mode of exodus. Impalement on branches and fence posts approached the commonplace, and several joy riders somehow found ways to run over themselves. Many of the devout, however, appeared to believe that only child sacrifice would be enough to appease the gods of summer. Therefore, up to three young offspring were often loaded onto the front of a vehicle, effectively serving as the driver's "crumple zone" when a resolute tree trunk chose to make its appearance. Others situated their children on the rear of their conveyances, from whence the tikes could be lofted skyward like clay pigeons fired from their traps as the speeding vehicle cleared a berm. But the most Darwinian method of execution was to hand the keys over to one's progeny, often no older than eight, and send him or her off into the merciless woods, often with their younger brothers and sisters in tow.

To Ryan, it was all tantamount to child abuse, no better than handing the kids a loaded pistol or simply beating them to death. And by mid-August, he'd had enough. It had been a miserable summer. Death and destruction reigned supreme: brains swelling out of heads, blood filling the shoes, broken this, broken that, paralysis, aphasia, families wailing, rows of comatose teenagers filling the ICUs, and incoming helicopters arriving in a nonstop conga line.

But on a hot, sticky, on-call Saturday afternoon, he found himself reclining on his bed, drifting in and out of sleep, totally protected from any malignant incursions into his dreams by his catcher just a few feet away. Wafting up into the summer air was the gleeful sound of his three girls running about the backyard, perhaps along with an additional neighbor child or two. They were busy at some form of tag, or so it sounded from all the proclamations, declarations, and negotiations. Ryan soaked in the sweet melody of his happy, healthy children at play, and smiled as his eyes again began to close.

Suddenly, a bright flash violated his setting lids immediately followed by an eruption from an apparent nearby volcano. His heart leaped. He bolted upright, reflexive fear clutching him by the throat. But he calmed quickly upon hearing the continuation of the girls' laughter and chatter. Worried about future strikes, he leaned toward a backyard-facing window and shouted, "Hey guys, get out of the yard. Get inside. *Okay*?"

There was no response, just continued jabbering and giggling. Just before he could call out again, his text signal went off. He grabbed the ever-spiteful cell phone and checked the screen. It was the dreaded call number of the never-sated emergency room.

"Typical," he mumbled. "Just when I thought I could catch a few *z*'s." He punched in the number and paced, awaiting a response. As the phone rang through, he heard the girls again, still carrying on out in the yard, surrounded by fifty-foot, lightning-avid trees. "Hey girls, I mean it. Get inside—right now!" he barked, in his deepest, most fatherly register directly into the ear of someone who finally picked up on the other end of the line.

As he started to apologize for the assault, there was a deafening roar from the heavens that seemed to precede a brilliant blue flash of lightning. A nanosecond later, a child screamed. Ryan threw down the phone, sprang to the back window, and leaned out to assess the situation, heart spasming with every parent's most dreaded fear.

The scene was hideous. Five contorted child-sized corpses lay scattered on the ground at the base of a smoking tulip poplar tree. Ryan jerked upright, hitting his head on the sash, and fell backward. He thought he might pass out, but his primal brain leaped into gear, all but completely shutting off his cognitive centers. He sprang to his feet, bolted to the front hallway, and bounded down the stairs like an Olympic triple jumper. He crashed through the front door and rounded the wrap-around porch as rain pelted down in cup-sized droplets.

Sprinting toward the backyard, his thinking brain rebooted as he prepared to perform CPR on the victims. But who first? His youngest? His oldest? His darling Riley? The children of strangers? They all were down. What the hell was he going to do? How could a loving god do such a thing to him? But on arrival, the ground was clear. The yard was empty. There were no scorch marks on the tree, no collection of deep-fried pediatric carcasses— just a soccer goal and a size-four ball. He stood and stared for the next several minutes, hands on hips, chest heaving, all the while being assaulted by a wrathful rain. He then walked about the yard inspecting every corner, as if somehow the five dead children had lured him into a ghastly game of hide-and-go-seek.

"Oh, screw you, and screw this," he cursed as he shook his fist at the bile-green sky. "You're going to throw my own kids into the mix, eh? My own kids? Oh, I'm coming after you, you pricks. I'm gonna get to the bottom of this and you're gonna regret ever messing with me, I swear."

Muttering a string of expletives, Ryan headed to his bedroom and wrestled out of his saturated clothing, toweled off, and re-dressed, all in the dark. The strike had knocked out the house's power. He located his phone, now sporting a laceration on its face, and called again into the emergency room. There, lying on an ER gurney awaiting his evaluation, was a sixteen-year-old girl paralyzed from a motorcycle accident.

"Right. I'll be there in a couple of minutes," remarked Ryan, putting the phone in his pocket. He slipped into his loafers; grabbed his ID card, wallet, and keys; and made for the stairs. He walked quickly through the bottom floor of the house and into the family room. There, all three girls were sprawled on the floor, reading or working on projects by candlelight. None looked up. Ryan broke into their collective trance.

"Hey guys, where's Mom?"

"In the basement," answered Ava. "She said she was going to check the fuse box."

"Did you hear that thunder, Daddy?" asked Erin. "It scared me."

"Oh Erin, don't be such a baby!" admonished Riley.

"I'm not being a baby," replied Erin. "It felt like the lightning was hitting the house, didn't it, Daddy?"

"It sure felt close to me, sweetie," replied Ryan. "But guys, I've got to run to the hospital. Tell Mom I'll probably be there for a while, okay?"

"Okay, Dad," came the choral reply.

Ryan started to leave but hesitated at the door and turned back to his daughters. "And goddamn it, girls, when I tell you to get inside during a thunderstorm—get inside! Right away! Okay?"

"But Dad," protested Riley. "We weren't outs—"

Ryan was out the door and headed for the jeep before she could finish, heart still tearing at his ribs.

CHAPTER 32

GUN CONTROL

The sixteen-year-old girl, Janean Rogers, lay in a trauma bay: head, neck, and body strapped down to a long fiberglass "back board." She was drunk, and so had been her boyfriend, who now lay dead in the next bay. The boyfriend had run his motorcycle into a telephone pole at a high speed. He was thrown into the pole; Janean had missed it completely but was hurled thirty yards out into an adjacent field. She sustained multiple injuries, the worst of which was a broken neck. Her cervical spinal column was a smashed-up mess, and she was paralyzed from the neck down. Soon she was in the operating room.

Ryan and Lisa LeClair made short work of realigning and stabilizing the scrambled vertebrae with multiple titanium screws and rods but were sickened to see that the girl's spinal cord had been sliced in two by the shattered bone.

"So, guys," he noted to a couple of nursing students. "This poor girl is paralyzed and she'll never get better—at least at our current level of medical technology. Her best bet will lie in the realm of bioelectronic interface technologies. Or maybe stem cells or something, someday. But for now she's screwed."

After finishing up, Ryan left to deliver the grim news to yet another in the endless series of shocked and grieving families. Soon he was with another family, explaining how a simple fall from sitting could result in a mortal injury—the victim, a man in his early sixties, had leaned back in his kitchen chair and the legs had kicked out. His head hit the terra cotta floor with a sickening crack. Ryan had emergently evacuated the resultant brain hemorrhage, but the guy was too far gone for there to be any optimism about his prognosis.

Next up were "bookend" families of bookend elderly women. Both were on brand-new and "guaranteed to be safer" blood-thinning medicines. Both had keeled over suddenly at home. Both sported massive deep brain hemorrhages. Both were in deep coma. Both were too far gone to be helped by any sort of surgical intervention, but neither was far gone enough to be declared brain-dead.

"Sheesh," Ryan mumbled to himself after addressing a waiting room filled with tear-stained faces. "A half hour more and they both would have been dead. *Dead.* No need for decisions, no family turmoil about pulling the plug, no guilt, no remorse. Now we'll end up keeping their hearts beating until they decompose from within, get all discolored and bloated, and become unrecognizable as their former selves. How freaking lovely."

Several more families of several more profoundly ill or severely injured patients followed, with a couple of surgeries thrown into the mix. Saturday afternoon morphed into Sunday night with no further sleep or sustenance—other than some graham crackers and peanut butter stolen from an ICU nurses' station. Ryan and Cara Klein were just finishing up an emergency craniotomy on a ten-year-old boy—he had rapidly gone blind from a huge tumor pressing on his eye nerves—when the ER called about another young boy, his story as gruesome and unignorable as his injury.

Twelve-year-old Alex Stark was hanging out in his basement with three friends. The group had entered into a heated debate about suicide and the most efficacious methods of its execution. They all agreed that firearms reigned supreme as a mode of exodus but had not come to a consensus on technique. Liam

Goldring favored shooting oneself in the temple. Alex vehemently disagreed. He had read on various suicide sites that placing a gun in one's mouth and aiming straight backward would destroy one's brainstem, resulting in an instant and pain-free death. The group countered that if one flinched while employing said technique the barrel could tip upward and sublethally blow off one's face. They pulled up multiple graphic pictures of such wounds on their phones. Alex retorted that it would be easy to maintain the correct barrel orientation by clenching it with one's teeth. To better demonstrate, he retrieved the Glock 43 his father, a methamphetamine dealer, kept in a bedside table, placed its barrel in his mouth, bit down on it, and pulled the trigger. In doing so, he had not accounted for the possibility that his father might keep the gun loaded, off safety, and cocked, in anticipation of unfriendly incursions from business rivals.

Alex must have indeed tilted the barrel upward as he squeezed the trigger, for the bullet failed to traverse his brainstem. Rather, it exploded through the floor of his skull, through the front part of his brain, and out of the top of his head. The blast shattered both eye sockets, blew apart both eye nerves, and pulverized both frontal lobes.

"Well, Dana, we'll be real lucky if we get this kid out of here alive," commented Ryan to a medical student as he rapidly prepped Alex's scalp for surgery. "When someone's shot in the head, in an instant the tissue behind the passing bullet widely separates and then slaps back together. An associated shock wave is sent out in all directions. Thus the damage extends far beyond the bullet's path. This was a 9mm bullet fired at point blank range—it's going to be a royal mess in there."

Ryan and Cara removed the front of skull and, within a few minutes, had evacuated huge clots of blood and scattered chips of bone from both frontal lobes of Alex's brain. Next they had to contend with profuse bleeding from deep within the resultant cavity. This proved to be an increasing challenge as Alex's expanding brain surged out of his head.

"Yep," remarked Ryan. "It's a disaster, all right. The brain's swelling like crazy, as it is wont to do. And of course, he's not clotting. Gunshot wounds to the brain release all sorts of materials that mess up the body's ability to clot blood."

The two surgeons proceeded to suck away large swaths of pulped-up brain, but it proved a losing battle. For every centimeter they removed, the brain swelled two.

"So, this poor kid's going to die," Ryan announced matter-of-factly, although his chest was constricting and he was fighting off waves of nausea. "We had to give it a try, but we're getting our butts kicked. His brain has given up. If we don't get out of here now, we won't even be able to get his scalp closed."

Ryan turned to Cara. "What do you think, Cara, get out of Dodge?"

"Holy shit, Dr. Brenan. I thought you'd never ask."

"Good idea, Ryan," came a voice from behind the anesthesia screen. "He's getting pretty unstable over here."

The two surgeons stretched the scalp back over the surging brain. They had to shoehorn large portions of it under the stretched skin. They sliced away the lobules of brain tissue that refused to be shoved back in, and unceremoniously tossed them into a stainless-steel kick-bucket on the floor with a sickening "plop." They then stitched the scalp closed, as further brain material squeezed out between the stitches, and tightly wrapped the head to discourage further oozing. The boy was then rushed up to the PICU before his heart could stop beating there on the operating table.

CHAPTER 33

PROWLER

Monday proved no real respite, but at least there were more team members about to help share the load. Ryan had kept the elective surgery schedule limited to a couple of one-hour spine operations, and it was a good thing. In addition to addressing a newly diagnosed brain tumor from the weekend, he ended up with two more emergency craniotomies for head injuries. In between operations, he surveyed the wreckage from the weekend. Eight teenagers with severe head injuries and a handful of post-op emergency craniotomy patients lay in ICU beds, all in coma. Two aneurysm patients who had been treated by the catheter team were still barely clinging to life. Five elderly patients with deep brain hemorrhages were dead, but their families had yet to accept it. Several multiple-trauma patients had disappeared off the list, suggesting they had succumbed to their injuries. Sixteen-year-old Janean Rogers remained paralyzed. Alex Stark, the self-inflicted gunshot victim, was brain-dead, but his young heart was still stubbornly beating. This was perhaps a blessing in that the transplant team had designs on a host of his youthful organs, if they could ever track down his father for permission.

All in all, it was a grim harvest. As Ryan finally lay his head on the pillow that night, he tried to follow Reverend Ron's advice and focus on the uplifts from the weekend but came up short. Instead he was subjected to a congress of mind-chatter relentlessly critiquing every nuance of his surgeries and his patient management. The critique was interrupted by crying echoing down the upstairs hallway. His first thought was the girls. He jumped to the floor and tiptoed to their room. Nope, all were nestled in their beds, hopefully dreaming of sugar plum fairies and other happy things. He kissed each one on the forehead and slipped back out into the hallway.

The crying reasserted itself but now seemed to be coming from the backyard. He looked out the window and his subconscious brain locked onto a hint of movement in the right lower corner of his peripheral vision. Someone, something, was moving among the hydrangea bushes by the barn. He strained to see better. Then there was no need to strain. A woman appeared. It had to be his dark lady. Who else would be out there at this hour, wandering around his backyard all dressed in black? She—it— moved out into the yard as if following a curving pathway. She walked slowly and deliberately, all the while looking at the house. Just outside of the screened-in porch she came to a halt, leaned forward, and peered inside.

Ryan exploded down the front stairs, sprinted into the kitchen, burst through the French doors out to the porch, and pressed his face against the outer screen. Nothing.

"Christ!"

As his eyes adjusted to the darkness he spotted her again. She was moving among the forsythia bushes on the far side of the yard. He blew out of the screen door and dashed toward her. She moved into the moonlight shadow of a towering hemlock. Ryan dove into the darkness and grabbed madly at the lightless air. He came up with nothing. Then he spotted her again, now on the front porch, her dark form strobed by a sputtering streetlamp out on Salisbury Road. She appeared to be trying to open the front door.

"Jesus!" blurted Ryan, launching himself through the bushes to the front walkway. On arrival she was gone, but he could hear her footsteps in the gravel of the driveway. He rounded the front of the house and saw her turning the knob of the side door.

"Hey, lady!" erupted out of his chest as his body prepared to lunge forward.

The specter turned and raised an index finger to her veiled face, as if to say, "Shhh." Ryan froze. She turned back to the door and, again, reached for the knob.

"Christ!"

Ryan broke through the paralysis and hurled himself in her direction. But now she was up by the barn, opening one of its large doors. He closed the distance in a couple of seconds but, on arrival, could see her exiting the back door.

"Oh, screw this," choked out Ryan, his chest heaving. "I'm not going to chase this thing around in circles . . ."

He charged back down the driveway and rounded the front, hoping he would catch her coming in the opposite direction. Once he caught up with her, he had no idea what he would do with her but he had to do something. He wasn't going to tolerate her skulking about the yard or sauntering into the house. He made it around the front corner and reentered the backyard. But she was gone. All that was left of her was some muffled sobbing, emanating from somewhere, and yet nowhere.

Ryan stood in the middle of the backyard, soaked to the skin by a frigid sweat, hyperventilating and bleeding. He had made this late-night foray with nothing on his feet. They had been sliced to pieces by the gravel of the driveway and the various pine cones, twigs, and thorns scattered like booby traps about the property's bushes and trees.

"Christ . . ."

CHAPTER 34

OCD

Ryan limped into the house and ran immediately into Kelly, who was standing in the kitchen, arms crossed.

"Ryan, what the heck were you doing out there at this hou—oh my God, look at your feet."

"Yeah, I cut them up a little," replied Ryan. He was doing his best not to bleed all over the floor.

"How? Why? What's going on?"

"I thought I heard something."

"But how did you cut up your feet so badly?" pressed Kelly as she grabbed a dog towel and pushed it under Ryan.

"I thought I saw someone, a prowler, so I chased her—him."

"With no shoes? Could you have imagined it? Could you have been sleepwalking?"

"No, I was wide awake. The dream catcher seems to be holding that sort of thing in check."

"Other than chasing imaginary prowlers all over the yard?"

"Honestly, honey, I thought I saw someone out there. You know there's been a bunch of break-ins in the neighborhood. I had to do something."

"And it didn't cross your mind to call the police? Instead you go charging around the property shoeless and without anything to protect yourself—a baseball bat, a fire iron?"

Oh god, why did I marry a lawyer, thought Ryan. He shrugged at Kelly and headed, without further word, upstairs. There, in the master bathroom, he stepped into the bathtub and washed his macerated feet under the faucet. *Jesus. She knows I'm full of it. I'm going to have to tell her about the ghosts.*

But he still couldn't do it. Not yet. He needed a practice run. A practice run to make sure he didn't come across as totally insane. He needed to have his facts all lined up, his analysis perfectly supported, his rationale airtight or she would rip it all to shreds. She had to believe him or telling her would cause no end of problems. No, he needed a dry run. And with someone more stable than Ariana. Like Matt. If anyone could give him a dispassionate, no-nonsense, nonjudgmental response, it would be Matt. Matt was inherently pragmatic. There was no room for nonlinear flights of fancy in his world—at the pharmaceutical plant—or else there would be explosions, poisoned pills, toxic leaks, or other dreadful things. He would go with Matt. Then, maybe he could address the good counselor.

He was on the phone with Matt the next day. Their schedules failed to mesh until early September, however, so Ryan resubmerged into his work. In the interim, he had all intentions of taking some time to organize his thoughts into a cogent presentation for Matt but found himself with no opportunity to do so right up to the evening before their meeting. And, as luck would have it, he was on call. And, the second the clock struck 5:00 p.m. his phone exploded. He spent the next several hours in the operating room, fielding one disaster after another. He made it home at three and collapsed onto the couch. Half an hour later, Cam Carlson was calling.

"Hey, Dr. Brenan. Sorry if I woke you."

"No sweat, Cam. What's up?"

"Got a big problem with a post-op kid," replied Cam.

"Okay . . ." responded Ryan.

"You're not going to like it, sir," warned Cam.

"I'm not going to like what, Cam?"

"You're not going to like what I have to tell you . . . about the case . . ."

"You're freaking me out, Cam," responded Ryan. "Spill the beans, buddy."

"Well, you know the pineal kid Cara and I did this morning with Dr. Corll?" asked Cam.

Ryan had been aware of the case. The trio had operated on a nasty-looking tumor of the pineal gland in the morning. The pineal gland is a tiny lump of tissue, situated at the very center of the head. For a surgeon, there's no easy way to get there. There are several potential ways—ways that every neurosurgical resident has to know by heart—but each one is via a long, narrow corridor, barely skirting hypercritical structures, and fraught with lethal booby traps along the way.

Ten-year-old John Calhoun had arrived with increasing headaches and visual loss, and it turned out he had a large tumor in the gland, pressing on his brainstem. Dr. Corll was a veteran pediatric neurosurgeon but had little experience operating on the gland. The procedure had reportedly gone well, however, and the child had been recovering nicely in the Pediatric ICU.

"Yeah, I remember. What's going on?" asked Ryan.

"He was doing fine, but in the last half hour he's crashed and burned," explained Cam. "We're talking coma, flexor, sunset eyes, pinpoint pupils. We re-intubated him. I'm down in CT right now. Scan shows a massive bleed in the tumor bed. Pics should be on your phone."

Ryan took a quick look.

"Holy crap, Cam. What's Dr. Corll wanna do?" asked Ryan, but he suspected he already knew the answer.

"Well, that's the thing, Dr. Brenan, he's gone out of state. Left last night for the Outer Banks," replied Cam.

"He left town immediately after a pineal? What the—" Ryan caught himself. He couldn't conceive of leaving the *hospital* for a few days after such a complex operation. And only then if the patient was doing amazingly well. Leaving the state the day of surgery without discussing the patient with your partners was tantamount to . . . well, it was definitely bad form. His hands were shaking and stomach acid percolated up his throat, so he shifted his focus to the problem at hand as he headed for the door. "Well then, Cam, what do *you* want to do?"

"We need to go back in, but the kid's probably screwed."

"Probably, but not definitely," responded Ryan as he reached the jeep. "Hey Cam, I thought Cara said you guys got all of the tumor."

"Shit, Dr. Brenan, there was no way to know. The damn thing was so bloody we had to keep cramming antibleeding stuff in the bed to get control. I think we left more crap in there than we took out."

"That's the thing, Cam," said Ryan as he steered out of the driveway. "Usually the bleeding will stop once you have all the tumor out. I would bet there's still a fair amount left in there. What approach did you use?"

"Sub-tent, supra-cerebellar." Cam was referring to one method of getting to the tumor.

"Ugh," grunted Ryan.

"Why'd you say that, sir? Would you've used a different approach?"

"Yeah, probably. I bet you had quite a reach in the end."

"Sure seemed to be. So, what approach would you've taken?"

"I like occipital trans-tentorial," replied Ryan, referring to a different route to the tumor. "So, what approach should we use now?" asked Ryan.

"Well, I thought we'd go back through this morning's dissection," said Cam. "But I bet you're gonna want to go your way, aren't you?"

"Roger that, my friend."

Not long thereafter, the two were working in the child's head under a microscope. They had quickly accessed and removed the large clot of blood that was killing the boy and were now attending to brisk bleeding at the depths of a long, narrow excavation.

"See, Cam, tons of tumor left over," observed Ryan. "By coming at it from behind, you had no choice but to work on it from inside out. That can be a living hell in a deep, bloody tumor. It can spook even the best of surgeons."

"And Dr. Corll ain't the best of surgeons," mumbled Cam, not low enough to be inaudible.

The resection of the remaining tumor went quickly, and soon the two surgeons were closing.

"Shit, Dr. Brenan," observed Cam, "I have to say, I thought you were nuts not to just go back through the original dissection, but that was pretty slick."

"Yeah, well, the bleed probably did most of the work for us. But I was worried that if we just repeated the approach you guys took, we would've run into the same problems."

"You think the kid's screwed?" asked Cam.

"Well, he wasn't dead, so there's hope, bud."

"You pretty pissed off at Dr. Corll?"

Ryan chose not to answer the question with a room full of gossip-adoring ears. The OR was a hotbed of unconstructive chatter, a regular viper's den. The slightest negative comment could make its rounds in seconds and be wildly distorted by the time it made its way back to its origin. Ryan wasn't happy at all with Dr. Corll, but he was darned if he would air his grievances before this voracious court of public opinion. Instead he just shook his head.

And they wonder why I'm so OCD.

CHAPTER 35

SERIAL KILLER

The kid ended up making a remarkable recovery. He was awake by noon. By 5:00 p.m., he was extubated and asking for food. The dramatic "save" bolstered Ryan's spirits, so when he got together with Matt Wolfe later that evening at a local sports bar, he felt emboldened to share everything about his paranormal predicament.

"Hey buddy, I don't have a clue what to make of this whole ghost thing, but is it any wonder you're having a hard time?" asked Matt after listening wide-eyed to Ryan's disclosure.

"What do you mean 'is it any wonder' I'm having a hard time?" responded a scowling Ryan.

"I mean, look at you," said Matt, taking a swig from a bottle of beer. "You're not your everyday run of the mill, super-elitist, self-important, sociopathic neurosurgeon, are you? You know what you are?"

"I'm afraid to ask."

"You shouldn't be. What you are is a regular guy." Matt gestured toward Ryan with his bottle. "You don't run around all puffed up about what you do—you actually seem embarrassed by it. And you don't go around quoting Chaucer or attending operas and poetry recitals—you're 100 percent happy playing with your kids or running around a soccer field with a bunch of third-rate has-beens. You even like hanging out with my extended family of meatheads."

"And your point is?"

"My point is that you're a normal guy thrown into the deep end of an insanely abnormal world, or perhaps, an abnormally insane world. Take your pick."

"But Matt, so are all neurosurgeons, and they're not all hanging out with dead people," replied Ryan, glancing around to make sure other patrons of the bar hadn't overheard him.

"They may not be seeing ghosts, but they're plenty screwed up, all right. I've met your partners at your parties. I've never encountered a more twisted group of narcissistic pricks in all my life. They're all infatuated with the trappings of the profession. They adore the title, the adulation, the control over other people's destinies. They're more immune to the stuff that weighs *you* down. I mean, you've got to give a damn about your fellow man for human suffering to get to you." Matt took another swig of beer. "But you, you're just this regular guy who lives in a world full of nasty, awful, wretched stuff—stuff that would break most people."

"Oh, really?" replied Ryan, a little too sarcastically.

"Yeah, really, Ryan. Think about how often you deal with some horrible tragedy or dispense some god-awful news to someone—"

"But Matt, that's my job."

"Exactly. I'd maintain that what you're experiencing, what's become the daily beat for you, has little parallel in the modern world. I know *I'm* not confronted with that sort of thing every day. Nor is anyone else that I know, including most docs. I mean, we don't live in the Middle Ages," said Matt, gesturing to the large flat-screen TV on the wall above the bar. "Most people forget that death even exists. They got a nasty reminder during the pandemic and didn't like it much. Remember how all you heard about back then was how docs and nurses were 'burning out' from the carnage? But it never stopped for you, did it? The deaths, the tragedies?"

Ryan took a sip from his bottle of beer. "You get used to it."

"Your psycho colleagues get used to it, but you're a regular guy. *You* don't get used to it. *You* swallow it, suppress it, bury it . . ."

"Maybe. But it's the price of admission."

Matt held up his palm. "Wait now, I'm not finished."

"Okay," responded Ryan with a sigh.

"Tell me this," started Matt, lowering his voice. "Have you, as a surgeon, ever killed someone? I mean, you operated on someone who was living and they left the hospital . . . dead."

"Yeah," replied Ryan, turning a bottle cap over and over in his hand. "I hate to say it, but it happens. One neurosurgeon wrote that every brain surgeon carries with them a graveyard of patients who he or she put there."

"Yeah, exactly, you're making my argument for me."

"Which is . . . ?"

"Well," said Matt, his eyes brightening as if he was on to something. "I read this article in the *New Yorker* once about people who, through no ill-intent, *killed* other people—mostly through car accidents. The article called them 'accidental killers.'"

"Okay . . ."

Matt scooted forward, closing the distance on Ryan. "Well, these poor bastards were wrecked by the experience—I mean, totally wrecked. Many became shut-ins. Many couldn't get back into a car again. Those who could, drove hyperaware, hyper-nervous, terrified it might happen again. Some moved to different states, or even countries, to escape their guilt and pain."

"So?" Ryan found it hard to avoid Matt's intense stare.

"So, Ryan, that's what you are. You're an 'accidental killer,'" replied Matt, making air quotation marks. "You're also an 'accidental maimer.' 'Cause you've hurt some people with your surgery, I'm sure. Hurt some pretty badly."

"Gee, thanks."

Matt took a large pull from his bottle and inched even closer. "Oh, it gets worse, my friend. You're not just an accidental killer, you're a *serial* accidental killer, and a *serial* accidental maimer. You've done it multiple times, I'm sure. And when you do kill someone, or hurt someone, you don't have the luxury to collapse into a cocoon, or take a six-month break, or stop operating altogether. You just saddle up and wade into the next case—day after day—knowing for sure that it *will* happen again, knowing that it *could* happen in your very next operation."

"I get it, Matt, but that's what we do."

"Ah, but you're a regular guy," said Matt, holding up an index finger and poking it in Ryan's chest. "And regular guys don't take too well to knocking off their fellow citizens, and paralyzing others."

"So, you're saying I have a great excuse for going off my rocker—because I'm a regular guy?"

"I'm not saying you're going off your rocker. I'm just saying that it's no wonder that you might be having troubles." Matt paused for a few moments to let things sink in. "And you never talk about it, but I know you had a pretty rough time in Afghanistan as well. This shit mounts up, buddy."

Ryan looked down and began peeling the label off his beer bottle. "So, you think all of this has to do with post-traumatic stress."

"Your whole life is post-traumatic stress," replied Matt, his voice raising a few semitones. "No, it's *nonstop* traumatic stress. You don't even have a chance for it to become 'post-traumatic.' There is no 'post.' You face it in real time, every day, with no end in sight. For goodness sake, Ryan, any normal guy would start to come unglued facing that."

"So, you think I *am* coming unglued?" challenged Ryan, reestablishing eye contact.

"Sure you are, buddy," replied Matt, gesturing again with his beer bottle. "You're certainly not the guy I first met. You don't seem happy, you don't get out nearly as much, you don't even seem to pay much attention to your daughters anymore."

"I'm busy as hell, Matt."

"I know you are, man. But that's the thing. Your weirdo colleagues may be able to sustain this for years on end, but I don't think a normal guy, a Ryan Brenan, can. Something's got to give. I think you normal guys need to take oodles of time off every year, and take sabbaticals from it all every so often."

Ryan took a deep breath in and then let it out very slowly. "So, you think I'm seeing ghosts because I'm not getting enough breaks in the action, getting combat fatigue, cracking under the pressure?"

Matt reached for Ryan's shoulder. "I'm not talking about ghosts, buddy. I'm talking about your overall health."

"Okay then, what about the ghosts?" said Ryan, slowly shrinking away from the touch.

"I have no idea what the ghost angle is. You told me you saw a shrink and a bunch of neurologists, and they found nothing wrong with you—so, you're apparently *not* cracking up."

"Any thoughts then?"

Matt paused. "Well, if I were going to get all metaphysical on you, I might argue that you spend an awful amount of time hanging out on . . . well, let's call it a bridge. A bridge between the living and the dead. You spend so much time there, maybe those who are milling around it see you as a buddy, or a guide or something. Maybe they're reaching out to you, asking for help, or even inviting you to join them."

Ryan's eyes widened. "You're scaring me, Matt. It might be better if you just told me you thought I was crazy. I thought you didn't believe in any of that sort of crap anyway."

"Hey, brother," replied Matt, holding up his palms. "If you're brought up in a strict Catholic family, you can't help but believe in a lot of spooky things. And if my good buddy says he's seeing ghosts, and has proof that they were once actual living people, who am I to argue? The point is, if you spent less time with the dead, maybe they might lose interest in you and move on to haunt someone else."

"I could handle that. I mean, it's not like I knew any of them," replied Ryan. He finished peeling the label off his beer and then looked up at Matt. "I guess I would understand if a former patient or two showed up at the door wanting to discuss their care. Or a long-lost relative or something. But they're all total strangers. And sheesh, if strangers have to visit, why can't I choose who? I mean, why not Lincoln, or Shakespeare, or *John Lennon* for God's sake?"

"Be careful what you wish for, buddy," replied Matt.

CHAPTER 36

BULLSEYE

While Ryan didn't run into a historical figure such as Lincoln, Shakespeare, or John Lennon, he did go on to encounter a soldier from the Battle of the Bulge. Only, this unfortunate combatant, twenty-year-old Penn State student, Malcolm Singer, was of flesh and blood. Malcolm was apparently an avid gamer. Bored with always conducting his wars online, he and several buddies created a club in which members reenacted historical battles out in the rural environs of State College. The principal weapons employed were CO_2-powered paintball guns. They donned shorts and T-shirts so hits could be experienced in their full savagery, realistically dropping the recipient to the ground in a groaning, writhing heap. In the interest of safety, though, close-range discharges were forbidden, and they wore goggles and helmets at all times.

So, on a late September Saturday afternoon, the crew had set up in a pine forest to reenact the famous World War II battle. Malcolm, a Wehrmacht Lieutenant had led his unit deep behind enemy lines without apparent detection. Peter Robinson of the US 101st Airborne Division, however, had spotted one of Malcolm's scouts and drew a bead on the German's chest. As Robinson prepared to shoot, Malcolm swung around a tree trunk and gutted him with a rubber knife. Unfortunately, Malcolm's sudden incursion shocked Robinson into pulling the trigger of his weapon. It dutifully discharged, and Malcolm was hit, point blank, in the left side of the neck. Malcolm dropped to the ground and rolled about clutching his throat—the red paint oozing between his fingers, taking on the appearance of profuse bleeding. Seeing this, Robinson fainted. But within a short amount of time, both soldiers were up and reengaged in their martial duties.

Later that evening, Malcolm hung out with his friends, reenacting the day's clashes under virtual reality goggles. At midnight, he took his leave and headed back to an empty dorm room. He was discovered there, Sunday afternoon, in coma. Not long thereafter, he was lying in the Carriere emergency room.

"It's crazy, Dr. Brenan," noted Cara Klein on the phone, "the paintball must have hit right over the kid's carotid. There's a big dissection in the artery and it's totally blocked. He's got a huge left-brain stroke with tons of hemorrhage. Films are in your phone. All I'm getting out of him is a flicker of movement to pain. Pupils are fixed and dilated." Cara was noting that the paintball had damaged one of the two main arteries feeding Malcolm's brain. This had caused a large area of brain to die and then bleed into the dead tissue. The brain was swelling against the skull and was killing itself off. The only treatment option was to surgically take pressure off the brain and hope for the best.

"Sheesh. What do you want to do, Cara?"

"The guy's screwed, Dr. B. I would just let him die. But I know you're going to want to give him the ol' Dr. Brenan one-in-a-thousand shot."

"Sounds more like one in a million. But let's do it."

Forty-five minutes later, Ryan and Cara had created a large opening in Malcolm's skull, and Malcom's boggy dusky brain was expanding well beyond its confines. Ryan and Cara pulled the scalp back over the mess and began to close.

"I know, I know, Cara," remarked Ryan. "Given another hour or two, he would have succumbed. Now he's going to hang around in coma for weeks until it's painfully obvious to everyone that he's gone. But it's what we do . . ."

The next call came in shortly after the two surgeons had dropped Malcolm off in the Neuro-trauma ICU, and it involved another gut-wrenching tale of sick happenstance. According to the trauma service, somewhere out in the outer reaches of Tioga County, nine-year-old Kevin Summerlake was annoying his fifteen-year-old sister and her nineteen-year-old boyfriend. Kevin had insisted on assaulting the two lovers with a nerf gun every time they tried to make out in a secluded den. After several such incursions, the boyfriend had launched into a blistering oration of profanity and hauled Kevin outside by the scruff of the neck. There, he ordered the boy to play quietly with some rusted old Tonka trucks or face certain evisceration. Only, Kevin failed to heed his orders. He slipped into his bedroom and procured a digital camera. He then secured an observation post with a straight line of sight to the couple and began snapping pictures. While capturing a host of potentially incriminating images, he managed to knock over a lamp.

The boyfriend alerted and leaped at the fleeing photographer. But Kevin juked past him and burst out into the backyard. As the boyfriend gave chase, Kevin rounded the house. This brought the two into proximity of the boyfriend's pickup truck where a high-tech bow and arrow set was prominently displayed on a specialized rack in the rear windshield. The boyfriend acquired the weapon, threatening to take Kevin down easier than a senescent doe. In full pursuit, he loaded the bow and pulled the nock of the arrow into shooting position, intent, according to the EMTs at the scene, on firing a warning shot over Kevin's head. Only, he stumbled on a rock and let go of the nock.

The arrow hit Kevin squarely in the center of his back. The high-carbon-steel, field-pointed arrowhead made short work of his skin and spinal bone, lanced through the underlying spinal cord, and embedded itself in his seventh thoracic vertebral body. Kevin went down in a heap, legs instantly paralyzed. Soon he was on a Carriere operating table.

"What the hell could the moron have been thinking?" asked Ryan, using a high-speed drill to cut away the majority of the arrow protruding from Kevin's back like a prop from an old Western movie.

"Dumbass," replied Cara. "Chalk another one up to Darwinism."

"Except it's not poor Kevin here who shouldn't be reproducing. It's the boyfriend's genes that should be kept from jumping into the pool."

The two dissected through Kevin's back down to the backs of the vertebrae. They removed the bone surrounding the arrow and opened the bag of fluid in which the spinal cord sat.

"Cripes, almost dead midline through the cord," commented Ryan.

"Ever see anything like this before, Dr. B.?" asked Cara.

"Oh yeah, sure. Back in my Army days—you know, during the French and Indian War—tons of arrows in the spine."

The arrow showed no intention of budging with traction, so Ryan acquired a sterile wrench and slowly rotated its shaft. It took some patience, but it began to free up from the vertebral body. Soon it lay in a metal kidney basin and the surgeons were closing the wound, both certain that the boy would never walk again.

As was often the case, neurosurgical pathologies—even rare ones—seemed to come in clusters. So it came as only a limited surprise to Ryan when he was soon called down to the emergency room to see thirty-eight-year-old Ralph Mickelson. Mickelson was bedecked from head to toe in camouflage gear and had an arrow sticking out of his forehead.

The attending trauma surgeon felt compelled to share the

story. Mickelson had been out bowhunting with friends. After downing several six-packs, the group had tracked a herd of deer to a wooded area just outside of Mittinburg. There, they split into two flanking parties and fanned out among the trees. Mickelson wasn't the best shot with a bow and arrow and, for the last several years, had suffered the indignity of hitting a deer but then losing track of the traumatized animal as it screeched its way into the engulfing forest. So upon spotting a target this time, he was determined to drop it with a shot right through the heart. Such a shot, though, was best achieved by close-range targeting, so he crept through the underbrush and closed the gap on his prey to just thirty feet. He hid behind a downed tree trunk and slowly raised his head. Unfortunately, to fellow member of the hunting party, Joey Nicely, Mickelson's mousy hair appeared no different from that on the flank of a white-tailed deer.

The arrow struck Mickelson a couple of inches above his right eye socket. He never lost consciousness and, after a careful chopper flight, he found himself in the Carriere trauma bay with half the ER peering in on him, all trying to resist the temptation to commemorate the occasion on their cell phones. Further spectacle was at hand when the trauma team cut his clothing away, as was the practice for all "gold alerts," revealing a remarkable collection vitriolic anti-Semite, anti-African American, and anti-homosexual tattoos flanked by graphically naked women brandishing confederate flags.

Ryan and Cara made short work of the surgery. The wound to the brain was narrow and clean, and there was no associated bleeding. Soon Mickelson was awake and swearing up a storm, taking swings at the recovery room nurses.

"Well, once again the old adage has been proven correct, Dr. B.," remarked Cara as the two surgeons walked away from the scene.

"Oh, and which one is that?" asked Ryan.

"I mean, that poor college kid earlier today was killed by a paintball, and that sweet little boy was paralyzed by one-in-a-million freak accident, while this misogynistic, bigoted Nazi prick took an arrow right in the brain and is fine. And I can guarantee he'll remain fine."

"All right, so what's your adage?"

"You can't kill shit, Dr. B.," said Cara, shaking her head. "You can't kill shit."

CHAPTER 37

WHEN THE CAT'S AWAY

Ryan wanted to challenge the point. He wanted to press Cara on whether harboring such uncharitable thoughts might affect her care of her patients. He certainly worried that it might affect his own. You love some of your patients. You like most. But there are some that no matter how you tried, you just couldn't warm up to them. And Mickleson checked several of his boxes. Hunter—check. Ryan just couldn't stand people who seemed to take pleasure in killing. Misogynist—check. White supremacist—check. All-around dickhead—check. But you had to swallow such reactions to your patients, didn't you? Be as dispassionate as possible. Give everyone the best care possible. Right? He was about to pose such questions to Cara when his mind abruptly switched to another. Why the hell didn't the undead choose to haunt all-around dickheads like Ralph Mickelson instead of the Ryan Brenans of the world?

It was a pressing question. It had been a bad few weeks. It seemed like the spirit world was upping its game. Ryan calculated that, on average, he was logging in some sort of "experience" every three or four days. Not that he was certain every sighting was the real thing, or the *surreal* thing. He just couldn't be sure with some. But others were unequivocal. Like the guy he spotted standing on a ladder over on Spruce Street, noose around his neck, the proximal end of the rope looped around the high limb of a sugar maple. Ryan, driving by, slammed on his breaks and opened his door just as the guy kicked the ladder away and jitterbugged in the cool evening air like a drunken marionette. But as soon as Ryan emerged from the jeep, the guy, the rope, and the ladder were gone.

And then there was the little old lady with the feathered hat and walker, coming out of Fennyman's Pharmacy. She was dressed for Easter Sunday mass, but it was a Wednesday evening in late September. And just as Ryan drove by, she rolled her eyes up into her head and keeled over—stiff, like a falling tree—her head bouncing upon the concrete at least three times. She, too, was gone by the time Ryan had stopped the jeep, leaving behind a single feather that scampered down a side ally.

The uncertain encounters were more plentiful, but they could be pretty darn nebulous. Just a funny look from a passing stranger. Or a group of kids on bikes that seemed awfully antiquated (the bikes, not the kids). Or a young couple in a canoe out on the river, when the river was a little too angry. Nonetheless, such sightings set off Ryan's internal spook detector. And it was going off far too frequently.

The initial thrill of tracking down so many of his ethereal visitors had dissipated. So what if he knew who they were, or once were? What good did it do him? Sure, it convinced him that he wasn't crazy, that the spooks weren't hallucinations. But that only intensified the mystery surrounding them. And frankly, it only made things more unsettling. These were ghosts, bona fide ghosts. Truth be told, the visitations were scaring the heck out of him. He had no idea where and when the next encounter would take place, but he was certain that it *would* take place. Even his own home proved an insufficient respite, particularly with respect to visits from the "dark lady." The only safe space was within the protective ramparts of the medical center. The spooks never dared bother him there. But the minute he lowered the draw bridge and ventured out into the real world he was fair game, a bone to be chewed by the spirit world.

It was as if the undead were determined to become regular fixtures in his life. Perhaps it was New Bethany, though, and not him. Perhaps the place was overrepresented in the metaphysical world. Or could it have something to do with the jeep? He seemed to experience so many of his "interfaces" when in the jeep. It had been his father's. When his father died, his mother put it in storage until he could drive. He loved the beat-up old thing, but could it be some sort of spook receiver? Who knew? The only thing of which Ryan was certain was that he needed a break, a reprieve, an armistice with the world of the dead. His wits were fraying; his pistons, overheating. So he clung to the promise of an upcoming escape—only a couple of weeks away—a neurosurgical meeting in Miami. Seven glorious days away from the apparently very haunted Susquehanna Valley. Surely the spirit world couldn't flourish in the bright sun and salty air of South Beach. It wouldn't be long and he would be in another world altogether— one bursting with life and youth and play. And as icing on the cake, he'd be accompanied by Kelly.

———

"They what?" Ryan barked into the phone, the Miami Beach offshore wind whipping his thick black hair into his darkening eyes. He and Kelly had been strolling along the boardwalk, headed for a fashionably late dinner.

"They narc'd him up and extubated him earlier today, sir. He passed about an hour ago."

It was Cara Klein. She was referring to a thirty-seven-year-old man, Jules LeBlanc, who had sustained a fracture dislocation of the neck in a bicycling accident earlier in the week. He was paralyzed in the arms and legs. Ryan had operated on him right away hoping for a miracle, but not anticipating one. None came.

Ryan and Kelly had left for Miami several days later. Reportedly, shortly after Ryan's departure, Mr. Le Blanc made it known that he didn't want to live if there was no hope for a full neurological recovery. How this was ascertained was not entirely clear in that Mr. LeBlanc couldn't write due to his paralysis and couldn't speak due to a breathing tube still down his throat. Nonetheless, the trauma team had gone ahead and disconnected him from the ventilator and removed his breathing tube. To preclude any discomfort or emotional distress in the process (and to accelerate his demise), they sedated him and gave him heavy doses of narcotic pain killers. Such a practice was common across the country, though it was usually reserved for terminal elderly patients who were dying a little too slowly for everyone's liking.

"What the hell are you talking about, Cara?" screamed Ryan, half out of rage, half to overcome the howling winds. "He was in no goddamned condition to make that decision. He was still in shock. Christ, he was still on a blower."

"Believe me, Dr. Brenan, we did all we could to block it, but those fuck-heads started in on it the minute you left the hospital. They brought in the shrinks, the grief counselors, the ethics team, the end-of-life team, the administration—you name it.

"I don't care who goddamned saw him; it was too early to grant any request for withdrawal of care. Christ, it wasn't withdrawal, it was assassination!"

This comment drew stares from passers-by.

"I know sir, I know. Honestly, Dr. Brenan, we did everything we could, but the pricks were bound and determined. They kept commenting how neurosurgery was always trying to keep corpses alive—"

"Corpses? *Corpses?* He wasn't a goddamned corpse. His brain was fine. He had no incurable disease. He could have adjusted. Why did they need to move so goddamned fast?"

"I think they saw his pulmonary injuries as a window, an opportunity to let him go. I mean, once his lungs healed up they would have had to put a pillow over his face to get him to die. This way, I think they felt they were simply withdrawing care per his wishes—"

"Yeah, by blasting him with Ativan and fentanyl, I'm sure. It might as well have been a goddamned pillow. And you say the shrinks and the ethics board all approved?"

"Yeah, every one of them."

"Idiots, morons . . ."

"But the trauma team laid it on thick, Dr. Ryan—how his life would be an utter misery, how he might never come off the blower, how he would have to be in a nursing home forever—"

"What a bunch of crap! Which idiot trauma attending was leading the charge?"

"Ahem . . . that would be Dr. Flintstone."

"Christ, I should have known." The trauma doctor in question was not actually a Dr. Flintstone. His real name was Dr. Kearney, but he had acquired the moniker due to his distinct resemblance to the cartoon character, Fred Flintstone. Dr. Kearney had once been a Philadelphia Fireman and was big, broad, and burly. He threw his weight around whenever he saw fit and loved to butt heads with the neurosurgical team over the care of the seriously injured. He was forever bludgeoning the residents with arguments to disconnect one coma patient or another from their ventilators. He maintained that essentially no one with a severe neurological injury stood a chance of meaningful recovery, so there was no point in wasting precious resources on their care. In his book, if you weren't up and dancing within two to three days of your admission, you should be prepared for organ harvest. Shaking with rage, Ryan signed off the call and then struggled to punch up Kearney's number.

"Kearney here."

"Yeah, Pat, it's Ryan. Ryan Brenan."

"What's up, Brenan? I thought you were off lazing about in the Miami surf," commented Kearney, with, as always, a demeaning tone.

Ryan couldn't contain himself. "Goddamn it, Pat, what motivated you all to knock off Mr. LeBlanc? You know god-damned well he could—"

"Now wait a minute, Brenan. We didn't 'knock off' anyone. The guy was toast. He knew it, we knew it, you should have known it!"

"That's bullshit, Pat. He was a perfectly viable human being."

"The guy absolutely *was* toast," replied Kearney. "Everyone agreed. I even had the ethics board weigh in. It was the right thing to do."

"To what, euthanize an entirely salvageable patient? For all we knew, he could have even gotten better."

"You know fucking well he had no chance of recovery. The guy was going nowhere, and he made it clear that he didn't want to live that way—"

"Did you consider for one moment that he might have been concussed, or situationally depressed; that he might not be capable of rational decisions?"

"Of course we did. The shrinks declared him 100 percent compos mentis—"

"So, we just execute him?" growled Ryan.

"Hey, buddy, you better watch the words you're throwing around there. They're pretty loaded stuff."

"Pretty loaded stuff? What about killing off a guy with decades of life still ahead of him? Is that not 'loaded stuff'?"

By now, a small crowd had gathered around Ryan to watch the show. He took no notice as Kearney retorted.

"Listen Brenan, I've taken enough shit from you. You want to say things like that, get back up here and say them to my face."

"I'd be delighted, Pat," replied Ryan, shuddering with fury. "You think you can bully everyone into doing what you want. Well, not me, buddy. Belligerence is no compensation for lousy care. You had no right to kill Mr. LeBlanc, no right at all. So, name the time and place and I'd be delighted to explain it to you face to face."

"Fuck off, Brenan. I'd squash you like the little stink bug you are. You're not worth the trouble." Kearney hung up.

Ryan turned to Kelly to vent. But she was gone. He looked past the dozen or so onlookers who had gathered around him but saw no sign of her. He broke free of their circle and searched the general area. No luck. He walked up and down the boardwalk several hundred feet in both directions to no avail. He hit her number on his phone, but she failed to answer. Finally, he scanned the water's edge and spotted her. She was seated just beyond the ocean's reach, hugging her knees. He staggered through the sand and sat down beside her.

"Sorry, honey. You just wouldn't believe what went on back at the shop."

"I know what went on, Ryan. I heard it all—as did half of Miami."

"Well, never mind. Let's go have some seafood and wine, and forget about it."

"I've kind of lost my appetite. Let's just get a snack at the hotel and head to bed."

"Oh, come on. Let's go get some dinner and then go out dancing," pleaded Ryan, unconvinced that this sounded in any way desirable.

"No, Ryan. I'm really not in the mood. I think I may take a long soak in the bath."

"I could join you."

"Have you seen the bathtub? I can barely fit in it myself. Besides, you'd be too itchy. After that call you'll need to move. Why don't you take a nice long walk and I'll go soak."

Half an hour later, after dropping Kelly back off at their room, Ryan made his way down the beach; stumbling and lurching alongside the breakers; mumbling, fretting, twitching, clenching and unclenching his fists; kicking sand, cursing, and condemning; carrying on like a moon-incensed madman.

CHAPTER 38

SHATTERED DREAMS

"**A**nd that was it, Dianne. From that point on, he was gone," remarked Kelly. She was discussing her ill-fated trip to Miami with Dianne O'Connor as the two walked along the periphery of the O'Connor farm on a cold, blustery October Saturday afternoon. "I guess I could've tried to resuscitate things, but to be frank, I was pretty pissed off."

"Because he made such a scene in public?"

"No, I get that. But why did he have to make the call in the first place? Why did he have to try to manage his patients from a thousand miles away? And why couldn't he have regrouped after it? Why couldn't he have shelved the issue for the rest of the trip and enjoyed himself, enjoyed me? But as soon as the phone call started to deteriorate, I knew I'd lost him."

"I'm so sorry, Kelly. I know you were hoping it would be a healing experience."

"Yeah, I was," replied Kelly, coming to a stop. "But I was being unrealistic, wasn't I? I mean, I guess I thought a week of the two of us together, no kids, a fancy hotel, the beach . . . well, you know . . . might resurrect things, might resurrect my Ryan. But no, he had to bring a third wheel along."

"His job," surmised Dianne.

"Yeah, his job. Only, I think *I* was the third wheel," replied Kelly, one foot on some fencing, staring off at hawk in flight.

"Come on now, Kelly. That's—"

"Oh, there's no two ways about it," interrupted Kelly. She turned to Dianne, eyes flashing. "I play second fiddle for sure. Not even second fiddle. I'm some sort of a junior understudy. It's not working, Di. If it weren't for the kids . . ."

The two talked for another hour, but the more they talked the more Kelly sank into feelings of helplessness and hopelessness. Driving home in her van, she tried to recall the last time she truly enjoyed being with Ryan but came up empty. She dreaded facing him in her current mood. At least the girls were home. They and the dogs would lift her spirits with their usual frenzied greeting when she came through the door. She smiled and bathed in the warmth of their love. Only, when she did get home she found the girls huddled on the couch crying, and the dogs hiding in the coat closet.

"Girls, what's wrong? What happened?"

"Dad's really mad at us," replied Erin between shuddered breaths.

"I don't think he'll ever speak to us again," added Riley.

"And we never touched it, Mom. We never even go in your room," added Ava.

"What are you talking about? Touch what?" asked Kelly, sitting down and gathering the girls into a soothing hug.

"His dream catcher thing," replied Riley. "It's all broken—"

"And Dad says it had to be one of us who broke it," said Erin.

"And he said one of us was lying. But we're not, Mom. We never touched it. We're kind of scared of the thing," explained Ava.

Kelly spent the next fifteen minutes tending to the girls and then strode up the stairs, her face reddening and her chest constricting. She entered the bedroom ready for a fight but found Ryan slumped and shrunken on the floor. He was holding the tangled mess of the former dream catcher and a container of glue. Several of his fingers were cut and bleeding.

"Goodness, Ryan. What happened?" asked Kelly.

"Huh? I don't know," replied Ryan, his face ashen. "One of the girls must have smashed it for some reason."

"What? You know they wouldn't do that."

"Yeah, well, how else would you explain this then?" replied Ryan, scowling. "I was downstairs watching a game. They were all up here in the playroom. One of them is lying."

"Come on, Ryan. They're afraid of that thing. They're not going to get near it. It's really windy out there today; maybe it just got blown to the floor."

"And that did this?" asked Ryan, holding up the tangled jumble of broken wood, torn sinew, and denuded feathers.

"What's the big deal anyway, honey? It's just a toy," asked Kelly, resisting the impulse to touch Ryan's shoulder.

"Just a toy?" responded a wide-eyed Ryan. "It's saved our sleep for how long now?"

"Come on, Ryan. You know it has noth—"

Ryan stood up, slammed the former dream catcher into a wastebasket, and stormed down the stairs and out of the house without a word.

He returned three hours later clutching a large paper bag.

"Ryan, where've you been?" asked Kelly, following him upstairs.

"I took care of things," grunted Ryan as he emptied six dream catchers of various sizes and configurations onto the bed.

"What the? You can't be ser—"

"I drove out to that Native American place out on eighty."

"Oh, Ryan. That's a tourist trap. Those things were probably made in China. You're acting craz—"

"Don't say it, Kelly." Ryan held up an index finger. "I need these."

"Ryan, I think what you need is an appointment with your psychia—"

Ryan held up a palm toward Kelly and hurried out of the room holding two of the dream catchers. Kelly followed him and watched as he hung one at the end of the long hallway and another in the girls' room. He then hung one in the master bedroom window and one over the bed. He stowed the other two in the closet. He went downstairs, poured himself a tall bourbon, and plonked down onto the couch. Kelly shook her head, gathered the girls for bed, poured her own glass of bour-bon, and read in bed until she drifted off into fitful sleep.

———

Downstairs Ryan had turned off his mind completely and sat staring blankly at the TV. He ran through a Civil War documentary, then a World War II documentary, then a Vietnam War documentary. It was well after midnight when he went upstairs. First he tiptoed into the girls' room and watched them sleep, tears streaming down his face for calling their honesty into question. After kissing each of them, he headed off to bed. The night had turned unseasonably cold for October, dropping into the twenties, and his poorly insulated bedroom reflected it. Slipping into bed, he cranked up the electric blanket and tried to snuggle up to Kelly. Even in her sleep, though, her response connoted deep annoyance. He flipped onto his back, chilled to the bone. It took some time, but he eventually drifted off, assisted by some mortally boring readings from his neurosurgical journals.

He awoke an hour later with a start. He was shivering violently and noticed the covers on his side of the bed had taken their leave of him and had spilled onto the floor. Kelly's side was somehow left undisturbed.

Well, damn, he thought. *It's gonna take forever to warm up.* He sat up and shimmied his way to the end of the bed to retrieve the truant covers.

"Holy fuck!" he blurted as he retreated to the headboard. Before him was a figure seated in the bedroom's chintz upholstered chair. A female figure. A female figure bedecked in funeral attire. She sat motionless, hands crossed on her lap, watching Ryan from behind her veil, her chest rising and falling with each ghostly breath.

Ryan collapsed himself around Kelly. "Kelly, Kelly, wake up! Wake up! She's here! Look! She's here!"

Kelly mumbled and turned her back to him more emphatically.

"Kelly, please! Wake up, for Christ's sake! Please look. She's here!" pleaded Ryan. In a frost-covered panic, he grabbed the nearest object that could be weaponized, a glass of water off the bedside table. "Get away from us, you fucking bitch!" he screamed as he hurled it at his visitor. It hit the back of the chair and bounced halfway back to the bed, shattering on the painted pine floor.

Kelly awoke with the explosion of glass. "Ryan, what the heck?"

He was shaking furiously. He tried to wrap himself in Kelly's warmth, but she squirmed free.

"Ryan, don't. Please, you're an absolute icicle."

He pulled the bedclothes around himself and sat shuddering, teeth hammering out Morse Code.

"What's up, Ryan?" queried Kelly. "I heard glass break and you yelling something about me being a bitch."

"No honey, I wasn't yelling at you. I was yelling at—" He stopped. "Um, I must have had a terror."

"A terror? It would sure be unlike any of the others you've

had. You've *physically* assaulted me plenty of times, but never *verbally*."

"I wasn't yelling at you, Kelly. Honestly."

"How would you know? You never remember anything after a terror. And what was the crash?"

"Um, I threw my water glass at your chair."

"What? Why?"

"I don't know, Kelly. I have no memory—"

"You can remember you *weren't* calling me a bitch and that you threw your glass at the chair, but you can't remember why?"

"Jeez, honey, I don't know. I think it was somewhere between a nightmare and a terror. I guess the new dream catchers didn't do the trick."

CHAPTER 39

TRICK OR TREAT

The new dream catchers proved remarkably impotent. For the following two weeks, the household awoke to Ryan's screeching almost every night. Everyone's nerves became frayed. The household became bleak and antagonistic. Even John and Paul skulked about, afraid that someone would take offense at their presence.

But it was Halloween night and everyone tried to rally. The girls were attired in their regalia and were raring to go: Ava as a zombie soccer player, Riley as a zombie witch, and Erin as a zombie ballerina. The crew was off to a late start, though. Kelly was getting barraged by a series of work-related phone calls and kept signaling to the anxious bunch to give her just a few more minutes. Ryan and the girls decided to wait for her out in the backyard. The girls occupied themselves by jumping into a six-foot-tall pile of leaves completely void of any sticks or twigs greater than a centimeter in length and a millimeter in diameter. Ryan had made sure of this. He had meticulously sifted through the pile earlier in the evening—a behavior that had been precipitated by an operative case from the past week, that of little Jimmy Preston.

Seven-year-old Jimmy had, himself, been leaf-pile-jumping in the safety of his own backyard. On his fourth plunge, however, he managed to drive a dogwood branch into his left eye socket. The wayward branch skirted the eyeball altogether but pierced the thin bone of the roof of the socket and sank many inches into Jimmy's brain. There, it caused substantial hemorrhaging. He came in to the medical center dying. Ryan and a resident removed a large clot of blood and the errant piece of wood from deep within Jimmy's cerebrum in less time than it would have taken to go downtown for a burger. Jimmy survived but was rendered neurologically devastated. The case left Ryan suspicious of the intentions of every leaf pile in town. And now his own sweet babies were daring fate right in front of him. He found himself wincing every time they vanished into the clutches of the capricious mound. His heart would stop beating until they resurfaced, laughing uproariously and bearing no grotesque wounds. So he was most relieved when Kelly finally exited the house and made her way over to the group.

With the raiding party now assembled, the Brenans set off up the alley behind the house, and then turned onto Avenue G. The group soon reached a target-rich region of New Bethany. Upon crossing each home's property line, the girls would break into a sprint to contest the honor of ringing the doorbell. Meanwhile, Kelly and Ryan would hang back at the curbside. The two, however, seemed to be enjoying the festivities in parallel. They moved as if there was a force field between them and exchanged no words. It was a relief to both when Kelly's work caught up with her and she broke away from the pack and slipped home.

After a brief protest, the girls went back to plying their trade. Ryan settled into a trance of parental bliss as he watched his girls flit about, falling deeper in love with each of them.

"Ryan . . . oh, Ryan . . ."

First it was little more than a whisper.

"Ryan . . . oh Ryan, honey . . ."

The voice started to seep into his pleasantly numbed consciousness.

"Ryan . . . I seeee you."

He scanned the area. A three-quarter moon assured good

visibility well beyond the light cast by a couple of anemic streetlamps.

"Ryan honey, I'm over here."

"What? Now you're addressing me by name?" said Ryan. He oriented to a field behind a row of widely spaced houses on the opposite side of the street and spotted her. And it was definitely a her. Medium height, slim, shapely. He heard a faint giggle as he moved toward her. But as he closed the distance, she moved farther out into the field.

"This way, honey."

Ryan entered the field. The woman matched his pace as she drifted toward an adjacent wooded area.

Another giggle.

"You naughty boy," tickled his ear.

He hastened his pace, but the woman slipped into the woods and disappeared. He came to a halt. He peered into the woods but couldn't imagine anyone easily making their way through the thick underbrush. He turned his head and strained so hard to listen for any rustling, that when the girls called out to him he jumped several feet into the air.

"Where're you going, Dad?" called the trio of sopranos.

Ryan turned. All three had entered the field behind him.

"Girls, did you see a lady go into the woods here?" blurted a wide-eyed Ryan.

"What lady? Where?" came the choral response.

"A lady—shorter than mom. You didn't see her, or hear her calling out to me?" inquired Ryan, accusingly.

"No, Dad," came the response.

"Okay, okay . . . well, let's get back to trick-or-treating, eh?" said Ryan as he strode toward Ninth Street, still looking back over his shoulder at the woods.

"Oh Ryan, did you forget about me? Don't leave, baby."

"What the fuck?" blurted Ryan. "Girls, surely you heard the voice that time!"

"Stop it, Dad, that's not funny. You're scaring me," whined Riley.

Ava and Erin chimed in, "Yeah, Dad, stop it. It's not funny."

Ryan realized the girls thought he was pulling a Halloween prank on them. It wouldn't have been past the Ryan of old to do so. But he was the only one shuddering and breaking out in a cold sweat. He rapidly ushered the girls away.

"Why are we going this way, Dad?" asked Ava as Ryan swept the girls down toward a different section of the neighborhood.

"Uh, we're going to track down some better candy, sweetie."

"Why are you running away from me, Ryan?" called out the voice.

"Fuck!" exclaimed Ryan as he whisked up all three girls and ran across Salisbury Road.

Forty-five minutes later the band arrived home, bags overflowing with treats. Kelly, still on the phone, broke off her call and kneeled on the ground to hug her returning zombies.

"How did it go, my scary trio?"

"Super fun, except Dad kept trying to scare us," said Riley.

"And he kept saying 'fuck,'" said Erin.

"Erin! That's inappropriate language. I don't want you using that word again, okay?" admonished Kelly.

"But I didn't, Mom. Dad did—twice!" replied Erin.

Kelly shot Ryan a withering glare. All Ryan could do was shrug, palms turned toward the ceiling, and grin as if the girls must have been mistaken. Kelly shook her head and turned her back to him as she continued to relive with the girls the positive, scare-free, swear-free, highlights of the excursion.

"Fuck," said Ryan under his breath.

CHAPTER 40

COMPLICATIONS

With the spirit world now speaking to him and addressing him by name, Ryan had to seek fresh counsel. Someone with whom he could probe the metaphysical implications and ramifications of his otherworldly encounters. He therefore arranged an audience with Reverend Ron. The two met in a dingy sports bar in Mid-November, and Ryan gave a full account of all that was happening to him.

"And you haven't told Kelly about these . . . hallucinations? Holy Hannah, Ryan, I thought you brain surgeons were supposed to be smart," remarked Reverend Ron.

"I told you, Ron. They're not hallucinations. I'm pretty sure they're the real thing."

"Hmm," said Reverend Ron, right eye twitching the way it always did when he was concerned. "Are you sure you ruled out all *natural* explanations for your 'real thing' before you went off looking for *super*-natural ones?"

"I've spent the past year eliminating all the 'natural explanations.'"

"Yeah, well, I think you cut some corners, my friend," replied Reverend Ron, pointing a finger at Ryan. "I think you tried a few interventions, then leaped to the conclusion that it was all an external phenomenon rather than an internal one."

Ryan frowned. "An internal one? Like me being crazy?"

"Well, my friend, it would be the cleanest explanation, the

shortest distance between two points. But short of that, why couldn't your apparitions be some form of seizures?"

"I discussed that with Whitehead, and had several EEGs."

"But you never completely eliminated the possibility, did you? That would require several days in a monitoring unit, wouldn't it? But you never went through with it, did you?"

"It's just so darned inconvenient," replied Ryan, breaking eye contact.

"Inconvenient, huh? Or is it that you're worried they'll find something wrong with you—with that amazing brain of yours—prove that you're not some kind of immortal?"

"Of course not," said Ryan, now looking down into his beer.

"And then there's the other gaping hole in your grand investigation," challenged Reverend Ron, leaning into the conversation.

"And that is?"

"What about your sleep? There's no doubt you suffer from a profound sleep disorder—probably several. I mean, sleep starvation, insomnia, night terrors, parasomnias, disruptive nightmares, you name it. What if your dreams are somehow spilling out into your conscious mind?"

"I'm not an idiot, Ron," said Ryan with a roll of his eyes. "I know all about sleep disorders. I mean, I had terrible bouts of sleep paralysis as a kid. But I've gone over that possibility with Whitehead *and* Larkin."

"But you didn't follow up on it, did you?" challenged Reverend Ron, forcing eye contact. "You never went ahead and got any formal sleep evaluations. A dream catcher allegedly takes away the worst of your nighttime troubles and you assume a supernatural explanation—"

"But Ron, how do you explain the fact that the grand majority of the ghosts I've seen can be traced back to real people—living people—people who actually walked this earth?"

"You never dream about family members, friends, patients, coworkers, acquaintances?" Reverend Ron took a slug of beer, some of the foam remaining in his thick black mustache.

"Ron, I had never heard of any of them before all this. Most died decades ago."

Reverend Ron shrugged. "I don't have all the answers, Ryan. I still suspect they were in there somewhere, in the deep recess of that thick head of yours, biding their time for a few-second interlude of daytime sleepwalking."

"But the apparitions can last for extended periods of time," replied Ryan. "Yet, I never lose consciousness, never fall over, never find myself asleep somewhere, never run off the road, or anything."

"Maybe sleep is flickering into your wakefulness," hypothesized Reverend Ron, "like an old movie projector—frames of sleep and wakefulness alternating so fast you don't notice anything unusual, other than the apparitions."

"Really, Ron?" said Ryan with an eyebrow raised.

"I don't know, Ryan. I'm making this up. I'm not an expert." Reverend Ron pushed his index finger into Ryan's chest. "But nor are you."

"I guess I'm getting your point. But—"

"My point is," interrupted Reverend Ron with a scowl, "there are still too many stones to turn over before we can accept *any* explanation for this—medical, psychological, or metaphysical. And I'm urging you to get on it, because whatever's going on is bringing you down, my friend."

"All right, Ronald, Scout's honor." Ryan made the sign of an oath with his right hand. "I'll get on it."

"Excellent."

"So, see a couple more neurologists, get some sleep studies and some more EEGs, and I'm good to go, right?" proposed Ryan.

"Jeez no, Ryan." Reverend Ron's right eye twitched harder. "Forget the ghosts for now. You're a freakin' mess. You're killing yourself. Right in front of us. Physically, I would bet, but most certainly emotionally. You're at serious risk, my friend, of all sorts of bad stuff—substance abuse, infidelity, major behavioral issues, mental illness, loss of job, loss of your family."

Ryan shifted uncomfortably on his bench. "What would you have me do, Ron? The work just keeps coming. It's relentless."

"Listen, Ryan, have you ventured out around the front of the hospital any time recently?" asked Reverend Ron, gesturing in the general direction of the hospital.

"Uh, I suppose so."

"Did you happen to see them building a freaking statue of you out there?"

"I get what you're saying," replied Ryan with a frown. "But I don't do this for Carriere. It's just that the patients keep coming."

"And you, Ryan Brenan, must single-handedly cure them all."

"Were that only the case. It feels like every other patient is leaving in a coffin, anymore."

Reverend Ron's bushy black eyebrows raised with this comment. He took a gulp of beer. "And you help put some of them there, don't you, Ryan?"

"Yep, Ronald, I do," replied Ryan, chin lifting in the air. "Matt Wolfe says I'm a serial killer; a serial *accidental* killer, that is. And a serial accidental maimer."

"A what?"

"You know, I hurt people now and then with my surgery, through complications—sometimes pretty bad complications."

"So, how does that make you feel?" asked Reverend Ron, leaning forward and fixing his eyes on Ryan's.

"Jesus, Ron, can you sound any more like a shrink?"

"Be that as it may, answer the question." Reverend Ron maintained unblinking eye contact with Ryan. "How does it make you feel when you hurt one of your patients?"

"Like crap, of course," replied Ryan, looking into his beer.

"Can you elaborate?"

"Sure. Like, I know it's unrealistic, but you go into every operation hoping, and somehow expecting, for it to go perfectly—exactly to plan. The slightest deviation from perfect, even in hopeless situations, is stressful. The worse the deviation, the greater the stress. Throw in a bad complication and it gets ugly."

"In what way?" asked Reverend Ron.

Ryan took a large gulp of beer and wiped his mouth with the back of his wrist. "Well, you ruminate about it nonstop. You replay the case in your head over and over again: your technique, your decision-making, your attention to detail. You see the operative field in your mind's eye before you go to sleep at night—like it's burned into your retinas. And you dream about it, night after night."

Reverend Ron nodded as if to say, "Go on."

Ryan hesitated, then frowned. "And at the risk of sounding too much like a raving narcissist, you begin to frame the whole miserable experience around how it makes *you* feel, rather than grieving for the patient and their family. You walk around feeling all sorry for yourself. And you feel like everyone in the hospital knows about the complication and thinks less of you for it."

"Got you," offered Reverend Ron, leaning further over the table and resting his chin on his fists.

Ryan continued. "And you feel physically ill. And the closer you get to the hospital, and to the ward the patient's on, the sicker you feel. You dread seeing the patient. You begin to hate the guy for existing, for surviving your folly. You hate how he keeps shoving your own incompetence in your face. And you hate yourself for hating him. And you wanna know when such feelings finally start to dissipate, Ron?"

"Tell me," answered Reverend Ron, right eye nearly swollen closed from constant twitching.

"Not until the guy leaves the hospital."

"Makes sense," said Ron, slowly nodding his head.

"Only, he doesn't leave the hospital," jumped in Ryan. "Because he's so messed up, because you've set off a chain reaction of other complications in him. So, he lies there and rots from within, on *your* service, under *your* charge. And you reach a point where you would actually feel better if he would just die. And you wish, if he's going to die anyway, that he just goes ahead and gets it over with—so you can be rid of him, and rid of the dreadful feelings he causes in you. And then you feel wretched about ever thinking such things. But it doesn't stop you for thinking them."

Ryan paused for a moment and sat back in his bench. "That's how it makes me feel, Ron."

"Sheesh, Ryan," responded Reverend Ron with an extended exhalation. "I'm so sorry." He shook his head slowly. "I think, you just gave me enough material for three doctoral theses. Have you ever discussed these feelings with Kelly?"

"Not really." Ryan drained his mug of beer. "I guess I didn't want her to think she's married to a sociopath."

"But, Ryan, this is the stuff you need to share with her. This is the stuff of true intimacy within a marriage."

"Yeah, well, why bring all that crap home and dump it on her? It's not her problem."

"Of course it's her problem." Reverend Ron grabbed the table edge with both hands. "Because of how it affects you and how it affects your relationship. She needs to know what a screwed-up world you inhabit, what you go through day to day, why you come home the way you do."

"But that's neurosurgery, Ron. At least for the guys who take on the big stuff. And there are plenty of other docs in plenty of other fields who have to deal with similar things."

"Well, then you can understand why I'm so busy," said Reverend Ron, eyes fixed again on Ryan's. "Don't you see how corrosive to one's psyche such a way of life has to be? I mean, if one doesn't get away from it enough, one begins to see such a screwed-up existence as being normal; and a normal, happy, invigorating existence as being deviant. I don't care how tough, or resilient, or above-it-all you guys think you are. No one can process such emotions effectively without regular respite. No wonder your sleep is so haunted; you're giving your brain no chance to wipe the slate clean of all the awfulness of the day."

Ryan shrugged. "And how am I supposed to do that?"

Reverend Ron drained his own mug. "You need to get out, to engage, interact, and enjoy the outside world—the real world, the world of your wife, your family, your friends. Give your mind things to play with other than all the horror shows that go on in the hospital."

"You don't think that I want to spend more time with Kelly, with the girls, with you bunch of knuckleheads?"

"I don't know, Ryan. If you want to so bad, why don't you?" said Reverend Ron, glaring at Ryan with his one open eye.

"Because there's not enough time in the day, the week, the year. Believe me."

"Oh, bull-shevism, Ryan!" replied Reverend Ron loudly enough to make other patrons in the bar turn. "If there isn't the time, then you need to make it."

"Easier said than done."

Reverend Ron sneered. "Because the great brain surgeon, Ryan Brenan, has to be on call every minute of every day for every dreadful eventuality. What are you, Ryan, a masochist? Or are you just stupid? Is it hubris? Ego? Self-infatuation? A hero complex? You're bearing too much of the load. I don't care how good you are, or how good you think you are. You can't do it all on your own."

"Ron, truly, I can handle my work. I—"

"Christmas, Ryan." Reverend Ron smacked his palms on the table. "Do you believe you're above the rules? You keep this up and you won't have to wait for visits from the other side; you'll be over there with them. And when that happens, do you think Carriere will give a damn? Do you think the system will skip a beat? Do you think they'll throw that statue up of you?"

"Nope," replied Ryan, shaking his head with certainty.

"You're darn right, 'nope.' The only one left devastated will be Kelly—if she's still part of your life at all. Because, brother—and please listen to me—no marriage survives without regular attention and fertilization."

"Oh, I get that one, Ron. I'm doing so much better with Kelly lately."

"Bull-shevism again, Ryan," barked Reverend Ron. "You're a stranger in your own home. You barely show up, and when you do, you act more like one of your ghost friends than a living, breathing, vital partner. You've got to do better than that, mister, much better."

"I want to, Ron, but—"

"But nothing, you failure of a footballer," Reverend Ron again pounded the table and then pointed his finger at Ryan. "Find a way, Ryan, while you still can."

"But there *are* logistics to all this, Ron—"

"Screw the logistics, Ryan," interrupted Reverend Ron. "This is your family we're talking about here. They need you every bit as much as do your patients. A happy medium can be reached with a little effort on your part. You'll still get to work ridiculous hours, and work way too hard, and lose oodles of sleep, but you'll be much happier. And you'll be a better doctor for it, believe me. And maybe, just maybe, your dead friends will leave you alone."

"I could live with that," replied Ryan, eyebrows knit as he looked over the other beings scattered around the bar.

CHAPTER 41

THE HAUNTING OF HILL HOUSE

Ryan took Reverend Ron's admonitions to heart, and drove over to Lamington the following Saturday morning to secure a peace offering for his beleaguered wife. The mission was magnificently successful. At a quaint used bookstore just off the Buckley College Campus, he had found and bought a signed first-edition Shirley Jackson novel. Ryan had never read any of the author's works, but he knew Kelly was an ardent fan. The irony of it being a ghost story wasn't lost on him, but he was certain that Kelly would be thrilled with the gift. He was now happily hurdling home past denuded cornfields and leafless forests as an occasional snow flurry was shaken out of a light-starved sky. As the jeep crested a small hill, however, he was forced to hit the brakes as he closed the distance on a lumbering flat-bedded tow truck. The truck was hauling a totaled 1990s Ford station wagon, remarkable only for its vintage.

For the next few miles, Ryan was stuck behind the truck. Time, being by far the most precious commodity in his life, he impatiently sought to find a way around the heaving vehicle. He was so engrossed in the task that he paid no attention to the fossilized conveyance sitting upon it. On hitting a stretch of road that was so curvy that passing would be impossible, he settled into his seat, let up a little on the gas, and looked up to study the accordioned Ford. The primeval land yacht featured a long-extinct, avocado-green paint job, faux-wood side paneling, and travel stickers from every conceivable tourist trap east of the Mississippi. On scanning the car further, he was shocked to see two unbelted children at the back window, peering out at him. He recognized that it all had to be some sort of metaphysical bullshit, and sneered back at the ghosts. When he finally hit a straightaway, he mouthed something profane at the kids and accelerated. As he began to pass, he looked up and was greeted by a toddler standing on the middle seat, banging on the side window, his phantom mother beside him only partially restraining him. He pulled forward and there was the dad, a satisfied look on his face, pipe in mouth, hands on the steering wheel.

"Jesus," was all Ryan could come up with. He studied the guy, or ghoul, bedecked as he was in a bright-orange bowling shirt. The ghost must have sensed the attention because he turned to Ryan, nodded, and tipped his pork pie hat. Ryan responded by giving the specter the finger. Suddenly, he alerted to the prolonged blast of an airhorn. His eyes widened as he looked ahead. An oversized semi was bearing down on him from the opposite direction. He slammed on his brakes. The ancient jeep deaccelerated commendably, shooting Kelly's gift off the passenger seat, slamming it against the glove compartment, avulsing its binding, and scattering pages all over the footwell. With a centimeter to spare, Ryan ducked back behind the tow truck as the semi barreled by, its driver delivering his own gesture of incivility.

Ryan fell back several hundred yards, shaking from head to toe. He eventually accelerated, his curiosity overcoming his post-traumatic terror. When he reached the truck, the kids, the toddler, the mom, the pipe-smoking dad, and, indeed, the station wagon, were nowhere to be seen.

"Jesus," he remarked to the passing scenery. "Are they trying to kill me?"

CHAPTER 42

MAYHEM

The near-death experience left Ryan shaken and agitated. He found it impossible to enjoy the weekend, trying to affect an air of carefree joviality for Kelly and the girls while his heart still tore at his chest wall. It wasn't until Monday morning, back in the embrace of the hospital, back among the strokes and head injuries, that his breathing settled and he lost his awareness of the minute-to-minute function of his cardiovascular system. Soon he was cheerfully attacking brain tumors and piecing shattered spines back together. Call, however, sucked some of the contentment out of the day. The first trauma alert came in at 6:00 p.m. sharp. The associated story was as dreadful as it was unavoidable, and would be repeated in all its graphic detail until it was seared into Ryan's memory banks.

Rick Hart was a devoted and doting father. He and his partner, Brandon Renfro, had adopted identical twin babies, Joy and Clarice, five years ago almost to the day. Brandon was an anthropology professor, and Rick a classicist, at Buckley University in Lamington, but Rick had put his academic career on hold to act as a stay-at-home parent. From day one, he watched over the children's safety like a militant guardian angel. Not a molecule of artificial foodstuff ever passed their lips. Their medical checkups and vaccinations were attended to with Aryan compulsivity. Top-of-the-line helmets were employed for every activity—outdoor or indoor—that involved any form of locomotion. And for their sorties out of their maximum-security compound, the two were strapped like astronauts about to lift off from Cape Canaveral, into state-of-the-art children's car seats.

In selecting a home, Rick made the children's physical well-being the number one priority. The house sat at the very end of a long cul-de-sac, thus minimizing traffic. It was only two blocks away from a superior K–12 private school, obviating the need for any seatbelt-deficient school bus rides. It was single-leveled, eliminating the risk of stairs. It was light-years beyond code in its infrastructure, security systems, wiring, ventilation, and environmental control. And all its surface paints and caulking were triple-certified toxin-free.

In the midafternoon, Rick was busy making an organic, non-GMO vegetable soup for the family's dinner while the twins colored in the adjacent family room. Across town, John Jourbert, a corrections officer at the Lamington Federal Penitentiary, was at a bar anesthetizing the pain of his current existence. He had recently been laid off. To make matters worse, he'd had yet another argument with his on-again off-again—but currently off-again—girlfriend, Alex. After finishing off a dozen shots of Wild Turkey, he called Alex and told her he was coming over to reclaim his wall-sized, maximum-resolution flat-screen TV. He paid his tab, then stumbled out to his extended-cab pickup truck. He was off with a scream of tires and bullied his way through traffic toward "the bitch's" duplex.

Barreling along the main thoroughfare of Alex's part of town, country rock booming from his truck's elaborate sound system, Jourbert must have believed he had spotted the stand of maple trees that graced the entrance into Alex's neighborhood. Only the trees weren't maples; they were sourwoods. And the street wasn't Alex's—Jourbert had overshot hers by several blocks. Nonetheless he made the turn and bombed down an extended cul-de-sac.

The truck hit the curb in front of Rick and Jonathan's house at sixty-five miles an hour, launching three tons of furious steel into the crisp November air. It cleared the lawn and plowed into the front wall of the house.

———

In New Bethany, Ryan was notified by the trauma team that two children were coming in with severe head injuries, both in coma, one "with brain coming out of her head." So he settled into his office and caught up on emails as he awaited their arrival. Lamington was a half-hour drive away, but Ryan knew that with the kids coming by air, it would be a good hour and a half before they arrived. It had something to do with their "packaging," and it was an endless source of irritation to him. When he finally heard the helicopters approaching, he ambled down to the trauma bays. To his surprise, the first victim through the doors was an adult: one John Jourbert.

"Who the heck is this? Where're the kids?" Ryan challenged Bill Geer, chief of the helicopter crew.

"He was the one in the worst shape, so he got scooped first," came the reply.

"Worse than a kid with brain coming out of her head?" challenged Ryan.

Geer shrugged. Ryan ignored him and squeezed in between the dozen doctors, nurses, and technicians attending to the mangled body. He stooped down to examine the barely identifiable human form. After a few moments, he looked up at the crowd. "I'm sorry, but you're all wasting your time. This guy's brain-dead."

Ten minutes later, the two children arrived. On initial survey, Clarice was found to be in deep coma and was exhibiting a dilated left pupil. On CT scan, she sported a huge collection of blood just outside of the brain that was shoving the underlying left hemisphere up against the right. Joy, with the reported brain tissue matting down her angel-fine blonde hair, was actually less of an immediate concern. CT scans demonstrated a large wedge of skull driven into the brain tissue, but there were no associated collections of blood that could kill her in the next few minutes or hours. She would have to undergo surgery to clean things up, but she was relatively stable and could wait a little while, as she had at the time of her birth, for her sister to get through her ordeal first.

Ryan and Lisa LeClair spirited Clarice away to the OR. Within minutes they had created a huge window in her skull and had opened the tight and bulging brain coverings. Underneath they encountered a dark-red Jell-O mold of clotted blood, a subdural hematoma. Ryan and Lisa irrigated the large lump of clotted blood off the brain's surface. The condition of the underlying tissue was appalling. It was bruised all over, boggy and swollen, and bleeding in multiple areas. The two surgeons went about their business, though, and within another half hour were closing.

An hour later, Ryan was in another operating room cleaning up Joy's gruesome but less devastating injury. It went quickly. He fished the imploded bone out of the brain, stopped any bleeding, washed out the wound with gallons of antibiotic-infused saline, pieced the shattered skull back together with tiny titanium plates and screws, and sewed up the jagged scalp laceration as aesthetically as he could. He had performed the procedure for all-too-many unfortunate children through the years—and plenty of adults. The list of offending agents was near endless: table corners, doorknobs, car doors, horses' hooves, horseshoes sans horses, baseball bats, golf clubs, pool cues, billiard balls, foul balls, lacrosse balls, lacrosse sticks, lawn darts, javelins, discuses, shot puts, garden gnomes, ball-peen hammers, claw hammers, drones, and, just the week before, a bronze figurine of Jesus holding a lamb.

A priest had given the statue to a young couple upon their baby's baptism. The baby's father had placed it on the back deck of the family sedan on the way home from the ceremony. Unfortunately, a coked-up college administrator ran a red light in his BMW just as the family's car crossed the intersection. The car T-boned the BMW, launching the holy effigy at the baby's head. The baby's entire forehead was caved in. The actual brain damage, however, was blessedly limited, and Ryan and his team had the child put back together and out of the hospital within a couple of days.

A similar outcome was likely for Joy. She had sustained her fractures in the right-front part of her skull. Thus, it was a portion of her right frontal lobe that had oozed out of her wound and, as Ryan was fond of pointing out to students, "God gave everyone a right frontal lobe so neurosurgeons could take it out." Often such injuries left no obvious neurological residue—no paralysis, no speech loss, no loss of the proverbial "fourth grade piano lessons."

Joy indeed made a wonderful recovery. Within a day her breathing tube was removed, and she was soon up and walking. The blessings fell shorter for Clarice. She remained in deep coma and trending toward brain death. Family discussions were agonizing and protracted. Rick and Brandon, as do so many aggrieved parents, held on to unrealistic expectations of a miraculous turnaround. Ryan spent much time with them every day, explaining and re-explaining the grim nature of the situation and the need to prepare for the worst.

On Thanksgiving Day, the worst was realized. Ryan pronounced Clarice brain-dead. He broke the news to Rick and Brandon, who both accepted it with preternatural grace. Both, however, were clearly devastated—their lives to be forever profoundly impacted by the ordeal: the specter of arbitrary mayhem to forever threaten any period of peace, Thanksgiving to forever be a source of pain, trust and respect for their fellow man to forever be jaded, happiness and joy to forever carry a footnote, a disclaimer.

The following afternoon, Clarice was back on an operating room table having several of her fresh young organs harvested for transplant. At the end of the procedure, all life support would be discontinued and she would cease to exist. During the procedure, Ryan headed to the PICU waiting room to check in on Rick and Jonathan. They were on the edges of their chairs, fists in their teeth, looking like they were expecting word to come out of the OR that it had all been a terrible mistake, that Clarice was just fine and would be up and about in no time. When Ryan came into the room, the two surged forth and nearly tackled him with desperate hugs. They clung to him and thanked him for all he had done, and had tried to do, and sobbed into his shoulders for the better part of an hour.

On returning home that night, Ryan wordlessly collected his three girls on the couch and clutched them under his arms, as if this might somehow protect them from the gratuitous assaults of a merciless world. Kelly entered the room.

"Ryan. What's up?"

Ryan failed to answer and just buried his bloodless face in the back of Ava's head. Kelly sat down in front of him and put her hands on his.

"Hey, honey," she whispered with a subtle tilt of her head. "You might want to ease up on your grip a little. I think the girls need to breathe, don't you?"

Ryan found himself unable to do this, so Kelly slowly parted his hands. Suddenly he released, stood up, and shuffled toward the front staircase. Kelly started to follow, but when the sound of the girls' crying chased down the hallway after her, she pivoted, leaving Ryan to scale the front staircase alone.

CHAPTER 43

BARRY DEELE

Ryan avoided Kelly for the rest of the evening. Well after midnight, he climbed into bed but didn't sleep for fear of agitating the already unsettled household with a night terror. He was off to the hospital the next morning before anyone was up. After extending his rounds into the afternoon, he headed to the hardware store to shop for nothing. On exiting, he decided to see if he could raise the sagging spirits of his family by bringing home an assortment of baked goods. The Rising, a Christian bake shop, was just a few blocks away in the main business district of town, so Ryan made his way there on foot. He reflexively took an alley connecting View Street and Main Street.

With its sweating brick walls and three out of its four lamps out of commission, the passageway could have been torn out of the pages of a Dickens novel. A dense fog completed the picture. Ryan had made it a third of the way down when he froze in place and started to tremble. *Jesus*, he thought, *what a perfect setting for another goddamned visit. Let's get the hell out of here.* He turned around and started to head back to View Street when a voice coming from that end of the alleyway smacked him in the face.

"Ryan! Ryan Brenan? Is that you?"

Ryan looked around and saw no one.

"Christ . . ."

He turned back toward Main Street and set off at a quickened pace.

"Hey, Ryan! Come on, man. Wait up!" The voice was clearly in the alley now.

Ryan came to a halt and turned, resolved to face the unheavenly music. And there it was. A dark figure hobbling in his direction. It wore a long, tattered overcoat; a sagging bucket hat; and a pair of stained canvas pants. With every other step, it leaned upon a gnarled hickory cane. It was outlined by the wane light coming from the alleyway entrance. Ryan began to tremble, largely out of fear but also out of anger. The bastards were getting entirely too brazen with their assaults on his psyche. *Son of a bitch.* He thought. *Maybe I'll just punch this prick in the fac*e. He clenched his fists and spread his stance.

The phantom came to a halt just out of Ryan's striking range. Breathing heavily, it rasped, wheezed, and sputtered. It tried to speak, but this set off a violent coughing fit that sent plumes of alcohol-laden spray Ryan's way. Finally, it brought up a thick wad of phlegm, which it dispatched to the alleyway wall. It then looked up at Ryan with jaundiced eyes and offered a nearly toothless grin.

"Whew, you really made me work there, Ryan," remarked the thing. "How are you, champ? Remember me?"

"Um . . ." choked out Ryan.

"I should think you would," it went on, its voice half growl and half gravel running over rotting wood. "Remember? I died on your table."

Ryan could only sputter in response, "Um . . . I'm sorry . . . I'm not sure. I—"

"What? People dying on you right there as you're slicing through their brain doesn't ring a bell? Come on, Ryan-boy, think. Barry Deele? I've been wanting to catch up with you for the longest time. I've got something for you." The specter rummaged through its pockets for something—a shiv, perhaps? "Something I've dreamed about giving you for years. Then I saw ya—right there, coming out of the hardware store—as big as day. But you scampered down this alley like a frightened jackrabbit!"

Ryan stood wordless for a few more moments, then the penny dropped. *Barry Deele . . . "the Big Deele." Of course.* Barry Deele had been a journeyman carpenter up in the Williamston region. He was known in the various drinking establishments of the area as the Big Deele for a comically oversized pelvic appendage, to which he put to good, or at least frequent, use. One day, he was discovered in the missionary position with the wife of a Baptist missionary. The good minister, speaking in tongues, was moved by a less-than-forgiving spirit to shoot Barry. The bullet hit him in the left temple and exited his right forehead. From there, it struck his lover in the low-left forehead, tumbling through her brainstem before coming to rest in the back of her head. She died instantly. Barry did all he could to follow suit.

Upon his arrival at Carriere, he was rushed to surgery where Ryan and a resident removed huge clots of blood from his frontal lobes, and then cleaned up the associated mess. But Barry wasn't the healthiest lothario in the area and had undiagnosed coronary artery disease. The blood loss and the autonomic outpouring of his violated brain stressed his heart into a bad rhythm from whence it decided to stop altogether, right in the middle of the operation. Thus, he was most accurate about his death upon the operating table. CPR was initiated and he was shocked multiple times. Eventually, his heart kicked back into gear. Ryan and his resident finished up the operation in a hurry but weren't expecting much out of their patient. To everyone's surprise, though, Barry survived and came out of coma. As he lacked insurance, it took four additional months to get him placed in a long-term care facility with rehabilitative capabilities, so he became a regular fixture on daily rounds.

"My gosh, Barry Deele," gasped Ryan, not sure whether the

Barry Deele before him was truly still among the living. "I do remember. I'm so sorry I didn't recognize you."

"Yep, it's me in the flesh," replied Barry. "I've probably changed a little since you last saw me, Ryan. I've been through some tough times since that Jesus-freak-fuck-up shot me." He then volunteered a summary of all that had transpired since he left Ryan's care. After his discharge from rehab, he ended up at a sister's house in Toledo. He stayed there until he was divested of all sisterly charity after having tried to introduce his sixteen-year-old niece to his singular attraction. He then led the life of an alcoholic vagabond, collecting drinks and change from anyone who would buy his story that he had sustained his head injury fighting in Afghanistan, or Iraq, or Kuwait, or some other "Middle Eastern shithole," as he put it.

"Well, my goodness, Mr. Deele. I'm so sorry it's been such rough sledding for you. But you look . . . good."

"Now, don't you bullshit me, Ryan-boy. I look like shit. I know. But I'm fucking alive and kicking, thanks to you. I've wanted to catch up with you for years, to thank you. To really thank you. Remember, I couldn't talk too good back when I left the hospital."

"No thanks needed, Mr. Deele. It's my honor. It's amazing to see you again—up and functioning so well."

"I'd be functioning much better if I laid off the booze and stopped chasing tail, I'm sure. It sometimes seems like I'm on a mission to fuck up all your good work. And it was good work, my friend, great work. Who gets shot in the head point-blank and lives to tell about it? Not my sweet little Frannie . . . or was it Annie? Well shit, doesn't matter, does it? I'm here because you saved me, and I'll never forget it. I tell everyone: 'If you're planning to get shot in the head, do it near the Carriere Clinic and ask for my main man, Ryan Brenan. He'll patch you up good!'"

"Well, thanks for the endorsement, Mr. Deele, but let's keep such stuff down to a minimum, eh?"

"You won't hear an argument from me, Ryan-boy! But listen, man; I meant it. I have something for you." Barry searched his pockets and pulled out a crusty, moth-eaten handkerchief. He opened it and revealed a bright, gleaming, silver cross. "Yeah, I got this at some holy-roller mission out in Gatlinburg. The priest, or minister, or whatever the fuck he was, gave me this and told me it would inspire me to do good works. I told myself it wouldn't do me no good, so why not give it to someone who truly does do good works? Someone who could probably use all the help he could get dealing with the likes of me."

"Oh, Mr. Deele, I can't take that from—"

"Not another word, Ryan," said Barry. "It's for you. It's always been for you. Use it to ward off evil spirits, keep the demons away . . ."

Ryan was concerned about the reality of this bizarre exchange, but the cross had weight and density as it dropped out of Barry's hand into his own, and the bear hug that ensued was of full weight, and density, and earthly stench.

"Well, thank you so much, Mr. Deele. I'm honored."

"No, *I'm* honored, Ryan, to have you as my brain-cutter. But don't let me hold you up any longer. You get home to your family. I'm headed for some Bingo at, of all places, the Baptist church!"

Barry hugged Ryan again. Upon release, Ryan pulled out his wallet and emptied it of two twenties and a five, offering the bills to Barry.

"I can't take that, Ryan."

"Of course you can, Mr. Deele. Go take Bingo by storm."

"Well, if you insist," grinned Barry, snatching the cash. He turned and limped back toward View Street.

Ryan watched Barry hobble out of the alley before turning toward Main Street, clutching his new silver cross in his right hand. His eyes fixed on another figure close to the alley's exit. In the hazy darkness, it could have been Barry's twin. Similar stature, similar posture, similar attire, but bearing a knitted skullcap rather than a bucket hat. As Ryan approached, the figure spoke.

"Got any for me, buddy?"

"Sheesh, I'm sorry," replied Ryan. "I just gave away my last bit of cash."

"You should be more parsimonious with your donations, Ryan. There are others of us around, you know. Others who weren't as lucky as Barry."

"I'm sorry, what? Do I know . . . I'm not quite sure . . ." stumbled Ryan.

"Yes, Barry's not the only one to get caught *in flagrante delicto*," laughed the figure. "And sometimes the husbands are armed with shotguns rather than .22s. You don't even try to fix some of us, do you, Ryan, old boy?"

The figure removed his hat, revealing a bloody mix of skull fragments, shredded scalp, and pulverized brain.

Ryan jumped back up against the alley wall, heart clawing at his ribs, silver cross spilling out onto the wet cobblestones below.

He blinked once, and the figure was gone.

CHAPTER 44

CONFESSION

A shaken Ryan retrieved his cross and stumbled his way to the bakery, finding some comfort in the large mural there depicting Jesus feeding the multitude. Why, he didn't know. On his way back to the jeep, he skirted the alleyway altogether, taking Market Street to get to View Street. He was soon home being celebrated by the girls for the fresh bear claws and cheese Danishes. Kelly held back, eyeing him suspiciously.

The ensuing couple of weeks were punctuated by busy call nights but, blessedly, no night terrors. So, it came as a shock on a Friday night in mid-December when a particularly dramatic one practically shook the house off its foundation. It took a good hour and a half to get everyone back to sleep. Everyone, except Ryan, who was too wound up. He couldn't shake an overwhelming sense of dread and foreboding, so he slipped downstairs and flipped on the TV. Finding nothing to hold his interest in the scores of available stations, he leafed through a couple of magazines left on the coffee table.

As he tried to read some football nonsense in a Sports Illustrated, he heard a squeak in the flooring overhead. Then pacing. Someone seemed to be moving between the bathroom, the guest room, and the sewing room. The footfalls were too heavy for the girls, who moved about the house with the silent grace of ballerinas. A sickening chill ran through him.

The woman. The dark lady.

He was certain it was her. And it made him shake with rage. He was damned if he would leave his family alone upstairs with that being, that creature, that thing. He crept up the back stairs, hands poised to grab the thing by the throat and strangle out of it any life it may or may not still possess. The stairway brought him up to the landing populated by Kelly's creepy Victorian dolls—both staring at him with menace. He eased past the gruesome pair and looked inside the sewing room. Nothing. He turned and peered down the short hallway leading to the girl's bathroom. And there she was.

Same out-of-focus, shimmering texture. Same black funeral attire. Same veiled face. Standing this close, Ryan could make out for certain that she was quite tall and slim. Were she alive, he thought, you might even describe her as being lithesome. But is it appropriate to use such a descriptor for someone who's dead? Ryan almost chuckled at the question. But as it crossed his mind, the specter took a couple of steps toward him, freezing him in his spot. She seemed oblivious to his presence, though, and turned to her left, down the long hallway and out of sight. As she made her way, her leather-soled shoes echoed back at him, mocking his immobility. He listened desperately, unable to move a finger. Then the footsteps paused, and a door moaned on its nineteenth-century hinges. He knew immediately which door it was—each one had its own distinctive cry.

"Christ, the girls!"

He shattered free of the icy grasp that held him, exploded down the hallway, and made the turn, feet digging at the floorboards like a cartoon character. He skidded to a halt at the doorway of the girls' room and spotted the specter. She was bent over his youngest daughter, Erin, stroking her hair. In a blind panic he ripped Barry Deele's cross from around his neck and threw it at her.

"Get the hell away from my girls!" erupted from his chest.

He ruptured into the room, screaming that he was going to rip the "fucking bitch" apart as he clawed at her departed flesh. But the dark lady dissolved into wisps of vapor that swirled upward, spread out over the ceiling, and dispersed into nothingness like smoke from a burning cigarette.

The girls awakened to see their screeching father madly tearing at empty air and burst into howls of terror. Ryan collapsed onto the bed with Erin, sobbing, and nearly suffocating her in a defensive embrace. Kelly was in the room in seconds, eyes wild with primal alert, the girls greeting her with frantic tales of a homicidal father.

"Ryan!" detonated from her mouth. "What the hell's going on?"

————

It took hours to settle the girls down. And vats of ice cream. And dozens of cartoons. Finally, they were asleep. Ryan and Kelly were too wired to even try, so they made their way to the kitchen and sat at the table. Ryan provided healthy pours of Irish whiskey for them both. There, Ryan felt the full weight of Kelly's cobalt-blue eyes upon his own.

"Okay, mister, out with it," ordered Kelly. "What the hell is going on? We're not leaving this table until I know *everything.*"

Ryan took in a deep breath. This was not the way he had planned to broach the subject. His discussion with Reverend Ron had injected enough doubt into his assessments that he wanted to do further research, eliminate further variables, collect more evidence before delivering his thesis. A presentation now would lack the necessary coherency and facts that would satisfy his brilliant, logical, and always skeptical spouse. Nonetheless, one look at her expression and he knew he had better come clean.

"Kelly ... I've been seeing ghosts."

"What?" Kelly's eyes appeared twice their size.

"I've been seeing ghosts. Lots of ghosts."

"Ghosts? What the heck do you mean 'ghosts?'" Kelly leaned forward and held Ryan in a steely gaze.

"I mean ghosts, Kelly. The undead, members of the spirit realm, the disembodied, the dearly departed, spirits, specters . . . ghosts," replied Ryan, trying to affect as sincere and as sane an expression as possible.

Kelly leaned further forward. "Ryan, do you mean you've been hallucinating? Are you worried you're having a nervous breakdown?"

"No, Kelly," replied Ryan, "I'm certain that what I've been seeing, experiencing, is real. I've researched them all, all the ghosts. Even the five kids killed by a lightning strike were real. Back in the 2000s, in New York State—"

"Ryan," erupted Kelly, popping up out of her chair and pacing back and forth. "You're not making any sense. I think you could be having a breakdown right now. You need help, honey. Real help."

"No, Kelly, listen. I know I sound crazy, but I'm not. My mind is functioning fine. But I'm seeing beings who are dead; people who are no longer with us, but somehow are; actual people who have walked the earth at some time but who are no longer alive. I've researched it all."

Kelly stopped pacing and stood with arms crossed over her chest. "Is this why you've been acting so strange, always on edge, jumping at every creak of the house—because you think you're seeing ghosts?"

"I guess, but—"

"And how long have you been seeing these . . . these ghosts?"

Ryan hesitated for a moment, then answered, "Since the little girl and the fire truck two Halloweens ago."

"What? Two Halloweens ago?" asked Kelly, now leaning over the table. "Ryan, honey, listen to me. I don't mean to be blunt, but you need get back to seeing your psychiatrist—right away—maybe even tonight. I think you're having a psychotic break."

"I've been seeing him pretty regularly, Kelly. I even saw him this week. He's not bad for a shrink. He knows about everything."

Kelly's brows furrowed.

"Look," continued Ryan, his speech becoming pressured. "I know it sounds ridiculous. But I've investigated it—extensively. I've found most of the ghosts in news accounts online. I mean, when they were people—living people. I made a spreadsheet of it. I can show you. I have no idea why they're appearing to me, but they are, and they're real. And they were real, real living beings. I don't know what it all means, but I've been researching every possible angle. I think I could be seeing the residue of people with ties to the area. I don't know. I need time, real time, to figure it out. But work's been so darned busy. I just need—"

"I'm sorry, Ryan," interrupted Kelly, dropping back in the chair opposite Ryan, "but what you need is medication. Maybe to be admitted for a while."

"Please, Kelly, listen—"

"And." Interrupted Kelly, "what you needed to have done was discuss this with your wife—right from the start."

"Kelly, I get it. But I wanted to have everything figured out before I discussed it with you. I'm closing in on it—I'm sure—but I'm not there yet."

"So, tonight you thought you saw a ghost in the girls' room," said Kelly, again popping out of her chair. "And that's why you went berserk."

"Exactly. One I've seen several times. A woman in funeral clothing." Ryan's eyes followed Kelly about the kitchen.

"Several times, huh? And are these . . . these apparitions getting more or less frequent?"

Ryan looked down at his lap. "I'm afraid, more."

"Christ, Ryan."

A red-faced Kelly took a deep cleansing breath, clearly trying to calm herself. She downed a shot of whiskey and poured herself another one. Then sat back down. "Well, then tell me about it. All of it. Everything. And please, start from the beginning."

Ryan nodded and proceeded to tell Kelly about all his otherworldly encounters and his efforts to understand them. Kelly listened intently, eyes fixed on Ryan's, periodically shaking her head, shivering all the time despite the warmth in the kitchen.

"Ryan, what does the psychiatrist think?" asked Kelly in a lull. "Surely, he's worried about your sanity?"

"That's just it, Kelly. He thinks I'm perfectly sane. So do Matt and Ron. They all—"

"Matt and Ron?" Kelly stood up and started pacing again. "Jesus, Ryan, Matt and Ron are drinking buddies. What exactly did the psychiatrist say?

"He believes I'm depressed and that I have some post-traumatic stress, but that I'm sane. He says that I fit no classic severe psychological disorder, that I passed every test he can give—"

"Except for seeing the undead," interrupted Kelly.

"Except for seeing the undead," repeated Ryan.

"Then he's an idiot," said Kelly, the rapidity of her pacing increasing.

"He's a decent guy, Kelly."

"Screw him."

"Look, Kelly—"

She came to a halt and leaned over the table. "Ryan, what about brain illnesses, tumors, infections? Shouldn't you get some scans, do some tests?"

"It's all been done. Our best neurologist has run MRIs, PET

scans, EEGs on me. Even did an LP—all normal," replied a nodding Ryan, as if the news would mollify his agitated spouse.

Kelly grabbed the table with both hands and stared into the backs of Ryan's eyes. "You told these supposed experts you were seeing ghosts and they didn't think to take you off duty, to admit you to the hospital, to do something?"

"They can't, Kelly. Not if there's isn't any evidence that I would be a threat to myself or my patients."

Kelly threw up her arms. "How about to your family?"

"Come on, Kelly, you know I'd never hurt you guys," pleaded Ryan.

"Oh bullshit, Ryan," exploded Kelly, smacking the table with an open hand. "You just scared the crap out of your girls. Do you honestly believe that won't leave a permanent scar in their psyches?"

This silenced Ryan. It was a direct hit, right to the midship. God, she was right. No matter how bad things might get with the undead, he had to a better job insulating his family from it all. He so often told the families of brain-tumor patients that it would be tragic if their loved one's disease claimed more than one victim, ruined the lives of other family members, but he was doing a miserable job applying the advice to his own situation.

"I promise you," offered Ryan, looking up at Kelly standing before him. "No matter what, that will never happen again. I swear on all that's sacred. I won't say another word, and I won't act out of the ordinary in any way. If I do, I'll be the first to have myself committed."

"I think you're being selfish, Ryan," responded Kelly, hands on hips. "Ridiculously selfish. I mean, what if you have an out-and-out breakdown in the middle of an operation or something? You could really hurt someone."

"I won't, Kelly. I haven't missed a beat at work. I'm okay. I'm not physically or even psychologically ill, according to the ex—"

"The goddamned experts have their heads up their asses, Ryan." Kelly plopped back down in her chair, arms crossed. "How the hell can they tell you there's nothing wrong with you? I want to talk to them myself. I want to speak with these supposed experts."

"We can arrange that," replied Ryan, holding out his hands in a calming gesture. "Just realize, everything's okay. Everything'll be okay."

"Oh?" started Kelly, piercing Ryan's reassurance with her gaze. "And what happens when your friends start visiting you in the hospital, in the middle of an operation?"

"They won't, Kelly. They never have. It's like they can't get in there."

"Because there's no death or tragedy going on behind those sacred walls?"

CHAPTER 45

WHO'S THE CRAZIEST OF THEM ALL?

After Ryan's startling revelation, Kelly went on the offensive. She demanded that he undergo extensive evaluation and treatment by "competent professionals," somewhere well away from the apparent lunacy of New Bethany, and exiled him to the guest room until he did. When he refused to take a leave of absence from work, she contacted several of her law school mentors to explore what legal recourse might exist to compel him to "do the right thing." But they had little to offer. They all noted that unless he demonstrated definitive professional dysfunction or went directly to the authorities and removed himself from practice, there wasn't much that could be done. Several were far more focused on protecting her assets than protecting Ryan's patients, and everyone recommended marriage counseling, which only served to infuriate her. Frustrated, she followed through on her vow to speak with his psychiatrist.

"Mrs. Brenan," started Larkin after some opening pleasantries on an oppressively gray late December afternoon. "This is highly irregular, but your husband insisted I speak with you, and he waved all rights to privacy."

"I'm sure it stretches your professional limits, Dr. Larkin," replied Kelly. "I greatly appreciate you doing this for me. But I'm at my wits' end. I need your insight and advice."

"I'll do what I can, but Ryan is still my patient. You and I both will have to respect that. Trust is so critical in my field," remarked a clearly hesitant Larkin.

"I understand. But anything you can share will be so very helpful," replied Kelly, who was working hard to hide the annoyance that was creeping into her chest. "So, what *can* you tell me, Dr. Larkin."

"Well, let's start with the fact that your husband is an extraordinarily bright man."

Kelly nodded with a look that said without words: *Well, of course he is. But that doesn't immunize him from mental illness, now, does it?*

"In fact, Mrs. Brenan," Larkin continued as he pressed his fingertips together and leaned back in his leather swivel chair, "in some areas of critical thinking, information analysis, and adaptive processing, he's simply off the charts. And that creates a bit of a challenge for a psychiatrist."

Kelly remained quiet, willing Larkin to get on with it.

"You see," Larkin continued, "he is so perceptive, and so many steps ahead in any conversation, that he could easily simulate normal cognitive, emotional, and psychological function, were he to so need."

"So, he's crazy—oh, excuse me, mentally ill—but he's faking sanity," said Kelly.

"No," replied Larkin, "I think he's quite sane and doesn't have to fake it. But were he to be suffering from severe mental illness, even psychosis, he's gifted enough to hide it, and hide it well."

"But surely he's fighting some mental illness, Dr. Larkin," pressed Kelly, inching forward in her chair.

Larkin smiled what was to Kelly a condescending smile, the smile of someone who believes he is the smartest person in the room. "I do believe he's constantly fighting a pretty severe situational depression, Mrs. Brenan. And he, of course, has his war experience ladled on top of that. But he exhibits no overt signs of profound mental illness or psychosis. He's fully functional in a most challenging profession. He's unequivocally known as the best neurosurgeon in the system, probably one of the best in the state, and he's maintained this level of performance all along. His judgment and cognition are spot on. He exhibits no impulsive behavior. His speech and thought processes are clear, goal-oriented, and precise. He's passed with flying colors every written battery I've thrown at him. There are absolutely no indicators for loss of reality testing. He experiences no delusions or hallucinations—other than, of course, the ghosts—"

Kelly broke in. "Other than the ghosts? Other than the ghosts? I would have to define that as some form of hallucination. I would have to say that's a pretty strong indicator of some loss of 'reality testing,' wouldn't you, Dr. Larkin?"

Larkin took off his glasses, cleaned them with a microfiber cloth from a drawer, put them back on, and then answered. "I'll be honest with you, Mrs. Brenan. I don't exactly know how to classify his experiences. Perhaps his hyper-processing mind is overinterpreting certain environmental cues—over-shooting on what's actually there. Goodness knows, he sees enough dead and near-dead people in his everyday dealings. Maybe that's carrying over to his experiences outside of the hospital. Maybe it's mixing with a twilight state of consciousness brought on by sleep deprivation. The man's a sleep disaster, isn't he? His neurologist is certainly quite worried about it. One way or the other, though, every other aspect of his cognitive and psychological function is perfect. If you take away the perception of apparitions from his interface with his environment, there's absolutely nothing else to suggest a loss of connection with reality."

"But that's a mighty big 'if,' isn't it?" retorted Kelly, fidgeting as she resisted the urge to launch herself from her chair. "And knowing he's been seeing things—things that you and I know darn well aren't there—isn't it your responsibility, your duty, to restrict him from working, to sign him off any patient care duties until things have been worked out, to put him on some sort of medication? Isn't there a huge risk of him having a full psychotic break and harming someone, or harming himself? Shouldn't you do *something*?"

"I'm afraid it's more complicated than that, Mrs. Brenan. Unless I deem him to be non compos mentis, or an imminent threat to himself or others—which in good faith, I cannot—I would have no grounds to do so, no medical or legal leg to stand on. And if I did take such an action, he could deny everything. And I guarantee a panel of the best psychiatrists in the world would find nothing wrong with him."

"So, we just have to sit around and wait for him to come off the rails?" asked Kelly, whose growing frustration was forcing tears to form in her eyes. "He did tell you how he scared the hell out of his daughters in the middle of the night a couple of weeks ago, didn't he?"

"He did, indeed. But honestly, I'm convinced he won't have a 'psychotic break,' Mrs. Brenan." Larkin again began cleaning his glasses. "And the fact that he's told you about his apparitions is a huge step in decompressing any negative psychological energy that he's been building up. Simply airing troublesome thoughts in a supportive environment helps dissipate them. I think releasing this phenomenon to you, to his friends, is extraordinarily healthy for him, and will accelerate the healing process—if there's indeed something to heal. In fact, he seems to already be responding. He told me he's had no further encounters since that night with your children."

"And you believe him?" countered Kelly, now at the very edge of her chair, both feet jiggling below her. "He's clearly lying. I can see it in his face after every one of his 'episodes,' now that I know what's going on. But wait a minute. You said, '*if* there's something to heal.' Surely, Dr. Larkin, there *is* something in there that needs healing. I mean, we can't just sweep under the rug the fact that he's been hallucinating for over a year, can we?"

"Think about this, Mrs. Brenan. Billions proclaim a definitive *knowledge* of the existence of a god. Many hold regular conversations with *their* specific god. Heck, many Christians believe they're literally ingesting the body and blood of Christ when they take the Eucharist. An argument could be made that this is all delusional behavior, even hallucinatory behavior. Yet no one is firing up the MRIs, EEGs, and psychiatric exams for any of these people. No one is putting them on Haldol or Fentazin. No one is serving up committal papers or banning them from doing their daily work. And half the people of England believe that they've experienced ghosts in one way or another, but they function pretty well as a society. So, I don't know for sure what Ryan's been experiencing, but I'm truly not concerned that he'll decompensate. He sees me with some regularity. He seems to be working through things quite well. If he stumbles, I'll be all over it."

Holy shit, thought Kelly. *This guy is just as crazy as Ryan—probably more.*

CHAPTER 46

ASININE

Despite Larkin's optimism, Ryan was having increasing difficulty "working through things." The interdimensional visits persisted, and his sleep deficit continued to accrue. His psyche began to twist and buckle. He contracted his world down to his professional duties and scattered minutes of strained interaction with his family. Even in the hospital, he found projecting his usual gregarious persona to be a challenge. He had become perpetually jittery and was suspicious of any stranger he encountered. He avoided sparsely populated areas of the medical center—particularly at night—but became nervous and agitated around crowds. In the OR, he would flinch every time someone new entered the room, and he would find himself studying them to make sure they were of living flesh and blood. Finally, on a fine Saturday morning in early January, a fissure ripped open in his finely honed professional mantle.

The meltdown revolved around the management of patient Andy Saunders. Mr. Saunders had presented to the medical center the previous evening after collapsing face-first into a plate of spaghetti. By the time he had made it to the hospital, he had come around but was found to have a shockingly elevated blood pressure. What was more, a CT scan demonstrated a sizable intraventricular hemorrhage, or IVH, a bleed into the sacs of fluid in the center of the brain.

"Anyway, Dr. Brenan, the guy's 100 percent intact," reported resident Lisa LeClair over the phone. "Neurology's gonna admit him. I think all he needs from our perspective is close follow in the ICU, major blood pressure control, ventric kit at the bedside, and a follow-up CT in the morning."

Ryan was hunkered down in the guest room of his house. "Anything else you want?" he challenged.

"I asked for a vascular study, but the ER team said the neurologists didn't want one. Why? Do you think we should insist?"

"Yeah, I would," replied Ryan, reviewing the CTs on his computer. "We need to rule out a vascular lesion."

"Gotcha. I'll go ahead and order a CTA." A CTA, short for CT Angiogram, is a radiological study of the brain's blood vessels.

The following morning, sitting at the nurses' station in the Cerebrovascular ICU, Ryan went over with his team the suffocating list of the forty-nine patients they had to see. When they got to Mr. Saunders, Ryan asked, "CTA show anything?"

"Well, Dr. Brenan," reported Lisa, shifting her gaze to the floor, "it never got done."

"What's up? Bad kidneys?" asked Ryan. He was referring to the fact that the IV dye required for a CTA could further damage the kidneys of someone who already had kidney disease.

"Um, no, sir. Dr. Woodfield canceled our orders for it."

"For what reason?" asked Ryan with a scowl.

"Well, he apparently was certain that the hemorrhage was caused by the guy's blood pressure and, with the blood pressure under control, required no further workup."

Ryan sat up in his chair. "No further workup?"

"You might want to read his note, Dr. Brenan. But I have to warn you, it's a bit inflammatory."

"Inflammatory?" said Ryan, one eyebrow raised.

"Here, sir. I pulled it up for you."

Ryan slid his chair over to the computer terminal and read the note out loud. "Assessment: This gentleman sustained an intraventricular hemorrhage. He is demonstrating no neurological sequela, and there is no associated ventricular dilation. Treatment is supportive unless he develops hydrocephalus. Blood pressure must remain strictly controlled. The hemorrhage was unequivocally secondary to an acute exacerbation of poorly controlled chronic hypertension. This is a classic case. Further evaluation of the brain parenchyma, or its vasculature, would be asinine; and would be yet another example of our current culture of undisciplined medical prodigality. Randall H. Woodfield, MD, PhD, FAAN. Professor of Neurology."

"'Undisciplined medical prodigality?'" questioned Ryan.

"I had to look it up," replied Lisa. "It means 'wasteful extravagance.'"

"I know what it means, but what the . . . ? Did you talk to him about this?" asked a scarlet-faced Ryan.

"Yes, sir, and I told him *you* specifically requested the study. He responded by lecturing me on the cost of healthcare, how it's driven in no small part by unnecessary testing, and how neurosurgeons are the worst offenders. Then he hung up on me."

Ryan stared at the screen. "What the f—" He caught himself and tried to remain calm. He almost succeeded. But just as he was about to take an all-forgiving cleansing breath, Woodfield paraded into the unit with a trailing entourage of PAs, residents, and medical students. Before Ryan knew what he was doing, he had pulled Woodfield into a charting area behind the nurses' station.

"Randy, why the hell did you cancel my CTA orders on the intraventricular hemorrhage guy?" Ryan blurted with pressured speech.

"Did you read my note, Dr. Brenan? I think I made myself abundantly clear on the matter," replied a defiant Woodfield, rolling his eyes for the sake of his audience.

"Note or no note, where the hell do you come off canceling my orders?"

"Well, he is *my* patient, Dr. Brenan," replied Woodfield, eyes fixed on the ceiling.

"I don't give a damn if he's a patient of the King of England, you don't go canceling a colleague's orders without discussing it with him or her. And you certainly don't write in the chart that the orders are 'asinine.'"

"If an order is such, Dr. Brenan, I have no problem identifying it as so. I do believe in practicing at least a modicum of fiscal responsibility. It's just too—"

"Listen here, you little gnome," interrupted Ryan, a finger in Woodfield's face. "You have to know a little something about a disease before you can address it with a 'modicum of fiscal responsibility.' The guy needs a goddamned vascular study."

"Well, I certainly know that in a classic hypertensive intraventricular hemorrhage, the chances of finding a causative vascular lesion is less than 1 percent. You should know that too, Dr. Brenan," said a now perspiring Woodfield.

"Jesus, Randy, you've got to start getting your medical edification out of something other than the *National Enquirer*— that's utter bullshit. This guy could easily have an AVM. We'd be nuts not to pursue it."

"Perhaps, Dr. Brenan, you should leave the diagnostics up to a cognitive specialty—" started Woodfield, referring to a notion that was particularly irksome to Ryan: that certain medical specialties were "thinking" or "cognitive" in nature, and that others—those that were procedure-based, like neurosurgery—were purely technical in nature, involving no real thinking, just some practice at "tinkering under the hood."

"Christ, Randy, don't give me that 'cognitive' bullshit. I'll tell you what, you come down to the OR when we deal with this guy's AVM and tell me it takes less thought, less 'cognitive effort,' than sitting around on your fat ass, mentally masturbating over some patient with the 'weak and dizzies.' The point is, you don't go around canceling your colleagues' goddamned orders."

"The patient's evaluation is 100 percent my prerogative, Dr. Brenan. I would be delighted to have the Medical Executive Committee clarify this for you."

"Listen here, you pompous ass. I don't give a crap what the MEC has to say about it. Here's what's going to happen: I'm going to reorder the CTA, and if you cancel it, I'm coming after you." Ryan leaned into Woodfield's face, Woodfield giving up a good six inches to Ryan.

"Are you physically threatening me, Dr. Brenan? May I remind you, I have a host of witnesses," said Woodfield, gesturing toward his entourage, precipitating in them reflexive flinches as if he were spraying them with acid.

"No, Randy. But you can consider it a professional warning—"

"Oh, there will be professional ramifications for this encounter, Dr. Brenan. I can assure you. Good day, sir!" Woodfield turned on his heel and scurried out of the unit.

The following Friday, Ryan found himself in the Chief Medical Officer's office, engaged in a heated discussion with CMO, Patricia Ingles, and Department of Neurosurgery Chairman, Aaron McNeal. He had remained standing at attention throughout the exchange.

"For God's sake, Ryan. Sit down, will you? You're making me nervous," said a red-faced Ingles with a gesture to a nearby chair.

"Thank you, but I'd prefer to stand."

"You do realize, if Woodfield's complaint were to reach the MEC, it could get you canned, don't you?" continued Ingles. "I mean, you went off on him in front of the whole damned ICU."

"He's lucky I didn't deck him in front of the whole ICU," replied Ryan.

"Good god, Ryan, would you listen to yourself? This isn't you. What the heck is going on?" remarked McNeal.

"You did happen to read the little prick's note, didn't you?" asked Ryan, teeth gritted, fist clenched.

"We did, but—" started McNeal.

"And you saw that the patient *did* in fact have an AVM, and that we *did* successfully remove it yesterday?"

"We did," replied Ingles with an angry nod. "And that's what's saving your ass right now. Woodfield is hardly going to follow up on this with egg all over his face. But what if you were wrong? What if the bleed was just secondary to his high blood pressure? Where would that have left you?"

"It would have left me still doing the right thing, and that public nuisance still being 1,000 percent wrong. He's the one that needs to be called to the carpet. Christ, the goddamned guy needs to lose his license."

"The point is, Ryan, we can't have our physicians threatening physical harm to one another," responded Ingles.

"I never threatened physical harm, although I wish I had."

"Ryan," said a standing McNeal, putting a hand on Ryan's rigid shoulder. "This isn't you, buddy. I've never seen you like this. What's going on? Are there problems on the home front? Is that why Kelly set up an appointment with me?"

"She what?" snapped Ryan, eyes widened.

"She asked to see me last week, but then canceled a couple of days later," reported McNeal.

"Jeez, I don't know. Maybe it had something to do with a departmental party, or something," replied Ryan, seething even more with the news.

"The point is, buddy," said McNeal. "You haven't been yourself lately. Frankly, you haven't seemed yourself for months."

"Oh, so my output has tailed off, has it? My outcomes have tanked? My complication rates have skyrocketed?"

"Come on, Ryan. You know that's not the case. We just—" started McNeal.

"Look, Ryan," interrupted Ingles from behind her imposing mahogany desk. "We know how productive you are. But there is such a thing as being over-productive. It can burn out the best. We think you've earned yourself some rest. You didn't even take any time off over the holidays."

"Yeah, well, it wasn't my turn."

"Be that as it may, we think you need a break," continued Ingles. "What about taking a few weeks off . . . starting Monday? Maybe see Ron Anderson for a session or two—"

"Good God, so now I'm a 'disruptive physician?' I need a time-out?" barked Ryan, who had spread his stance.

Ingles held out her hands in a calming gesture. "We didn't say that. We're just thinking you're due a break."

"Okay, sure. I'll get on the horn right now and cancel, what— thirty, forty operations?" said Ryan with a sneer. "Oh, and who shall I have look after the kids—you, Aaron? You do know Leslie and Jim are both off next week?"

"Come on, Ryan. We're worried about you. We only want the best for you," reassured McNeal.

"Tell you what. If you want the best for me, fire incompetent boobs like Woodfield. I'd have to spend far less time cleaning up messes around here."

"Actually," started McNeal, clearing his throat and shifting his feet, "we need you to *apologize* to Woodfield . . . to help make this all blow away."

"You're kidding, right?" replied Ryan, face turning a new shade of crimson. "The guy's a goddamned menace. He needs to be—"

"That's enough, Ryan," said Ingles, pounding her desk and rising from her chair. "You *will* take a few weeks off, and you *will* apologize to Dr. Woodfield or—"

"Or what? Last I checked, I'm no longer in the Army. You want to fire me, go ahead. But don't think you're going to give me orders. You both know I was in the goddamned right on this. I'm sorry I lost my temper with the little prick around a bunch of impressionable youngsters. But it wouldn't happen if we didn't hang on to dead wood like him."

McNeal clasped Ryan on the shoulder and maneuvered him toward the door. "Come on, Ryan. Let's go get a cup of coffee." He turned back to Ingles, who looked like she might detonate. "You heard him, Patricia. A heartfelt apology. Case closed."

CHAPTER 47

LOVER'S LEAP

Kelly's heart almost stopped when Ryan reported to her what had transpired in the CMO's office. It was, perhaps, the first time in their marriage that he had disclosed such detailed information about an incident at work. She realized it was more to warn her that he could end up getting fired than to actually share anything from behind the iron curtain, but it was shocking nonetheless.

"Jesus, Ryan."

"Yeah, I know. But screw them. And screw Carriere if they're going to kowtow to the Woodfields of the world and fire people like me."

"Oh, they'll never fire you," noted Kelly with a steely calmness. "I know organizations like Carriere all too well. They're fully aware of what side their bread is buttered. You're one of their lead cash cows. You would need to have sliced Woodfield's throat for them to truly consider getting rid of you; and even then, they'd think twice about it. That's why Aaron went for coffee with you afterward. To put a punctuation on the matter. They just wanted to rein you in a little. Keep you within the navigational beacons."

"I don't know. I was pretty rough on old Patricia," remarked Ryan, shaking his head slowly.

"Nothing she can't handle, I'm sure. I guarantee, you're probably one of the least disruptive, disruptive physicians she's got over there. They know what a good Boy Scout you are."

Ryan smiled at this and looked Kelly directly in the eye.

Odd, she thought, just that brief flash of connection felt so electric, so . . . energizing. But it didn't last. It couldn't have been fifteen minutes later when Ryan's phone went off. His face, which had softened in their conversation, went rigid. After a terse exchange with whoever was on the other end—something about a vomiting kid—he put the phone in his pocket, stood up, and moved toward the door.

"I'm going back in," he said, pulling on a winter coat.

"But you're not on call."

"Christ, Kelly," snapped Ryan. "Since when do I have to be *on call*?" And he was off with a spray of gravel. When he returned hours later, he headed for the couch without a word.

The following morning, Ryan disappeared into the hospital, offering no estimation of when he might return. The family, however, was slated to go to the Stravinsky Concert Hall of Salisbury University for a regional youth dance competition in the early afternoon. Riley had been preparing for the event for months. Two hours before curtain time, Ryan had yet to return. Kelly was livid. It was a Saturday, for goodness sake. As time accelerated, Riley had become apoplectic, incessantly pestering Kelly to get going—Dad or no Dad. Kelly held out until the last second and then relented. She ushered the girls into the van and was just pulling out of the driveway when Ryan skidded in. He ditched the jeep and hopped into the front passenger seat of the van. He was not an especially welcome guest.

The van crossed the bridge and made its way through town in complete silence. Soon it was shooting out of the New Bethany environs, entering an area where the Laurel Ridge abruptly dove down to the edge of the highway in the form of steep cliffs.

The surrounding countryside was blanketed by a few inches of wet snow that had dropped the previous night, but the road was clear, save for a quarter inch of soggy brown salt. Agitated, Kelly accelerated to fifteen miles over the speed limit as Ryan stared blankly out of the passenger-side window.

Suddenly, he blurted out, "Jesus! Kelly, stop the car! *Stop the car!*"

"What the . . . why, Ryan?" responded Kelly, taking her foot off the gas.

"Stop the car, goddamn it! I saw something . . . back at Lover's Leap!"

"Okay, okay. What do you mean you saw some—?" pressed Kelly as she pulled to the side of the road. But Ryan was out of the van and plunging into the adjacent woods before she could bring the vehicle to a full halt. *My God, is this it,* she thought. Was this really happening? Was he having a psychotic break right there, right then—in front of the girls?

Lover's Leap was a geographic site along Laurel Ridge where the south-facing cliffs folded inward to a steep, creek-based ravine. Legend had it that back in the region's prehistory, a pair of Native American lovers from rival tribes had thrown themselves, hand in hand, into the ravine rather than endure forced separation. The Brenans had hiked to the location several times, and Ryan looked for it each time he passed by in the car. What he could have possibly seen to precipitate such a reaction in the millisecond the site flashed across his eyes, Kelly couldn't imagine. It had to be one of his apparitions. And he had reacted to it like a lunatic, probably again permanently traumatizing the girls. Goddamn it. This was exactly what she predicted would happen. Lucky it wasn't in the operating room, but what damage would it do to the girls to see their father come completely off the rails? Nonetheless, she felt compelled to follow, if only to make sure he didn't harm himself.

She jumped out of the van and started to give chase, then stopped short. The girls. She couldn't leave them there by the side of the road. She let them out of the van and had them follow her as she picked her way through the clawing underbrush. Ryan was easy to track. His shoes left prints in the soggy snow, pointing straight in the direction of Lover's Leap. Soon they were accompanied by scattered drops of blood. He must have cut himself crashing through the brush.

"Kelly! Kelly!" The voice came from just a few dozen yards ahead. "Kelly, I need my phone!"

Kelly hesitated for a moment. If Ryan was truly having a psychotic break, she didn't want the girls to witness it. Yet she couldn't ignore his pleading cries. She pressed on. A minute later, she broke through into a clearing at the foot of the cliffs and froze. The three girls, in near pursuit, followed, and upon witnessing the scene, accelerated toward their mother like startled ducklings. Ryan was kneeling in a stream by a crumpled body. It was a woman. Her right leg was contorted in an impossible position. She appeared to be young, probably in her teens. She was dressed in jeans and a yellow long-sleeved T-shirt. Both were torn and bloodied, as was her underlying skin. Her hair was long and scarlet blonde, the scarlet a new addition thanks to a serpentine laceration in the back of her head.

"Jesus, Kelly, don't let the girls come over here! Girls, back up, don't come near. Kelly, move them back!"

"What is it, Daddy?"

"Is it a girl?"

"What happened to her?"

"Did she fall?"

"Is that blood?"

"Is she dead?"

Kelly immediately processed the situation and shielded the

girls, moving them ten yards back into the woods. She made them all promise to stay there until told otherwise. Then she ran back to Ryan and the injured woman. Ryan jumped her before she could utter a syllable.

"Kelly, do you have your phone? Mine's in the car. She needs help right away."

Kelly felt her back pocket. With great relief, she sensed the slick presence of a late model Apple. She handed it to Ryan. He dialed in to the emergency room with bleeding fingers. Help would soon be on its way.

"What should we do for her until they get here?" asked Kelly.

"We can't move her. She could have all sorts of spinal injuries," replied Ryan. "At least for now, she's breathing and has an open airway. But she's going to get hypothermia for sure." He took off his coat and shirt, and covered her as best he could. He bolted into the woods, yelling over his shoulder, "I'll be right back." He returned within minutes, now bleeding from several slashes across his face, arms, and chest, carrying an old army blanket. He covered the shredded, distorted body and kneeled to again assess her pulse.

"Christ."

"Is she . . . dead?" asked Kelly, hand to mouth.

"No . . . not yet," replied Ryan. He looked at the girl for a few moments, then turned back to Kelly from his crouched position. "I'm sorry, honey. It was just a flash between the trees. I didn't know if it was real or . . ."

"A ghost?" slipped free from Kelly's lips.

Ryan ignored the comment.

"Why don't you get the girls back to the car? I don't want them exposed to this anymore than they've been. It'll be a circus here pretty soon," said Ryan as distant sirens grew louder.

And, soon, it was a circus. Being so close to the medical

center and town, three ambulance teams arrived on the scene simultaneously, as well as several fire trucks and four police cruisers. Within half an hour, the woman was extracted from the woods and was on her way to the Carriere trauma bays. Once the dust had settled, Ryan returned to the van. He was shirtless, filthy, and covered in blood—his own, and that of the fallen woman. The girls looked at him wide-eyed. Kelly thought he resembled some crazed psychopath from the West Virginia mountains. The stuff of one of his teenage cabin-in-the-Appalachian-woods slasher movies. She started up the van and turned the wheels eastward.

"Kelly, what about the competition?" asked Ryan.

"Oh, Ryan, we're way too late. And I doubt you want to go in looking like that."

"I can wait in the car . . ."

"I think after that, no one's heart is really going to be in it. Let's just go home and get calmed down and cleaned up."

"Oh jeez," sighed Ryan. He turned toward the back of the van and addressed Riley. "Riley, sweet pea, I'm so sorry to make you miss your competition. But I don't know what else we could have done. We had to help that poor girl. Maybe after we get all cleaned up, we can make some hot chocolate and play some Clue."

Ryan was clearly trying his best to affect a happy-go-lucky fun-daddy persona in the offer, but it came out of a wide-eyed face smeared with mud, perspiration, and blood.

CHAPTER 48

PROOF

When they arrived home, Kelly found herself softening again about her exasperating husband. He certainly played the hero well, and endearingly. And for one evening of playing board games with the girls in front of a blazing fire on a frigid winter's evening, he also played the part of a loving family man well. But he was gone physically when the family awoke the next morning, and mentally when he returned home in the late afternoon. The tension in the household rapidly returned to its new set point. So, Kelly was all too happy to see Monday arrive with its initiation of a new work week. Ryan had vanished into his alternate universe, and she and the girls could resume their calmer, less complicated existence as a single-parent family. The tranquility was abruptly upended, however, the following Wednesday evening.

"Mom, Mom, look at this, look at this!" came a squealing refrain from the three Brenan girls as they barreled down the stairs. Their voices and faces bore a mixture of excitement, thrill, and delighted terror. Ava, the eldest, was clutching an open laptop computer. The others were pointing feverishly to an image frozen upon it.

"What's going on, girls? What's this all about?" asked Kelly, only to be buffeted by a cacophony of competitive narratives. "Girls, girls, please, one at a time. I can't make any sense of what you're trying to tell me," responded Kelly, as she sought to pacify the quivering tower of babel before her.

"It's a ghost, Mom, a real ghost!" came a more unified response.

"See, Mom, Dad *did* see a ghost in our room that night!" blurted Ava.

"I'm scared, Mom," said Erin. "I don't want to live in this spooky old house anymore."

"Yeah, Mom, I want to move back to Washington. There weren't any ghosts there," said Ava.

"Yeah, Mom, can we move back to Washington? This whole town is haunted," added Riley.

The commentary was now coming in from every direction, at every pitch in the soprano range. Kelly had caught the gist of things, but was still in the dark about what had set off this mass panic. One thing was certain, though: Ryan was at its epicenter. He must have told the girls about his goddamned ghosts. Now she had a full-blown, five-alarm crisis on her hands. *Christ, Ryan, don't you have more sense than that?*

"Girls, girls, calm down, please," responded Kelly. "This house isn't haunted. It's a lovely old house. There's no ghosts here, or anywhere."

"But it *is* haunted!" came a three-part inharmonious reply. "Dad said so, and he's right!"

"Girls, what exactly did your father tell you?" asked Kelly, her cheeks flushing, her body tensing.

"He didn't tell us anything," replied Ava. "We heard him telling *you!* He told *you* he had been seeing ghosts, and *you* told him he was crazy."

"What? Wait a minute. When do you *think* you heard all that?"

"The night Dad came screaming into our room," answered Ava, blushing.

"Ava, what makes you think you heard us talking about ghosts?"

"Well, we were kind of spying on you," Ava admitted, looking down and shuffling her feet.

"Spying? How?"

"There's a grate over the fridge. It's connected to a grate in our closet. We can hear people talking in the kitchen if we uncover it," answered Ava.

Crap, thought Kelly, as she recalled the grates between some of the downstairs and upstairs rooms. They were used to spread warmth throughout the house before the advent of central heating. But they were now considered a fire hazard and were supposed to be sealed off. It was one of a million home-improvement projects she had yet to address. Currently, they had only unsecured sheets of linoleum over them, and apparently, they served as parenteral monitoring stations for the girls.

"Please don't be mad at us," pleaded Riley. "We were worried you were going to really yell at Dad after he scared us so badly."

"I'm not mad at you guys." And she wasn't. She was plenty mad at Ryan, but not at the girls. At least Ryan hadn't intentionally dropped all his ghostly craziness on them. But he was still responsible for the mess. She wasn't sure she could spin things in a way that would bring the girls' careening imaginations under some semblance of control. And she had yet to ascertain what had set off this current supernatural feeding frenzy. She tried to affect a calming posture and tone. "Okay, then tell me—and I mean only Ava for right now—what's with the laptop?"

"Well, we knew you didn't believe Dad about the lady ghost in the house," replied Ava. "So, we wanted to see if we could prove he was right. We found our old baby monitor up in the attic last week—the one with a camera—and set it up at the end of the long hallway. We connected it to Dad's old laptop and recorded from it each night. We didn't see any ghosts the first few nights, but last night we caught her! The lady ghost!"

Agitated chatter erupted. It took Kelly another fifteen minutes to settle things down.

"Okay," said Kelly. "Show me your ghost."

Ava set up the recording, and Kelly watched intently despite the barrage of excited jabber and the dozens of little index fingers pointing out the supposed phantasm on the screen. Kelly replayed the sequence over and over again. *Jesus,* she thought. *What the hell is that?* It definitely looked like a female form walking—no, floating—down the hallway. And it seemed to pause at the girls' room before disappearing. She studied the green monochromatic video closer. It was terribly grainy. Then with a great sigh of relief, she admonished herself: *Shoot, Kelly, you dope, you almost fell for it.* She was almost a victim of the power of suggestion. God, how easy it was to fool herself amid all this hysteria. She turned to her three vibrating daughters. "Girls, this isn't a ghost."

"But Mom . . ."

"Girls, girls, shush for a few minutes. Look and listen. Last night, a warm rain moved in over the cold snow and there was a thick fog, remember? You couldn't see the hand in front of your face. Even inside the house was kind of foggy, wasn't it? So, I'm sure what happened was a car over at the Sorgens' house was pulling out of the driveway and its lights cast shadows through the foggy air and into the hallway. As the car moved, the shadows moved down the hallway. If you look closely, it simply looks like light and shadows, doesn't it?"

The girls weren't so convinced.

"It sure looks like a lady to me."

"In a black dress."

"And she stops right at our door."

Crap, thought Kelly. This was going to be a real problem. She considered having Ryan speak to the girls when he got home. Explain to them that the house was in no way haunted, and that there were no such things as ghosts. But he would likely balk at the idea and counter that there *were* such things as ghosts, and that he had seen some—some in the very house he was supposed to claim wasn't haunted. She could hear his maddening reply already. And to make matters worse, he would insist on seeing the video. And all that would do is convince him further that his hallucinations were, in fact, actual entities. Paranormal entities. Ghosts. He would be insufferable. No, she would have to deal with this new wrinkle herself, as she did everything in the house. She cleared her throat.

"Listen, girls, you're going need to have faith that I would never mislead you. This is *not* a ghost, it's just an optical illusion, a trick of scattered light in the fog. I need you to be brave about this, especially for your dad. I don't want you discussing it with him or showing him the video. He's under enough stress right now. We don't need to add to it. It's important that we all remind ourselves that there are no such things as ghosts, and there are no ghosts here, or anywhere. We as a family have to be smart and rational, and forget all this ghost stuff, and have a nice, normal, happy life in this nice, normal, happy house, okay?"

The girls all nodded in skeptical acquiescence.

CHAPTER 49

REALLY?

As Kelly faced the girls' barrage, Ryan pulled into the driveway. He could see through the kitchen window the girls surrounding Kelly, frantically pointing at a computer. He was about to step inside and see what all the excitement was about when his phone went off.

"Hey, sir." It was Cam Carlson. "Sorry to bug you again so soon, but you're not going to believe this one."

"Oh? Do tell," replied Ryan.

"Remember Timmy Perdue—the motorhead we had to do a front-back on?"

"Sure. Didn't we just discharge him today?"

"Roger that. Well, he's back."

"Shoot, what is it? Wound problem? Pneumonia? Something else?"

"More like 'something else,'" replied Cam. "The dumbass rolled over another car and has ripped our repair to shreds. Fractured more vertebrae. Lots of spinal cord compression. Weak, but not fully paralyzed. Probably should go right away."

"For Christ's sake," replied Ryan, turning the key to restart the jeep. "Okay, Cam, I'll be right in."

Timothy Perdue was a forty-four-year-old man still working his way through adolescence. A major NASCAR fan, he made a hobby of stealing cars for their parts and using said booty to soup up his own impressive collection of muscle cars. One week prior to his current admission, he had been rocketing through the streets of Bloomsbury at 2:00 a.m. with no seatbelt on when he caught a curb, flipping his Camaro ZL1. He ended up slamming into a statue of Ronald McDonald outside of the eponymous restaurant. He escaped serious head injury, but shattered three successive vertebrae in his neck. He was all but completely paralyzed. Ryan and Cam removed the three destroyed blocks of bone from the front of Mr. Perdue's neck and replaced them with a cylindrical titanium cage. They positioned a titanium plate over this and secured it to the surrounding vertebrae with screws. They then turned him onto his belly and drove two parallel rows of screws into five successive vertebrae. Then they bolted the screws onto two parallel titanium rods that ran the length of the repair, and placed Perdue into a hard, plastic brace extending from his chin to his lower chest.

To everyone's delight, the guy made a full neurological recovery. He was up and walking two days after surgery. He had to remain in the hospital for several more days due to assorted other injuries, during which time he pestered Ryan about when he could drive again. Ryan repeatedly explained that it would be months and, upon returning to driving, Mr. Perdue would have to be far more judicious than he had been in the past—another high-speed accident would be devastating to his reconstructed neck.

On the evening of his release, however, fueled by beer, Jägermeister, and cocaine, Mr. Perdue took to the streets in a recently stolen Mustang GT. In West Salem, a police car gave chase. There, Perdue ran a red light only to encounter a semi bearing down on him from his right. He pulled the wheel hard, but the truck clipped the Mustang's rear end. It flipped multiple times, coming to rest in the dining area of another McDonald's. Perdue had again forgone the use of seatbelts and was thrown into the drinks and condiments counter. The force of the impact had ripped out the grand majority of his surgical screws, popped out his bone-filled titanium cage, and broke two more vertebrae. His neck took on the conformity of a demented snake.

As Ryan entered the ER, he was hit by an overwhelming sense of angry futility, and it surged to the surface when he laid eyes on Perdue.

"Mr. Perdue, what the hell happened?" barked Ryan.

"Yeah, Doc, who would've guessed I'd get into another accident so soon?" replied Perdue, lying flat on a stretcher.

"Well, frankly," growled a red-faced Ryan, "I would. How many times did we go over the fact that you weren't allowed to drive until you were out of your brace?"

"I know, I know, Doc. It was dumb of me, I know."

"More than dumb, Mr. Perdue. It was idiotic, criminally idiotic. And pathetic. I can't think of anything more *stupid* that you could've done."

"I get it, Doc. I'm sorry for fucking up all your good work."

"Hey—I'm not the one lying there in pieces. For Christ's sake, what were you thinking? The spinal cord doesn't have nine lives, you know. You were given one miracle already, a miracle most people are never granted."

"I know, I know. I'm so sorry."

"Sorry? To whom? I don't give a damn. It's just work to me. What if you'd hit another car, though, and killed some kids? How sorry would've you been then? Or would you be sorry at all?"

"Yeah, no, I do get it, Doc," replied Perdue. "Thank God it's only me who got fucked up."

"Yeah, thank God. All it means is dragging my team and me out of bed to put you back together again. Christ."

"I do appreciate it. Really."

"Yeah, well that's something, I guess," replied Ryan as he started to put orders into a computer.

"You know, Doc, I wasn't always a shithead," said Perdue.

"Huh?" replied Ryan, still focused on the computer screen.

"Yeah, way back when, I was gonna be you."

"Excuse me?" Ryan looked over at Perdue.

"Yep. I was gonna be a doc, just like you. Maybe a bone doc. I was an honor student and all that. Then I blew out my knee in football, and found I liked the narcs too much. Drugs and cars, they somehow gave me the thrill I used to get from hitting people. And, well, here I am today. But I was a good guy once—like you—not just another fucking dirtball."

Perdue broke down crying. Ryan watched, red-faced and hands clenched. But soon his shoulders sagged, his fingers loosened, and tears filled his eyes.

"Hey, Mr. Perdue. I'm the one who should be sorry," offered Ryan in a hushed tone. "I shouldn't have spoken to you like that. You don't deserve it."

"Oh yes, I do,' replied a sobbing Perdue. "I'm such a piece of shit. I know it. Seems like all I know how to do is fuck things up for everyone around me. Drove my wife and kids away. And any real friends I had. I deserve any shit I bring on myself."

"No, Mr. Perdue, no one deserves this," said Ryan, putting his hand on Perdue's shoulder. "But look, buddy, your neck is pretty messed up. We need to go to surgery right away. We'll do everything we can to get you in working order. But we're gonna need to find a way to get you to stop taking such terrible risks—it'll kill you some day."

"Thanks, Doc. I'm sorry you have to deal with dirtballs like me. It must suck the life right out of you."

"Hey, Mr. Perdue, it's my honor to take care of you. I'm the dirtball here. I should have never spoken to you the way I did.

I don't know what came over me. I guess . . . I guess I was just frustrated. You were doing *so* well. It freaked me out to see you back here. I'm so sorry to be so hard on you."

"Hey, I get it," replied Perdue. "Shit, if getting all irate at one of us pieces of shit is your worst crime, you got nothing to worry about."

Ryan left the room, choking back tears. He skirted Cam, who was out at the computers documenting another consult, and walked out into the frigid night air. He needed to breathe. He wasn't sure he could. *What the hell was that all about, Ryan,* he admonished himself. Yelling at a patient—a badly injured patient? He'd never done anything like that before. What was his problem? Where was his humanity? He began to shake and cry. "Oh God, what's happening to me?"

CHAPTER 50

TEENAGE DREAMS

When Ryan finally got home that night, he passed Kelly in the family room and strode wordlessly for the guest room. The pattern had taken full root. He would arrive home in darkness, usually after the girls had gone to bed, and either collapse onto the couch or go straight up to the guest room. He would make no attempt to interact with Kelly. He wouldn't eat. He wouldn't even have a drink. In fact, in a fit of temperance he had cleaned out the house of all alcohol, thinking that it might improve his perpetually sour mood. In the mornings, well before sunrise, and well before anyone else was up, he would leave for the hospital. His world was thrown entirely into darkness, both literally and figuratively, the only light appearing in the operating room. There, he still felt in control, still appreciated, still alive.

———

"You've gotta be kidding me," Ryan called out to the OR squawk box, the Friday morning of another weekend of call, some day—he couldn't remember which one—in early February. He and resident Eric Edmundson were working under a microscope on the exposed spinal cord of fifteen-year-old Jessi Faust.

"No, it's got everything, Ryan," came a disembodied voice through a haze of static, "areas of necrosis, pseudopalisading, hypertrophic vessels, severe anaplasia." The pathologist was describing the appearance of the tumor tissue under a microscope.

"Shoot. Thanks, Jon," replied Ryan.

"Well, that sucks," remarked Eric.

"Sure does," replied Ryan. "Hey, Eric . . . do me a favor and go take a look. Let's make sure we agree."

"Will do, sir. But you're not gonna take the whole thing out while I'm gone, are you?"

"Would I do that to you, Eric?" answered Ryan, without looking up.

"Yes, you would, sir. I've seen how fast you go when we're not around."

"Well, I guess you'd better not stop for coffee and doughnuts along the way, then."

Eric scrubbed out of the case and hurried out of the room. Ryan addressed a group of nursing students while he continued to work under the microscope.

"Well, guys, that was bad news, really bad news. As you can see, we've opened this young woman's spine and have been working on a tumor in the substance of her spinal cord. Tumors here aren't usually super nasty—if you can get them out without paralyzing the patient. But the pathologist sounds convinced that this tumor's a glioblastoma, or GBM. That's a highly malignant tumor, far more commonly found in the brains of adults. For all intents and purposes, it's a death sentence for this sweet girl."

Ryan continued to work, removing sizable portions of the tumor from the depths of Jessi's spinal cord. He had the grand majority of it out by the time Eric reentered the room, all scrubbed up and ready to re-gown.

"Well, Eric?" asked Ryan, continuing to work.

"I don't think there's any question, Dr. Brenan. Sure looks like a GBM."

"Crap."

"I know, sir," said Eric as he took over the position of the principal operator. "Good god, Dr. Brenan, you really went to town on the tumor. It's almost all out. I was only gone for fifteen minutes."

"Nah, plenty left for you to do."

Eric worked for another hour and a half removing the remainder of the visible tumor. Soon he was bandaging the wound as Ryan headed to the waiting rooms to break the grim news to Jessi's parents.

The weekend proceeded with its usual harvest of young and old bodies, some who would survive their ordeals and some who would not. Jessi's operation, however, tipped off a particularly disquieting string of cases, as if a malevolent force was deliberately toying with the law of medical averages. Over the next twenty-four hours, three separate teenage girls presented to the medical center, having experienced convulsions for the first time in their young lives. All three—Emma, age thirteen; Sophia, age fourteen; and Mia, age fifteen—proved to have glioblastomas. All three, after surgery with Ryan, were staring down the barrel of months of radiation treatments, chemotherapy, and assorted experimental protocols. All three would likely be dead before they could vote.

Late the following Thursday afternoon, the children's hospital called into the operating room with a request from Mia, the fifteen-year-old, for Ryan to stop by and discuss her diagnosis with her. Ryan had already broken the bad news to her and her family the previous evening. At about six thirty, he shook free of the OR and walked over to Mia's room. Mia's parents were waiting outside, their faces stained by tears.

"Hi, Dr. Brenan. Thank you so much for coming over," offered the stricken mother.

"Oh jeez, it's the least I can do, guys. Again, I can't tell you how sorry I am about the diagnosis. Have you met with the pediatric oncologist yet?"

"Yes, we have," replied the mother. "She was very nice but awfully matter-of-fact with all her statistics. I'm afraid that after a few minutes it all just became noise to me—an awful, horrible screeching noise." She broke down into sobs and buried her head into her husband's shoulder. Her husband took over.

"Anyway, Dr. Brenan, Mia's been researching her tumor online all afternoon and wanted to ask you some follow-up questions. We told her that perhaps the oncologist would be the better resource, but Mia asked to speak with you specifically. Do you mind?"

"Oh my gosh, of course not," answered Ryan. "Why don't you guys take a few moments to clear your thoughts, and we all can go in together."

"That's the thing, Dr. Brenan," responded the father. "Mia asked to speak with you alone. And we said it was all right. I think she's worried about what such a discussion would do to us. Here she is, three days out of surgery for brain cancer, and she's worried about *our* well-being."

The father now broke down into his own sobs, and the couple clutched one another, dissolving into a shuddering mass of agony. Ryan touched the couple's shoulders, not for the first time this week thinking about his own daughters, and then proceeded into the room.

"Hey there, Dr. Brenan," remarked the bright-eyed teenager in sweatpants and a pink hoodie, sitting in her hospital bed, tethered by two IVs. "I see you got past the sentries. Thanks for coming."

"No problem, Mia," replied Ryan, sitting down on a vinyl sofa. It's what I'm here for."

"How many heads you crack open today?"

"Oh, just a couple."

"Sounds like you're slacking," replied Mia, arms crossed.

"I know. Can't believe they pay me for this."

"Well, if you're looking to share any of it, let me know. But . . . I guess I won't have much time to spend, will I?" remarked Mia, the ends of her smile sagging. "Dr. Google says my tumor's pretty bad news."

Oh Jesus, thought Ryan as his eyes moistened. He tried to clear his throat of a large lump that had formed there and answered, "It can be, Mia, but you're young and healthy, and new treatments are coming into play every day. So, hang in there and be prepared to kick its butt."

"Yeah, well, we'll see whose butt gets kicked in the end, won't we?"

"We'll see, Mia," replied Ryan, reaching out to touch her hand.

Mia paused for a moment and tilted her head. "Tell me this, Dr. Brenan . . ."

"Yes?" replied Ryan, inching forward on the couch.

"Will it be painful? I mean, when I die."

Ryan swallowed hard. "Who says you're going to die?"

"Um, I checked the stats." Mia rolled her eyes. "They don't leave much doubt."

"Be careful of all those statistics, Mia. They sound wretched, but they're just an average of responses. No one says they'll apply to you. And there are always exceptions to the rule." Ryan shuddered at the thought of how empty his reassurances sounded.

"You don't have to be so gentle with me, Dr. Brenan," replied Mia, eyebrows furrowed a little. "I know the score. Please, just be as straight with me as you can, okay?"

"I am being straight with you, Mia. But you're right, the odds aren't great. We have a real tiger by the tail here." *Oh shit, Ryan,* thought Ryan, *must you persist with the vacuous clichés?*

"So . . . will it be painful?" asked Mia, locking her intense stare on him.

Ryan paused for a moment. "Generally, no, for those who do succumb."

"You mean for those who die."

"Okay, for those who die," replied Ryan. The words contorted his face.

"And will I . . . will I be me? Until then, I mean?" asked Mia. "Will I still think the way I do, and feel the way I do about others?"

"Yes," replied Ryan, nodding. "Most often, those who go on to die keep their faculties until the very end."

"And will I get all swollen and ugly?" asked Mia, frowning in disgust.

"Sometimes people who are in their last weeks are placed on steroid medicines that can cause a lot of swelling. Otherwise, there isn't necessarily any change in your physique or appearance— except you may lose your hair for a while."

"I never liked my hair anyway," remarked Mia. "I guess now I can have any color and style I want."

"Sounds like a deal."

"Can I still be a cheerleader?"

"I don't see why not. Just don't let anyone drop you on your head," replied Ryan with a forced smile.

"No worries there. I'm never on the top of the pyramid. What about going out on dates?"

"Ha! That one will be up to your parents."

"Yeah, well, I'd bet I can guilt them into letting me do just about anything," said Mia, with a sly smile. "I might even get a car out of the deal!"

"Hmm. I refuse to be complicit in that scheme."

"Only kidding, anyway. I couldn't do that to my parents. They're good people, Dr. Brenan."

"I agree."

"They're not going to get through this very well," said Mia, eyes glistening.

"They love you very much." The words nearly failed to make it past Ryan's vocal cords.

"I know. That's why I asked to speak with you privately."

"So they didn't have to hear us talk about the tumor?"

"No. They're going to have to deal with the cold hard facts at some point. But I wanted to ask a major favor of you," said Mia, locking her eyes on Ryan's.

"Anything," said Ryan, finding it hard to maintain the eye contact.

"Well, I can tell they trust you. After all, they let you operate on my brain."

"Okay..."

"Well, I know I'll be seeing dozens of other docs, and that *you* won't have much more to do for me. It'll be the chemo doctors, and the radiation doctors, and all."

"Yeah, but we'll absolutely follow along with you," replied Ryan, taking Mia's hand.

"Well, that's what I would want—to have you stick with me," replied Mia, patting Ryan's hand. "So my parents have someone, someone they trust, someone who will help them get through this, someone who they can turn to when they're scared or confused. Could you do that for me?"

"You have my word," replied Ryan, the lump in his throat doubling in size, causing his voice to waver.

"Can I come see you every month?"

"You can come see me every week. It would certainly brighten up my days."

"Nah, that would take too much time away from school and cheerleading. For now, let's settle on once a month."

"Deal."

The two shook hands. They spoke for another couple of hours, some of the time about managing the disease, some of the time about life in general. Finally, Ryan broke free and made his way to his jeep. He opened the door and climbed in. It was a tremendous relief to make it that far. His chest was tearing open and his feet had turned to stone.

After deep breathing in the jeep for a good half hour, he drove home. He cried throughout the ride, then again throughout a prolonged shower, and then again while creeping into the girls' room and kissing each on the forehead as they slept. He then stumbled down the stairs, moved silently past his wife seated in the kitchen, dropped into his corner of the couch, and stared into a blank TV screen. Kelly followed him into the room and started to say something, but then stopped, turned, and headed off to bed.

CHAPTER 51

COME AS YOU ARE

The next day was a blur. Ryan had stayed up far too late numbing his brain with war documentaries. He sleepwalked into the hospital and made his way through several unremarkable operations. Soon he found himself climbing back into the jeep. It felt like a century since the previous weekend's call, and a decade since his heart-wrenching discussion with Mia. It had been a merciless week. But it was Friday. And no matter how bleak, how abusive the week, there was something about Friday evenings after a weekend of call that lightened one's step and made one feel less bedraggled, less vulnerable. Technically, he didn't have to set foot back in the hospital again until Monday morning. Technically, the poor sucker on this weekend's call would round on his and everyone else's patients. Technically, Ryan *never* had to round on weekends when he wasn't on call. And yet he always did. But after mulling over all his recent discussions with Kelly, Larkin, Matt, Ron, Ingles, and McNeal, he had made a vow to himself that he would amend his ways, that he would take more time off, that he would regularly escape the constant beat of tragedy and death that permeated his life, that he would rekindle an outside life—an outside life he would joyfully share with Kelly and his girls. Yep, it was time to drive a stake into the ground, to draw a line in the sand, and proclaim to the world, "Here I stand," and begin this new approach, this new life, this new existence, right here and now.

Only he wouldn't. Not this weekend, at least. Nope, there were too many broken bodies in the various ICUs, too many sick kids, too many adults who were hanging by a thread, too many sweet teenage girls dealing with the private hells of their biological death sentences, to entrust their care to his less-than-compulsive partners. No, it wouldn't work. He would have to go in. But he would do it in a new, more abbreviated fashion. He would slip in early on Saturday and Sunday mornings, lay eyes on the five, or six, or seven sickest patients, and then sneak out before anyone ever realized he was there.

With a surge of enthusiasm from this new conviction, he steered the jeep out the doctor's parking lot. Breaking free of the Carriere campus, he turned on the radio. The jeep's thirty-five-year-old electronics, however, left something to be desired. After some static, some garbled voices from a sports show, and then some more static, the radio flatlined. Ryan smiled and rolled down his window, letting the crisp winter air embrace him—such a pleasant change from the foul, stale fetor of the hospital.

As he came off the hill and steered toward downtown, the jeep hit a refrigerator-sized pothole in the road, its fossilized suspension not much better than a couple of bricks shoved between the axle and the main body. The shockwave sparked the moribund radio back to life, and now it clearly played "Come As You Are" by Nirvana as he turned down Main Street.

"What the—" Ryan came to a sudden stop. Traffic was backed up for several blocks. What was more, the sidewalks were abuzz with people. This was most odd. What the heck was going on? Was it a holiday? Was there any holiday in early February? It was February, wasn't it?

Ryan watched the pedestrians pass by, and several returned his gaze. Some nodded, a few even smiled. It was the smiles that shocked his numbed brain into alertness. There was something dark about them. Something harsh and accusatory. It made his skin crawl.

Then recognition started to kick in. "Jesus, is that Mr. Abramson?"

Mr. Abramson had been a local pharmacist. He had died the previous year from a ruptured aneurysm.

"And Jimmy Bader?"

James (Jimmy) Bader had been a New Bethany High School senior, who had died four weeks after catapulting through the windshield of his father's Lexus on Thanksgiving Day.

"Christ, that's Ms. Klinger."

Frances Klinger, an English teacher from Bloomsbury, had died over the Christmas holiday after a five-year battle with metastatic melanoma.

"And there's Mr. Granger. What the fu—?"

Matthew Granger, a handyman at Grenoble's Amusement Park, had his head crushed in freak accident while repairing the Tornado, a renown wooden roller coaster.

Now, too many former citizens turned their heads to look his way, some stopping dead in their tracks and gawking, others pointing him out to their ghastly acquaintances. All the while, the disorienting music of Nirvana played on.

"Good god, that's enough of "Kurt Cobain." With trembling fingers, Ryan hit a button to change the station. The red digital call numbers whirled past on the small LED screen and again landed on the same station, playing the same song. He tried the same maneuver again, with the same result. He hit the off button. It obeyed. But only for a moment. The radio flashed back to life. Same song, from the beginning. The left front and right rear speakers, which had been deceased for at least a decade, now came back to life. He hit the off switch again, and then again, and one more time—always with the same results. He jabbed at the device with a closed fist, only to affect an increase in the volume.

"Goddamn it!" barked Ryan as he punched the recalcitrant radio with all his might, only to affect an increase in distortion and a boxer's fracture of his right little finger.

The jeep was still pinned in by stop-and-go traffic. "Christ, do I make a run for the bridge?" wondered Ryan as he tried to shake the pain out of his injured hand. But hell, there were so many of them wandering out there, where would he go?

No. Stay in the jeep, Ryan. Don't acknowledge them. Don't even look at them. And for God's sake, stop hyperventilating. You don't want to freaking pass out.

His locked his eyes on the car in front and willed his auditory centers to close out the repetitive grunge rock. He had gone through six or seven full replayings of what was once a favorite song when he was finally able to hit the gas and scream across the bridge.

Arriving home, he was drenched in sweat and shaking uncontrollably. Unable to communicate, he stumbled past the girls in the family room, and Kelly in the kitchen, and hit the liquor cabinet in the dining room only to recall he had recently emptied it. He headed back to the family room and collapsed into his corner of the sofa. The girls scattered and fluttered about the house like startled birds until finally coming to perch in the dining room.

Kelly tiptoed into the family room. Ryan glanced her way and then, without saying a word, turned his attention back to the TV. Kelly started to leave, but abruptly turned and walked toward him. She sat down on the coffee table in front of him, blocking his view of the TV, and touched his left knee.

"Ryan, what's up?" she whispered.

"Uh, nothing . . . just the usual," replied Ryan, trying to look around Kelly at a thirty-year-old sitcom.

"I don't think so, Ryan. You look awful. You've seen another one, haven't you? Another ghost."

"Uh . . . no, honey. Just the usual," repeated Ryan.

"Ryan, look at me," said Kelly. "Something's horribly wrong. I can tell. Are you going to share it with me, or not?"

"Uh, I'm okay. Just figuring out some stuff from work. Bad stuff. Nasty stuff," was all Ryan could offer.

"Look, Ryan," replied Kelly in a hushed tone that nonetheless betrayed an underlying irritation. "You swore to me you would share more, be straightforward with me, be honest about everything. I don't feel you're keeping your word. Something is really bothering you. Why don't you and I step outside and discuss it?"

"I'm okay, Kelly. Really. It was just a rough week," snapped Ryan, rising from the couch. "Think I'll go for a drive." He strode out the side entrance, the door slamming behind him.

CHAPTER 52

LAST DITCH

R yan didn't return until late Saturday afternoon. When pressed, he claimed to have gone back to the hospital out of concern for a patient and then stayed in a call room for the rest of the night. The remainder of the weekend passed without further incident. Ryan simply behaved, in Kelly's mind, like one of his ghosts: floating around the house, haunting various spots but never truly interacting with the living. Not that the living had much to do with him. The girls, and even the dogs, were giving him wide berth. Monday morning couldn't come soon enough. When it finally did, Kelly called Reverend Ron. They met in the late afternoon, and Kelly offered up her version of all that had been going on in the Brenan household

"Yeah, Kelly. He and I had a long talk back in November. We were supposed to get together every couple of weeks, but he always canceled out," remarked Reverend Ron, his right eye twitching.

"Then you've seen it, haven't you, Ron?" asked Kelly, eyes wide. "You've seen how crazy he is."

"I'm not sure, Kelly."

"Oh God, please don't tell me you think he's 'perfectly sane' like that idiot, Larkin," remarked Kelly, her face flushing.

"I'm not drawing any conclusions," said Reverend Ron, shaking his head and holding up his hands defensively. "I'd need more time with him. But I think all this might have something to do with his sleep disorders rather than true mental illness. Or perhaps some bizarre form of seizures. Both of which, in some ways, would make things easier to address. If he would only get on it."

"Well, he needs to get on it soon," said Kelly, using more dramatic hand gestures than she was happy with. "He's a disaster waiting to happen, and no one seems to recognize it."

"Has he had any further breakdowns since that night with the girls?"

"No. I have to admit he's not running about the place screaming at shadows anymore," said Kelly, forcing her hands to remain clutched together on her lap. "But he's just an empty shell when— or *if*—he comes home anymore. A zombie. And how long before he comes unglued on some dark and stormy night and shreds the girls' psyches for good? It's bound to happen, Ron."

"Why do think so, Kelly?"

"Because the guy's being utterly disingenuous about it all," replied Kelly, tossing her hands in the air again. "He swears up and down that the apparitions have stopped, but he's clearly lying. You can see it in his eyes after one of his hallucinations. And it's happening more and more frequently. The guy needs help, Ron, and I mean major-league professional help. And not here. Somewhere far away from the hallucinogenic miasma of the Susquehanna Valley. Everyone here is crazy. Larkin, his neurologists, his bosses, Matt. And frankly, now I'm worried about you."

"Well, I'm sorry you feel that way," replied Reverend Ron, averting his eyes.

"I'm so sorry, Ron," Kelly reached out to touch Reverend Ron's forearm. "I don't mean to insult you. It's just that I'm desperate. I don't know what to do—short of tasing the guy and dragging him to a psych ward. He needs help. He needs big-gun psychiatrists. Maybe you could convince him to get some real help in New York, or Philly, or Boston—"

"I did try, Kelly. He's not very open to *'real'* help," replied Reverend Ron, looking down at his shoes.

"I'm sorry. I insulted you again, didn't I? I know you're an expert on problem physicians, but Ryan isn't really a problem physician, is he? Not yet, at least. No, that will be the very last thing to go, his precious work. He's a problem husband, and a problem father, and a problem friend, but he sure as hell won't allow himself to be a problem physician." Kelly stood up from her chair and started pacing. "God, when I'm not worried about him I'm so pissed at him. I've had it with the ridiculous hours, the perpetual absences, the dismissiveness of all that's not neurosurgery, the bizarre behaviors, the withdrawl, and most of all, the lies."

"No offense taken, Kelly. But I have to note that the two spheres are intimately interconnected—his home life and his work life. One goes down—so will the other. So, maybe I can still be of assistance. Maybe, if I could help him with his work stressors, his extracurricular disturbances would settle down. Then maybe things on the home front would come more online. And, if I might be so bold, maybe you two could get your marriage back on track."

"Ha, what marriage?" replied Kelly with an upward jerk of her chin. "The guy's married to his job."

"I get it, Kelly. Truth be told, most life partners of neuro-surgeons have a real feces sandwich to swallow—if they value commitment and adult company over liquidity and material abundance. They put their own careers on a back burner and become single parents, facing all of life's challenges and crises on their own. And those thinking they can change the dynamic are usually left deeply disappointed and disaffected. I've seen this picture too many times. Neurosurgeons prove to be my most challenging clients—charter members of my 'frequent flyers club.'"

"Tell me about it," replied Kelly, picking up one of Reverend Ron's psychology textbooks and mindlessly leafing through it.

"Yeah, well, problem is, you face in spades. Ryan is one of the most committed doctors I've known. He's not married to neurosurgery. He's married to you. And I know he loves you very much. But neurosurgery's his mistress, and a most jealous one at that."

"Yeah, but I think it's the other way around." Kelly put the book down. "I think neurosurgery is his one and only love, and I'm a little bit on the side. Frankly, Ron, this marriage has been nothing but a double-cross since day one—a real bait and switch."

"Meaning?"

"Well . . ." Kelly examined the artifacts on Reverend Ron's bookshelves. "When we first got to know each other, he seemed as if he would be the most interesting and exciting person one could share a life with. And then nothing. Year after year. And it isn't just a physical absence, he's never there mentally. He threw up his ridiculous 'Iron Curtain' between the 99 percent of the week that represents his professional life, and the meager 1 percent that he shares with me."

"Look, Kelly," said Reverend Ron, guiding her back to her chair. "It's perfectly normal for you to be feeling a mix of emotions. Concern, fear, sadness. But also alienation, neglect, betrayal, resentment, and anger. You've been dealing with so much with Ryan. The guy's a mess. The depression, the PTSD, the sleep disorders, and whatever these apparitions are. But why not see if you can still find your empathy and love for the guy? Can't we try to get the old Ryan back? How about if we both put a full-court press on him to get some help? As you say, far away from here. With world experts. Can we try that before giving up the ship? You and I both think the world of Ryan, and love him dearly."

Kelly couldn't help but fire back a skeptical look. "Yeah, we love him, all right. But does he deserve it? How far can we go if he won't help himself? When does my tending to his crippled psyche compromise my care for my girls?"

The two continued to discuss the situation for another hour. No ground was gained on Kelly's indignation, but they both agreed that Ryan needed much intervention. When they parted, Reverend Ron promised to badger Ryan until the guy agreed to accept multidisciplinary assistance—outside of New Bethany.

"I can't thank you enough, Ron," said Kelly, stepping in for a long parting hug. "I should have come to you much sooner. I've known for a long time, at some level, that something was profoundly wrong. I kept challenging him, begging him to confide in me, but he kept denying he was having any troubles. He's such a prideful man. He's incapable of acknowledging his own weaknesses, his own frailty. He would never admit to anyone, least of all his life-partner, that he needed help—*never*. It's not in his DNA. Unless, of course, it threatened his precious work. Then he'd be all over it." Kelly paused for a moment. "No matter what, though, I do want the best for him."

Reverend Ron's right eye twitched furiously with this last remark. "Forgive me for saying this, Kelly, but I don't like the sounds of that. It sounds like you're not on a mission to repair your relationship, to rekindle your love, but are more like on a mission of mercy for a fellow human being—like throwing a life preserver to a drowning stranger.

"If the shoe fits, Ron," remarked Kelly as she turned and left the office.

CHAPTER 53

BREAKING POINT

S hortly after seven the same evening, Ryan received a series of text messages from Reverend Ron. He ignored them, preoccupied as he was with a new major problem. The family was preparing to leave for a ski trip in Vermont with the Wolfes, the O'Connors, and several other families. The excursion had been planned for months. Everyone was leaving Wednesday and wouldn't return until the following Thursday. They were staying at a quintessential ski lodge just to the Woodstock side of Killington. But one of Ryan's partners—the one taking that weekend's call—had a family emergency and asked Ryan to help cover for him. Ryan agreed, and now had to break the news to Kelly. He waited until after the girls had gone to bed and explained the situation to her in the family room.

"I don't get it, Ryan. Why now? Why at the very last minute?" challenged Kelly, springing up from the couch.

"I'm so sorry, Kelly, but you know stuff happens. Someone had to cover for Jim."

"And it had to be you, like always."

"He asked," said Ryan, holding his palms up. "What was I supposed to say: 'No way Jim, your dying brother's *your* problem. I have some important skiing to do.'"

"Don't be absurd," replied Kelly, pacing back and forth in front the fireplace. "But I don't understand why it always has to be *you* who takes the extra call."

"It's not just me. But Leslie's in Europe and with Jim out, it leaves only me to cover the children's hospital. Leslie's supposed to get back Saturday night, so she'll take over Sunday. And Jordan will pick up the adult side."

"Well, the girls are going to be heartbroken. They've been so excited about the trip." Kelly paused to poke at the coals of a dying fire. "And explain to me again why we have to cancel the whole thing? Couldn't we still head out at 6:00 a.m. Sunday—maybe stay a couple extra days?"

"You know perfectly well, Kell, that if we plan it that way, some kid will come in at five o'clock with a terrible tumor. It happens every time. Besides, it's not a good time for me to bug out of town. There are several sick kids in the PICU."

Kelly smacked the fire iron into her palm. "There's always 'several sick kids in the PICU,' Ryan—that's your excuse for everything."

"Well, pardon me for giving a damn," replied Ryan, raising his voice and standing up from the couch.

"You can get mad at me if you want, but this is ridiculous," said Kelly, poking the glowing coals in the fireplace more vigorously, sending showers of sparks up the chimney.

"I'll tell you what, then," growled a red-faced Ryan, "if it's so damned important, why don't you guys go ahead and make the trip without me."

"Maybe we should."

Ryan stood silently for a few moments, then softened his tone. "Actually, that's not a bad idea. It would probably do everyone some good. You guys go ahead and head out as planned, go have fun with Dianne and the crew. I'll crash here for a few days and recharge my batteries."

"I don't like it, Ryan." Kelly returned the fire iron to its stand and faced Ryan, arms crossed. "It's just another example of you backing out of any form of social engagement—any form of normal activity. It feels like all you want to do anymore is hang out with the sick and dying; and, apparently, the dead."

"Come on, Kelly, that's not fair," said Ryan, reaching for Kelly but then backing off.

"What's not fair is your abandonment of your family," replied Kelly.

"I'm doing my best."

Kelly froze Ryan with her eyes. "Well, your best isn't good enough. Your patients and your partners aren't the only ones who need you."

"I know, Kelly. And you know I love you and the girls more than anyth—"

"Oh bullshit," replied Kelly, making a cutting motion with her hand. "You love your job. You love being so goddamned important, and wanted, and needed over there in the hospital. It's an ego thing, isn't it? You can't get away from that titanic ego of yours, can you?"

Ryan shrank and looked at the floor. "Kelly, I think it's quite the opposite. I—"

"Are you kidding me?" replied Kelly. She began to pace again. "Your ego is massive. No one else at Carriere can do what you do. You have to take on every complex case, every tumor, every hemorrhage, every shattered spine. If you leave the place for five minutes, people go paralyzed, children die, the whole institution crumbles to the ground—"

"I think that's unfair, Kelly. I just—"

"You just believe you're the only real neurosurgeon there. Everyone else is second fiddle, so the place needs your constant presence. You go away for a weekend and expect the body count to mount, don't you?"

"Of course not. It's just—"

"It's just that you know I'm 100 percent right," interrupted Kelly, now coming to rest in front of Ryan. She pointed to his chest. "And that's a sad state of affairs. Because if it's true, if there are no other neurosurgeons as competent as the great Ryan Brenan there, then you should demand that the place hires five more Ryan Brenans. But you wouldn't want that, would you?" Kelly shook her head. "No, you like being the top dog, the go-to guy. You don't want anyone around to challenge your exalted position. And that's a sick soul who could do that, who could accept inferior partners and compromise patient care for the sake of their own ego."

"That's a low blow," replied Ryan, flopping back onto the couch. "You know I would never compromise their care. If I thought—"

Kelly's eyes flashed. "Oh, that's right, Dr. Brenan. Please forgive me. I forgot. You always put the patients first—that never-ending parade of sick and lame who occupy every minute of your nights and days. And what about the girls and me? We're left on the outside looking in. We're not here to be loved. We're here to patch you up and send you back into battle every day, aren't we?"

Ryan was cowed, and afraid to say anything further. Kelly took several cleansing breaths and spoke again, arms crossed over her chest.

"Look, Ryan, I'm sorry to be so harsh. You and I aren't in a good place right now. Maybe it *is* a good idea to get away from each other for several days. Get our thoughts together. We probably need a lot longer than that, but it's a start. So yeah, maybe I'll go ahead and leave on Wednesday. You stay in New Bethany and crash, or go out drinking with your soccer pals, or hang out with your ghost buddies. Do whatever floats your boat." She paused for a moment and locked eyes again with Ryan. "But no matter how you decide to occupy yourself, I suggest you do some good, hard, deep introspection and assessment of your situation. And I'll do the same."

Ryan didn't like the sound of this. It was separation talk. There were no "we's" or "us's" employed. She didn't offer a team approach. Both were to independently assess their "situations"— whatever that meant. Nonetheless, he couldn't think of another solution right now. He couldn't bear the thought of a captive several days of pretending he was feeling great and wanting to play. Besides, the goddamned ghosts would probably follow him to Vermont—introduce him to a whole new crew up there. Maybe a week apart would do both Kelly and him some good. Maybe they would get back together afterward with a new appreciation of what they had and what they needed to do to preserve things.

The two broke off the discussion and went their separate ways. Kelly and the girls would leave early Wednesday as planned. Ryan would do his call and then chill out at home for the remainder of their time away.

CHAPTER 54

BREACHING THE RAMPARTS

The house was empty. The family had departed on Wednesday as planned. What was more, John and Paul had been kenneled. Kelly was convinced that Ryan, left to his own devices, would completely forget to attend to even their most basic needs. Ryan had conceded the point, much as he would miss their presence in the big old house whenever he was home. But it turned out he wasn't home much. Wednesday and Thursday ran well into the nights. And then, with the start of call on Friday, the weekend exploded with a panoply of human disasters ranging from strokes, to hemorrhages, to broken spines; but ironically, to no pediatric cases. By late Saturday night, Ryan had lost track of the hour, and frankly, of the day. He had just finished up a craniotomy and was changing when he realized he had left his phone in the operating room. He changed back into scrubs and jogged over to OR 22. On entering the room, he was startled by something he caught out the corner of his eye. He would have sworn it was a young girl in street clothing. But when he flicked on the lights, the room was empty.

Jesus, Ryan. Don't do that to yourself. Don't let your imagination run wild. But, man, can these OR rooms be spooky in the middle of the night.

Heart pounding, he grabbed his phone off a stainless-steel table in the corner and headed out into the hallway at flank speed. Glancing down at the phone's face, he saw the emergency room had been calling. He called back. Apparently, an elderly women had garroted herself on wire fencing while snowmobiling in pitch darkness out in Whitly County.

Ryan reflexively walked toward the stairway at the back of Ward 6 East. With it, he could drop down directly into the rear of the ER immediately next to the trauma bay. Only he had forgotten that 6 East was out of commission. It had been undergoing refurbishing now for several months. The unit was cordoned off with hanging plastic veils and an array of access-forbidden signs. He would now have to double back and head to another staircase a few hundred feet to the west.

Shoot! You idiot, Ryan. He detested ever having to retrace his steps. Wasting time, any time, drove him crazy. Unnecessary repeated efforts at anything robbed him of the invaluable minutes, or even seconds, that could otherwise be spent doing something more constructive. After reproaching himself, he released a big sigh and plotted his new route to the carnage awaiting him in the ER. Just before making an about face, his momentum took him around a corner, and he happened to glance down the hallway leading to 6 East. There, all the signs of ongoing construction were gone. Six East was all lit up and open for business. He reconfigured his already reconfigured trajectory and hurried his way through the now busy unit, happy to be back around lots of people. He passed the brightly lit nurses' station, maneuvered his way around multiple medication carts, zipped past half a dozen nurses and aides, and arrived at the staircase in record time. He made it down the six flights in seconds, avoiding the last four or five steps before each landing. He hit the ER hard and fast, determined not to be "curbsided" by any stray docs, and burst into the trauma bay. Resident Ernest Nobleman was awaiting his arrival.

"Hey, sir," greeted Ernest.

"Hey, Ernest. What've you got?"

"Nothing good, sir. A seventy-two-year-old woman, multiple medical problems, cocaine, and alcohol on tox screen. Caught her neck on barbed wire while snowmobiling, arrested at the scene. She's in coma, pupils fixed and dilated, no corneals, no response to cold calorics, but still breathing over the vent. Severe fracture dislocation at C4-5 with associated carotid and vertebral artery injuries. Brain shows diffuse anoxal injury and probably ischemic strokes on top of that."

"Okay, then, what do you want to do?" asked Ryan.

"Well, she's not going to survive this, Dr. Brenan. I suppose we could put her in cervical traction, support her, and monitor her intracranial pressure, but I'd have to believe she'll be brain-dead by morning no matter what we do. So, I would probably just let her die."

"So, you don't want to decompress her brain or fix her neck?" asked Ryan.

"No, sir. There'd be no point. I'll show you her scans."

Sheesh, thought Ryan, *what a difference a year makes.*

The two looked over the patient and her scans, and Ryan complimented Ernest for his thorough evaluation and accurate assessment. They sat down at adjacent computers to document their findings. After a few minutes, Ryan finished up and stood. He was going to make one more foray to the 8 North Medical ICU and then head back to the changing room. He started for the stairs but stopped. He turned to his resident. "Hey, Ernest, since when did they open up 6 East?"

"Huh?" replied Ernest, looking up from his computer monitor. "I don't think they have. It was all full of workmen and dust last time I went by a day or two ago."

"Really? I just went through—" Ryan stopped short and broke out in a cold sweat. "Shit."

"What's that, sir?" asked Ernest.

Ryan looked down at his shoes. They were covered in chalky white material, the kind that accumulates in a worksite where new sheet rocking is being cut and hung. "Shit." He reconstructed in his mind his recent walk through the ward. It was obvious now, but at the time, in his hurry, he had failed to note the unquestionable skew deviation of reality there. Something was definitely not right. The arrangement of structures, the colors, even the pictures on the walls were a far cry from the oppressively utilitarian decor of modern-day mega medical centers. The lighting was off as well. It was of the brilliant, sunlike, analog kind via incandescent bulbs—not LED or fluorescent ones. And no one was in scrubs. The nurses were in tight-fitting, starched-white dresses. And all donned those weird little caps. And were heavily made up. And the patients were in tailored and pressed pajamas and smart-looking robes—not the one-size-fits-no-one, modern-day, embarrassingly gaping gowns. The equipment wasn't right either. Wire-basket medication carts, paper charts hanging by every patient room, naked IV poles without boxy electronic pumps attached.

Shit, was all Ryan could think as he bounded up the stairs, the hair on the back of his neck standing on end, cold sweat running down his back. Now he stood before the door to 6 East, wondering if he had the guts to step inside and see what was going on. But he had to do it, he had to know. He grabbed the handle and projected himself forward. Only, he ran his face into the door. The handle was locked. He swore, and then dropped down a floor via the staircase. He blew through 5 East and made for a distant central staircase. From there he re-alighted onto the sixth floor and steered at top speed toward 6 East. At the ward's entrance stood the usual construction barricade and warning signs. Ryan stepped past them. Inside, he found nothing but the detritus of a busy construction area, and his own footprints through the dusty central hallway.

"Shit."

Ryan began to wretch. He had seen the hospital as an unassailable stronghold, somehow impregnable to the agents of the undead. And this wasn't just a strange face in a window or flash of something in an operating room. It was so goddamned elaborate and concrete.

Jesus, he thought as the world began to spin. Kelly was right. Whatever it was that was going on out *there* had now spilled into *here*. His fortress. His sanctuary. His professional world. It had only altered his movements this time, but could it interfere with his patient care? Was Kelly right about that too? Would it make him a danger to his patients?

He stumbled to one of the call rooms, curled up into a ball, and pulled the sheet over his head. But he was left undisturbed for only a few minutes. Soon he was back in the operating room, piecing a fifty-two-year-old man's head back together. A sizable ice-laden branch had severed itself from its parent oak tree and crashed into the guy's house. The guy had been asleep in bed when the deadly invader plunged through the roof and into his head, leaving his nearby wife entirely unscathed. Surgery went smoothly enough, but Ryan couldn't help repeatedly scanning the room for unwelcome visitors.

Several more emergency consults poured in, and before Ryan knew it, it was Sunday morning and relief was on its way. He and Cam Carlson made some rounds, then made their way to the coffee shop. Ryan was buoyed by the lack of further ghostly incursions and by his release from call duties. He talked himself into believing that the girl in the operating room was a figment of his overheated imagination, and the 6 East occurrence was some sort of interdimensional glitch. He reassured himself that the natural order of the universe, at least within the hospital, had been restored. He therefore chatted with Cam about the Olympics and other innocuous subjects, and savored his unhurried cup of coffee. He eventually wished Cam good luck with the rest of the weekend and headed for the stairs.

After changing out of his scrubs, he made his way to the 8 North ICU to do a final check on several of his "sickos," then blitzed through 8 West toward a back staircase that led to the doctor's parking lot. Halfway down the hallway, he almost ran over a woman in an all-too-familiar cancer turban. It was Delores Sopena. Mrs. Sopena was a beautiful African American woman of thirty-two when she first presented to the medical center with convulsions. She was found to have a fungating left-sided brain tumor which proved to be a gliosarcoma—an evil relative of glioblastoma. With Ryan, she went through surgery, chemotherapy, radiation, and experimental gene therapy. The experimental therapy had been so ineffective in other patients that the residents had christened it "glioma-chow." To everyone's delight, though, Mrs. Sopena went five years with no signs of tumor recurrence. Ryan saw her in his clinic monthly. She was such a delightful person and was so full of gratitude for every additional minute of life, that every time she came in, Ryan found himself praying to a God he didn't necessarily believe existed to please, oh please, deliver her from her disease.

And it seemed to work. Until it didn't. Until Ryan's god dropped the ball. Five years and two weeks after her original surgery, after years of "clean" MRIs, she had another seizure. The tumor had made its reappearance and was now double its original size. Ryan reoperated and cleaned out all visible tumor; but then after three months, it was back and was streaming into the opposite side of Mrs. Sopena's brain. Her goose was cooked. No further surgery would be of any benefit: radiation had been used up, and any further chemotherapy regimen was likely only to make her miserably sick. After two more months, the tumor was everywhere, and the only thing that kept Mrs. Sopena going was increasing doses of medicinal steroids. Two weeks prior to this evening, she had missed an appointment and Ryan assumed the worse. But here she was in the hospital, looking worn, bloated, hairless; and yet, beautiful, due to an inextinguishable inner radiance.

"Hey there, Mrs. Sopena! Jeez, I almost tripped over you," said Ryan.

"Hi there, Dr. Brenan!" responded Mrs. Sopena, her incandescent smile lighting up the ward. "How's my favorite man on God's own Earth—other than my husband, that is."

"I'm fine, but what are you doing in the hospital?"

"Oh, I'm having seizures. They can't seem to get them under control. I think I'm on four anticonvulsants now, but they keep coming—every so many hours. And they've been nasty ones."

"Sheesh, I'm so sorry," said Ryan. "Who's taking care of you?"

"Um, I think it's supposed to be Dr. Woodfield from Neurology, but I've never laid eyes on the man."

"Christ," said Ryan, cringing.

"What was that, Dr. Brenan?"

"Nothing," replied Ryan, shaking his head. "How are you feeling?"

"Oh, Dr. Brenan, I do believe it's my time," said Mrs. Sopena with a smile and tilt of the head.

"Don't say that. You look great. This is just a bump in the road," said Ryan, reaching out to Mrs. Sopena, not at all convinced by his own words.

"No, Dr. Brenan, I can feel it. My spirit is leaving my body as we speak. And that's all right, I'm ready to be with Jesus."

"No, Mrs. Sopena, you'll be fine," replied Ryan, gently holding

Mrs. Sopena's withered shoulder. "They just need to get the seizures under control. I'll take a look at your meds myself. I'm sure we can get things worked out and get you home."

"It's all right, my sweet man," replied Mrs. Sopena, patting Ryan's hand. "I've made my peace with it. Gabriel calls and who am I to argue? But I am so filled with joy that I got to see you this one last time. I worried that I wouldn't after I missed my appointment. But I was so sick to my stomach that day. I didn't want you to see me that way, to remember me that way."

"Ah, come on, Ms. Sopena, we'll have many more visits together. I'll make sure of it. I'll call the office tomorrow and get them all scheduled up—every couple of weeks suit you?"

"You're such a wonderful man, Dr. Brenan," said Mrs. Sopena, eyes sparkling. "I really will miss you. But we'll be reunited one day. I'm certain of it." She stepped into Ryan and gave him a hug so filled with love and gratitude that it took his breath away. "You go now, Dr. Brenan. You go see your beautiful family." She broke away and entered her room.

Ryan, with no family to see, turned and made his way to the nurses' station, intent on looking up the medications the moron Woodfield had placed her on. Hopefully, he could get them straightened out. He sat down and fired up the electronic medical records program and pulled up her chart.

"What the fuck?" The words burst from his lips.

He sat transfixed. At the top of the chart, flanking Mrs. Sopena's name, in bold, bright-red lettering, was the word: "Deceased."

"It's not possible." He hit the Google icon on the home screen and punched in Delores Sopena, Eliasburg, Pennsylvania. And there it was.

"Mrs. Delores Sopena, beloved wife and mother, was united with our Lord and Savior, Jesus Christ, after a five-year battle with brain cancer on Tuesday, the seventh of February. Mrs. Sopena, originally of Asheville, North Carolina is survived by . . ."

Ryan couldn't read on due to the thick screen of tears in his eyes. He pushed himself away from the keyboard and made his way to Mrs. Sopena's room. It was empty of all beings—dead or alive.

"Jesus."

CHAPTER 55

COME JOIN US

Ryan stumbled out of the hospital and fell into the jeep. He was soon home on the couch, unable to recall how he got there. He flipped through scores of stations on the TV but soon turned it off with a disgusted sigh. He then leafed through several catalogues until a creak in the upstairs hallway threw him off the couch. Mouth dry, cold sweat dripping into his eyes, he picked up a fire iron and scaled the back staircase. Again, on the landing, he encountered the Victorian dolls. He lifted the poker and prepared to take a swing at them but thought better of it and went about scouring the upstairs. When finally convinced that the place was free of spectral intruders, he reminded himself that the house was fond of creaking and groaning as the temperatures outside made their February swings. He headed back to the family room where he tried playing some guitar but couldn't seem to form any chords. He flopped back onto the couch and turned on an English soccer game. He put his feet up on the coffee table and watched, through sagging lids, twenty-two grown men in shorts run about a rainy pasture.

He awoke sometime later, sensing a presence in the room. He sat up with a start and looked over at the kitchen doorway. Standing there was a sandy-haired boy of perhaps five or six. Ryan stared at the child for a while, finally grumbling, "Well . . . ?"

The boy looked up at him. "Can I have a glass of water, Daddy?"

Ryan erupted off the sofa.

"Listen here, you little prick. *You're dead,*" he sneered, shaking his index finger at the boy. "So no, you can't have a drink of water—because you can't drink. You can't eat, you can't sleep, you can't take a pee. You can't even blow your goddamned nose. So, get the hell out of my house!"

The boy stood motionless for a few seconds. Then something appeared on his face. It was a tear, and it took a run down his left cheek and dropped to the floor. He lowered his head, turned, and shuffled off into the kitchen.

"Crap," mumbled Ryan to himself. "Why'd you have to be such a prick to the kid? He's already got a world of problems, being dead and all." Ryan leaped forward to catch up with the ghost. Maybe to apologize. Maybe to get him a glass of water. Only, when he reached the kitchen, the kid was gone.

Despite the innocuous nature of the apparition, his heart had climbed halfway up his throat and his entire body shook. He craved a cigarette despite never having smoked. He paced the ground floor for some time before firing up his phone, trying to reach any and all of his soccer and band buddies. But he struck out. "Well," he tried to reassure himself, "I've probably hit my spook quota for the day anyway. Not bad really. I think I scared the little bastard more than he did me."

He reentered the family room, dropped into the couch, and tried to enjoy the latest edition of the *New Yorker* only to find the articles overly verbose and the cartoons annoyingly obtuse. He tried watching TV again, but even his favored war documentaries couldn't hold his attention. Finally, to his great relief, he heard a car crunch along the gravel driveway and come to a stop by the side entrance.

Thank God, some company. Maybe it was Ron. He rose and moved to the side-entrance doorway. Out in the driveway sat a sparkling new top-of-the-line Lexus. Ryan strained to see the driver. It looked like Ronnie Garber, an old buddy from med school.

What the hell? What was Ronnie doing here? And was that Mitch Harriot, an old friend from high school, riding shotgun?

The old wooden storm door squealed at the press of his hand. He stepped out onto the side porch and drank in the splendid sight before him. He watched as Ronnie rolled down the window and motioned for him to come over. As if hypnotized, he complied. He reached the car and, as he placed his left hand on the door, stooped to catch a glimpse of the back-seat passenger who was scooting over to make room for him. It was none other than Bob Jessup— the very same sunset-loving Colonel Robert Jessup who had been blown to pieces when his helicopter was hit by that insurgent rocket in Afghanistan.

The penny dropped. Ryan hadn't kept up with the two in the front but had read years before about their independent demises: Ronnie from a fall while mountain climbing in the Andes; and Mitch, from blowing his own brains out with a shotgun.

"You gotta be kidding me," he choked out.

He looked down and noted that his hand was still grasping the car door, and that sitting on top of it was Ronnie's. It was large, meaty, strong, and frigid.

"Climb aboard, partner," offered the grinning ghost.

Ryan backpedaled furiously to the side porch, tripping over its steps. He sprang to his feet and scanned the vicinity for any object that might be weaponized. He seized an iron-framed piece of porch furniture, hoisted it over his head, and lurched toward the Lexus. Surprise registered on Ronnie's face. He raised his arms to shield his head from the impending violence. Ryan heaved the chair with all his might, and the car vanished. Then, as if plotted by Hollywood screenwriters, a rumble of rare February thunder galloped across the sky and heavy droplets of artic-cold rain began to pelt the earth.

"Well, at least this is a more appropriate setting," sighed Ryan as he turned back toward the house. Overcome by an uncontrollable bout of the jitters, he scoured the place for alcohol—even one of those little airplane bottles would do—but found none. He ransacked the refrigerator, praying to find an ancient can of PBR in an archaeological dig at the back of its lower shelves, but came up empty. Then his eyes fell on two bottles on the lower door, two bottles of cooking wine.

"Not ideal . . . but any port in a storm!" he commented as he unscrewed the cap on the bottle of white and took a couple of healthy slugs. It was vile stuff, but it sure felt good going down. He took a couple more gulps.

Oh man, he thought, *that's what I needed! Freaking pricks. This is ridiculous . . .*

After what felt like only a couple of minutes, he looked down into the kitchen sink to find two spent bottles.

"Huh? How did that happen?" he slurred.

He turned away from the sink and took a step. Or rather, a stumble.

"Oh crap, I'm drunk. Well, at least it calmed the shaking." He moved to the family room and put on a winter coat. "Let's get the fuck out of here. There's no way I'm gonna be one of those morons who doesn't have the sense to get out of a god damned haunted house. Think I'll mosey on over to Ron's . . ."

As he prepared to leave, the front doorbell rang. He hurried out the side door and sprinted toward the jeep.

"Screw that," he blurted. "Probably a bunch of dead Girl Scouts, selling hundred-year-old Thin Mints . . ."

Soon he was flying down Salisbury Road, making for the bridge.

The entrance, however, was blocked by a police car. Strobed by the vehicle's dancing lights, a hardy young patrolman leaned into the teeming rain. The guy looked more like a Maine lobsterman than an agent of the law. The sodden policeman waved an oversized flashlight toward an alternate route, but Ryan ignored the gesture and pulled up alongside him.

"What's up, Officer?" asked Ryan, struggling to sound sober.

"Sorry, Doc. West Main Street's flooded."

"But it only just started raining. How could it be flooded so soon?" challenged Ryan.

"Dunno, Doc. Maybe melted snow. But I've got my orders," replied the policeman, water sluicing off his hat and spilling into the jeep.

"Hey—you're not one of them, are you?" asked Ryan as he reached out the window to poke the patrolman.

The drenched young officer reared back a step.

"What's the matter, Doc? Got an emergency? You gotta get to the hospital?" He directed a bright halogen beam into Ryan's face.

"No, not really. But don't you think I could get through with the jeep?"

"No can do, Doc," replied the policeman as a capricious wind did its best to dash off with his hat. "That's how people drown. They misjudge the depth and flow of the water. You don't want to end up dead tonight, do you?"

Ryan shook his head, offered a perfunctory thanks, made a K turn, and accelerated in the direction of Shamaqua. Hydroplaning his way west, he passed Hunter's farm stand and went into a series of hairpin turns as the road scaled the first of several abrupt ridges. He only made it another mile when he came upon a fallen poplar lying across the road.

"It's a freaking conspiracy," Ryan growled as he turned the jeep around. "Well then, next stop, Catamount."

He was back in town within minutes. He blew past the slickered policeman, past the paint store, past the ice-cream stand and gas station, and ruptured out of the southern end of New Bethany. He sped up to sixty coming off a curve when, suddenly, he found himself slamming on the breaks. There, walking in the middle of the road, were four children.

The slashing rain darkened the children's silhouettes, but the jeep's antiquated headlights illuminated them well enough. They were all in dressed in Halloween costumes. Three sheeted ghosts and a surgeon. They made no attempt to get out of the way. They simply turned, looked up at Ryan, held out their bags, and cheered, "Trick or treat!"

"Little bastards. They've got to be ghosts; after all, it *is* February," reasoned Ryan. "Maybe I should just run 'em over and continue on. Oh crap, though, what if they hitch a ride?"

Ryan turned the jeep around on spinning wheels back toward town. Now his only remaining exit out of New Bethany was Avenue G. This would lead him to points southwest. Driving that way as fast as possible, he pulled out his phone and called Kelly. She didn't answer, so he left a message in her voicemail.

"Hey, Kell. I hope you guys are having a great time. Weird stuff going on here. I mean really weird. Not sure what they want from me. Tryin' to get out of here, but they don't seem to want that for some damned reason. If I can, I'll find a way to get up to you guys. Tell the girls I'll always love them. And Kell, just know . . . shit. What the hell?"

Coming upon another obstruction, Ryan slipped the phone back into his coat pocket. A mile and a half out of town, an SUV lay on its side, blocking the road. Torn-up torsos lay strewn about the scene like toy soldiers emptied out onto a playroom floor. Ryan was certain this was all phantasmagoric bullshit—the body count was preposterously high. But the doctor in him wouldn't allow him to retreat without checking. He slipped out of the jeep into the deluge and touched the first victim. Stone cold. He went to the next. Same. He tried one more. Frigid, like it had fallen out of a meat truck. Yep, utter crap. The spirit world was in rare form tonight.

This time, he decided he would just go ahead and plow through the mess as he stepped over one of the many frozen carcasses. He was sure that every component of this scene was made up of nothing but horse shit, unearthly pseudo-matter. Suddenly, a collection of said pseudo-matter grabbed him by the ankle and tore at his flesh. He heard himself scream as he kicked the thing in the head. It released, and he scrambled back toward the jeep, slipping, sliding, and falling to the ground several times until he was finally able to clamber back inside.

"Oh, screw this," he said. "Clearly these sons of bitches don't want me leaving home. At least they were friendly there. I guess I'll go back, keep an axe by my side, and keep trying to get a hold of someone, anyone . . ." Unfortunately, though, in his mad scramble, his phone had leaped out of his pocket, slid several yards across the wet asphalt, and dropped into an adjacent sewer.

Soon, he was skidding to a halt in his driveway. He then stumbled though the side door into the family room where a new surprise awaited him. On the couch sat an attractive woman of about twenty-five. She had long blonde hair and doll-like facial features, and a slim but curvy body. She was attired only a bikini—modest but revealing enough. And she was soaking wet. She looked like she had just stepped out of the ocean. She turned and smiled.

"Hey there, handsome."

"Hi there . . . ma'am," slurred Ryan.

"Come sit by me," said the phantom Barbie, patting the cushion beside her.

"Poor girl," mumbled Ryan. "I wonder if she even knows she's dead. Probably drowned surfing or something. Jesus, I hope she wasn't eaten by a shark. Wouldn't that be a nasty memory to carry with you for eternity?"

"Come join me, big boy," said the women. Again, she patted the seat beside her.

"Um, I don't think it's the best idea. I'm a little old for you. Don't you think?" croaked Ryan, hiding behind the coffee table.

"Oh, come on, sweetie. I won't bite . . . hard. Besides, Kelly's far away."

"Well, I'm sure she wouldn't approve of you dripping all over her couch. The girls get in trouble for it all the time."

"You're funny, Ryan. We could have a lot of laughs together— don't you think?" said the smiling ghost.

"I don't know about that. The point is, ma'am, you and I don't have much in common. I mean, you're dea—"

"Don't be such a prude, Ryan," admonished the ghost. "You know you'd love it. Come on, let's have some fun!"

"Um, I'm not sure what the rules are for such a thing, Ms.—"

"Mindy. My name's Mindy. Come on, Ryan, sweetie. Come be with us."

With this, Mindy the ghost stood up and moved toward Ryan.

"Sheesh," mumbled Ryan, backing up. "If I'm going nuts, I guess there could be worse ways."

"You're not going nuts, Ryan. You're just lonely. But you don't have to be lonely anymore. You'll never have to be lonely again," whispered Mindy. She took another step toward Ryan and took hold of his hand.

Ryan recoiled. Her hand was cold, and waxy, and dead.

"Uh, gotta go, Mindy. Nice talking with ya. Uh ... show yourself out, okay?" said Ryan backing away.

"Oh, Ryan, come back here. I haven't even shown you my tattoo," coaxed a pouting Mindy as she started to lower an edge of her bikini top.

Ryan looked away, whipped around, and scurried for the front stairway. As he crossed the kitchen, though, there was furious knocking at the front door and out the kitchen window, headlights flooded the driveway. Car doors then opened and shut, and a commotion of voices approached the side entrance. Ryan turned and headed for the back staircase. For the thousandth time, at the top, he was startled by the pair of creepy Victorian dolls and their glassy eyes. He seized them both by the throats and chucked them into the sewing room, slamming the door behind them. He stumbled down the short hallway, not sure where to go or what to do as several voices called to him from the outside.

"Come on, Ryan. Open up!"

"Come out, come out, wherever you are, Ryan!"

"Come on, Ryan. Let's have a party!"

"Let us in, Ryan, we've been looking so forward to this."

Then the front and side doors popped open, and dozens of revelers poured in. "Fucking Mindy," slurred Ryan.

He crept along the hallway and looked into the guest room. He thought about his father's old shotgun, hidden behind some of Kelly's old DC gowns in the closet. He wasn't sure how much good it would be against the bastards, but it would sure feel good in his hands. And, he could get some shells for it in his room. *Let's see how jolly these pricks are in the face of some buck shot.*

He entered the guest room and then its the cedar-lined walk-in closet. He took hold of the Remington, shut off the light, and reentered the guest room.

"What the fuck?"

There on the bed sat a tall, dark, middle-aged man with black hair. He was dressed in scrubs. He looked up at Ryan with a sad smile, then put a pistol in his mouth and pulled the trigger. Ryan averted his eyes at the last second but felt the percussion of the blast. He staggered out of the room, clutching the shotgun. As the echoes of the discharge cleared, the noise from downstairs grew louder. The player piano started up, and drunken singing assaulted every inch of the house. The raucous crew addressed each song to Ryan, changing the lyrics of old standards to include his name and various highlights of his life. They particularly enjoyed misappropriating Beatles songs.

"Bastards," said Ryan. "They know what buttons to push."

The raucous crowd then started in on Kelly. Only the wording became harsh, condemning, and vile. Between songs, they called out to Ryan and begged him to join in the festivities.

"Come on, Ryan. Stop playing hide-and-seek up there."

"Ryan, forget that slut wife of yours. Come meet some real women!"

"Come play, Ryan. Everyone's expecting you!"

"Come on, Ryan. We're here for you!"

It was too much to take. Every word pounded Ryan's crumbling psyche. He cried and he cursed and begged them to stop. But every time he did, the rabble downstairs laughed and guffawed and catcalled at him. He became increasingly disoriented but tried to make his way to the master bedroom. All the while, the noise escalated as the revelers approached both staircases. As he passed the girls' room, he glanced inside. There, another black-haired man in scrubs was sitting on Erin's bed, Glock to his temple. Ryan looked away.

Bang!

"Jesus! Stop it, will you?" cried Ryan.

The voices were starting up the stairs.

"Come on, Ryan, let's do some shots of Jameson's!"

"We're coming to get you, baby!"

"You're all ours now, Ryan!"

He glanced into the playroom. Another man, tall and dark. This one with a shotgun in his mouth.

"Christ!"

Another deafening explosion. Then more voices, more cajoling. They had to be halfway up the stairs.

He somehow made it to the master bedroom and fell inside. There, he looked up and realized he was in the presence of another uninvited guest. A woman. A woman in black funeral attire. The dark lady. Crisp and clearly outlined this time. Fully three dimensional. Tall, slim, athletic. She moved with the fluidity and grace of the living. She had her back to him and was opening his closet. She parted the clothes upon the rail and found a hidden panel at the back. She slid the panel open and removed an object out of an alcove recessed into the plaster wall.

Ryan knew what it was before she turned. It was a lockbox full of shotgun shells. She turned toward him.

"Oh, I get it," he said. "That's what this is all about, isn't it? That's what the whole last year of bullshit's been all about, isn't it? You all want me, don't you? On your side of Matt's bridge. Or whatever it is. Why? Who the fuck knows? But that's what the peep shows were for, wasn't it? And little Mindy's invitations. And the ride in your fucking Lexus. It's what everyone down there's hoping for, isn't it? I mean, no one's mincing words tonight, are they? 'Come join us,' 'Come be with us.'"

The specter spun the combination on the lockbox. It popped open, revealing several cartons of shells. She held the box up to Ryan. He made no motion toward it.

"You want me to take some, huh?" he said. "What, you want

me to do it here? In the bedroom? Where my little girls could find me? You've got to be kidding me. You're crazier than I am. I mean, if I *were* to do it. And don't get me wrong, it's not like I haven't considered it. I mean, I didn't need you bastards to plant the seed. That son of a bitch was planted a long time ago. I mean, it's not like Kelly loves me anymore. And with her goes the girls . . . and my whole world. So, who needed you all to come up with the idea? Did you really think I needed my hand held every step of the way? But like I was saying, if I were to do it, there'd have to be *no* chance the girls would find me . . . after."

The dark lady lifted the box higher.

"Hold your horses, will you? I know what you're after, but you don't have to be so pushy. We have to think this through better. The point is, it could never be in the house. Top floor of the barn, you say? I suppose that would make sense. The girls never go up there. They're terrified of the place. Yeah, I suppose I could go up there with a bunch of towels and sheets and a shower curtain—to limit the mess. Leave a note. Make sure Kelly sends Matt or Ron up there. Yeah, Matt and Ron. I don't want Kelly seeing me like . . . like that. But listen, it's not like I've agreed to this. It's you guys who are so goddamned sure. It's you guys with the master plan. What the fuck is the deal, anyway? Why do you have your hearts so set on this? You can't be that wanting for company. I mean, there are billions of you. Aren't there?"

The dark lady stepped closer and touched Ryan's chest with the lockbox. Ryan found himself removing a carton, tearing it open, and taking hold of several shells.

"Okay, okay, I get it. Jeez, late for a funeral or something, lady?" challenged Ryan as he moved to load the gun. "What is it with you guys—"

He froze. The specter, the dark lady, had taken hold of his hand. He flinched, expecting the cold, ceraceous contact of the dead. But her hand was warm, soft, and moist. It was gentle and deft, and it moved his hand bearing the shells away from the gun. She then stepped closer, took hold of Ryan's arms just above the elbows, and leaned forward to rest her head against his chest.

After an indeterminate passage of otherworldly time, she took a step away and looked up. As she did, she slowly removed her hat and veil. Long, sumptuous, auburn hair tumbled out with a release of an overwhelming scent—a most pleasant scent, a scent familiar to Ryan but just out of the grasp of his recognition. Her hair framed a rising face, a beautiful face, a cherubic face—Kelly's face. Kelly.

Ryan slammed up against a wall as if he had been hit by an explosion. The shotgun and its shells scattered across the floor. He slid down to the ground, desperately clinging to a retreating consciousness.

"Jesus, no! Not Kelly."

CHAPTER 56

MEMORY

For much of the trip, Kelly had done her best to ignore the invasive absence of her husband. Somehow despite the distance, despite the fun distractions, he was still loitering about her mind, like a bad taste in the mouth that refuses to clear. For a guy who was never around, his residue was annoyingly persistent. Perhaps it was a matter of habituation. She was used to his prolonged absences punctuated by rare but unignorable appearances. He would routinely go three, four, five days at a clip without being around, then just materialize and expect the family to gleefully pick up exactly where they had left off. It was as if they were duty-bound to go into some sort of suspended animation, then immediately snap back to life upon his return.

What really was the difference, then, between her situation now and that back in New Bethany? What was stopping him from appearing out of the blue and filling her with guilt—guilt for living her own life; guilt for enjoying herself; guilt for not sharing his stress, his fatigue, his misery. But God, she had needed the escape, the separation. She had needed the respite from that grim stranger who had taken up residence in her home. She had so desperately needed the guy to refrain from haunting her thoughts, her feelings, her existence.

But now she was telling herself to be careful of what she wished for as she hit the redial on her phone for the fifth straight time. Something was wrong. She couldn't feel his intrusive presence anymore. A dark gaping chasm had opened between him and her. It was crazy to be so unnerved, but she was certain something bad was happening. The girls had called him late in the evening to tell him about their day, as they had each night of the trip. But tonight he failed to pick up. No one picked up. This was unprecedented. The guy lived with the phone perpetually by his side. Every second of every day. Even when on vacation. Even when out of the country. If he couldn't answer because he was in surgery, or attending to an emergency, he always made sure that *someone* did. If he was in the middle of speaking to a patient, he would always fire off an acknowledging text. And if the phone went down, he would obtain a spare from the hospital within minutes.

An icy chill seized her body. She ushered the girls to bed and tried to reach him herself. Several times. When there was no answer, she paced for half an hour awaiting some sort of return communication.

He had to be in the hospital, doing God knows what. Doing what he always did. Probably operating. No shock there. Operating when he was supposed to be off was his thing. The circulator was probably too busy to pick up. A sick kid. A real sick kid. Yeah, that had to be it.

She waited another half hour but no messages came in. Her chest tightened. Something bad was happening.

She remembered that he had rung earlier. She had ignored the call at the time. She checked her voicemail and, with a sense of relief, saw that he had left a message. She listened. It was immediately obvious that he was drunk. God, he could get so down when he was drunk. And there was no doubt about it, he was down now. Despondent would be a better descriptor. And Jesus, he was driving.

His message stopped mid-sentence. Then there was muffled speaking, as if he had put the phone in a pocket. Something to the effect of: "What the hell . . . No fucking way. What a bunch of bullshit. What do they want from me?" Then he was out of the car. She could hear his footsteps. Then, in succession: "Nope, cold as ice. And you too. And you . . . Nope, utter bullshit." Then there was some sort of scuffle and Ryan had let out a yelp, one of pain and panic. Then the phone hit the ground and cut out.

Kelly listened to the recording several times. Along with a growing sense of terror, she was buffeted by wave after wave of paralyzing guilt. *Oh my God,* she thought. Something horrible was going on. Ryan was in trouble. Big trouble. She knew it in her soul. And she'd left him there. Alone. *Fucking Larkin, fucking Ron, fucking everyone, acting like he was perfectly fine. And fuck you, Kelly. You absolutely knew he was in trouble, but all you did was attack him.* What if he was worse than anyone thought? What if he was going to do something to himself, drunk, behind the wheel? He *was* going to do something. She could feel it. *Jesus, I'm going to lose him.*

She sought to relax her breathing.

Panic's not going to help anyone, Kelly. You have to remain calm, and do something. Right away. Get home. Get to his side. Help him through whatever this was. Help him through this illness. Help him get better. For however long it might take. Get home now. Before it's too late.

She grabbed her friend Dianne and explained. If all was well, she would return the next day. If not, well . . . they would cross that bridge as they needed to. Dianne told her not to worry, she would watch over the girls and get them home.

Within minutes, Kelly was off. It was a six-hour drive in the best of conditions, and it wasn't the best of conditions. It was snowing. Hard. But the van had all-wheel drive and snow tires, and Kelly was determined. Thankfully, the weather app showed that the precipitation turned to rain somewhere near the

Pennsylvania border. As she drove, she called the Carriere operating room to check if any emergency neurosurgery was under way. Nope, none. She called Ron, but he didn't answer. She called the New Bethany police and inquired about any bad accidents in the vicinity. There had been none, as far as they were aware. She asked if they could check in on Ryan, and they told her they would do their best. They called back an hour later and noted that the house was all lit up and there was a jeep in the driveway. This eased her mind about drunken crashes at least, but not about what else he might do.

As she contemplated the unthinkable, she was flooded with memories: vivid memories, insistent memories. Their years together before kids. His stricken face when Ava's delivery put her through thirty hours of hell. His adolescent pranks. His stupid band practices. The feel of his arm around her on the couch. His body pressed up against her back as she slept. His quiet crying in the middle of the night over a dying child. His obvious infatuation with his own children. His obvious infatuation for her. His million little gestures of adoration. A touch on the arm. Some little gift on no special occasion. A throw blanket wrapped around her shoulders on a cold winter evening. His forever incompetent attempts at loading the dishwasher. An unsolicited back rub. A kiss on top of her head. The unspoken happiness in his eyes at finding her home every night on his return from work.

So many memories. Too many memories. They were blurring her vision with tears. Yet she needed to recall them all. Now more than ever.

Strange, she thought as she drove on, *how love depends so much on memory.* Every minute of every day can't be infused with overwhelming throes of passion and heart-stopping moments of wonder, no matter how much you love someone. Those were the peaks of a relationship, not its baseline. And memories of the peaks had to carry you through the valleys. Ignore the memories, let them be swallowed into the depths of time, and what happens? You forget *why* you love someone. You forget that you *do* love them. Hold on to the memories, and the many seemingly inconsequential interactions you have throughout the day help to reinforce those peaks, raise them to even higher levels. Let the memories go, and the same interactions serve only as annoyances—fingernails on the marital chalkboard—and serve only to plain down the peaks.

And that's what she'd done. Let go of the memories. Let them be smothered by the day-to-day irritations. She had forgotten, forgotten the view from the peaks. Those glorious views. She had defaulted to the valleys. She had forgotten the whys of her love for Ryan. She had convinced herself that she no longer loved him. But, she was wrong. She never stopped loving him. She had just forgotten, literally forgotten. And so had he. They were both complicit. They both had taken their love for granted and allowed themselves to run on diverging tracks. And now their love was in big trouble. It all might be lost, never to be recaptured. But it *could* be recaptured. The memories *could* be restored. The peaks *could* be rebuilt. It was far from guaranteed—their relationship had suffered much neglect. There were changes that needed to be made. Much needed fixing. But they could figure a way. Together. They could leap off those diverging tracks and intertwine again. It *was* doable. It *was* worth it. If only they could have another shot at it.

Please, God, give us another shot at it.

CHAPTER 57

NOT TODAY

Ryan looked up from the floor in shock. Something had happened to Kelly. Something unthinkable. After all, he was looking at her ghost. He burst into tears. Kelly was dead. She was gone. Forever. He begged, and cajoled, and even threatened God not to take her away. He violently shook his head, praying it would clear his brain of the entity before him, awaken him from whatever alcohol-induced nightmare he was having. But the ghost remained. And it was definitely Kelly. His Kelly. And she was gone. Gone from the ranks of the living. All that was left was this vestige of her. This specter. This ghost. And wherever she was, he couldn't join her. There was no way he could cross the bridge now, no matter how much he might need to, no matter how much the rabble downstairs might want him to, no matter how much *he* might want to. No, he had to stay on this side for the girls. His now motherless girls. How he would go on, he didn't know. He couldn't imagine facing the world without Kelly. A tidal wave of grief fell upon him, crushing him against the wall. *Please, God, give us another chance.*

He tried to stand, tried to reach for her, hoping to seize her, hold on to her so she couldn't leave. But his limbs failed him. Nothing moved. Nothing. He tried to speak, tried to tell her that he loved her with everything that he was, that she was the center of his universe, that she *was* his universe—not his work, not his profession—but no words came out. He wasn't sure he was actually breathing. All he could do was look at her. Follow her. Drink her in. Savor her presence for perhaps the very last time. It wasn't easy through the tears. He was crying harder than he ever had in his life, realizing all that he had lost.

Then it hit him. At first he thought it was the tears. Or the alcohol. They must have been blurring his perception. But as he took in every angle, every curve, every nuance of Kelly's face, it dawned on him that it wasn't Kelly at all. A near-perfect copy of her, for sure, but not her. It possessed all her features. But from when she was eighteen, or twenty-two, or maybe fourteen—it was impossible to gauge. It was, somehow, a newly minted Kelly, a Kelly freshly stamped from the die. It was adult in size and figure, and yet its features were childlike. It bore no signs of an adult life lived: no freckles, no blemishes, no laugh-lines, no fine wrinkles, no small scar on the left side of the chin. No, the features that made Kelly, Kelly; the small imperfections that bespoke a life of hard work, concern for others, struggle, worry, caring, strength, gratitude, grace, love of family, love of life—all the features that made her so beautiful—had yet to be etched into this being's newly cast visage.

He reassured himself that it definitely wasn't Kelly, or worse yet Kelly's ghost, just some sort of phantasmal approximation of her. A facsimile, but not her. And with this realization, all the cumulative fear and despair of the night, of the past year, of the past several years, washed out of his body. A sense of clarity lanced through the fog of all that had been happening to him. And he believed he knew the answer. He had spent so long engaged in a dance with death that he had forgotten all the beauty and wonder of life. He had been seduced by death, drawn in by the stark, absolute nature of its being. It was so binary—you existed, or you didn't. It made engagement with death, doing battle with it, all the more desperate, all the more heroic. Every other human endeavor, every other pursuit, paled in comparison; lacking as they did the terror, the gravity, the pathos, the honor, the sacrifice, the intimacy, the trill. And it wasn't entirely his own doing, his own folly. Death enjoyed playing with you, toying with you, making you believe you had some agency, allowing you to swim in the addictive waters of hope. But there was no such thing as hope when confronting this adversary. The outcome was never in doubt. The winner was pre-determined. And yet, you were sucked in, deeper and deeper, as Death purposefully pulled you away from all that you cared about, all that you loved, until the struggle was all that mattered. A cosmic joke on you. An eternal bait and switch. Pulling you away from life and love and community, and leading you to nothingness.

Yes, it was Death who had drawn him away from the loves of his life. And it was Death who had made him forget. Forget his love for Kelly. Forget his adoration of his girls. Forget his delight in his friendships. Forget his joy in living and being. And it was Death who filled him with guilt, guilt whenever he disengaged from the sacred fight. He had played completely by Death's rules. He had followed Death across Matt's bridge and had wandered so far into Death's kingdom of emptiness that he had lost the way back.

But seeing Kelly's ghost, believing that Kelly had died, shocked him out of his fugue, opened his eyes to where he was, and pierced the darkness with brilliant light. Thinking the unthinkable forced him to recognize how far he had wandered away and how much he longed to be back on the other side. On the side of the living. With Kelly and his girls. Blackness and nothingness, Death could have them. Suddenly he craved light, and color, and sound. Birdsong and fragrant summer breezes, wind and rain and chilly nights, crashing surf, babbling brooks, music, laughter, art, chatter, spice, hugs, kisses . . . and love. Unabashed, unbridled, inextinguishable love.

Yes, the answer was appallingly easy: reject Death, break out of its embrace, step out of its dance, and immerse oneself in life. Revel in and celebrate life. Spurn the dead and embrace the living. Surround oneself with the living, the vital; the quick, and *not* the dead. He needed to kick the dead out, send them on their way, and welcome back into his house, into his home, into his heart, the living.

He scanned the room to gain his bearings and then looked up again at the specter. She knelt and collected the scattered shells. She then stood and watched him. She was smiling at him, head tilted to the right. And she was fading. Her outline became hazy, her features blurred. And as she became less and less distinct, the shells in her left hand did so as well. A tear ran down her face as she lifted her right hand and brought it to her lips. And as she dissolved into the bedroom air, she blew him a kiss. A warm floral breeze rushed over Ryan's face, and she was gone.

With the spirit's disappearance, the noise from downstairs crashed in around him. He hadn't heard a peep out of them when he was in the presence of the dark lady. But now, the revelers called out to him again, and again they sang their sick ditties. Again, they made their way up the stairs. Again, there was much jocularity and laughter. Again, they beckoned Ryan to join them. And again, they started in on Kelly.

That was the final straw. Ryan sprang to his feet, grabbed the shotgun by its barrel, and made for the front staircase. As he strode into the hallway, he bellowed: "I know what you want, you pricks, but you're not getting it! I'm staying here, with the living; with my wife, with my babies. You want to party, you dead freaks? Let's party!"

He started down the stairs, meeting several formally attired spirits along the way. They reacted in horror as he swung the butt end of the Remington at them and screamed as the stock of the heavy gun careened through their skulls. And with each swing, one uninvited guest, then another, atomized. In response, a mass panic ensued, reminiscent of an old black-and-white Godzilla movie. Spook merrymakers scattered in every direction. A graveyard's worth of revelers frantically made for the front doorway, scratching and clawing and trampling one another to get out. Ryan scythed through the clambering throng with a vengeance, screaming all the while: "Go back to your own kind, you freaks! Nothing here but the living. So, clear the fuck off!"

Those that could, squeezed out of the door and spilled out onto the street where they dissolved into the supersaturated February air. Those that could not were dispatched by Ryan's mad swings. Soon he had cleared the entranceway and was continuing his rampage into the music room where several spirits cowered behind the player piano. The dining room was clean, but another jam of ghosts backed up into the kitchen as too many tried to scramble out of the side door in the family room. Why they didn't just pass through the walls, Ryan had no clue. But who among the living can claim to understand the ways of the dead?

Soon, the air was fetid with their dematerialized protoplasm. The whole house reeked of death. Ryan threw open several windows to clear the stench, then continued with his room-to-room interdimensional treasure hunt. After clearing the downstairs and the basement, he stode upstairs via the front staircase. There he found no one in the kids' bedroom or the playroom but did catch a spook hiding behind the gowns in the guest room closet, and several behind the shower curtain in the girls' bathroom. There were none in the sewing room, although he went ahead and smashed to pieces the two Victorian dolls just in case.

He then marched out to the outbuildings where he found a number in the upstairs of the barn, apparently waiting for a show. Had they not heard all the commotion coming from the house?

Were these things not all interconnected? *I guess not*, he thought, as he sliced and diced his way through them all like an overeager reaper at the harvest. He grabbed a flashlight from the barn and inspected every corner of the property. Finishing this, he let out a big sigh of relief as he grew satisfied that all supernatural elements had been exorcised. But then he stopped short.

The attic. There, of all people—or non-people—he found the sweet, briny Mindy. Feeling somehow connected with this one, or perhaps guilty for having appreciated her formidable physique a little too much, he popped open a large round window in the front gable.

"All right, Mindy, out you go. And please, don't ever come back, or I won't be so hospitable."

Mindy clambered out through the vent without saying a word and dropped to the ground, dissolving into the ether before she impacted.

Enlivened, and still drunkenly agitated, Ryan needed to dissipate his residual murderous energy, so he decided to go for a run. The pain would do him good. It would remind him of how alive he was. He changed into exercise attire, leaped out of the ghoul-free front door, and hit the road toward town. At the bridge there was no blockade or passed-on policeman, and he crossed over the river, joyfully recalling his many walks there with Kelly and the girls. After running along the levee and rounding the moribund football stadium, he headed into town via West High Street. Passing its stately row of Victorian mansions, he gleefully peered into each of their softly lit parlors. He ran up and down Main Street looking into the storefronts, thanking each one for being there. Had anyone ventured out into the driving rain, he would have been engulfed them in a grateful bear hug. But none did—both the living and the dead apparently deeming it prudent to keep their distance. Finally, he crossed the Susquehanna again and retraced his girls' Halloween route, blowing kisses to each of the small, understated, but always generous homes along the way.

Happy, aching, and exhausted, Ryan arrived back at the house. He stumbled up the driveway, retrieved the porch furniture, and returned it to its rightful place. He opened the side entrance's storm door, delighting in its evocative squeal, entered the family room and collapsed onto the couch. Hugging the girl's favorite throw pillow, he plunged into a dreamless slumber.

At 5:00 a.m. he surfaced. He sensed Kelly was near. Her scent enveloped him. Not her perfume, but the faint sweet smell that was Kelly, and only Kelly. The scent that the spirit world failed to fully replicate. Her facial features framed by her cascading hair came into focus. Her facial features, with all the glorious imperfections she had earned through living a full, loving life. He felt her lips on his. And something else. Something warm and wet, dropping onto his face like a gentle summer rain. Tears. Sweet, salty tears.

Suddenly he was wide awake. He bolted upright with a start. Kelly rocked back and then threw her arms around his neck, whispering, "Don't be frightened, baby. It's me. I'm home. Everything's all right. Everything's going to be all right."

"Kelly? What . . . is it you? You're not one of them, are you? Is it you? What . . . what are you doing here?" His neurons kicked in. "It *is* you, isn't it, Kelly? I mean, you're not cold. I can feel you. I can feel the life in you." He stroked a small scar on her chin. "And it's your face, your beautiful, lovely face . . . It *is* you, isn't it, Kelly? It's truly you."

Kelly, holding his head in her hands, brought her face again to his and looked into his eyes. "Of course, it's me. I came back. I was so worried about you. I had to come. I'm sorry I scared you. I just wanted to feel you. I need you, Ryan. And you need me. We can do so much better. We just need to recommit to each other. Stop taking each other for granted. Work at it. Together." She held his chin with her left hand, brushed the hair from his forehead with her right, traced his scar, and kissed it. "I know you've been hurting. I know I pulled away. But please know that I never stopped loving you. And I never will."

The two kissed in hungry desperation, Kelly squeezing all the breath out of Ryan's lungs. Through short gasps, he eked out, "Kelly, the girls . . . where are they?

"They're fine, honey," whispered Kelly. "They're with Dianne. She'll bring them back Thursday. Or we can go up and get them, together. Everything's all right, baby."

CHAPTER 58

ANGELS AND DEVILS

"So, Ronald, we're back to meeting in pubs again, eh?" asked Ryan as he devoured his friend in a hungry bear hug, a year and a half after his fateful night with the spirit world. "Is this my new confessional?" The two were connecting in a dive bar halfway to Bloomsbury that still clung to the smoke of cigarettes consumed in the past century.

"I'm not a priest, Ryan. I don't do confessionals. But we're here to knock out one of your sessions. I figured meeting in a place like this was the only way to get you back on track there, buddy."

The two sat down opposite each other. "You make it sound like I've been avoiding you'" replied Ryan. "I've only missed a few sessions."

"A few sessions? It's been over a year, now," replied Reverend Ron with a roll of his eyes.

"A year? Hmm. I would have sworn we just did one—"

"Um, Ryan, it's October. If I'm not mistaken, our last formal session was in July, last year. You were still in the midst of all your UPenn workups."

"Sheesh, it has been a while, hasn't it? I guess I counted seeing you out on the soccer fields," remarked Ryan, looking off to his right. He then refocused on Reverend Ron. "But the reality is, I'm doing so much better. And Kelly and I are doing so much better. I'm not sure we need to meet regularly anymore."

"Ha! We never did meet 'regularly.' But you need to be meeting with someone—and I've heard you've blown off the marriage counselor *and* the UPenn psychiatrists."

"Yeah, well, the marriage counselor was a bit of a man-hater. And I didn't blow off the UPenn shrinks. They discharged me," said Ryan, holding up a mug of beer in a toasting fashion and then taking a large swig.

"And you were honest with them—about everything?"

"I was, indeed, Ronald," said Ryan with exaggerated indignity. "But they were like old Larkin. They couldn't find a single thing wrong with me and were very pleased with the fact that there were no further visitations after that godforsaken weekend."

"And that's the honest-to-God truth, Ryan, no further visitations—for over a year and a half now?"

"Honest to God and scout's honor, Ronald," pledged Ryan, holding up his right hand.

"Did they have a final hypothesis on the apparitions?"

"Oh, they were kind of like you. They attributed them to 'sleep starvation' and a host of sleep pathologies—some form of 'narcoleptic hallucinations' or something," remarked Ryan, using air quotations.

"What did the sleep specialists say?"

"Passing grades. And they really went to town on me: five separate sessions with them. They said I showed multiple severe sleep disturbance patterns—some, pretty darned atypical."

"Atypical?" Reverend Ron's right eye began to twitch.

"Yeah, that's why they kept repeating the 'sleep-ins.' They said my sleep EEG patterns were bizarre. They're going to write me up as a case study!"

"So, that was it all along, eh? Like I hypothesized—a sleep pathology," said Reverend Ron, relaxing his shoulders and taking a large gulp of beer.

"They said no. In all their runs, I exhibited no signs of

sleepwalking or mixed states of consciousness. In the end, they believed the apparitions were some form of seizure activity."

Reverend Ron's right eye twitched harder. "Hmm. What did the neurologists think?"

"Oh, they put me through the ringer too. Everything—short of rectal probes. But in the end, they gave me a complete clean bill of health as well: 'No evidence of seizure activity or any other neurogenic dysfunction,'" recalled Ryan, again using air quotations.

"And their interpretation of the apparitions?"

"They thought it was a fatigue and stress-related 'transient psychological state' that had 'clearly dissipated.'"

Reverend Ron's right eye was now twitching furiously, and he leaned forward over the table. "So, let me get this straight: the psychiatrists thought the apparitions were due to your sleep disorders, the sleep specialists thought they were due to seizures, and the seizure specialists thought they were psychiatric?"

"That's about the size of it."

"Wonderful," responded Reverend Ron, throwing his hands into the air.

Ryan chuckled. "Everything's all right, Ron. Stop fretting. It's over. It's truly over. I know it. I can feel it in my bones. And overall, I think I'm light-years better than I was, don't you?"

"I *do* think you're light-years better, but it doesn't mean you're not still at risk. That you can't still screw everything up. Addicts are never truly cured," said Reverend Ron with a pointed finger.

"Addicts?"

"Absolutely. I liken you to a junkie—clean, for now, but at high risk of running back to the embrace of your drug."

Ryan frowned. "That's a little harsh, Ronald."

"Is it? There's no two ways about it, Ryan. You're addicted to your profession, or its intensity, or its adrenaline rush, or the succor it gives to your ego—your need to be needed, your need to be a hero, your need to be 'the man.' Probably, all the above." Reverend Ron took another large gulp of beer.

"Yeah, well then, that's problematic, isn't it? There'll be no twelve-step program for me then."

"Oh, and why not?"

"Because I can't cold turkey *my* drug. I'm immersed in it every day."

"Well . . . you could," said Reverend Ron, fixing his eyes on Ryan's.

Ryan shifted in his seat. "Well, yes. I guess I could. But I don't want to."

"I know," said Reverend Ron, leaning forward and poking Ryan in the chest. "But that means it'll be all too easy for you to lapse back into your old patterns of counter-dependency, overcommitment, self-neglect, marital-neglect, social isolation, psychic energy depletion, sleep pathology, burnout, depression, and despair; and I would suspect, back to your spectral interactions."

"It's all right, Ron," said Ryan, chuckling again, and drinking from his mug. "I've got this. Really. I'm a different person. And I've scaled way back on my schedule."

"Way back?" asked Reverend Ron with a raised eyebrow.

"Well, a fair amount back."

"And that's working?"

"Most of the time. Kelly thinks I'm still a little overcommitted."

"I don't like the sound of 'a little overcommitted.'" Reverend Ron lowered his head but kept his gaze fixed on Ryan's eyes.

"Come on, Ron. I've got to do what I've got to do," replied Ryan with open palms.

Reverend Ron shook his head. "Sounds like mission creep to me, Ryan. Sounds like the old Ryan resurfacing."

"I'm trying, Ron. I'm trying really hard. What else would you have me do?"

"Ha!" replied Ron, again poking his index finger into Ryan's chest. "You poor excuse for a footballer, you fell right into my trap! You can start by making our sessions sacrosanct. You cut out all other counseling opportunities, my man. You need someone keeping you within the navigational beacons."

"Well then, Ron, I'll start making it to our sessions."

"Great!" replied Reverend Ron, raising his mug to Ryan and then taking a celebratory slug of beer.

"*If* . . ."

"If . . . ?" replied Reverend Ron, lowering his mug.

"If, one: we continue to hold them here."

"Sounds perfect to me," Reverend Ron again made a cheers gesture to Ryan.

"And two . . ."

"Two? How many provisos are there going to be?"

"Just the two."

"All right, shoot."

"Two: you make it to our Halloween bash next week."

"I don't know about that one, Ryan. You know I hate those dress-up things," replied Reverend Ron with a look of mild disgust.

"I'll make sure there are bevvies of eligible nurses."

"Including the Neuro-ICU team?" Reverend Ron's eyes had noticeably brightened.

"If you wish."

"Deal."

The two clinked mugs and drained their beers.

After several minutes of letting the commentary of a college football game fill the space between them, Reverend Ron broke in. "So, Ryan . . ."

"Yeah?"

"I've been thinking about that night." said Reverend Ron, again fixing his eyes on Ryan's.

"What night?"

"The one in February."

"You mean when the entire spook world descended on me?" replied Ryan with a shiver.

"Yeah. I still have to ask, why couldn't it all have just been a dream?"

Ryan frowned. "How so?"

"Well, I remember you saying that it all started after you fell asleep on the couch."

Ryan shook his head definitively. "No. I said it all started when I *woke up* from sleeping on the couch."

"I know, but keeping with your sleep pathologies, why couldn't you have fallen into a deep sleep and dreamed it all, finally waking up when Kelly got to you?"

"Well, if you're going to start using reasoning like that, maybe *everything* is a twisted dream. Maybe I'm still lying in a gully in Afghanistan, dying," replied Ryan with a touch of annoyance in his voice.

Reverend Ron smiled warmly. "Well, let's hope not. That would have some pretty unsettling implications about my own existence."

"You know, you surprise me, Ron," said Ryan.

"Oh?"

"Yeah. I mean, I know you're a man of deep faith, and yet you're having the hardest time accepting even the slightest possibility that what I went through could have been real. You once accused me of rejecting my scientific roots, but here you are rejecting your ecclesiastical roots. You so much want this to be related to a sleep disorder or some other cerebral short-circuiting. Where's your spiritualism, your mysticism, your belief in something beyond the scientific, beyond the explainable? Where's your belief in good and evil, in angels and devils?"

"And that's what you think the whole ghost thing was, the work of the devil?" asked Reverend Ron with raised eyebrows.

"Potentially. Although I think the Kelly ghost was playing for the good guys."

"By presenting you with a box full of shotgun shells?"

"That's the thing," replied Ryan with a note of excitement in his voice. "It was all an illusion, Ron. That next morning, I checked. There were no shells anywhere. The lockbox was on its shelf, locked, with no cartons missing. She never actually offered me any shells. I think her intention was to get me to the point of considering . . . well, considering something really stupid. Then when I saw her as Kelly, it stunned me back to my senses—like electroconvulsive shock therapy or something. And it worked! So, isn't that the kind of work you would expect out of an angel? Hell, maybe they all were playing for the good guys in some crazy way. Maybe they were trying to teach me some critical lesson about life, about living."

Reverend Ron took another big slug of beer. "Well, if that's the case, maybe you could still do with a visit from them now and then to help keep you on the straight and narrow."

Ryan cringed. "I think I'll take a pass on that, my friend."

CHAPTER 59

IMAGINE

The evening of the Brenan Halloween party was unseasonably balmy, affording the affair a loose and licentious atmosphere. Scantily costumed partygoers milled about the Brenan downstairs and backyard, congealing and recongealing into assorted collections of exposed flesh. Ryan had stationed his band out on the screened-in porch for maximum neighborhood projection. Kelly, bedecked in witch's garb, served drinks from behind an antique oak lectern-turned-bar in the adjacent study. The Brenan girls, mirroring their mother, were all witches of one form or another, and manned a bubbling cauldron of spiked punch. Reverend Ron swam among bevies of Halloween-sexy female revelers, the Neuro-ICU nurses included. Matt Wolfe assumed center stage on the porch and served as the evening's emcee, manipulating the crowd's excitement to a fever pitch.

The band members were dressed in matching mummy getups made of bandages purloined from the Carriere operating rooms. The night's performance was augmented by guest appearances from a jazz saxophonist and a professional Taylor Swift impersonator. Extra mics were positioned among the audience for group singalongs and live karaoke. They strategically placed multiple iPads to help the band with their lyrics and chord progressions.

For the first hour or so, the band played nothing but Halloween-themed songs—basically anything that mentioned ghosts, vampires, mummies, witches, spells, devils, cats, bats, pumpkins, the color black (or orange), the moon, owls, bones, thunder, nighttime, candy, crows, ravens, hounds, and the like. At ten, they shifted gears and unleashed their much beloved Beatles set. This, thanks to a peaking inebriation curve among the guests, packed the porch and surrounding rooms with clapping, dancing, and howling celebrants.

As Ryan, Matt, and the rest of the band cried out the lecherous lyrics to "When I Saw Her Standing There," Ryan's gaze was drawn to a young man illuminated by one of the many flashing stage lights strewn about the porch. He was standing well to the back, slouching up against a wall. He stood about five foot ten, was of medium build, and dressed in a black T-shirt and black leather jacket. His skin was pale; his eyes small, green, and impious; his brows, full and sardonic; his hair, sandy brown and shaggy. He nodded in time with the "music" and moved his lips along with the words, only wincing when Matt and Ryan would end up more than a semitone flat in their singing.

The young man locked eyes with Ryan and smiled. It was a warm smile, yet a wry one. He supplemented it with a lift of a pint glass full of beer and an approving nod. He took a large gulp, turned, and loped his way through the pulsating crowd toward the backyard door. Just before exiting, he turned again to Ryan, made another cheers gesture, winked, and stepped out into the darkness.

Ryan stood frozen in place, mouth agape.

"No freakin' way."

He looked over at Kelly through the open study doorway and saw that she too stood motionless, transfixed by the exiting young man, her supercomputer brain running through a thousand possible interpretations of what she had just experienced. She

ABOUT THE AUTHOR

Gary Simonds is a neurosurgeon who has treated tens of thousands of patients with devastating illnesses. He is a professor at the Virginia Tech Carilion School of Medicine and the Virginia Tech School of Neuroscience. He has published three nonfiction books on burnout and psychological distress in healthcare providers and routinely writes about, and gives talks on, neuroscience, neurosurgery, medical socioeconomics, medical humanism, medical ethics, and burnout.

Gary grew up in New Jersey and England, is an avid soccer fan, a guitar and banjo player; and lives with his wife, Cindy, and border collie, Hamish, in a log cabin in Black Mountain, North Carolina.

shook her head as if to wake herself out of a dream and blinked her eyes several times. Her cobalt-blue eyes locked in on Ryan's, wide and ablaze, her lips forming the words: "No freakin' way..."

She was thinking the same thing.

It had to be him.

Granted, it was Halloween and it could be a masterful costume. But the resemblance was uncanny. The off-center smile, the glint in the eye, the irreverent posture and gait. Could it be him? Could the Brenans have just been paid a visit by the one and only John Lennon?